FORTY DAYS
AT KAMAS
A NOVEL

PRESTON FLEMING

D1225597

Forty Days at Kamas
A Novel
Preston Fleming

PF Publishing, Boston

This eBook is a work of fiction. Names characters, places, and incidents are the product of the author's imagination or are used fictitiously. Any resemblance to actual events, locales, or persons, living or dead, is coincidental.

PF Publishing Boston, MA
http://www.prestonfleming.com
ISBN-10: 0-982-95949-4
ISBN-13: 978-0-9829594-9-7

Für Elise

CHAPTER 1

"Not believing in force is the same as not believing in gravity."
—Leon Trotsky

Wednesday, March 6, 2024

The train lurched forward. I reached out to steady myself and my hand closed around the cold ankle of the sickly high school teacher who had boarded the train four days earlier in St. Louis. He had been oddly silent through the night and I felt a fleeting pang of guilt for the sleep I had enjoyed when his coughing finally stopped. After six days of sitting on the floor of an unheated prison compartment with twenty other prisoners, I felt little else. Anyway, the teacher's suffering was over.

Still only half-awake, I sensed that the prison car had been nudged from behind, as when a train switches engines. Then all was silent except for the sniffling and wheezing of the men packed in around me. Before I could be sure what had happened, a twinge of pain darted up my spine from the pinched discs in my lower back. It was like no other pain I had ever known. A glowing fireball roared up through my neck, filled my skull, burst out the crown of my head and pierced the ceiling of the compartment, propelling me with it into the clear moonlit sky. The fire and I became one, soaring over the icy rail yard where the prison train had come to rest.

Suddenly the pain and the cold were gone. Below me, rock-strewn hills rippled out in all directions, meeting a line of jagged mountains in the distance. Halfway between the rail yard and the mountains was a scene that both disturbed and attracted me. A string of brilliant flood lamps atop tall poles outlined the perimeter of a vast prison camp. The camp's wire fence enclosed a neat quadrangle, marked at intervals by wooden guard towers and surrounded by a broad swath of ploughed no-man's-land. Transverse walls divided the camp into five equal sections. Three of these sections housed row upon row of elongated single-story lodges. The other two held an assortment of structures resembling workshops, administration buildings, and utility sheds.

A steady wind blasted the camp from the north, creating swirls of snow and waist-high drifts in the lee of the tightly strung barbed-wire fences. I directed my attention toward the lodges in the center of the camp and saw them loom larger. Now I could hear the whistle of the gusts more clearly. As I hovered above the camp, a surge of terror overtook me, followed by waves of hatred, despair, and grief, each frightening in its power, yet unfocused and without object, as if the collective anguish of all the camp's inhabitants had risen up to meet me in a whirlwind of human misery. I turned my gaze from the camp and climbed higher until the fear subsided.

When I looked down I noticed a solitary road leading from the camp past a cluster of sandbag bunkers. I followed the road beyond an administration compound and motor pool, over a line of hills and into the next valley, where a concentration of street lamps and neon signs marked the outskirts of a town. The instant I focused my gaze on the town, I closed in on it at astonishing speed. Below me lay the same darkened rail yard where a locomotive had shunted our four battered prison cars onto a siding before towing the civilian coaches to the terminal.

The flashing red and white lights of a shunting engine illuminated a half-dozen canvas-topped troop trucks that disgorged black-uniformed guards in helmets and body armor. Some of the guards led snarling attack dogs on short leather leashes. As the shunting engine retreated toward the passenger terminal, the guards switched on their flashlights and formed a skirmish line opposite the coaches.

Not the dogs again, I grumbled. But before the fear of mauling could grip me, I realized that I was dropping back down to earth at an angle that seemed certain to land me on the roof of the last prison car. Just before impact I looked away.

A tremendous blow shook the car's exterior wall. Then it struck again. But I felt no impact. When I opened my eyes, I saw huddled forms all around me rising slowly and painfully from the compartment floor. In the gray light filtering in through the compartment's dust-caked windows, I saw that some did not stir at all.

More crashing blows struck the sides of the rail car. It took me a moment to recognize that these came from the banging of clubs and rifle butts signifying that the time had come to unload. Almost in unison, our crowd of shivering, half-starved public enemies began pressing itself against the barred door of the compartment.

Because I had occupied a place far from the door, the crowd's shoving toward the exit gave me enough room for the first time in days to stretch out my cramped limbs. As I stretched, I felt lice crawling down my legs and suppressed an urge to scratch. With only a few seconds left before the guards would slide open the door to the corridor, there was no time to waste hunting lice, much less to think about my strange vision of the landscape outside.

Casting aside all thoughts other than how to haul my feeble body off the train, I rolled sideways onto my hands and knees, trying to tuck my right foot under me to stand. But there was no feeling in either leg. Apart from being debilitated from hunger and cold, the endless hours of sitting with my back propped against my fellow prisoners had cut off circulation to my legs.

The pounding of clubs and rifle butts began again at the head of the train and moved quickly down the line toward our car. From earlier stops I knew that once the door rolled open, anyone too slow to join the initial rush off the train would risk a thrashing about his head and shoulders. Fear came over me that I couldn't scuttle fast enough to avoid a beating.

I made another frantic attempt to get on my feet, but I fell back against the schoolteacher's stiffened corpse.

I had forgotten about him in the odd fascination of my dream and the urgency of leaving the train. Now I wondered whether there was time to scavenge anything useful from him. I patted down his pockets and the usual places where prisoners tended to stash a bread roll or an uneaten ration bar, and then searched for a bag or a bundle. It was no use; while I had slept the prisoners behind us must have noticed the schoolteacher turn cold and seized his belongings. For a moment I envied them; then I felt ashamed.

Outside the compartment a key turned the deadbolt in the steel door. Under power from the guards' beefy shoulders, the door slid open and reached its limit with a heavy thud. A moment of silence followed.

Then began the hellish din of rifle butts on sheet metal, cruel rasping curses, and discordant music playing from worn-out loudspeakers outside. The music, I knew, was required by convoy regulations to mask the cries of prisoners and the blows of nightsticks and rubber truncheons. Why the music was invariably an atonal modern symphony, none of us knew.

I was still on hands and knees at the edge of the crowd when the rush began and gained my footing in time to join the scrum as it heaved forward. The guards shouted and cursed at us as they drove us outside.

"Pile out, you sorry turds!" one yelled over the frenzied barking of his well-fed German shepherd. "On the double to the blacktop! And plant your raggedy butts inside the markers!"

Through the filthy window, I could see a thinly spread line of guards with submachine guns leveled at the hip. Closer in, plainclothes thugs armed with truncheons, pepper gas canisters, and other non-lethal weapons herded the swift-moving stream of prisoners toward an assembly zone marked by orange traffic pylons.

The few stragglers who didn't sit promptly upon reaching the icy blacktop received a sudden kick in the leg or a sharp jab in the ribs from a guard's rifle butt. Still another detachment of guards armed with sinister-looking jointed truncheons lurked further on, walloping any inattentive prisoner who failed to link arms with his neighbors. As the guards waited for the rail cars to empty, a flurry of snowflakes fell, diffusing the yellowish glare of the floodlights over the railyard.

Anxious for my legs to recover in time to drop to the platform without injury, I hung back and let others pass. To jump without full control of my legs might cost me a broken limb, which in a labor camp could lead to reduced rations and eventual starvation. Yet to be last out the door meant a beating and damage that might be just as bad. With each second I prayed for my circulation to return. Then I heard Will Roesemann's voice coming from the next compartment.

"Paul, quick—I need your help."

Preoccupied with my legs, I had forgotten about my former cellmate at the Susquehanna interrogation facility. My first impulse was to refuse, but Roesemann had come to my aid many times and he had never asked anything in return.

"Give me a second, Will," I told him. "My legs aren't quite right yet."

I dropped out of the packed corridor into the compartment where Roesemann knelt at the side of a bruised and bloodied prisoner.

The night before, at an unscheduled stop near the Colorado border, a squad of security men had tossed the prisoner aboard like a sack of potatoes. Word spread through the sleeper car that his name was Glenn Reineke and that he had escaped from a corrective labor camp at Kamas, somewhere in the Wasatch Range east of the Great Salt Lake. He and his partner had managed to evade capture for two weeks before a logging crew spotted them and held them at bay. The security force that finally took the fugitives into custody had given them an exceptionally brutal handling because both had escaped from Kamas before.

Roesemann pulled one of Reineke's arms over his shoulder and offered the other arm to me. He was surprisingly heavy for so lean a figure and I could feel the thickness of his arm and shoulder muscles. During his time on the run he had grown a full black beard flecked with gray that matched heavy eyebrows knitted together at the bridge of a prominent nose. Reineke's eyes were shut and his body completely limp. I wondered if he was even alive.

"This is pointless, Will. He's a goner," I said.

Suddenly the wounded man stiffened and raised his head. He mumbled something unintelligible.

"He thinks he's back at Kamas," Roesemann said with a troubled look.

"I'm not sure I can handle this, Will," I replied. "I can barely walk myself."

"Try anyway."

"Will, this guy is trouble..."

"Goddamnit, Paul, stop whining and give me a hand."

I swallowed hard and took Reineke's arm.

The shouting of the guards outside became frenzied, their grunts and howls making them sound more like victims than aggressors. As prisoners we knew better than to cry out when hit because that only provoked the guards to beat us harder.

When we reached the car's exit, by some miracle no guards remained on hand to harass us other than a dog handler stationed five yards back from the tracks. Roesemann jumped out and put his arms around Reineke's chest while I lowered myself to the ground holding the wounded man's legs.

At that moment a pair of guards looked our way from the edge of the blacktop and started toward us, clubs raised to strike. Roesemann and I put our heads down and rushed forward, prepared to meet their blows. But the guards were not after us.

Without a word, the pair lit into a shuffling graybeard just ahead. They rained blows upon his distinguished bald pate until his scalp was awash with blood. He scrambled desperately to break free but a vicious kick in the gut promptly felled him. He lay motionless a few feet short of the blacktop, rivulets of blood streaming onto the thin layer of new snow. Then two other guards seized him by the feet and dragged him between the orange pylons, his bald head bouncing across the frozen ground with sickening thuds.

Throughout the beating, Roesemann and I kept lugging Reineke between us, evading all blows except for a few glancing kicks from a young guard who stopped pursuing us the moment we reached the pylons.

"Get down and link arms!" the uniformed youth threatened from a spot safely beyond reach.

Behind us a truck engine roared and I turned around to look. At that instant a rubber truncheon caught me behind the ear and sent my knit cap flying from my head. Though dazed, I tucked my chin into my chest to protect my throat from additional blows. When none followed, a murderous rage well up inside me, not only at the pain and humiliation, but at the absence of any warning. The guards treated us not like fellow humans but like domestic animals that responded to physical correction rather than to words.

We waited anxiously on the snow-covered blacktop until the guards were satisfied that no prisoners remained in or underneath the coaches and none were concealed anywhere else in the rail yard. My lice stirred again, this time in my scalp and up and down my neck. I caught one and crushed it against my boot, but left the others alone. It was pointless—no matter how many I destroyed, more always appeared.

"Get up! De-link arms and form a single column four abreast!"

Having performed this operation many times, we succeeded in forming a workable column within seconds. Roesemann and I lifted Reineke and held him between us.

"Prisoners, prepare to march at my command!"

With guards flanking us on either side, we crossed the tracks and followed a deeply rutted path through a patchwork of open fields for fifteen or twenty minutes before it intersected a four-lane paved road that led toward town. Carrying Reineke had depleted my last reserves of strength, and the pain in my lower back had become nearly unbearable.

"Keep to the road! One step to the right or left and I'll fire without warning!"

I spotted a line of six unmarked tractor-trailer rigs parked two hundred yards ahead along the shoulder and resolved to hold out until we reached them. When we closed to within a hundred yards of the nearest truck, Reineke suddenly began to mutter and shuffle his feet. Roesemann and I looked at each other, unsure of what to do, and in that split second of hesitation, the man twisted out of our grip and broke away toward the fields.

Without thinking, I left the column and tackled him around the waist. Someone fired a warning shot and a half dozen guards swarmed after us. I lay still, anticipating a shower of blows. But to my amazement, the prisoners nearest to us closed in around us to form a protective screen. All Roesemann and I needed were a few seconds to pull the breathless fugitive onto his feet and we all managed to keep moving. The guards withdrew.

After the scuffle, I let go of Reineke for a moment to see whether he could walk without my support. It was only because of my odd position that I was able to see someone keeping pace with us among the trees. A moment later an old woman carrying a basket and a duffel and a young girl wearing a canvas backpack emerged from a thicket onto the road's shoulder.

At first the guards failed to see them. The woman made the sign of the cross, then calmly stepped into the road, removed the cloth covering from her basket and began handing out bread rolls. The half-starved men broke ranks and collided with each other to get their hands on a precious roll.

A burst of submachine-gun fire erupted, aiming over our heads. Dogs whined and barked, straining at their leashes to attack.

"Everybody on the ground! Sit! Link arms!"

The command rang out again and again as prisoners dropped to the ground, stuffing precious bread into their clothing.

"You! Woman! Freeze!" screamed the enraged dog handler closest to the old woman. But the woman had already taken the girl's hand and was leading her back into the trees with remarkable speed and agility.

Without a moment's hesitation the handler reached down to unleash his dog. In a flash a black German shepherd was racing alongside the column in headlong pursuit. Having seen dogs like these maul prisoners many times, I shuddered at the thought of what would happen to the unfortunate woman or her child. For an instant I considered stepping between the dog and its quarry but I lacked the nerve. The beast galloped past me at top speed.

Then I heard a high-pitched canine yelp followed by shouts and cries of animal pain. I turned my head in time to see a broad-shouldered prisoner sitting astride the black shepherd dog, one forearm locked firmly in the dog's jaws and the other pinning the dog's windpipe against the icy road. Guards converged upon the man and beat him senseless but the dog remained limp when they pulled it away from the prisoner's inert body. Angry murmurs spread among us but another burst of gunfire silenced the crowd immediately.

"Major Whiting! Sir! Request permission to track the women!"

A young dog handler stood at attention before the convoy leader, a lean, sinewy man of about forty.

"Stand down, Rogers," Whiting responded with an Oklahoma twang. "We have prisoners to deliver. Leave the women, and help move these vermin onto the trucks."

Whiting waved off the eager young soldier and strode back to where one of the guards was directing two prisoners to drag the dog slayer's body to the nearest tractor-trailer.

"Is he still alive?" Whiting asked the guard.

"He was a minute ago."

"Then tie his hands and feet. If he lives, send him to the isolator with Reineke."

"Yes, Sir!" the guard answered.

"And next time, son, when you open fire, don't waste your bullets firing into thin air. Hit somebody."

Roesemann and I looked at each other in mute fury. On command we hoisted Reineke between us and lifted him onto the truck.

CHAPTER 2

"Whoever can conquer the street will one day conquer the state, for every form of power politics and any dictatorship-run state has its roots in the street."

—Joseph Goebbels

Saturday, November 12, 2016

Our stone farmhouse atop a forested knoll commanded a sweeping view of the hills along the Ohio River to the southwest. The south end of the house projected just beyond a line of towering maples, the French doors of our old glassed-in porch opening onto a flagstone veranda. Beyond the boxwood hedge that enclosed the veranda on three sides, the hill sloped gradually at first, then more steeply, past our neighbor's horse paddock to the two-lane state road that connected downtown Sewickley with Interstate 79.

I finished my mug of tea and joined my wife on the veranda. Juliet had begun covering the boxwood with burlap slipcovers and called me over to shovel mulch around the roots. I pulled a long-handled shovel from the wheelbarrow to join her. Meanwhile, our two daughters, Louisa and Claire, aged three and nearly five, busied themselves collecting fallen twigs for the woodpile. The sun was already high in a cloudless sky and the morning frost had melted nearly everywhere.

It was the second Saturday in November, only four days since the national elections in which the President was re-elected under the banner of his newly formed Unionist Party. The Unionists also took both houses of Congress, which had come as a complete surprise to me. I had been spending sixty-hour weeks at the office and had not paid much attention to the persistent reports of large-scale voter registration fraud, voting machine hacking, pre-stuffed ballot boxes, and voter intimidation at polling places in major cities across the country. Even with a government-imposed blackout on live television and radio coverage at polling places, rumors of a stolen election had quickly spread to nearly every household with a phone or a computer. But like too many others, I did not understand what was happening until the damage had already been done.

"Where do we put the sticks, Daddy? " my older daughter Claire asked, bringing my thoughts back to the present.

"By the woodpile, sweetie," I replied. "Break them up in pieces about so big and make a stack with them."

"This one's too big to break." She was dragging an eight-foot branch across the grass. "Will you help me?"

"Of course." I lay down my shovel to give her a hand, but when I reached her, Claire had dropped the branch and was pointing toward the road at the bottom of the hill.

"Who are those people, Daddy, and where are they going?" she asked. "Are they going camping?"

I looked up and saw the road clogged with a slow-moving procession of cars, pickup trucks, trailers, Amish-style horse carts, bicyclists, backpackers, even big-wheeled garden carts pulled rickshaw-style. Those on foot were trailed by a pack of underfed dogs. It reminded me of World War II newsreels of the Dutch fleeing the bombing of Rotterdam, or German refugees retreating from the advancing Red Army. Most of the cars and trucks were far from new and many of the foot travelers shabbily dressed, though most gave the impression of being strong, hardy people who had once belonged to America's middle class.

A trio of deer peered out from behind a copse of trees near the road and hesitated, unable to find a break in the uninterrupted stream of traffic. A few of the dogs looked up, as if catching a scent, but none gave chase.

"Where are they going, Daddy?" Claire repeated.

"I think some are headed north to Canada, darling, like the Moores." The Moores were our neighbors who, having lost their savings to inflation and having failed to sell their horse farm before the mortgage company gave notice of foreclosure, abandoned the farm and their unpaid tax obligations and moved in with their son in Ottawa.

"The ones in the fancy cars are probably driving to the Toronto airport to catch a flight overseas. The rest are probably headed south, where there are more jobs and it's cheaper to live."

"Are we going away, too?" Claire asked, turning to me with a look of disapproval.

I heard footsteps behind me and felt my wife grip my arm. She held on with both hands as if what she saw on the road had given her a chill.

I looked into her eyes and saw the fear of losing our business, our savings, our house and everything in it—and not being able to start over. Not in America, anyway. Not with the Unionists in power. I glanced over to Claire, hoping that she had not sensed Juliet's fear.

"Not today, sweetie," I replied. "We're staying right here at home. Mommy and Daddy have work to do. And so do you and Louisa. Here, let me pull that branch over to the woodpile for you. Now, break up the small twigs, like this." I used more force than necessary to break one of the tender twigs in half. "But leave the big sticks for me, okay?"

My wife squeezed my arm once more and let go to take my hand.

"Jeff's car just pulled in," she said softly. "I'll brew a fresh pot of tea. Why don't you carry some chairs onto the veranda?"

****

Jeff Fisher had been my personal attorney and business advisor for nearly fifteen years. He was sharp, strong-willed, and experienced, but also honest and utterly down to earth. Jeff had studied law at Columbia and could have risen to partner at any of the big law firms in downtown Pittsburgh, but instead chose to join his father's small practice in Sewickley. I was happy he did. His advice was worth far more than I paid for it.

"Any news from the Germans?" I asked, handing him a mug of Lapsang Souchong laced with a shot of twelve-year-old rum.

"Well, they've made you an offer," Jeff said without enthusiasm.

"That's more than I've had from anyone else in the last three years," I replied. "I'll give them credit for that much."

"Don't get too excited, Paul. Their offer is half of what we expected and a third of what the company is worth even in today's market. They don't want to buy the company; they're out to steal it. Still, it's an offer. And it might even be worth taking, depending on what you expect from the economy under a Unionist administration."

"You and I both know that wage and price controls have been a complete disaster for small manufacturers like us," I responded. "The Germans, on the other hand, seem quite comfortable with government controls. With the European economy in the toilet and foreign trade down to a trickle, they seem almost desperate for a foothold in the U.S. I'd say that's good news for us."

"But the bad news is that they think we're even desperate to sell than they are to buy," Jeff replied.

"Do you think we might be able negotiate a better price?"

"I doubt it. They're talking to some of our competitors. They seem pretty confident that at least one of us will decide to take the money and run."

"Damned Europeans! They see the Unionists come to power and now they think they have us on our knees. They're certain that the president will go to Brussels, swallow his pride, and give special trade and investment concessions to the EU. It makes me want to—"

"Not so fast, Paul. If you're right about the Unionists and they do put the economy into a coma, this may be the last offer you'll see for a very long time. And if you have to liquidate, you could wind up buried under a landslide of unpaid bills and tax liens. The Unionists play rough with tax defaulters, Paul. You could be looking at federal prison."

"But if I sell, then what? This is the only business I know, and I am making a living in spite of it all. If I hang in there, the company might grow its way back to profitability somehow. If I sell now, and if there's anything left afterward, where could I invest the proceeds and be able to live off the income? The only option I see would be to emigrate and start over—"

"Father says it would be crazy to emigrate now," Juliet interrupted with surprising vehemence. "His contacts in Washington insist this is a once-in-a-lifetime opportunity to buy assets at the bottom. And they also point out that when things get better—as they are bound to do eventually—anyone who emigrates will get a very chilly reception on his return." Juliet looked at me as she continued. "Paul, both of our families have been in Pennsylvania for nearly a hundred and fifty years. You wouldn't really give it all up, would you?"

Jeff spoke up before I could respond.

"Juliet, if you'll remember," he said gently, "the Jews had been living in Germany and Poland quite a bit longer than a couple hundred years. The Jewish families who emigrated survived. Same with the Russian aristocracy in 1918. And the French nobility during the Reign of Terror. The risks—"

"Jeff, you don't honestly consider the Unionists to belong in the same category as the Nazis or the Bolsheviks?" she replied.

"You've heard their speeches, Juliet. A person is either with them or against them. To the Unionist mobs, you and I are class enemies."

"But we're all Americans," Juliet protested. "Some of our neighbors are Unionists. They're not bad people. I'm certain they wouldn't do anything to harm us…"

"Maybe so," I interjected. "But how can we be sure there aren't others who would stone our Volvo the way they stoned Sally Zimmermann's Lexus in Ambridge last week?" I asked. "Her children were in that car, for

God's sake. All the crazies saw was a shiny new SUV. Sally and the boys were lucky to get away with their lives."

Juliet put down her teacup. When she raised her eyes I could see that she remained unmoved. In matters like this, she still looked to her parents for leadership. Even after fourteen years of marriage... I let the thought drop.

"Paul," she addressed me in a conciliatory voice. "I hear what you're saying. But if it's a decision between emigrating and finding a way to make things work here in Sewickley, then in my mind the choice is clear. We both know life isn't always easy. It was hard back in Washington's day and in Lincoln's day and during the Depression. If the wealthy and educated had emigrated then, America would have failed as a country long ago. I think we have a duty to stay."

I paused to refill my cup before responding and didn't spare the rum.

"I know how you feel, Juliet. I don't like the idea of running away any more than you do. But deep in my gut I don't trust the Unionists. Think about it: if we sold the business, we would have enough to start over somewhere—Australia, Ireland, maybe Costa Rica or some place in South America. It might be a little rough on the two of us, but the girls would do just fine. We could—"

"And walk away from everything we know—the company, our house, our community, our parents? Could you really do that, Paul? I don't think I could look at myself in the mirror if I did. I don't want to be a refugee..."

She lowered her gaze and her eyes seemed fixed on some frightful vision inside her head.

Jeff sighed, then let out a deep breath before looking to me for a decision.

"I suppose I can't put it off any longer, can I?" I asked with a weak smile. "You both need an answer..."

Jeff nodded.

"The Germans want a response today. Should I schedule a meeting or tell them you're not interested?"

My wife raised her head and I felt the burden of her gaze.

"Well, it's a tough call. Very tough," I repeated, looking directly at my wife, then staring out past the trees to the rolling hills beyond.

"But in the end, I don't see how I can run out on Washington, Lincoln, FDR, and a hundred and fifty years of venerable ancestors. As much as I'd like to tell the Unionists to drop dead, I suppose the principled approach is to stay and tell the Germans to drop dead instead."

Jeff rose without showing approval or disapproval, merely giving me a pat on the shoulder as he left his cup on the tea tray. Juliet smiled, palpably relieved, then rose to carry the tray back to the kitchen while I escorted Jeff to his car.

CHAPTER 3

"Those who plot against us in the dark will vanish in the dark."
—Mohammed Taraki, Pro-Soviet Afghan coup leader

Wednesday, March 6, 2024

Claire Wagner removed her backpack and set it beside her on the long station bench. The train that had brought her to Heber, Utah, had rolled on toward Ogden a half hour earlier and she was now the only person left in the double-wide trailer that served as the town's passenger railway terminal. The puffy-faced woman in the Amtrak ticket window glanced at her disapprovingly every two or three minutes as if to convey that she was ready to close the station and go home.

Claire wore the same navy corduroy trousers, white turtleneck, and navy sweater that she had worn to the Philadelphia airport a week earlier with her mother and eleven-year-old sister, Louisa. Her clothes were no longer clean after a week of travel and her hooded red parka was torn in front where she had brushed against a nail on the train. But her outfit was warm and durable and she was glad that it had distinguished her from the bands of homeless children she had seen at each stop along her westward journey.

Claire's mind wandered and her soft brown eyes welled with tears as she tried to figure out for the thousandth time how she had become separated from her mother and her sister at the emigration counter in Philadelphia. She remembered clearly going through the emigration line ahead of them, handing her ticket, passport, exit visa, and exit tax papers to the man behind the counter, who stamped them and returned ticket and passport to her. She needed to go to the bathroom, and her Mom told her to meet them at the gate when she was finished. She found a place to sit on the waiting room floor, but when the ticket agent announced pre-boarding ten minutes later, Mom and Louisa were nowhere in sight. That's when Claire started to worry and decided to search for them back at the emigration counter.

When she got there, the men behind the counter were not the ones who had stamped her passport. None of them knew anything about her mother or Louisa. At Claire's insistence, they shuffled through the papers in their outboxes but her mother's and sister's papers were not there. She considered boarding the flight alone but decided against it. She didn't know anyone in London; if her grandparents failed to meet her at Gatwick airport, she might be in even worse trouble than she faced now. She decided to stay at the gate and wait for her mother and sister to come looking for her.

A few seconds later a woman with a kindly round face, dressed in an elegant but threadbare camel's hair coat of the kind her grandmother always wore, knelt beside her. Claire saw the sadness in her eyes and sensed that the woman did not find it easy to speak.

"Please listen to me, dear, and don't say anything until I'm finished. I was in the line behind you and I saw them take your mother and sister into the security office. Please don't stay a minute longer. Leave the airport right away and go find some relatives or friends who can take care of you. Here—take this money for your cab ride. And don't bother about your luggage. Just go quickly and don't ask questions."

Claire took the woman's advice and the cab fare, too. It was a lot of money, enough for ten cab rides to downtown Philadelphia.

That had been exactly one week ago. Since then, Claire had made her way to the Philadelphia railway station, then back to Pittsburgh and to Cleveland before the long train ride to Utah. Once she had known relatives in each of these cities, but all of them had left the country. The only one who had refused to leave was her father. But all she knew about him was that he had been in prison for a year and that a special court had sentenced him to five years hard labor at a camp somewhere in Utah.

Now that she was here, Claire was determined to find her dad and to stay close by him until he was free again. But from what she had learned on the train, there were dozens of labor camps in what they called the Utah Security District, and there were even more camps to the north, in the former states of Wyoming, Idaho, and Montana. Some people spoke of Utah as if it contained nothing but Restricted Zones, military bases, and labor camps. And what she had heard about the camps terrified her. To think of her dad as a prisoner working outdoors all day in these Wasatch Mountains during the dead of winter made her desperately sad, despite her lingering anger at him for having been arrested and having left her and her mother and sister all alone in Pittsburgh. Why, she asked herself, hadn't she stayed in Philadelphia or Pittsburgh instead of buying the train ticket to Utah?

Claire was so preoccupied with her thoughts that she failed to notice the ticket lady approach and sit beside her.

"Excuse me, young lady, but it's time to close the station. Don't you have a place to spend the night? The next train doesn't leave until tomorrow morning and it's awfully cold out there."

"I'm not taking another train," Claire replied. "I'm staying right here. My father is in Utah and I've got to find him."

The woman furrowed her brow and gazed around the empty room before answering.

"Do you mind if I ask how old you are?"

"I turned twelve last month but my dad says I'm very mature for my age."

"Well, I'll be honest with you. Heber used to be a pretty nice town but I'm afraid that's not so anymore. And it's certainly no place for a twelve-year-old girl in pigtails to be running loose. Do you have any money for food?"

"I had some, but I spent all of it getting here."

The woman frowned, then held out her hand to Claire.

"Come with me. The woman who sells food to the passengers has an extra room in her cabin. Sometimes she lets it out for the night. Maybe she'll take you home with her."

Claire slung her backpack across her shoulder and followed the ticket agent down the length of the passenger platform to an unmarked cinder block building. Inside, four lean and weather-beaten workmen in quilted coveralls shared a dinner of cold beans and rice.

At a counter nearby, a woman in an ankle-length down overcoat covered her wicker breadbasket with a checkered napkin and raised her duffel as if preparing to leave. A tartan scarf covered her hair and was knotted under her chin, babushka-style.

When the woman turned to wish the workmen a good night, Claire saw that she was not as old as one might have expected, perhaps only forty or so, like her own mother. Though not tall, her face was long and narrow, with a straight nose and a cleft chin. Her complexion was ruddy from the cold and weathered from wind and sun. She smiled at Claire and then at the ticket agent.

"Let me guess. Did you come here for the skiing? Or perhaps for a snowmobiling tour? March used to be a big month for tourists around here."

Claire said nothing but the woman continued to smile at her.

"Helen is joking with you," the ticket agent interjected. "The ski resorts closed years ago. And the last snowmobiles around here were handed over to the Army around the time of the Manchurian War."

"Which is precisely your good luck," the woman continued. "Because the shortage of tourists means I happen to have some extra room over at my place. Now you wouldn't be looking for somewhere to stay, would you?"

"Yes, I would, Ma'am," Claire said.

"Call me Helen. And your name is...?"

"Claire. I don't have much money, though. All I have is..."

Helen waved aside the objection and picked up her basket.

"Don't let that trouble you. I don't have much, either."

Helen turned to the ticket agent and smiled.

"Dorothy, don't you worry about Claire tonight. We'll come by again tomorrow. Come along, Claire, we've got a long walk ahead of us and it looks like it's going to snow again. Good thing you're a strong-looking girl, because that backpack of yours may grow a bit heavy when we start up into the hills."

Claire thanked the ticket lady, then followed Helen outside. They walked silently in single file along the tracks toward the freight yard. In the distance Claire could see a string of vacant passenger coaches, including four unmarked sleepers at the far end of the yard. Men in shiny black helmets and dark uniforms shone spotlights at the cars, as if preparing to move in for a closer look.

Between gusts of wind they could hear bits and snatches of music— odd music that Claire found unnatural and disturbing. But before long they crossed the tracks to where the music no longer reached them.

"My cabin is in those hills beyond the pine grove. We're going to follow this path for a while, cross a road or two and, before you know it, we'll be there."

They continued for a mile or more when Helen stopped abruptly and raised her hand to signal for silence. She stepped off the path into the trees and beckoned Claire to join her.

"We've got company," she told Claire in a whisper. "I see trucks parked ahead. I think they're picking up prisoners for Kamas."

"Prisoners?"

"Yes. Kamas is only about ten miles from here."

"Do we have to take a different way to your cabin?"

"No, we sure don't," Helen answered firmly. "Now, keep your eyes open, follow close behind me and do exactly as I do. This is still America, by God, and we have a right to use the roads like everyone else."

"Is Kamas a labor camp?"

Helen turned to Claire with a quizzical look.

"Aren't you a little young to know about labor camps? When I was your age, places like Kamas didn't exist in this country and none of us believed they ever would. But things have—"

"They've sent my father to a labor camp," Claire interrupted. "They told my mom it was in Utah. I came here to find him."

Helen reached out both hands and held Claire by the shoulders.

"I don't know your father, Claire, but let me tell you something just between the two of us. People can say what they want, but it's nothing to be ashamed of to have a father who's been arrested. Camps like Kamas are filled with fine and decent men. My husband has been in Kamas for nearly five years and Alec is one of the best. These days it's the people outside the wire you have to watch out for."

"Maybe my dad came here on the same train as I did. And maybe they took him to the same place where your husband is."

As soon as she heard herself say it, Claire felt more discouraged than ever. The corners of her mouth turned downward and quivered despite her best efforts to stay composed.

"It's too late in the evening for thoughts like that, sweetheart. Save your worries for the morning, when you're stronger. Besides, there's something we need to do right now and we ought to have our wits about us to do it."

She nodded toward the wicker basket.

"Do you see this leftover bread? Sometimes I drop it where the convoy prisoners can pick it up. The guards don't like it but I do it anyway in the hope that perhaps one day somebody will do the same for my Alec. Here, stuff some of these in your pockets and watch me for the right time to drop them."

Claire did as she was told and followed Helen along a wooded path that ran parallel to the road. Through the trees and falling snow she could see the light of kerosene lanterns and flashlights and hear deep-chested dogs barking. As they emerged from the woods, she saw a parade of men in dirty orange coveralls trudging four abreast along the road. To her right she heard shouts and scuffling among the prisoners and saw a squad of black-uniformed guards run forward alongside the column.

"Now! Follow me across the road and, when you reach the middle, empty your pockets!"

Helen waited for a dog handler to pass, made the sign of the cross on her chest, then set off brazenly across the road. The prisoners were stunned to see a civilian, much less a woman, in their midst and cautiously broke ranks to give her space. She pretended to stumble and let a dozen or more hard-crusted rolls tumble onto the snow-covered road. The prisoners closest to her pounced on the bread like starving wolves, then those at the rear of the column rushed forward to claim the leftovers. Claire took this as her cue to empty her pockets.

The last roll was gone when Claire saw the black German shepherd streaking toward her. Before she could think, Helen had seized her hand and pulled her back along the wooded path as fast as they could run. The two of them didn't stop running until they were completely out of breath. Only then did they pause to wonder why the dog had not pressed its attack.

It was nearly an hour later when they reached Helen's cabin, a one-story frame cabin nestled among scrub oaks in a shallow ravine facing southeast over the Heber Valley. The road that had once led to the cabin was difficult to trace now, overgrown as it was with saplings and covered with two feet of fluffy snow.

The moment they entered, Claire's half-numbed cheeks felt the warmth left by the last smoldering coals in the wood stove. With stiff fingers she removed her snow-encrusted boots. Once Claire's parka was hung up to dry, Helen promptly led her into a tiny bedroom with twin cots.

The room was clean and orderly except for a dozen bunches of dried flowers hanging from the rafters and a paint-spattered, wooden easel in the corner. On the nightstand was a framed photograph of a giggling blonde girl in a bathing suit not much older than Claire.

"Do you live here all alone?" Claire asked as Helen gave her a fresh T-shirt for a nightdress.

Helen nodded and grinned with obvious pride.

"Yep. It's mine by squatter's rights."

"Can I ask you a big favor?"

"Of course, sweetheart. I don't know if it's in my power, but I'll try."

"Would it be okay if I stay with you till I find my dad?"

Helen laughed gently and gave Claire a motherly hug.

"You're welcome to stay as long as you need to. From now on this room is yours. But there is one catch: if you want to eat around here, you're going to have to work. And work starts first thing in the morning."

CHAPTER 4

"You are not brought here to live but to suffer and die... If you live, it means that you are guilty of one of two things: either you worked less than was assigned you or you ate more than was your proper due."
—Soviet labor camp doctor, 1930s

Thursday, March 7, 2024

I opened my eyes in the pre-dawn darkness and looked out upon row after row of triple-deck bunk beds. I lay on a top berth, my kit bag tucked between my head and the plywood slab. Although I had no blanket, my prison coveralls kept me warm enough in the airless barracks.

I counted five rows of beds, each row twelve beds long, for a total of 180 berths, all of which appeared to be occupied. The floor was covered with sleeping men, too. If each of the four prison cars had delivered a hundred live prisoners to Heber, then the 400 of us occupied a dwelling intended for 180.

At the sound of a distant electric school bell, the prisoners began to stir. A low murmur rose as men spoke to each other in apprehensive whispers.

I looked down at the bunk directly below and saw Will Roesemann staring back at me.

"Next bell will be roll call," he said sleepily. "What do you suppose they'll do with us?"

"Whatever it is, anything is better than interrogation. Right now all I care about is getting fed."

"I could eat sawdust," Roesemann agreed.

I slid off my bunk and sat beside him.

"I saw them take Reineke away after you fell asleep." I could tell he was replaying the scene in his mind as he spoke. "They took the guy who brought down the dog, too."

"Thank God they didn't haul us off for helping him," I said. "With our luck, we're probably on some blacklist already."

"Stay cool, Paul. I'll bet they couldn't care less about us."

I had lost count of the number of times Will had told me to stay cool. He always seemed to have things figured out several steps in advance.

As I climbed down from my bunk a trio of warders in goose down greatcoats entered the room. Each carried a two-foot nightstick and rapped it rhythmically against a wooden bed frame. Each was hatless and had a shaven head that accentuated his thick neck and beetled brow. Their theatrical belligerence combined with a pathetic need for attention reminded me of bullies on a high school football team.

"Listen up, you pukes," shouted the shortest of the three, a heavy-jawed, bullet-headed gorilla. The room fell silent.

"In exactly two minutes, I want every one of you standing at attention on the parade ground. Deputy Mills will show you how to assemble for roll call."

He pointed to a sullen thug a few feet away.

"When roll call ends," he continued, "I want to see you march single file to the latrines where you will have five minutes to do your thing. Then Deputy Mills and his men will lead you to the transit center for disinfecting, de-lousing, and registration. Is that clear?"

"How about food?" The question came from the rear of the barracks. "We haven't eaten since yesterday morning."

"You'll get a ration bar at registration and another at the end of the day when you finish your work," the warder answered. "No hot meals till tomorrow."

"And who the hell are you?" someone mumbled.

The bullet-headed warder scanned the group angrily for the man who spoke.

"My name is Renaud but you'll call me Deputy Renaud if you don't want to spit teeth. I'm chief warder for new prisoners. And anybody who doesn't like the way I do things can step forward right now. There's plenty of room for you in the isolator."

Silence followed. Renaud looked around the crowded barracks as if to spot future troublemakers.

"Alright then, when I say 'go,' I want you to line up outside in single file. No stragglers—the last ten in line lose their morning rations."

Renaud gestured for Mills and the other warder to leave and then followed them to the door.

"Go!"

All four hundred of us rushed for the door at once, crushing the weak and the unlucky against the walls and against bunks bolted firmly to the floor. But once outside and under Mills's direction, it took us only a few minutes to line up in formation, most of us having been drilled in prison yard protocol at detention facilities all across the country.

Roll call went swiftly. Out of habit, I counted the number of names reported as missing. The total exceeded forty, which meant that hunger, dehydration, exposure, and illness had reduced the size of our transit convoy by nearly ten percent. Natural selection had already begun and I wondered how long my own strength would hold out.

Mills counted off the first forty prisoners to enter the transit center. I was among them. He ushered us into a concrete-floored shower room with sprinkler heads mounted along three walls. A fleet of wheeled laundry hampers was parked near the entrance.

Renaud rejoined us, followed by Mills and a third warder who appeared to be in his early forties. His freckled face wore a permanent expression of skepticism and disapproval that aroused my immediate dislike. His name was Grady and, as I learned later, he had once been a partner in a well-known accounting firm before he, Renaud, and Mills had all been convicted of looting the company where Renaud and Mills had been executives.

Renaud then resumed the briefing he had begun before roll call: "Listen up, scum! It's shower time. Yes, these are real showers and to prove it, I will be staying here with you to supervise. You will have exactly two minutes, timed by my watch, to get undressed. In these two minutes, you will deposit every possession and article of clothing you have into one of these hampers, taking with you only eyeglasses, artificial limbs, and other medical prostheses. Your prostheses will be x-rayed and searched by hand. So if any of you think you are clever enough to smuggle in drugs, weapons, money, or other contraband, I urge you to come over here right now and deposit your treasures in the hamper. I will personally hang from the watchtower anybody caught smuggling. Camp rules permit me to do it—I've done it before, and I'll do it as many times as I must to keep contraband out of this camp. Am I making myself clear? Good. Your two minutes start—...now!"

Some of us wore the orange coveralls issued at transit camps. Others were still dressed in civilian clothes or in prison denims. Regardless of what we wore, when Renaud signaled that our time was up, every one of us stood naked while the hampers brimmed with our filthy, louse-infested clothing.

In the disinfecting room, trusties with shaved heads worked us over with electric clippers, shaving our scalps and removing every vestige of beard and body hair. Next we had five minutes to shower. Orderlies then handed out antiseptic ointment to spread on any sores or wounds and dusted us with de-lousing powder before we stepped onto the scales.

There we stood, naked, hairless and utterly undignified, waiting in single file to enter the next phase of our initiation. I noticed that many of the men bore the scars of past beatings and interrogations, while others bore war wounds. It was equally sobering to see so many prostheses, especially among the younger men, some of whom had seen combat in Iraq or Afghanistan or Civil War II or had fought in the Russian Far East against the Chinese.

I turned around in the queue and looked Will Roesemann over from top to bottom. He was thirty-two years old, just short of six feet, small-boned, and moved with the grace of a former college soccer forward. But now he weighed twenty pounds less than he had in college and displayed the sagging shoulders and bony ribcage of an idle and malnourished prisoner.

If Will appeared unfit for a life at hard labor, I did not look much better. Though I had been reasonably well muscled in my youth, endurance had never been my strong suit; twenty years behind a desk had not done anything to improve it. Now, after dropping some thirty pounds since my arrest, I had no stamina, and with my forty-sixth birthday fast approaching, my recuperative powers were well past their peak.

Will looked at me and stifled a laugh. I looked back at him and at the other pale scarecrows. Our powdered skins made us all look like horror-movie zombies—I, too, let out a quiet laugh.

After that I stumbled through the rest of in-processing with more curiosity than dread. In the next room, a stock clerk handed me a set of six patches with my newly assigned identification number, W-0885, a sewing kit, a well-worn but clean set of poly/cotton-blend underwear, thin white acrylic socks, an orange acrylic watch cap, and faded orange winter coveralls. The insulated coveralls resembled a one-piece snowmobiling outfit and were similar in construction to the coveralls used by U.S. troops in the Russian Far East. I soon came to appreciate how important this garment was to a prisoner's survival. Without it, the cold would have killed most of us within days. Finally, each of us was issued a used pair of felt-lined rubberized leather boots.

My assignment to the general labor pool held no special significance for me yet, as all of us had been assigned to general labor and I did not yet appreciate the survival value of non-manual labor. Similarly, my identification card, number patches, and ration card held no meaning to me beyond the humiliating realization that from now on, the camp authorities would know me only by the numbers sewn onto my hat and uniform.

The event I remember most vividly from the final stages of in-processing was receiving my first ration bar. I had become so accustomed to the transport feeding schedule that the delay in my morning meal had left my stomach in knots. Now I chewed each bite of the fortified meal bar slowly and savored its flavor and texture. It was a vanilla bar, but it tasted nothing like vanilla, its recipe having apparently been adulterated beyond recognition from the original formula.

Those of us who finished in-processing first were made to sit cross-legged outside on the snow-covered parade ground. Not far away, the warders huddled around an oil drum trying to stay warm over the wood fire inside.

Will Roesemann and I sat next to each other and speculated quietly about what might be in store for us at Kamas. Will had heard rumors of Asian-style re-education and brainwashing, while I expected hard labor building airfields or military bases.

Before our discussion had gone very far, I felt a tap on my shoulder. I turned around and saw a slim, long-legged prisoner not much older than twenty-five with a flat, open face and a broad grin. His sparkling blue eyes revealed a raw vitality that seemed oddly misplaced in a camp like Kamas.

"Are you the fellows who helped Major Reineke off the train last night? I looked for you when we got to the barracks but I lost you in the dark."

From his accent I surmised that he was a Texan.

"I wish you'd found us when we were still on the road," I grumbled. "We could have used your help. That last couple hundred yards nearly killed me."

"I would have pitched in," the Texan replied, still grinning, "except I was at the back of the line where the bread was. I scored five pieces and was fixing to give the extras to you. But I was so damned hungry I couldn't keep from eating them all. And good thing I did, because if I'd still had them this morning, they would have gone straight into the hamper."

"Well, I'm glad they did somebody some good," I groused.

Will laughed at my sour disposition. Then he introduced us and asked where the man was from.

"Galveston. Name's Jerry Lee," he replied. "How about you fellas?"

"Pennsylvania. We shipped in from Susquehanna. Tell me, how do you know Reineke?"

"I served in his unit during the Manchurian War. He was battalion commander when the Chinks attacked us across the Ussuri River. If it hadn't been for the Major, the Chinks would have overrun our sector big time. Later on, I heard he stayed on all the way through the withdrawal to Sakhalin Island and the airlift back to Alaska. Man, he was a hell of a fighter! I couldn't hardly believe it when I heard he deserted."

"Hold on," Roesemann interrupted. "How do you know he deserted? From what I've been told, State Security arrested just about everybody who made it back from Sakhalin. I've met troops accused of desertion who swore that the DSS rolled up their entire unit the moment they stepped ashore in Anchorage. The desertion rap stinks, if you ask me."

Jerry Lee shrugged sympathetically.

"So maybe he didn't desert. All I can say is that when I was in Alaska just after the Armistice, some buddies of mine told me Reineke had tried to resign but the brass wouldn't let him. A couple of days later somebody at field headquarters tipped him off that he was about to be arrested. So he hightailed it for the Yukon."

Another voice spoke up from the row in front of us. It was a knowing voice with a Long Island accent. "I know Glenn Reineke. What he did may have been desertion under the law, but it had nothing to do with cowardice. He escaped twice from this camp. No coward would ever do that, knowing what the warders do to people who get caught."

"Do you know the guy who stopped the dog?" Roesemann asked.

"Yup. Reineke's escape partner. A former Navy SEAL by the name of Toth. Hard-bitten as they come. My guess is he'll leave the isolator even stronger than he went in."

The speaker had a long, gaunt face that was deeply creased with leathery wrinkles. His doleful eyes and drooping eyelids gave him an almost funereal expression. It was an intelligent face, but not an honest one. I introduced myself and met Steve Bernstein, a forty-four-year-old pharmaceutical rep from Manhasset. This was his fourth year in the camps. After nearly a year at Green River, he had been transferred back to Kamas to work as a hospital orderly.

When we learned that Bernstein had been in Kamas before, we peppered him with questions about camp conditions, work assignments, the guards and warders, and every aspect of camp life. Will Roesemann only listened carefully and watched Bernstein with the skeptical demeanor of an attorney hearing trial testimony from a hostile witness. I assumed that Will had picked up the same whiff of dishonesty in Bernstein that I had detected. But after a few minutes he joined in to ask Bernstein what percentage of Kamas inmates consisted of drug dealers, armed robbers, and sex offenders, criminals of the kind who tyrannized the holding prisons and transit camps.

Roesemann seemed pleased when Bernstein reported that the only non-political prisoners in the camp were white-collar criminals like Renaud, Grady, and Mills. These men had agreed to serve out their sentences as warders in a labor camp rather than as prisoners in conventional lock-ups in exchange for being given two years credit for every year served. I knew that the presence of violent career criminals at Kamas was a matter of vital concern to Roesemann. The felons had not given him a moment of peace in the holding prisons.

Jerry Lee asked about work categories at Kamas. Mines were universally feared because of their reputation as death traps. Logging camps and quarries did not rank much higher. Federal safety regulations were not enforced at any of the worksites in the camp system. Bernstein told us that he had spent six months at a gold placer facility in the Yukon where conditions were as primitive as the days of the original Yukon gold rush a century before. Prisoners perished daily from exposure, disease, and exhaustion.

Fortunately, Kamas offered a variety of work specialties, including military and civilian recycling, road-building, logging, snow-clearing, and silver mining. Recycling employed by far the largest number of prisoners. The military recycling site, located on the road to Heber, salvaged destroyed or damaged military equipment left over from Civil War II and the invasion of Mexico. With so much weaponry and supplies having been lost in Russia, and industrial capacity stalled at less than half of what it had been before the Events, recycling was essential to rearming the military.

The civilian recycling site, located near the burned-out village of Oakley along the Weber River, specialized in truck and auto parts as well as building materials and fixtures removed from forfeited properties around Park City. According to Bernstein, camp engineers estimated that it would take more than a decade before the Kamas-based salvage crews could exhaust the potential of the former Park City and Deer Valley resort areas, once rebel strongholds. The high price of auto parts and plumbing and electrical fixtures on the black market meant that the government would make a fortune from stripping the confiscated properties of its once-prosperous citizens.

Jerry Lee followed up with a question about work quotas and food rations and the margin for survival between them. Was it possible to outlive your sentence if you stayed on full rations? Or was the system rigged against a prisoner's survival?

Bernstein answered that Kamas was not as corrupt as other labor camps, where guards and warders grew fat on extra rations stolen from starving prisoners. Still, quotas and rations were calculated with precious little margin for error. For that reason, the constant struggle for survival led to rampant theft, cheating, fighting, extortion, and every other means of ensuring one's own survival at the expense of the next man.

Bernstein's theory was that State Security considered political prisoners fundamentally incapable of rehabilitation or re-entry into Unionist society. But if so many prisoners were to remain in custody indefinitely, the camps had to be self-financing. And since a prisoner's value to the state depended on his contribution to the camp's output, his continued receipt of rations depended upon his meeting the work quota. Anyone who failed to meet the quota saw his rations cut. The problem was that anything less than a full ration was insufficient to sustain life.

When asked how camp veterans managed to beat these odds, Bernstein replied simply that they were willing to do whatever it took to survive. New prisoners, he said, tended to harbor unrealistic hopes of a last-minute reprieve or clung to pre-arrest values and standards. Veteran prisoners had learned to cast aside their old morals and cared only about the preservation of their lives, however humble or crude that life might be. Whoever looked backward risked slipping irrevocably into the abyss.

Bernstein's commentary had a sobering effect on us. But he seemed so eager to gain our confidence that I decided not to give it to him just yet.

When the last of the new prisoners emerged from the transit center in their fresh orange coveralls, the warders ordered us to count off by threes and divided us into teams to shovel snow from the entrance roads, walkways, and parade grounds around the camp.

Renaud led one team to the Service Yard, which contained workshops, storage sheds and maintenance facilities and served as a buffer zone between the women's camp in Division 1 and the men's camp in Divisions 2 and 3. Grady took another team, including Will Roesemann and Bernstein, to Division 2, where the foreigners' barracks were located. Jerry Lee and I remained in Division 3 with Mills.

In less than an hour of shoveling snow, blisters formed on my hands and my entire upper body began to ache. Nearly a year and a half of captivity without exercise had made me quite unfit for hard labor. I found myself moving more slowly, using less effort, and faking it as much as I could without drawing Mills's attention. I observed how the others paced their work and learned to follow their example. By the third hour I had become an energy-efficient robot.

As the sun hid behind the western hills, an icy wind arose and poked its way under our collars and up our sleeves and pant legs. Despite my blistered hands, aching shoulders, and the shooting pain in my lower back, I shoveled faster just to stay warm. I kept my head down, glancing up only occasionally to watch the advance of leaden clouds across the darkening sky.

Suddenly I heard the sharp crack of a rifle shot and instinctively hit the dirt. Craning my neck around to see what had happened, I watched a pair of uniformed guards clamber down the ladder from the nearest watchtower, enter the gate in the inner perimeter wall, and draw their pistols from their holsters. One covered the other as the latter knelt beside the fallen figure of a young woman in coveralls a few yards from the wall. The kneeling guard rolled her body over, revealing that the entire back of her skull had exploded from the force of a rifle shot exiting her head. Then the guard waved to the watchtower and the marksman inside fired a second shot into the air. This was the belated warning shot. The official report required a second bullet casing as evidence that the warning shot had been fired.

Once satisfied that the woman posed no further threat to camp security, the two guards holstered their sidearms and dragged her body by the ankles through the open gate into Division 2. Then they ordered the rest of us to resume shoveling while they retreated to the warmth of the heated watchtower. It was all over so quickly that none of us had time to react. One minute the girl was scribbling on her clipboard, the next moment she was carrion.

Within minutes, word spread among the hushed shovelers that the girl's name was Lillian, that she had been a work scheduler from the women's camp, and that she was in the habit of leaving her hat and scarf near the perimeter wire while she worked. Someone remarked that the guards had warned Lillian many times to keep her distance from the wire, but this time they had not bothered with courtesies. Even in the context of a corrective labor camp, such a brazen act of premeditated murder was an outrage.

As the news spread, the prisoners seethed with resentment and made only a pretense of work, unless a warder was within arm's reach to enforce it. With less and less snow being shoveled, portions of the entrance roads, walkways, and assembly areas remained uncleared as the sun set and the first column of prisoners returned from worksites outside the camp. Mills cursed at us to keep working and shoved several idlers whose shovels remained at their sides but he stopped short of using his nightstick on them, likely for fear of being overpowered. So while the prisoners stood their ground and refused to work, the warders conferred and the guards looked on warily from their high towers.

Mills returned after a few minutes with Renaud and six additional warders wielding ax handles. Behind them was the black-uniformed DSS officer I had seen during the march from the railway station. It was Major Jack Whiting, the camp's security chief. Whiting stepped ahead of the two warders carrying a battery-powered bullhorn and stopped at the very spot where Lillian had fallen.

"Listen up, prisoners, in this camp you follow the rules. If you don't, you will face the consequences." He paused, surveying the crowd before him. "If you don't work, you don't eat, you don't sleep, you don't get shelter from the cold. Until your work is done, you will stay here in this yard and receive no evening ration. I will be back in one hour to check on your progress."

As soon as Whiting lowered the bullhorn and turned to leave, the warders moved among us in pairs, whacking any prisoner who did not make a vigorous display of shoveling. They bashed a dozen or more of us to the ground before we resumed our work, shoveling slowly but without interruption, taking extra care to stay away from the wire.

An hour later, Whiting returned, and even though the wind had scattered much of the piled snow across the camp yard once more, he was satisfied. The warders looked on impassively as we lined up to receive our second meal bar of the day. When the last man had received his ration, we were dismissed to report to our permanent barracks. I looked for Roesemann without success. I was beyond exhaustion, beneath depression.

By the time I arrived at my new home in Barracks C-14, no vacant berths were left. Too tired and cold even to get angry, I found a space on the floor under a bed near the center of the room, gnawed at my ration bar and settled in for the night. Lights went out moments later.

The last thing I heard before falling asleep was a muffled cry, a momentary creaking of a nearby bed, and the sound of bare feet dropping to the floor and padding quickly across the room. Whatever they were doing to each other sounded dreadful, but I was too spent to care.

CHAPTER 5

"Reactionaries must be deprived of the right to voice their opinions. Only the people have that right."
—Mao Zedong

Thursday, March 7, 2024

When Claire opened her eyes, she found herself curled between crisp white sheets. She wore the fresh T-shirt Helen had given her and clutched in one arm the gray velour elephant that had traveled in her backpack all the way from Philadelphia. Her body was shivering and when she closed her eyes, she remembered that she had been dreaming about last night's walk through the snowy hills and her encounter with the men in orange overalls.

In her dream, she thought she had recognized her father among the column of prisoners and had tried to pursue him through loose, knee-deep snow up a steep mountain path much like the one that had led to Helen's cabin. The men in her dream were moving much more slowly than the men she had seen on the road, but no matter how hard she tried, she couldn't keep pace with them. Time after time she strained to get a better look at the prisoner who looked like her father, but most of the time his back was turned to her, and besides, he looked too skinny to be her dad.

Still, there was something about the way he held his head and the way he stooped when he walked that made her pretty sure it was Dad.

But she kept falling behind and it made her terribly unhappy because she wanted so desperately to catch up to him and wrap her arms around him and take him home to someplace where they could be a family and she wouldn't need to be afraid anymore.

Helen knocked gently on the half-open door before she entered the dimly lit bedroom.

"You've slept for nearly twelve hours, Claire."

Claire gave a weak smile.

"Do you remember where you are, sweetheart?" She asked as she sat down at the foot of the bed. The girl nodded.

"I have some breakfast for you in the kitchen. It's not much, but it will keep you going till we get to town. Are you hungry?"

Another nod.

"Come with me then. I think we need some talking time."

Helen gathered Claire's dirty clothing and carried it out with her. In the kitchen, she had filled a plastic tub with hot soapy water and began washing the corduroy trousers by hand. She picked the turtleneck off the floor but hesitated before dropping it into the tub. Tucked inside was a zippered travel wallet that contained Claire's passport, national I.D. card, photocopies of correspondence with her grandparents, and two folded one-dollar bills. Helen removed the passport, examined it quickly and stuffed it back into the wallet. Then she tucked the wallet inside a cereal box at the rear of the kitchen cabinet and closed the door.

Claire took a seat at the kitchen counter opposite a bowl of hot oatmeal. Without looking up or testing the first spoonful she began to eat.

"Claire, I wish we had lots of time for this but I'm afraid we don't."

Seeing her guest stop eating long enough to look up at her, Helen continued.

"I know it's hard to know whom to trust sometimes. Without your mom and dad around, it's extra hard. I may not be your mother, but once, a long time ago, I had a daughter your age. If my little girl were ever lost in a strange place, the thing I'd want more than anything in the world would be for some good person to take her in for a while and help her find her way back to me.

"So here you are, and here I am, and you need help getting back to where you belong, and I'm ready to help you. But for me to do that, you need to tell me some more about yourself. Do you think you could do that?"

Claire let out a demure burp, covered her mouth with her hand and giggled.

"I guess I can," she answered. "But could I have some more oatmeal first?"

Guided by Helen's gentle questioning, Claire told the story of her twelve-year-old life. She told of a contented childhood in a small town with plenty of friends and of her room in the stone farmhouse near Sewickley with a sweeping view of forest and farmland. She mentioned how much she had liked school, and that nearly every adult on both sides of her family had earned an advanced degree and achieved success in business, engineering, or law.

Then she told of how her father had cut his own pay to keep his company from going out of business and of her mother's return to work in Pittsburgh when taxes and inflation made it impossible for the family to survive on her father's earnings alone. And she told of how she had missed her friends after the private school they attended had been forced to close its doors under the President-for-Life's latest education reform plan.

When Helen asked what had made her leave Pennsylvania and travel all the way to Utah, Claire explained that, for as long as she could remember, her grandparents and aunts and uncles had been fighting with the government over money and taxes. During the Events, her grandparents had been forced to sell their landholdings to the state of Pennsylvania and, not long afterward, every one of her adult relatives had decided to emigrate to England or Chile. Everyone except her mom and dad, and they would have gone, too, if her dad had been able to sell his company.

After years on the edge of insolvency, he finally locked the factory doors and sold what was left for enough to cover the family's emigration taxes and exit visas. But when he went to the bank to collect, the security police arrested him and canceled the family's exit visas. Claire's mother managed to get new exit visas for herself and her children, only to be detained at the Philadelphia airport along with Claire's little sister, Louisa.

Helen reached out and clasped Claire's hands in hers.

"Don't worry, Claire, we'll find them. It took me a while to learn where they took my husband, Alec, but I found him. We can find your dad, too, if we try."

"Do you really think so? You're not just saying that to make me feel better?"

"Honest. Scouts' honor."

Claire looked puzzled.

"Sorry, I guess you're too young to remember the Girl Scouts. Anyway, it may take a little time before we figure things out. Meanwhile, we'll need to put you to work. So, tell me, what sorts of things do you know how to do? Have you ever done chores around the house or odd jobs for your neighbors?"

"I've done some babysitting for the family across the street. And I help Mom in the kitchen sometimes."

"What sort of things in the kitchen?"

"I know how to set the table and wash dishes and clean up after dinner. And polish the silver. And I can cook a little."

"I wouldn't mention the silver polishing if I were you. But what dishes can you cook? Eggs? Bacon? Pancakes?"

"All of those. And just about anything kids like to eat. You know, hamburgers, hot dogs, homemade pizza."

"Can you sew?"

"I took some lessons once. And my mom taught me how to make napkins and pillow cases on her sewing machine."

" Sounds like you're very qualified," Helen laughed. "You know, a hundred years ago, well-bred girls not much older than you were sent off to wealthy people's homes to learn how to run a proper household before they married. Of course, since the Events, there aren't many homes like that around, but with all the government people posted in the valley, perhaps there might be a general's wife or a colonel's wife who could use some help. How would that kind of work suit you?"

"Okay, I guess," Claire answered with downcast eyes. "But I'd much rather stay here with you. Couldn't I just live here and be your helper?"

"There's nothing I would like more, my dear. But my tiny business is barely enough to feed me, let alone the two of us. No, I think what we need to do is to find us a good home where you can work for a while to earn your keep. Let's talk to Dorothy this afternoon, shall we?"

"Couldn't we wait just a few more days? I'm kind of..." Her voice trailed off.

"...scared?" Helen finished her sentence. "A brave girl like you who's come out here alone all the way from Philadelphia?"

"What if the police come for me like they did for my dad? They'll put me in jail, won't they? Then I'll never be able to find my parents."

Claire's eyes brimmed with tears and she hid her face in her hands. Helen drew an arm around Claire's shoulder to console her.

"I understand. It's natural to be afraid when you've been separated from your parents. But let's look at your choices: If you go back to Philadelphia or start looking for your dad on your own, sooner or later the police will pick you up. When they discover who you are, they may send you to where they're holding your mother and sister or they may decide to put you in a juvenile detention facility somewhere. Not a good idea. On the other hand, if you stay here and let me help you, we can reach out to your grandparents overseas and let them know where you are while we're looking for your parents. Then, together, maybe we can sort things out. But for that to happen, we need to buy some time. So, are you with me?"

Claire frowned as she considered the decision.

"I'm with you," she replied, then slowly wiped away her tears.

"Okay, then. We have a deal," Helen answered with a cheerful smile. "Come, now, finish your oatmeal so we can find you some clean clothes to wear till yours are dry. Then you can start helping me prepare the things we're going to sell tonight at the railway station."

CHAPTER 6

"In any country, there must be people who have to die. They are the sacrifice any nation has to make to achieve law and order."
—Idi Amin Dada, Ugandan dictator

Friday, March 8, 2024

An electric school bell mounted on the barracks wall erupted to harass me out of a deep and dreamless sleep. The clanging penetrated every corner of my brain, distracting me from the throbbing pain in my lower back and the ache in my arms and shoulders from the previous day's work. I rolled slowly out from under the bunk and surveyed my new home in the pre-dawn darkness.

Like the transit barracks, it was a simple rectangular box of flimsy prefabricated construction with no interior walls or partitions. It was smaller than the transit barracks, however, designed to sleep little more than half the number of prisoners. I counted three closely packed columns of triple-decker bunks, twelve beds to a column. The interior walls were covered with graffiti and riddled with holes stuffed with rags and straw.

A murmur arose from an adjacent row of bunks. I turned to see a knot of prisoners gathering to look at something in a lower berth just across the aisle. One of the men stepped aside long enough for me to see a pool of dried blood on the bare wood floor. A moment later I caught a glimpse of a bloody arm hanging down from the bunk.

"They slit his goddamned throat," I heard someone say with disgust. "Served him right."

"I knew there was something fishy about that guy," another voice added nervously. "He gave me the creeps the minute I saw him."

"Maybe so," a third voice countered. "But every time somebody goes killing a stoolie, the bosses take it out on the rest of us. Just you wait, they'll be shooting another poor bastard like that girl they shot up yesterday."

"Just a second. Maybe you don't remember the way things used to be around here," added a voice from the top bunk just behind me. "Whiting had stoolies in every work crew feeding him lies about us to save their own skins. Those rats sent the best of our men into the isolator or off to Canada or the mines. Without stoolies, the bosses can't control us and they know it. Personally, I'd rather take a bullet than go back to the way it was."

The speaker climbed down from his bunk and stood next to me. He was tall and rangy with a narrow face and tranquil blue eyes. He looked about ten years younger than I and seemed in good physical shape for someone who had been in the camps for very long. His accent sounded mid-Western, Wisconsin or Minnesota, and he spoke with the confidence I associated with higher education; I guessed he might be a high school or college instructor.

"I just arrived here yesterday, but I'm with you about the stoolies," I told him. "At Susquehanna there were more stoolies than lice and you couldn't say a word without hearing it played back to you during interrogation."

"Welcome to Kamas. Here at least we have the stoolies on the run," the man said, holding out his hand. "Ralph Knopfler's the name. Do you have a work assignment yet?"

I shook his hand. "Paul Wagner, and no. Any advice?"

"If you have a choice, go for the civilian recycling plant. They have plenty of work for new men and you don't run much of a risk of being reassigned to something worse later. Military recycling is not bad, either. But don't go near the silver mines in Park City. They're killers."

The bell rang a second time and we followed the crowd of prisoners onto the parade ground. After roll call a work scheduler read out the assignments for the new arrivals. Road construction, snow clearing, waste disposal, and the ore crushing plant were all read out before they reached recycling sites A and B. I was assigned to Recycling Site A, which recovered civilian building materials on a large scale. I congratulated myself on my good fortune and gave a high five to Will Roesemann, who was assigned to the same place.

Breakfast was served in Division 3 mess hall, a two-story factory-like building of cinder block construction. Each of us received a plastic bowl of watery oatmeal with a few elusive globules of margarine floating on top and a ration bar that we were supposed to save and eat at midday. I estimated the food's caloric value and wondered how I would survive until dinner.

Tucking the ration bar inside my coveralls, I picked up an enamel mug. Self-service urns contained a choice of cold water, weak tea, or a thin coffee substitute unlike any I had ever tasted. I opted for the tea and stepped into the dining area, which consisted of row upon row of metal picnic tables bolted to the floor.

I had learned from painful experience that selecting a seat in a prison or labor camp dining hall demanded extreme caution. Mealtime fistfights were commonplace. At Kamas the warders, easily identifiable by their sleekness and heft, sat at special tables near the windows. Foremen, work schedulers, and other high-ranking prisoners also sat together, as did prisoners under the age of twenty-one.

Here and there were tables of silent, slow-moving, painfully gaunt figures who could easily be diagnosed as goners or last-leggers—prisoners who lacked the physical strength to carry on much longer and already had lost the will to survive. I had known goners at Susquehanna and in the transit camps and had seen how quickly their final decline could take hold. Every self-respecting prisoner feared this fate for himself and his friends.

Being over forty, I chose a seat at a table of older prisoners with whom I imagined I might have something in common. One of them was the fellow at the barracks who had expressed fear of reprisals for the killing of stool pigeons. His furtive manner and yellowing front teeth made him resemble a rodent. My intuition told me that he might have been an alcoholic or drug abuser before entering the camps. He recognized me and held his hand out across the table.

"Just in from Susquehanna, eh? I was there once."

His name was D'Amato and he worked in the warehouse.

"You're lucky to be in recycling," D'Amato said. "Sometimes you can find stuff that you can sneak back to the camp and sell to the guards. I found a gold chain once. Traded it for a sack of ration bars."

"What's the warehouse like?" I asked.

"It's the best, believe me. I used to be in snow removal and I nearly froze more times than I can count. Lost the toes to prove it."

"How did you go about getting a change in duty? Was it hard?"

D'Amato's neighbor, a towering fifty-something whose aristocratic features showed several days of gray stubble, inclined his head to hear D'Amato's response. D'Amato gave him a sheepish smile and went on.

"Pure luck. One day you're at death's door, the next day you're in from the cold. There's no way I can explain it. Take Judge O'Rourke, here."

He nodded respectfully toward the man on his right, a small, ruddy-faced man of about sixty who wore silver wire-rimmed bifocals.

"The judge and his partner, Judge Richardson, used to be in waste disposal. Nasty, nasty work. Judge O'Rourke came down with cholera and nearly didn't make it. Now they're both appeals clerks and report directly to the deputy warden. Whenever anybody requests a case review, it goes through them."

"Every prisoner has the right to due process," Judge O'Rourke added gratuitously. "Oh, you'll hear petty grumbling about the appeals process from time to time, but in nearly twenty years as a judge, I have found that it is the criminal's nature to claim unfair treatment."

I looked at the man in amazement. To claim that due process existed at all for politicals charged under Title 18 rose to the level of a psychotic break with reality.

"And what might your offense be?" I inquired. "If you don't mind my asking."

The judge pulled himself upright and cast a disapproving look my way.

"Title 18, Section 2384."

"Seditious conspiracy," I noted. We all knew the sections of Title 18 by heart. "Odd, but you hardly look like somebody who'd be involved in that sort of thing. Could it be that someone made a mistake?"

"There is a perfectly reasonable explanation for what happened in my case," the judge replied stiffly. "I'm sure it will all be straightened out in due course."

The man was either a Unionist stooge or certifiably insane. I shoveled down my oatmeal and chugged the rest of my tea to get away from them.

After breakfast, more than a thousand of us assembled at the eastern gate of Division 3 for our march to Recycling Site A. New snow had fallen overnight and knee-high drifts covered sections of the road leading north. Iron gray clouds hung low in the sky as they advanced steadily to the east.

I felt a mixture of anticipation and fear as I set out for my first full day of work at Kamas. I had already calculated the precise number of days remaining in my sentence but had reassured myself that this was only the first of many work assignments I would have in my camp career. This one might last days or months, but in either case, the tedium would be broken by meeting people and gaining knowledge unlike any I had known before.

We marched a distance of nearly five miles in about an hour and a half. As we came within a mile of the recycling site its outlines became clearer. The place seemed indistinguishable from an ordinary junkyard except for its enormous size. Slowly certain sections of the site took on the form of auto salvage yards; others of lumberyards, brickyards, and plumbing supply yards, each specializing in the recovery of a different class of materials. To the rear, a huge structure the size of an airplane hangar opened to receive a flatbed tractor-trailer.

As the head of our column reached the site's outer perimeter fence, a metal gate slid open to admit us. Group by group, work teams peeled off to their regular worksites, leaving the newcomers behind. We halted and counted off by fives to form fresh squads. Roesemann and I ended up on different teams. Still, I found some familiar faces in my twenty-man work team, including the Texan, Jerry Lee. Our leader was Ralph Knopfler, whom I had met in the barracks before roll call.

In a speech as brief as it was blunt, Knopfler announced that, so long as we remained on his work team, we were to regard him as the final authority in all things at the site. It was he who kept attendance, made work assignments, set quotas, measured output, and determined who went on sick call and who was punished for shirking. He urged us to get to know each other and to work closely as a team because our collective output would from now on be the single biggest factor in our individual survival at Kamas.

Knopfler then led us to a nearby section of the yard where dump trucks had delivered a towering heap of bricks, cinder blocks, paving stones, and stone building blocks. For the rest of the day our group's task would be to carry the bricks and blocks to an assembly area where we were to sort them by shape, size, and color, and stack them onto wooden pallets. He and two of his foremen would instruct us in the proper way to carry out our tasks.

For the next nine hours, we picked bricks and blocks from the heap and carried them across the yard on our shoulders or in hods, then stacked them onto pallets. Other than a ten-minute lunch break to eat our ration bars, we labored without interruption from morning till after dusk. I watched my teammates closely, matching my pace to that of the men who worked neither fastest nor slowest. It was punishing work and every muscle and sinew in my middle-aged body cried out for relief, but somehow I survived until the end of the shift. When the whistle blew, we dropped bricks and hods where we stood and assembled for the march back to camp.

As our brickyard work team was one of the first to reach the site's main gate, we lined up near the head of the column and waited for the gate to open. We sat cross-legged on the ground, close enough to link arms if ordered to do so. I allowed my mind to idle, studying the landscape and surveying the compound's guard towers and perimeter fence for blind spots and other weaknesses.

The convoy guards seemed unusually quiet and tense. I reasoned that they might still be in a state of heightened alert following yesterday's shooting and work stoppage.

But this did not fully explain the behavior of the warders, who milled about nervously at a great distance. From past experience, I would have expected them to pace up and down the road, giving a whack to anyone who stepped out of line. I turned around and faced the rear of the column to gain a better view of the work teams behind me.

One group was waiting in a spot where the road passed particularly close to the perimeter fence and an adjacent watchtower. One of the guards in the tower bantered with the prisoners below as if they were wagering on something. Then suddenly a prisoner seated nearby pointed excitedly toward the tower, where one of the guards had tossed what appeared to be a tobacco pouch into the yard.

A murmur rose from the group nearest the tower, then silence as one of the prisoners broke away from the column and strode toward the pouch. From where I sat, I recognized the prisoner as a stout little Chinese POW who also worked in the brickyard. He spoke little English but was a natural comedian, resorting to gestures and mimicry when words failed him. The Chinaman looked back at his teammates with a broad grin and made a rude gesture with his corncob pipe to show how manly he was to accept the dare.

He approached the tobacco pouch gingerly, then stooped to snatch it off the ground. As he strutted back toward the column, the POW waved it over his head in triumph then tucked it into his coveralls. Suddenly he did a little jig and an instant later we heard a single gunshot. The Chinaman spun around and fell with a bullet wound in his thigh. He looked up at the tower plaintively and dragged himself back toward the column lest the guards shoot him again.

Without warning, a prisoner broke out of the column and ran toward the Chinaman to help. It was Will Roesemann. He knelt at the wounded man's side, pulled his arm around his shoulder and lifted him the same way he and I had lifted Glenn Reineke two days earlier. It was a noble gesture, but it didn't get him or the Chinaman far. The pair hadn't taken more than three paces before a burst of machine-gun fire slammed into Will's back and blew a gaping hole through his chest. A round from the same burst hit the Chinaman in the neck and nearly tore off his head. Those of us who saw it gasped but did not dare break ranks.

As always, Will had done the right thing by his fellow man. Only this time it had cost him his life.

And now I was more alone than ever.

As if on cue, the convoy guards raced down the length of the column and took up positions spaced precisely ten yards apart. They barked orders for us to stay seated on the ground and link arms or be shot. Warders arrived moments later, swinging their clubs wildly at any prisoner who sat even slightly out of alignment with the column. I felt a glancing blow strike my shoulder and needed all my self-control not to lash out at the warder who hit me. Other prisoners looked daggers at their attackers but none dared raise a hand against them.

While the guards and warders were busy enforcing order, Major Jack Whiting climbed down from the watchtower with an assault rifle slung over his shoulder. His face held a look of animal satisfaction that sent a shudder up my spine because it told me that he had shot the Chinaman for sport.

The march back to camp was highly charged, since we all knew that at any moment a sudden movement might incite the guards to fire upon us. We closed ranks as if we could hide from their bullets behind our fellow marchers. When we came within a mile of camp, we saw armored vans stationed at intervals along the side of the road, their swivel-mounted machine guns trained upon us. Inside the camp, more machine-gunners drew beads on us from watchtowers and roofs. Instead of being released to the mess hall for dinner, the warders led us to our barracks in small groups and padlocked the doors behind us.

Since every barracks had at least one inmate in Recycling Site A, the news that Roesemann and the Chinaman had been shot spread rapidly throughout Division 3. The shootings aroused a sense of dread in the veteran prisoners, who had seen camp conditions slowly improve over the past year but feared a crackdown in response to the recent spate of stoolie killings. Most prisoners wanted desperately to believe that the security organs were gradually becoming more humane since the President-for-Life had died one year before. But now it seemed that worse days lay ahead.

I found a vacant bunk and lay back, contemplating a bleak future given such dire omens on my first two days at Kamas. But I was soon distracted by a raging debate in the next bunk.

I recognized John D'Amato's voice.

"Look what your stoolie-hunting has brought us to! You guys hit a stoolie, they shoot Lillian. You guys hit another stoolie, they shoot Fong and the new guy Roesemann. You'll never win!"

"So you think that if we stop killing Whiting's spies, he'll stop shooting prisoners?" Ralph Knopfler answered. "What kind of numbskulls do you take us for? When has State Security ever shown respect for our lives? When they're not shooting us, they're starving us, freezing us, or burying us in the mines. First let them stop the spying. Then we'll have no need to whack stoolies."

Others, most of them siding with Knopfler, joined the debate. They seemed to recognize no middle ground between murdering suspected informants and allowing them to denounce us. My sympathies were generally with Knopfler but I had no stomach for the throat slitting. And the last thing I wanted was for the bosses to tag me as a rebel. So I listened to the discussion a few minutes longer, lost interest, and dozed off.

CHAPTER 7

"In a time of deceit, telling the truth is a revolutionary act."
—George Orwell

Wednesday, November 16, 2022

I stepped out of the taxi in front of the Union Bank building on Grant Street and immediately felt the bite of the west wind sweeping across the Allegheny. My wife Juliet stepped onto the curb next, followed by Claire and Louisa. The girls, now aged eleven and nine, respectively, huddled close behind their mother to stay out of the wind while I fumbled in my wallet with half-frozen fingers to pay the fare.

"You're short," the driver objected. "The fare is forty-five bucks with the fuel surcharge."

"But the meter includes the surcharge," I replied irritably. "I gave you forty, and that's with a five-dollar tip."

"Sorry, mister. Maybe you don't ride cabs much lately. They make us run the meter, but nobody pays the metered rate any more. I know there's price controls and all, but if cabbies could only collect what was on the meter, these here streets would be empty. "

I fished out an extra five-dollar bill. Welcome to the Third World, I thought.

"Sorry, I didn't know that," I told the driver. "Here's the extra, and have a nice day."

I followed Juliet and the girls into the lobby, where they stamped their feet to stay warm. It was only marginally warmer inside. The wind whistled through the joints of the plywood sheets that had replaced the massive windows all along the front of the high-rise office block despite being sheltered by eight-foot-high sandbag barriers on three sides of the building. The plywood and the sandbags were a legacy of summer street battles between wildcat strikers and the National Guard, followed by student riots in September and October.

The lobby seemed far darker than normal, even allowing for the overcast skies and the boarded-up windows toward the north. I looked up and saw that only a third of the lighting fixtures were lit, apparently to conserve electricity. As it was nearly ten, the morning rush was already over and foot traffic was surprisingly sparse.

The overall atmosphere reminded me of a trip I had made as a young man to the Russian Far East in the years following the fall of the Soviet Union. Every city looked and smelled the same: near-empty sidewalks, urine-soaked stairwells, parks choked with weeds, decrepit smoke-belching buses, long queues outside ill-stocked grocery stores, and dour faces on everyone except small children and the rare appearance of a young couple in love. Only now, Pittsburgh had the added charm of rows of vacant or shuttered storefronts. Though Thanksgiving was only a week away, there were no holiday decorations anywhere.

I stepped up to the reception desk with Juliet and the girls in tow.

"We have an appointment with Stephen Daly in Commercial Lending at ten," I said to an expressionless woman of about fifty in a knitted beret, ski gloves, and full-length quilted parka.

"Sign in," she replied, pulling off a glove to peck with her index finger at a touchscreen monitor. "You'll each need a badge."

She handed over four visitor badges and watched as we clipped them to our lapels.

"It's on the eleventh floor," she added, dismissing us. "Stay in the reception area until someone comes to get you."

The elevator started with a jolt and Juliet reached out instinctively for Louisa's arm. Juliet had been sleeping badly for more than a week and, in the harsh glare of the elevator's overhead light, I could see the dark circles under her eyes. Her mouth had taken on a grim set in recent weeks and, except when alone with the girls, she had become increasingly reserved, perhaps even depressed.

It had been nearly a year since her parents had emigrated to England. Since then she devoted most of her time—when not managing the house, home-schooling the girls or taking them to visit other home-schooled students in Sewickley—attempting to sell our house, our cars, our furniture, and all the tangible personal property that we could not take with us on the plane when we, too, left the Unionist State behind.

Having failed to find a buyer for my business after posting losses for six straight years, I closed the factory, paid off the remaining workforce, and sold the remaining assets to settle obligations to lenders, lawyers, and the tax authorities. Now, with today's closing on the sale of the company's real estate and payoff of the last remaining commercial indebtedness, there would be just enough funds to cover the family's exit tax and to leave a few tens of thousands in cash to embark on our new life overseas.

The exit tax was a recent invention of the Unionist administration, intended to stem the flow of affluent citizens out of the country. Like the federal estate and gift tax, the exit tax was levied on the transfer of property—in this case, on transfers of cash to overseas accounts by American citizens. The tax rate was steeply progressive and, for those with total assets valued at more than a few thousand dollars, it was tantamount to confiscation.

We stepped out of the elevator opposite a pair of doors with frosted glass panels. The doors opened and Jeff Fisher stepped out to greet us with a brave but weary smile.

Jeff had guided me through the entire ordeal of liquidating our family's business and personal assets, settling our debts and taxes, and then applying for exit visas. The latter was a neat trick the Unionists had borrowed from the playbook of other totalitarian regimes around the world. Ostensibly designed to prevent the flight of criminals and terrorists, the real purpose of the exit visa was to prevent the flight of capital and skilled labor, and the formation of a powerful opposition in exile. For if, in arranging one's affairs, one did not give full satisfaction to the Unionist authorities, they would refuse to issue the visa. And to attempt departure without an exit visa was a serious federal crime akin to sedition or treason.

Perhaps Jeff felt guilty for not having convinced me to sell out six years earlier, when German bidders had offered to pay several million for the business, and when the exit tax was still two years from going into effect. By the time we realized that the Unionists would close the door to emigration, Juliet's parents were already preparing to leave and Juliet had lifted her objection to emigrating, as well. But by that time, there were no bidders left for businesses like mine. I kept it running as long as I could, and in that endeavor Jeff was always ready to help. Even after he closed his own law practice in Sewickley and joined a larger practice downtown, Jeff gave me discounted rates for legal work that increasingly meant the difference between economic survival and destitution and possibly also between freedom and imprisonment.

"Come on in and let me get you something warm to drink," Jeff greeted us as he held open the door.

We stepped into a small meeting room that held a conference table set for eight and a sideboard where a tray with carafes of coffee and hot water was waiting. Jeff poured Juliet a mug of tea and opened two packets of hot cocoa for the girls before pouring black coffee for him and me.

"Were you and Daly able to finish all the tax forms last night?" I was trying my best not to betray any lingering anxiety that some critical detail had been overlooked. "Juliet wants to make sure we allow enough time to collect our bags at the hotel on our way to the airport."

"That shouldn't be a problem," Jeff replied. "Steve had to make some minor revisions this morning based on some revised tax calculations but I expect him here with the documentation in a few minutes. The Loan Committee was happy to get the amount they did to close out the debt.

They were also able to persuade the Tax Department to go along with most of our proposals. These days the bank is practically an extension of the IRS, so I don't expect any complications there."

"Jeff, if you don't mind my asking an impertinent question, how will they pay us the balance?" Juliet inquired. "Were we able to get it paid in gold, the way my father did when he emigrated?"

"I'm afraid that's no longer possible, Juliet. The foreign exchange regulations changed last year. Officially, the U.S. dollar is still a convertible currency. So you'll be getting greenbacks."

"Not redbacks?" she asked with a look of concern. "I thought that greenbacks were only for domestic circulation and that redbacks were the only dollars allowed overseas…"

"Technically, yes," Jeff replied with a weary shrug. "But I've been assured that you can convert your greenbacks to redbacks at any major overseas bank. The rules seem to change from week to week, so I called the Federal Reserve yesterday to confirm. To be completely safe, though, I suggest you take your money to the bank the minute you arrive in London."

At that moment the door opened and a tall man of about thirty opened the glass-paneled doors pushing a cart bearing neatly arranged stacks of legal documents.

Steven Daly gave the distinct impression of a man under pressure. He was thin and cerebral and, with his wire-rimmed glasses and well-tailored gray wool suit, seemed perfectly cast as the young loan officer working his way up the ranks in Western Pennsylvania's leading regional bank. But his smile of attempted reassurance lacked mirth and his broad forehead glistened with nervous perspiration as he stepped into the light.

"I hope I didn't keep you waiting long," Daly offered as he transferred the stacks of documents to the conference table.

Jeff Fisher introduced the banker to each of us, then immediately began checking off each set of documents against a list he took from his briefcase. Some documents he examined quickly, others he took the time to proofread line by line.

When he reached the end of his checklist he looked up.

"And will someone be bringing the cash?" he inquired. "It would be helpful for Paul to see how much space it's going to take in his carry-on bag. We will also need a Form 105F, of course, to get through Customs."

"Cash? Are you sure that was part of the agreement?" Daly reddened but kept his composure. "I'm sorry, Jeff, but I don't recall if the bank ever agreed to that. The settlement sheet indicates payment by cashier's check. That's generally how we do these transactions, unless, of course, you prefer a wire transfer."

"We've been over this a half dozen times, Steven. Paul has no account in London to receive the transfer. And we've made abundantly clear that a cashier's check is not acceptable. I'm afraid we must insist on cash."

Daly seemed to regain his composure and nodded to Jeff in acknowledgement, though without looking at Juliet or me.

He picked up the phone and dialed a four-digit extension.

"It's Steven. A cashier's check is not acceptable. They insist on cash."

Daly listened without changing his expression.

"All right," he replied after thirty or forty seconds. "I'll see what I can do."

He hung up the phone and turned to Jeff rather than to me.

"They're not sure they have enough large bills on hand right now. They want Paul to come down and see if what they have will be okay."

"Would you like me to go with you?" Jeff suggested.

I looked at Juliet, who had just fished a book out of her handbag for Louisa to read. She looked pale and her hands seemed to shake as she opened the book.

"No, please stay with Juliet. I'll make this as quick as I can."

Daly stood and I followed him out the door.

In the elevator Daly punched the button for the basement.

"Is the vault really in the basement?" I asked.

Daly smiled but did not speak. He punched the button again and the elevator began its descent.

When the elevator stopped, the door opened onto a dimly lit corridor. Daly turned left and told me to follow. We walked briskly for a minute or two and then stopped at a steel door marked only with the number B112, where Daly entered a code onto a keypad. The door opened and we followed another unmarked corridor through several right-angled turns without meeting another person.

"Are you sure this is the way to the vault?" I asked with mounting impatience as we set off through another double door.

"Come along," he answered without even a glance behind him. "You want your cash, don't you?"

In a few more steps we emerged through yet another steel door onto a loading dock. Two middle-aged men, also in gray suits, turned toward us as we entered.

"This is Mr. Wagner," Daly announced in a voice that was absolutely devoid of civility.

"If you'll come with us, Mr. Wagner, we'll be there in a jiffy," the taller one said. Unlike Daly, he spoke with an accent distinctive of Pittsburgh's working class. With his thick neck and hulking shoulders, he looked more like a professional wrestler than a banker.

He pointed to the open rear doors of a late-model panel truck backed up to the loading dock.

I caught of glimpse of Daly quietly retreating into the corridor from which we had come.

"Wait a second," I protested, suddenly alarmed at being hopelessly lost and at the mercy of my two thuggish-looking companions.

"Come on, pal, let's get going," the shorter man chimed in. "Don't you want your cash?"

He stepped toward the van and in the moment that I turned to follow him I felt the larger man grasp my right wrist and wrench it behind my body. In a matter of seconds both my wrists were handcuffed behind my back and I was being hustled forward into the van.

CHAPTER 8

"Under conditions of tyranny, it is far easier to act than to think."
—Hannah Arendt, philosopher and Holocaust scholar

Saturday, March 9, 2024

Helen and Claire sat at the white-tiled kitchen counter across from each other, staring at neatly stacked piles of dried herbs. Off to the side were an antique apothecary scale with a set of graduated brass weights, a box of plastic sandwich bags, a stack of newspapers, and handwritten labels showing plant names and instructions for their use.

"It'll go faster if we work as a team," Helen began. "I'm going to weigh out each herb and call out its name and the weight. What I want you to do is find the right label, write the weight on it, and stuff the herb and the label into the plastic bag. Got it?"

"I think so," Claire replied.

They went to work. In fifteen minutes they had bagged the echinacea and moved on to the chamomile flowers.

"Have you given much thought to what Dorothy said last night about places for you to work?" Helen asked a few minutes later. "It seems to me that it boils down to three families. You need to think about picking the one you like best. Then maybe we should visit them on our way to the station tonight. Would that be okay?"

"I suppose so," Claire replied, "but I don't know who to pick."

"I understand," Helen answered. "Would you like my opinion?"

Claire nodded silently.

"Here's how I see it. There's the older couple with the wife who gets around in a wheel chair. They seem nice, but a bit too old to know what to do with a girl like you. Then there's the Army colonel with five children. He'll likely know how to handle kids, but there's too many of them already. And then there's the third family, the important civilian with connections to the military. He and his wife have only one child and they also said they could arrange for you to go to school. Dorothy says the wife is young and quite sweet."

Claire fidgeted with a bag of chamomile, opening and resealing the zip-lock strip.

"What if we go to their house and I don't like them? Do I get a second pick?"

Helen breathed a deep sigh.

"Ah, there's the rub. In this town, all the government people know each other and are like members of a special club. If you agree to work for one of them and then change your mind, you can't count on having your pick of the others. The next one you interview will ask you where you interviewed before. Then he'll call the first one and when he hears you changed your mind he may not want to hire you. But if you lie about the first one and the others find out later, they might fire you for being dishonest."

Claire didn't respond.

"It used to be that a person had the right to work for whomever he pleased and if he didn't like it, he could quit and find another job. But that's not the way it is anymore. Especially in a government town like Heber."

Helen ground a chamomile blossom between her fingertips and let the dust fall onto the table.

"So there it is, Miss Claire. You'll need to make a choice before we leave tonight. And then let's hope to heaven it's a good one."

"Tonight? Can't we wait till after the weekend?"

"They all want someone right away. If you wait, somebody else may get there first."

Claire lowered her eyes and went back to packing herbs. She and Helen spent the rest of the afternoon on herbs and baking fresh rolls and getting Claire cleaned and dressed for her interview. Shortly before sunset, they set off down the hill toward Heber.

They stopped in a gated compound that contained some of Heber's better homes, most of which had once been vacation houses for wealthy residents of other states. Now the compound was reserved for the exclusive use of high-ranking government officials. The General Services Administration guard in the tiny gatehouse checked their names against a list on his clipboard and pointed them through the gate toward Lt. Col. Chambers's house.

"I thought the dad wasn't in the army," Claire remarked as they walked to the end of a cul-de-sac that contained a single log-and-stucco home.

"I thought so, too," Helen said.

Before Claire could reply, Helen knocked on the heavy oak door. Both of them heard loud music coming from inside. It sounded to Claire like the blues band her dad had listened to so often during the weeks before his arrest.

The door opened and Claire peered up at a tall dark-haired woman whose oval face, delicate features, and graceful carriage reminded her of the Russian ballerinas she had once seen on stage in Pittsburgh. The woman bore no trace of make-up other than pale lipstick, and she wore her sleek mahogany hair tied behind her head with a black ribbon. Under a white cotton chef's apron she wore a black wool turtleneck and neatly pressed tan slacks. She pulled the door open wide, shifted her baby on her hip and held her hand out to Claire in greeting.

"So you're the young lady Dottie has been saying so many wonderful things about. Please come in," she said in a husky voice. "And Helen, I'm so pleased to meet you. I'm Martha Chambers. I was just putting Marie to bed. Please excuse my husband, but Doug invited some friends from work to join us for a light supper. They're watching hockey in the family room. May I get you something to drink?"

Claire noticed Helen sizing up Martha Chambers as the woman spoke and wondered whether Helen noticed the sadness she saw in Martha's eyes.

"May I have some ginger ale, please?" Claire inquired.

"Water would be fine for me, if it's not too much trouble," Helen said.

"Not at all," Martha answered cheerfully before casting a sidelong glance at the baby, now fast asleep.

"Claire, would you like to try holding Marie?" she offered. "I don't think she'll wake up now that she's been fed."

Claire grinned and allowed Martha to place a cloth diaper across her shoulder before handing over her baby. The infant felt soft and warm and made her feel relaxed. Claire looked around the room at the massive stone fireplace, hardwood floors, lush draperies, and the leather chairs and sofa. She could not recall having seen such a beautiful living room since she was a small child, in the days before everyone around her had grown poor. She wondered how this young couple could afford such luxury when her parents had been reduced to living in far humbler surroundings.

Martha Chambers returned with a tray.

"I was so excited when Dottie called to tell me about Claire," she began. "It's not that I was looking for help, really. But our next baby is due in August and I don't know how long I'll be able to keep up the pace. With Marie I spent the last two months of my pregnancy flat on my back. I thought it might be nice to have a helper this time, someone who could keep me company and handle some of the simpler chores. After August, we could see about extending the arrangement."

Helen took a sip of her mineral water. Claire thought she looked tense.

"What kind of a schedule would you have in mind for Claire? Would she be free to attend school?" Helen asked.

"Oh, yes, of course! In fact, Doug thinks we might be able to get Claire into the federal school. I take it Claire hasn't enrolled anywhere yet?"

"Not exactly. Claire lost her I.D. on her way here from the East and it may take some time to issue a replacement. I don't know how long you and your husband have been in Heber but there's quite a bit of red tape living in a Restricted Zone."

"I know exactly what you mean," Martha replied easily. She looked past Helen to Claire, who had already finished her ginger ale and was rocking the baby gently as she strolled around the room.

"Claire, do you think you could manage to keep Marie asleep if you took her up to her room and tucked her in? If you do, I know where there are some fresh-baked chocolate chip cookies."

Claire's eyes widened.

"It's a deal!" she replied and started toward the stairs with Marie in her arms.

When Claire was out of earshot, Helen put down her glass and addressed Martha Chambers in a cool businesslike voice.

"Let me be frank, Mrs. Chambers. Claire is for all intents and purposes an orphan, as her parents are missing. She came to Heber from Pennsylvania without travel documents and has no residence permit to stay here. Also, the town schools are full and because Claire has no special ties to Heber, she won't be eligible to enroll until they reach her number on the waiting list, which is far from assured.

"My only purpose in saying all this is to do what's best for Claire. Though I hope we can eventually get her back to her family, it's just not possible for me to care for her indefinitely while we look for them. I sensed that you and your husband might be able to offer Claire something better. She's a very bright girl and has been raised well. If you would be willing to take her in as a sort of junior *au pair*, so to speak, I'm confident that she'll live up to your expectations."

Martha Chambers listened attentively.

"It takes a special sort of person to do what you've done for Claire," Martha replied. "And I want to thank you for bringing her to us first. But at this point I'd like to include my husband in the discussion."

Claire came bounding down the stairs as Martha finished. She stood beside Helen and tugged at her sleeve.

"Helen, you've got to see the upstairs," she said excitedly. "They have a huge bathroom with a whirlpool tub and a marble floor. And there's a sewing room right next to the baby's room. It's incredibly cool!"

Martha rose with a smile and took Claire by the hand.

"But you haven't seen the kitchen. Come on, let's find those chocolate chip cookies before Doug and the men eat them all."

The kitchen was grander than any Claire had seen since they moved out of the old stone house in Sewickley. There was a huge refrigerator-freezer, a full-size gas range, a microwave oven, and even a dishwasher.

Separated from the kitchen by a food-preparation island was a family room equipped with a massive sofa, stereo system, and flat-screen television.

Claire turned her attention to the five men seated on the sofa and adjacent easy chairs, drinking beer and raging at the television screen over a hockey goal just scored. She tried to guess which one was Mr. Chambers. She guessed wrong when the youngest-looking of the five men left his seat and joined the women in the kitchen. Claire was happy it was he because she didn't have very good feelings about any of the others. There was something hard and mean about their eyes. She looked over at Helen and saw that Helen had sensed it, too.

"Don't mind these guys," Doug Chambers began without introducing himself. "They're sore losers for the moment but they'll get over it when they accept the fact that the Avalanche are going to win the Stanley Cup again this year."

The other men paid no attention. Their eyes were on the next face-off.

"Say, can I offer you something to drink," he asked. "Or did Martha already take care of that?"

Doug flashed a charming smile lit up by sparkling blue eyes. He possessed a restless energy that made him appear boyish and impulsive.

Something about him made Claire think of her former gym teacher, a father of teenage girls who had coached girls soccer. The physical resemblance between the two men was remarkable: wiry blond hair, a broad forehead, dimpled chin, and a fleshy bow-shaped mouth. She pondered the prediction Mr. Chambers had made about the Avalanche and wondered if he was as fanatical about winning as her gym teacher had been.

"Doug, could you tear yourself away from the game for a moment so we can have a talk with Claire? Helen brought her over to meet us tonight because Dottie thought you might be out of town after the weekend."

"Be right with you," he answered, and then took a last peek at the television screen before following the women into the living room.

"Helen has been kind enough to tell me a bit about Claire's background," Martha began when all were seated, "and I can't think of a better match for us. But I know it's not easy for Helen to leave Claire with total strangers, or for Claire to decide to stay. I thought they might like to learn a little more about us."

Martha turned to her visitors.

"Do either of you have any questions about us?"

"Perhaps you could tell us a few words about where each of you came from and how the two of you met," Helen suggested with a polite smile.

Doug and Martha glanced at each other, each seeking a cue to begin. Martha spoke first.

"Well, I grew up in a small town in New Jersey. I had just finished a degree in art history when the Events came along. When the riots spread, my parents decided it might be better for me to leave the country until things settled down. So I flew to Paris, rented a room, and started taking lessons in figure painting and color. I was in my fourth year and happy as a bird when I met Doug at a dinner party.

"He was still in the Army then, posted to the Defense Attaché's office at the American Embassy. We were married six months later and had two more wonderful years in Paris before Doug was transferred back to the Pentagon. But I'll let Doug take up the story from there, because since we returned it's generally been a matter of where Doug's career has taken us."

The joy had left Martha's voice the moment she mentioned the transfer from Paris. Claire wondered whether love at first sight lasted as long in real life as it did in books. She examined Doug's face closely for clues.

"Okay, my turn," Doug began with relaxed good humor. "First of all, I have to confess that I only got the assignment to Paris on a fluke. If I hadn't still been on medical hold when the job opened up I'm sure they would have shipped me off to Vladivostok to fight the Chinese. So, for me, getting wounded by the Canucks in the border war turned out to be my lucky break."

He gave an uneasy laugh.

"So off to Paris I went. But as much as Martha and I enjoyed France, when it was time to come home, I couldn't stand working in the Pentagon. When I heard that State Security was looking for officers with combat experience, I resigned my commission and moved over to the DSS. That was two years ago. We were assigned to Heber last summer."

Claire looked at Helen and saw that her expression had suddenly hardened. She seemed to regard Doug Chambers as if he were a poisonous snake.

"And what sort of work are you doing now, Mr. Chambers, if you're at liberty to say?"

"I'm deputy chief at the labor facility over in Kamas."

"And do you enjoy that sort of work?" Helen's voice now had a brittle edge to it and Claire sensed that she wasn't the only person in the room to have noticed.

"Why, yes, Mrs..." His voice trailed off seeking her last name but Helen did not offer it up. "I find it highly rewarding. Since I joined the Department, I've had a hand in removing some of the most destructive elements from our society and have put them in camps where they can't do any more harm. I think camps like Kamas do the country an enormous service."

He returned Helen's icy stare.

"But perhaps you see it differently," he went on. "May I ask what sort of work you do?"

"I have a small trade in medicinal herbs and homemade baked goods. I gather the herbs and bake the breads and sell them both in town."

"Medicinal herbs," Doug replied. "How intriguing. Do you work at all with the local health clinic or the military hospital?"

"No. I'm not a doctor," Helen said.

"But still, isn't it a bit like practicing medicine?" he asked. "Doesn't it require a license to do that kind of thing?"

"Not at all. It's considered self-treatment."

Doug Chambers nodded slowly and settled back on the sofa with a predatory smile. "You know, Martha, I find this medicinal herb business fascinating. I can't imagine why the government isn't doing more to promote something like this. You know, I think I'll make some inquiries tomorrow morning at the military hospital about how this fits into the national health care program. And maybe I'll ring the EPA office in Denver. We wouldn't want to use any herbs that were on the endangered species list, now, would we?"

"Make whatever inquiries you like, Mr. Chambers," Helen answered coolly while casting a sidelong glance at Martha. "Now, if you'll excuse us, Claire and I have business to do at the station."

Helen took Claire firmly by the hand and rose to her feet.

Claire appealed with tearful eyes to Martha, who seemed bewildered at the sudden turn in the conversation.

"Helen, I was hoping that Claire would stay here tonight. Have we said something to make you think we wouldn't take good care of her?"

"Not at all, Mrs. Chambers, but we do have other interviews lined up tomorrow."

"But Dottie said we were your first choice. Did that change? I don't quite understand what's happening."

Doug Chambers whispered a question to his wife and his wife whispered back.

"Please don't go," he addressed Helen in a conciliatory tone. "I'm sorry if I was rude to you. I didn't mean to be threatening. After all, this is supposed to be about Claire, isn't it? It seems to me that Martha and I have a lot to offer Claire, advantages she might not get living with another family. Why not let her spend the weekend with us? I'll get out of the way and you and Martha can talk on Monday about where to go from there."

Claire lowered her eyes, folded her hands and prayed to God to give her just this one thing in exchange for all the things he'd taken away. When she looked up again, Helen seemed ready to speak. Her face was pale and her hands trembled ever so slightly.

"Sometimes it's difficult to put strong reservations aside, but for Claire I will."

She turned to Claire.

"My dear, it's time for me to go off to work. Be on your very best behavior for Mrs. Chambers. I'll try to come by tomorrow afternoon to visit. If not, I'll see you Monday morning."

Claire threw her arms around Helen's waist and buried her face in her dress to hide the tears of gratitude and relief that streamed down her cheeks.

"Thank you, thank you, thank you," she whispered quietly to herself before raising her eyes to meet Helen's loving gaze. Then Helen kissed Claire softly on the forehead and left.

CHAPTER 9

"Mankind is tired of liberty."
—Benito Mussolini

Monday, March 11, 2024

My fifth day at Kamas was a Monday. Sunday had been a day of rest, when all prisoners were confined to quarters except for meals. In Barracks C-14, most of us went back to sleep after breakfast and remained in bed until dinner to conserve our strength. I spent much of the day thinking about how much I would miss Will Roesemann. He had been a selfless friend and had brought out the best in me at times when, left to my own devices, I might have wallowed in depression and self-pity. Without him, I knew my path would be more treacherous and my chances of survival substantially worse.

At five o'clock Monday morning, we all dragged ourselves out of bed to prepare for roll call and another day of work. All except for one prisoner, a frail-looking fellow in his early twenties who had slit his wrists with a piece of broken glass during the night. The warders examined the corpse to satisfy themselves that this was not another stoolie execution, then ordered two prisoners to drag the remains off to the camp morgue. The rest of us hurried to the latrines so that we would not be late for breakfast or roll call. An hour later we stood in formation on the Division 3 parade ground and assembled for work.

By seven the metal gate had closed behind us at Recycling Site A. This was my third day in the brickyard. As soon as my work team arrived and received instructions from the foreman, I picked up my hod where I had left it Saturday evening and started filling it slowly with clay bricks from the heap near the perimeter fence. When the hod was full, I carried it on one shoulder to the pallet yard and lowered it to the ground. Then I knelt to stack the bricks on the nearest pallet and did it all over again. This was mind-numbing work that should have been done with a forklift. But forklifts were scarce and prisoners were not. So we continued.

At one o'clock, the foreman blew the whistle for our fifteen-minute lunch break. I felt the gnawing ache of hunger as I sat down on a pile of bricks to rest. For this was to be a lunch break without the lunch. As punishment for our hour-long work stoppage when Lillian was shot, Jack Whiting had ordered all new prisoners to be deprived of midday ration bars for three consecutive workdays. This was the third day and I had never experienced hunger as intensely.

So instead of breaking out a ration bar, I sat on a stack of bricks and contemplated what had become of my hands after three days at Recycling Site A. Working in the winter cold without gloves had given them a bluish-gray cast. Even at rest, my fingers remained curled into claws that required superhuman will to straighten. Tiny shreds of skin hung from my fingertips and the heel of my hand. And I looked with disgust at the pits and gouges, now infected, that had caused both my hands to swell. But I also felt relief that the skin was hardening into callus tissue and that none of the nicks was deep enough to cause much bleeding.

I heard a rustle in the dirt behind me and turned my head in time to see Jerry Lee and his friend D.J. Schultz approaching. At twenty-three, D.J. was several years younger than Jerry Lee and looked even younger than that. He was a total smart aleck and cracked jokes at every chance, often at the risk of a clubbing. Before his arrest, D.J. had worked as a mechanic at a government motor pool in Ohio, while Jerry Lee had been a long-haul driver for a nationalized trucking company in Dallas. Both shared a love for sixteen-wheeled tractor-trailers, stock-car racing, and the open road.

The two of them had met on the train to Heber and had become inseparable. All the same, I was surprised that both had managed to land spots at the same worksite and even on the same team. Either they were extremely lucky or they were shrewder operators that I had realized.

"Mind if we share your lunch?" Jerry Lee asked before sitting beside me.

"Sure," I replied. "How about a steaming bowl of three-alarm chili?"

"Don't get me started on chili. I won a chili-eating contest in Galveston once. I could eat the stuff every day."

"Pull up a brick, anyway, and get comfortable," I offered. "I've been meaning to ask you boys how both of you managed to get work at Site A when the work assignments were supposed to be handed out randomly."

"Well, not quite randomly," D.J. pointed out. "We figured that since they do everything by counting off, we'd find out how many worksites there were and sit that many spaces apart at roll call. So we got the answer from an old-timer and it worked. Then, once we got here, Jerry Lee switched places with another guy to get us on the same work team."

"You boys fit in here just fine. Bent minds in a bent system."

"Hell, they put me in here for conspiracy," Jerry Lee said. "The least I can do is live up to the label."

"Conspiracy, hell," D.J. snorted. "You just happened to mouth off to your boss one time too many."

"Well, what about your sabotage rap? All that means is that you were a total screw-up on the job."

"Screw-up, my ass," D.J. retorted. "I was the curve buster who made all the other jack-offs look bad. And now here I am working in a goddamned junkyard, hauling bricks with my bare hands. Some reward."

He wasn't laughing anymore.

Jerry Lee turned to me.

"How about you, Paul? How many years?"

"Same as you," I answered. "A fiver."

"Conspiracy?"

I nodded. "I used to own a vitamin company," I said. "Come the Events, business went downhill fast but by the time I made up my mind to sell, there weren't any buyers left. I closed it down and applied to emigrate. Apparently, the government hates quitters. State Security arrested me the day I paid the exit tax and planned to leave. 'Economic sabotage.'"

Before Jerry Lee or D.J. could respond, the foreman blew the whistle signaling the end of the lunch break.

"Tough break," D.J. quipped as they rose to leave. "But you'll survive. As long as you do what you're told around here, they leave you pretty much alone," he replied. "There's too many of us for them to do it any other way."

"Beneath all the craziness, there's a certain order to this place," Jerry Lee added. "You just have to take the time to figure it out. Hell, this morning they even let Major Reineke out of the isolator a day early. I saw him over in the lumberyard a while ago."

Jerry Lee pointed toward the fence. I spotted Glenn Reineke talking to Ralph Knopfler through the barbed wire. Reineke looked unsteady, but after a nearly a week in the isolator, it was a miracle he was on his feet at all. Even from a distance I could see that Reineke carried himself with the self-confidence of a natural leader. Beneath his inexpressive features I detected a powerful determination that would not be cowed nor diverted from its goal.

As the afternoon wore on, Knopfler stepped up the pace so that our work team would be sure to meet its quota before dinner. From time to time I had to stop and put my head between my knees to avoid feeling dizzy. But whenever I bent over, my lower back pain flared up again. I was feeling sorry for myself until I heard screams from across the yard and saw a warder beat a gray-haired prisoner to the ground with a rubber truncheon.

As bad as my afternoon might be, the newcomers on the adjacent work team appeared to have it even worse. Their usual foreman had not appeared for roll call and had been replaced by a warder who was notorious for the sadistic pleasure he took in driving his prisoners to the limit. I had been watching their ordeal for several hours. Any man who failed to keep up with the warder's relentless pace felt the bite of the truncheon. Those who complained were assigned heavier loads. Those who refused an order were beaten unconscious.

Several of the older prisoners collapsed and were carried off to the infirmary. More would doubtless have taken that escape route but for a rumor that prisoners beyond the age of sixty who reported to sickbay ran the risk of being euthanized by lethal injection. Some even claimed that the sound of bulldozers during the night came from mass graves being dug in the hills east of camp. Although we had no evidence to support the rumor, many believed it. Preposterous rumors swept through Kamas so often that even a sensible prisoner could become a conspiracy theorist over time.

When the workday finally ended, I was almost as relieved as the men in the neighboring work team to see the warder's abuse come to an end. Knowing that you could be at the mercy of such a sadist at any moment completely undermined the sense of order that good leaders like Knopfler labored to create.

My spirits sank further when I realized that the extra minutes we had taken to achieve our quota had landed our work team at the rear of the column for the march back to camp. The advantage of being at the head of the column was that one could maintain a steady marching pace without having to respond to the frequent stops and starts required when stragglers were beaten or pulled out of line. Being at the end, with its frequent double-time marching, required twice as much effort to get home.

Our work team was last in line waiting for the gate to open except for the team whose foreman had been replaced by the sadistic warder. After their day of torment, these men seemed barely able to stand. Two team members collapsed where they stood and were dragged off. The remaining men raised their voices in protest but the convoy guards merely summoned additional warders to bludgeon them into silence.

At last the gate opened and the column marched out. Ahead of us the western sky had turned shades of pink and purple. It was gorgeous; but owing to the suffering of the men behind us, a palpable tension remained in the air as we trudged along the icy road. That night the guards kept to the edge of the road, as if to maintain a greater distance from us. The extra warders who had whipped the hapless prisoners into shape at the end moved to the front of the column while a platoon of armed guards took their places in the rear. The guards and warders seemed edgier than ever. Something nasty was about to happen.

I heard an anguished cry from a prisoner somewhere behind me, then a warder's angry threat, and suddenly staccato bursts of gunfire filled the air. Guards on both sides of us let loose without warning. I dropped to the ground like everyone else and prayed that no bullet would find me. My eyes stayed shut until the shooting stopped and we were ordered to stand. I dreaded what I might see when I opened them.

When I finally dared raise my head I saw very little at first. Nearly all the casualties were behind me. Though we were forbidden to turn around, I couldn't resist stealing a glance to the rear, where more than a dozen bodies sprawled across the icy road, with crimson streaming from their wounds. Cries of pain shattered the stillness. If the previous week's shootings might have been explained away as the occasional excesses of overzealous individuals, this had the earmark of a systematic massacre.

Row by row the guards ordered us to rise and drove us at gunpoint some fifty yards further on, where the front of the column was waiting for us. Whether from shock or apathy, there wasn't so much as a whisper among us. When everyone who could walk had rejoined the main column, the guards ordered us to face front and resume the march to camp.

Later we would learn that eight men died in the incident and another dozen were treated for wounds at the camp infirmary. Still others had concealed their injuries to avoid being singled out for further punishment.

When at last we reached the outskirts of camp I spotted black-uniformed marksmen silhouetted against the pale sky, both in the watchtowers and atop snow-covered barracks roofs. As we came closer, I saw additional machine guns trained on us from either side of the camp gate. If the deaths of Lillian, Fong, and Roesemann had stirred unrest among the prisoners, this unprovoked massacre seemed likely to ignite something even worse. The camp bosses appeared to have anticipated our reaction and were prepared to meet it head on.

But, as it happened, the column passed through the gates without incident. We stood at rigid attention on the Division 3 parade ground while the roll was taken and remained there while the warders returned small groups of prisoners to their barracks. When our turn came, the unit marched off the parade ground in silence.

The barracks were dark when we arrived. I climbed into my bunk, and let out a sigh of relief when I heard the clatter of the door being padlocked behind us.

CHAPTER 10

"I keep my ideals because in spite of everything, I still believe that people are really good at heart."
—Anne Frank

Monday, March 11

Claire paced back and forth across the living room floor with baby Marie, stroking her tiny back and cooing in an attempt to stop her crying. She checked the diaper for wetness but it was dry. Then over the baby's wailing she heard the doorbell. It was Helen waiting on the doorstep.

"I was so worried!" Claire exclaimed as she opened the door. "When you didn't come yesterday I was afraid I might never see you again."

"Forgive me," Helen answered, wrapping her arms around both Claire and the baby. "I was on my way over when I met someone who needed my help. It took longer than I expected."

Helen released her grip and Claire noticed that the baby had nearly stopped crying.

"Marie likes you," Claire said. "Come inside and let me give her to you. Maybe she'll nap for you."

Helen removed her overcoat and hung it from a hook in the entryway. Then she took the baby in her arms and gave Claire a thorough once-over. A trace of pink had returned to Claire's pale cheeks and her thick brown hair was braided into gleaming pigtails. Her navy corduroy trousers, white turtleneck, and navy sweater were nowhere to be seen.

Instead, Claire wore a new blue denim jumper over an embroidered pink T-shirt.

Claire noticed Helen admiring the new outfit.

"There wasn't much worth buying in the stores, but Martha bought everything we could find that fit me. And wait till you see my room! I have my own closet and dresser and even my own bathroom!"

"You look happy," Helen said softly.

Helen's eyes started to glisten. Claire seized her around the waist and buried her face in Helen's coarse woolen sweater. The baby had fallen asleep in her arms.

"Is Martha around?" Helen asked when Claire had relaxed her grip.

"She's upstairs. Would you like me to get her for you?"

"Please do. I can't stay long today."

Claire raced up the stairs and disappeared for a few moments, then returned with Martha Chambers in tow.

"Helen, it's so good to see you. Claire missed you terribly. Did she tell you about our shopping trip?"

Helen nodded.

"She seems very happy here."

"She's adjusting well," Martha replied. "And Marie absolutely adores her." She held out her arms to take the sleeping baby and Helen deposited her on Martha's waiting shoulder.

"Martha, I'd like to apologize for my behavior on Saturday. I don't know what came over me. I don't normally snap at people."

Martha Chambers put out her hand to touch Helen's arm in sympathy.

"Don't say another word about it. Just know that Claire will be safe with us. Doug and I will take care of her just as if she were our own daughter."

Helen smiled at Martha and then at Claire and asked if there was a place where she and Claire might have a few minutes alone.

"You can stay right here. Marie and I need to go upstairs for her nap, anyway. Take as much time as you need."

For a few moments Helen and Claire sat holding hands in silence.

"So, how do you like it here, Claire?" Helen asked at last. "Do you think you'd like to stay awhile?"

Claire paused to think.

"It was a little strange at first, but now I really like it. It's kind of nice being so busy. It keeps me from thinking about other stuff."

"Like what other stuff?" Helen asked.

Claire's eyes welled with tears.

"You know. Mom and Dad. And my little sister. And my friends at home."

"I know. But there's not much we can do about that just yet." Helen said calmly. "Now, do tell me about Mr. and Mrs. Chambers. Are they good to you?"

"Martha is real nice," Claire replied, wiping away her tears with the back of her hand. And Doug's okay, too, I guess, only he's away most of the time. He's fine when he's around Martha and the baby. But I don't like it at all when he's with the men who come to visit him."

"The men who were in the kitchen Friday night?"

"Yeah, he works with them," Claire replied. "They drink too much whiskey and say really mean things about the prisoners. Except Mr. Rocco. He's Doug's boss. Mr. Rocco told me he has granddaughters in Texas and he asked me to read him a story the way his granddaughters do."

A cloud seemed to pass over Helen's face but disappeared quickly.

"Well, I'm happy that things are working out. It's good to know that you're in safe hands." She looked at Claire intently. "But tell me, have you talked to Martha or Doug or anybody else here about your mom and dad?"

"No, they've been too busy," Claire replied, staring at her folded hands. "Martha said she wanted to have a long talk with me last night, but the baby was acting up and we never got around to it."

"You haven't said anything about your mom and little sister being taken away at the airport or your dad being arrested, did you?"

"No."

"Good. Now think hard," Helen urged. "Have you told anyone in Heber or anyone on the train about what happened to your family? If you have, I need you to remember everything you said to them. Can you think back that far?"

"The only other person I've talked to is you. I remember saying something to Dottie at the station about my dad living in Utah. But that's all. I didn't say anything about him being arrested or put in a camp."

"You're certain of that?" Helen pressed.

"I'm certain."

"Okay, that's good. Now, Claire, I want you to listen very carefully. From now on, you must forget about trying to find your parents. I will take care of that for you. Your job is simply to take care of yourself. If anyone asks about your family, don't answer. If you're forced to say something, tell them you're an orphan. As for how you got here, say that you got on a train in Pennsylvania and kept going till you reached Heber." Claire wanted to say something, but Helen shook her head to silence her.

"As for your childhood, say nothing about the stone house with the view of the river, only about the small house you rented in town. I don't know how much you've picked up about what has happened in this country, but it's not safe anymore to be thought of as wealthy or educated. People like that get arrested and end up in the camps or worse."

"I don't understand. Look at Martha and Doug and their house and Doug's car and the way they live. Aren't they wealthy?"

"Ah, Claire!" Helen exclaimed. "You are so young! Doug works for the government, and in today's world, it's the government who decides who can live in a big house and who cannot. But that's not important right now. All that matters is that you sit tight until I can track down your family. Because no matter what anyone says, your parents are the ones who really love you and you belong with them. If it takes me a while to find them, at least you're safe here."

Claire stared at her hands in silence.

"What do you say?" Helen asked her. "Can you handle it?"

Claire nodded.

"Just keep visiting me, okay? And don't stop looking for my dad, no matter what."

CHAPTER 11

"To revolt is a natural tendency of life... In general, the vitality and relative dignity of an animal can be measured by the intensity of its instinct to rebel."
—Mikhail Bakunin, Russian anarchist

Tuesday, March 12

Soon after our return to the barracks, someone noted that the massacre had occurred on the first anniversary of William Barry's ouster as Secretary of State Security. Barry, a career-long confederate of the President-for-Life, had founded the corrective labor camp system and spent nearly a decade filling it. Camp veterans suspected strongly that the bosses had chosen this date to further intimidate us. For Barry had been not merely purged, but executed on orders from the incoming President within weeks of the President-for-Life's death. The ostensible reason had been Barry's messy handling of the Quebec uprising, but the security chief's enemies, many of whom had friends and relatives in the camps, appeared determined to bring the DSS to heel.

This, in turn, left those running the DSS anxious to preserve their power. Did Barry's ouster mean they were less needed now? What better way to show their usefulness than by responding to new disturbances? By this reasoning, many Kamas prisoners feared that the previous week's shootings had been deliberate provocations engineered by Rocco and Whiting to justify a massive crackdown. And yet, during the year of political uncertainty following the deaths of Barry and the President-for-Life, no warden or security chief had dared set the precedent of opening fire on massed prisoners inside a camp.

Tempers flared as prisoners gave vent to their outrage about the massacre. I had underestimated their passion. Ralph Knopfler gathered teammates and friends at the south end of the barracks and presented his case for a camp-wide strike. D'Amato tried to shout Knopfler down from a bunk three rows away, dismissing the idea that the incident had been premeditated. He warned Knopfler and other hard-liners that a strike would be futile and would provoke even more punishment.

But the hard-liners argued that State Security sought nothing less than to reintroduce Barry's reign of terror. They linked the massacre to the previous week's shootings and pointed out that few prisoners, if any, had ever left the Kamas facility as free men. Conditions had not improved since Barry's death; they had nothing left to lose.

D'Amato and his fellow Unionist sympathizers called for patience. They admitted disappointment that a long-rumored general amnesty had not been handed down as expected on the first anniversary of the President-for-Life's death but argued that such initiatives were complex and took time. Any act of open defiance would result in tightening the lid for months to come. To send a petition or even a delegation was one thing, if done in a respectful manner, but thrusting non-negotiable demands in the Warden's face would certainly fail.

The debate raged well into the night in Barracks C-14, as it did in most barracks within Division 3 and many in Division 2, as well. Notes thrown over the wall between the two camp divisions kept both sides informed of the debate's progress. By roll call the next morning, most prisoners had decided for themselves whether to appear for work, but none of us knew for certain what the other would do. All we could hope was that, if a majority opted to strike, the minority would go along. Any prisoner who worked in defiance of a strike risked being labeled a traitor and murdered in his sleep like a stoolie.

During breakfast, every prisoner watched his neighbors for signs of whether he favored or opposed the strike. Close friends whispered among themselves in an effort to predict what others would do when the time arrived to line up for work. Anxious prisoners milled around longer than usual to catch any last-minute portents of what was about to happen.

When the camp siren blew, it became evident at once that Division 3 had decided to strike. A note lobbed in from Division Two confirmed that it had done the same. Most prisoners who had returned to the barracks immediately after breakfast remained there while those who loitered outdoors or in the mess hall made a beeline for their bunks. No one wanted to be seen lining up on the parade ground.

I watched from the barracks door and could see the assemblage of guards and warders waiting for us under the flagpole. They stayed another half-hour before they withdrew en masse through the gate to Division 2 rather than risk following us to our barracks and being outnumbered should violence ensue. As soon as the last guard passed out of view, prisoners began to emerge cautiously from the barracks: first one at a time, then in small groups, then in torrents. It was clear that the bosses did not have enough troops to herd us all onto the parade ground. They would have to withdraw and come up with a Plan B. For the moment, we had won.

Freedom is an odd, uncomfortable feeling when you have gone without it for long. We hardly knew what to do with ourselves without being ordered around. Some prisoners were exuberant, tossing their orange caps into the air and offering high fives and victory hugs to everyone in sight. Others kept to their bunks.

We gathered to discuss next steps. In our barracks, it took less than an hour for a plan to emerge. Knopfler and other leaders had a very clear idea of what they wanted to happen next. Over the years, activists like these men had pieced together a loose system of camp self-governance that coexisted with the official camp administration but concerned itself primarily with issues over which the administration had no jurisdiction or control.

Messengers visited each barracks to propose that the inmates elect a representative within one hour for a division-wide meeting. The purpose of the meeting would be to assemble a delegation to deliver a message to the camp authorities before the end of the day. Division 2 would do the same.

An overwhelming majority voted for Ralph Knopfler to represent Barracks C-14. Knopfler circulated from bunk to bunk, seeking out the views of prisoners whom he knew and trusted. Having been in the barracks for only five days, I was flattered when Knopfler climbed up to speak to me. I was even more surprised when he made no reference at all to the strike.

"I've been watching you at the brickyard, Paul," he began. "You're a good worker. Maybe too good for a man your age. You ought to slow down a bit until you're in better shape. Believe me, if you try to keep pace with kids like Jerry Lee or D.J., you'll get sick. And you can't afford that here."

"How long does a new man usually need to get up to speed?"

"You're getting there," Knopfler said. "Another week or two."

"I wouldn't want the team to miss a quota on my account..."

"Screw the quota," Knopfler snorted. "The numbers are all fabricated, anyway. By the time a quota gets handed down to me, it's usually utter nonsense. As a team leader, what I do is make sure we beat the quota by a hair on some days and miss it by a mile on others. That way we get full rations the greatest number of days and short rations the fewest."

"Now I get it," I said.

"My friend, if the path is crooked, there's no point to walking straight," Knopfler replied.

I was eager to turn the conversation back to the work stoppage.

"Do you really believe a strike will end up doing us any good?" I asked. "I hate to admit it, but it seems to me the bosses hold all the cards."

"They always do, but we shouldn't let that stop us," Knopfler said with a self-assured smile. "Come watch the meeting. It's got to be the only democracy within a thousand miles of here."

"Are you sure there will even be a meeting? What if the bosses retaliate?"

"That's not how they operate," Knopfler replied confidently. "The camp administration has a chain of command. They are required to report an event on this scale to their headquarters before taking action. Knowing the DSS bureaucracy, it'll be the end of the day before they see a response. Don't worry, they'll meet with us."

The Division 3 meeting was held later that morning in the mess hall. A voting representative attended from each of the thirty-six barracks in our division, along with a dozen or more observers like me. But apart from the novelty of watching a representative democracy at work among rebellious political prisoners, I found the meeting disappointing. The debate in Barracks C-14 had displayed a higher level of argument and presented a far more compelling set of facts.

After two hours of inconclusive discussion, the informal body had elected a five-member delegation to draft a message to submit to the warden. Knopfler and Reineke were among the five. Their first action was to dispatch a note to a guard at the main gate inviting five officials of the Warden's choice to meet with them at three o'clock that afternoon.

In the meantime, our entire group remained in the mess hall for lunch. As Knopfler had predicted, there was no clear sign that we might be assaulted. The high level of tension felt earlier that morning had dissipated. And despite the strike, the kitchen continued to prepare food, since most of the kitchen workers were prisoners and the rest were contract laborers unwilling to lose a day's pay by failing to work.

The five elected delegates sat at a table normally reserved for warders. When they finished, Knopfler took me aside.

"Come back at about ten minutes before three if you want to see something interesting. That's when the Warden's crew will likely show up. Glenn will arrive early, too. He told me he'd like to talk to you."

The next two hours passed without incident, with most prisoners spending the time in their bunks or conversing outside under a sunny midday sky. When I arrived for the meeting at the appointed time Knopfler took me aside once again. He said he had good news.

"You're in luck. The Warden has come with six men. That gives us two more places at the table and we're a man short. Care to join us?"

"I was hoping to avoid that kind of notoriety."

"Too late for that," Knopfler replied. "After bringing Reineke into camp, I'm sure Jack Whiting knows exactly who you are."

"All the same, I'd rather not rub his nose in it."

"Believe me, Paul, you're much better off if Whiting thinks you're a hard-ass than a coward. Come on, big guy, we need you."

I hesitated, then followed Knopfler into the dining hall and took a seat at a mess table along with the other six prisoner delegates. Besides Knopfler, Reineke, three other elected delegates, and me, there was an Argentinean surgeon representing the foreign prisoners.

The other three elected delegates were men I knew primarily by reputation. Seated to Reineke's left was George Perkins, a bookish former Washington legislative aide who had been working as a lobbyist for the German chemical industry when he was arrested on espionage charges. Although I had been annoyed to hear him defending the Unionist Party line in discussions earlier that morning, he seemed an intelligent man who might bring balance to the debate.

To Reineke's right was Chuck Quayle, a thirty-five-year-old former plant manager for a frozen foods company in Indiana, who served as a team captain at the military recycling site. Quayle was highly popular in camp but he had such a generous and easygoing nature that some hard-liners considered him too soft to deal with the camp bosses.

The final elected member of the delegation was Pete Murphy, a recently retired Army officer from Kentucky who had served briefly with Reineke in the Manchurian War. He was generally a likeable fellow, but subject to frequent bouts of depression and was rumored to be a recovering alcoholic.

Kitchen workers were still delivering plastic water pitchers and mugs to our table and to the empty table directly opposite ours when the government delegation filed in.

Fred Rocco, the warden, a tall, trim, scholarly-looking man of about fifty-five dressed in a dark blue business suit, gazed at us through dark steady eyes that conveyed shrewd detachment. He was a survivor of bureaucratic intrigues in both the State Security Department and the Federal Bureau of Investigation, where he had spent most of his career. He had landed in Kamas as warden through a combination of luck and years of networking inside the Washington law enforcement community. Faced with imminent arrest when his chief backer in the Bureau fell victim to political intrigue, Rocco pulled off a defensive coup by engineering his own transfer into the Department of State Security.

Once in the Department, his new backers defended him against his enemies in the Bureau and reached a compromise that satisfied all concerned. Under the deal, Rocco retained his rank and salary and his right to retire with full pension in three years, but only if he left Washington and served out those years as Warden of a labor camp in a Restricted Zone. Since his arrival, Rocco had rarely set foot inside the camp compound and remained a shadowy figure to most prisoners. By reputation, he was neither liberal nor draconian but followed regulations closely and let his deputy warden handle most day-to-day matters. He approached the negotiating table with a relaxed smile, took a seat near the center and unzipped a leather writing portfolio.

Close behind Rocco was the Deputy Warden, Doug Chambers, a fair-haired man several years short of forty with a broad forehead and deep-set blue eyes. On the surface, he projected an air of unshakeable self-confidence. But something about the man's bravado didn't quite ring true. Beneath his black State Security uniform, Chambers appeared to have gone soft and fleshy and, to my mind, showed signs of dissipation.

Most prisoners were aware that the deputy warden had fought for the Unionists throughout the Events and later in Mexico and Canada. The veterans among them, however, regarded Chambers with a mixture of envy, mistrust, and hatred. Had it not been for a lucky wound that saved him from the Manchurian War, Chambers might well have ended up inside the wire. Instead, he had traded on his combat record to transfer into State Security, where he became just another self-promoting careerist whose job was to make their lives hell.

The third man at the Warden's table wore the same black uniform as Chambers, but his shoulder insignia indicated the higher rank of full colonel. He appeared to be in his early forties, but had a puffy, florid face that had turned jowly and double-chinned. He sat before us as silent and immovable as a roadblock and I recognized his pugnacious expression as that of the prototypical schoolyard bully. Before long we would learn that the colonel's name was Tracy and that he was as stubborn and cruel as he looked.

The camp security chief, Major Jack Whiting, nicknamed "The Wart" for a growth on his left cheek, sat next to Tracy. Whiting had once served on the police force in Denver, but soon after the Colorado riots he joined the newly formed State Security Department and rotated through a series of camps in security roles. Whiting was notorious at every labor camp west of the Rockies for being an enterprising sadist who never let go of a grudge.

The final two members of the Warden's delegation were anonymous staff aides whose role seemed limited to note taking and recording the meeting on tape.

Rocco banged his mug on the metal table as soon as his aides opened their notebooks. All eyes were upon him except mine. Instead I glanced down the table at my colleagues and saw their narrowed eyes and firmly set jaws, braced for the severest kinds of threats and reprisals from the Warden and his crew.

"Before anything else is said here today," Rocco began, "I want you all to know that I take full responsibility as Warden of this camp for the shooting of prisoners yesterday at Recycling Site A. I give you my personal assurance that nothing of the kind will ever happen again at this camp as long as I am in charge."

Rocco leaned forward on his elbows and looked at us serenely over his half-rimmed bifocals. From the expressions on the faces of others around the room, I could see that I was not the only one in shock.

Rocco continued.

"I have brought my senior deputies here today to express our sincere regret for this tragic loss of life, to listen to your accounts of how the shooting happened, and to receive your proposals for how we ought to deal with it. So unless Doug or Jack or Colonel Tracy here has anything to add, what I'd like to do is listen to what your side has to say."

To all appearances, Rocco's words were well intentioned, sincere, and delivered with sensitivity. But coming from a man with Rocco's history, none of us was quite ready to believe them.

"Warden, I'll be the first to admit that what you've said comes as a welcome surprise," Glenn Reineke replied. "If State Security is genuinely willing to take responsibility for what happened and to prevent any more unprovoked shootings, this meeting might go more smoothly than I had expected."

"I certainly hope so," Rocco answered.

"But just to make sure we don't misunderstand each other, I'd like to read out a number of points that were raised this morning among the barracks representatives."

Rocco nodded amiably.

"What our fellow prisoners want is summarized in the following points:

"One. Suspension without pay of any camp official who fired on a prisoner or issued a command to fire, pending a full investigation.

"Two. A joint commission of camp officials and prisoners to report on their investigation within two weeks.

"Three. Prompt trial of anyone charged with wrongdoing and punishment of anyone convicted.

"Four. Compensation to the families of dead prisoners and full medical care for the wounded, along with disability pay.

"If you are willing to grant us those four items, Warden, along with the apology that you've already given us, I think we might convince the men to go back to work."

Rocco listened patiently and Chambers did the same, showing no sign of agreement or disagreement. Whiting, however, curled his upper lip in disdain and looked off into the distance. Colonel Tracy's cheeks turned crimson with rage. He opened his mouth to speak but Rocco cut him off, responding to Reineke without so much as a glance at anyone else on his own side of the table.

"Well, I didn't hear anything so unreasonable in all that. You're asking for the officers involved to be suspended pending an investigation; for a report within two weeks; for swift trials and punishment of anyone found guilty; and for compensation to the victims. Is that it, or have I left something out?"

"That's the gist of it, Warden," Reineke replied.

"And if we agree to your terms, you will recommend an end to the strike and a return to work tomorrow morning? Do I have your word on that?"

"You've got mine. How about the rest of you? Ralph?"

"I'll agree to that," Knopfler said.

"Pete?"

"If you give us those four points, I think we have a deal," Murphy added.

"George?"

"Agreed."

"Chuck?"

"I'll go for it."

"Georg?"

"I do not object."

"Paul?"

"Since I'm appointed and not elected, I'll defer to my colleagues. Yes."

"In that case, maybe we can all forego the 'who-struck-John' portion of this meeting and get right to a deal," Reineke suggested.

The Warden came out from behind his table to offer his hand to Glenn Reineke. Reineke accepted the handshake. I looked back across the table and saw Doug Chambers scratch his chin with a puzzled look. Both Whiting and the red-faced Colonel looked as if they were about to have heart failure.

The rest of us were left speechless. The whole thing had lasted less than five minutes.

CHAPTER 12

"He who has a why to live can bear with almost any how."
—Friedrich Nietzsche

Wednesday, March 13

Immediately after the session with Rocco and the camp authorities, the five members of the prisoners' delegation met again with the three dozen barracks representatives. Reineke and Perkins explained that Rocco had agreed to every one of their demands on the condition that the strike was to end by morning. At first a cheer rose from the group, but within moments I sensed that many representatives did not accept the Warden's assurances at face value.

Having experienced countless times how fluently lies and false promises flowed from the bosses' lips, these seasoned camp veterans scoffed at assurances that the Warden would follow through. When had Rocco ever punished a guard for shooting a prisoner? What if it was all a fraud?

The more the delegates tried to allay their concerns, the more the representatives appeared to retreat into sullen apathy. The delegation had been hoodwinked, they moaned. Rocco and his ilk would say anything and promise anything to get the one thing that mattered: an end to the strike. Yet not one of the barracks representatives suggested repudiating the deal the delegation had struck. Unable to come up with solutions of their own, yet clinging to their cynicism, they accepted the Warden's offer under protest and resigned themselves to imminent disappointment.

By evening the barracks representatives had spread word of the meeting's results throughout Division 3. But unlike most of the representatives, who nurtured a deep hatred and distrust of the Unionist regime, most rank-and-file prisoners accepted the recommendation to end the strike. These plain and honest folk cast aside the suspicions of their representatives and took into account only that Rocco had accepted the delegates' terms and had vowed to set things straight. Since a deal had been reached, they savored the promise of change, which Reineke's team appeared to have achieved without further sacrifice or risk of retribution. A buoyant air filled the mess hall that evening, with even the contract kitchen workers joining in the spirit and handing out extra helpings of soup and bread until supplies ran out.

We awakened to a harsher reality the next morning. During the night, strong winds heralded the approach of a frigid mass of arctic air. By roll call, the temperature had dropped to minus five degrees Fahrenheit, with steady winds up to thirty miles per hour. A line of prisoners claiming sudden illness and unfitness for work extended around three sides of the infirmary.

As I lined up for roll call, I assessed my own fitness for work that day. After a week at Kamas, my reserves of physical and mental strength were even lower than when I had arrived. Despite improved physical conditioning, more efficient work methods and partial adjustment to the 6,500 feet of altitude, the inadequate diet, long work hours, and exposure to the elements had worn me down. I had lost several more pounds, often found myself short of breath, and was never quite able to feel warm at the core, even after a meal of hot oatmeal or soup in the overheated mess hall. Prisoners who had survived camps in northern Canada claimed that the human body could adapt to far greater cold than we faced at Kamas, but I couldn't begin to imagine it.

After an uneventful roll call, with no more guards or warders than usual, and the latter showing unaccustomed restraint, the trek from camp to the recycling site strained our nerves to the breaking point. For as soon as we cleared the gate, our escort of armed guards suddenly doubled in number. At the head of our column was a canopied troop truck whose tailgate had been lowered to reveal a swivel-mounted, .50-caliber machine gun aimed straight down our throats. The guards who walked along our flanks, far from looking contrite, wore smug expressions that unnerved even the most optimistic among us. There would be no investigation, their eyes seemed to say, and we were at their mercy once again, having given up our strike without receiving anything tangible in return. And while they were dressed warmly in thick goose down parkas, heavy insulated gloves, and Arctic-rated snow boots, we wore the same patched and faded coveralls that we had slept in and in which we had awakened, still chilled to the bone.

Frequently that morning the members of our recycling team examined each other's faces and ears for signs of frostbite and treated the telltale white spots by breathing onto them or rubbing them with bare hands. We tried speeding up our rate of work, then slowing it down, in an attempt to find a pace that would produce the optimum balance between warmth and fatigue, but we could not solve the equation. No matter how hard we worked, we could not generate enough warmth to keep our limbs warm. And we all knew the horrors of frostbite from having seen the missing fingers and toes of prisoners who had survived previous winters in the Wasatch Range.

At mid-morning break I heard a whistle and followed the rest of the work team to a sheltered corner of the brickyard, where Ralph Knopfler had convened our work team. Knopfler told us that he had learned upon arrival at the recycling site that all Division 3 prisoners would face short rations for the next three days to make up for the meals we had eaten during the strike. Starting the next day, no ration bars would be issued for lunch. Furthermore, Knopfler announced, new calculations showed Recycling Site A to be further behind quarterly targets than expected. Daily work quotas would accordingly be raised until further notice. The ugly truth dawned on us that retaliation for the strike had already begun and that the Warden's promises of justice were worthless.

But the cold ensured that none of us dwelled very long upon the betrayal. All we cared about now was warming ourselves, returning to camp, and consuming hot soup, fresh bread, and sweet tea when we arrived. Little more was said among us until the closing whistle blew.

By the time we assembled at the main gate for the march back to camp, it became clear to many of us that the cold had done more than make us miserable. From time to time I would hear shouts and see a foreman or work group leader try to revive a prisoner who had collapsed, usually with shouts and kicks and blows from shovels. About half the time, the prisoner could not rise to his feet and had to be dragged by his ankles to the side of the road.

Four times that afternoon I heard rifle fire and twice watched prisoners commit suicide by running for the perimeter fence, where they were shot before reaching the electrified wire. When a man chose to end his life like this, it seemed to me no less murderous to shoot him than when the guards had tricked Lillian or Fong into approaching the wire. Yet today none of us raised his voice or took so much as a step out of line.

No shots were fired on the march back to camp. But the column stopped many more times than usual for the guards to deal with stragglers. A rumor spread before lights-out that Recycling Site A alone had lost more than a dozen men that day to exposure, exhaustion, or suicide. Still, no one proposed another work stoppage to protest the losses. For the moment, we had no cards left to play. Our spirit of resistance was tapped out.

A peculiar consequence of the one-day strike was that, for three days afterward, no one came around to padlock the barracks from the outside, as was normal camp procedure. Some, like Bernstein, were quick to call it a gesture of good faith by the warden, while others dismissed it as necessary for Whiting's stoolies to report to their case officers about prisoner morale. Several times during the first night the door to Barracks C-14 opened to admit visitors. Among them was Glenn Reineke.

Reineke sought directions to my bunk and asked me to join him for a short walk. In a nearby barracks a handful of his former comrades-in-arms and loyal friends had cleared the beds in one corner to offer us some privacy. Reineke asked me to take a seat next to him.

"I never had a chance to talk to you or the other fellow who carried me in from the train. If I'd been left in that rail car, there's no doubt the warders would have finished me off. I am in your debt."

His unblinking eyes were fixed on mine and possessed an almost hypnotic quality.

"But I also wanted to talk to you about something else. Knopfler tells me you're a hard worker and lead a clean life and aren't the kind who breaks when the cold and the hunger get you down. He said you'd be a good man for me to talk to, somebody whose mind is still fresh and uncorrupted by camp life."

He continued in low tones to ensure our privacy.

"You know, when I quit the Army, I was about as bitter as a man can be. The war with China was beyond anything I ever imagined. Not the fighting—after six years of combat I'd seen just about everything. But I never thought I'd see the day when our own government would sell out American fighting men in a foreign war. When we broke out from Khabarovsk and fought our way to the evacuation from Vanino, I was fed up taking responsibility for other men's lives. All I wanted was find a place where people weren't shooting and spoke English and had enough to eat and where I could get up in the morning without having to worry about anybody but myself, my wife and kids. And I wanted to see my family more than anything."

He paused for a moment, glancing around to make sure we were still alone.

"So I handed in my resignation and made my way overland from Alaska to Colorado. Within a week, they arrested me for desertion. State Security goons spent another year softening me up in an interrogation cell before they sent me here to die.

"In the beginning, the only thing I lived for was escape. I made my first attempt after about four months. They caught me, flogged me half to death and sent me underground to work the silver mines. It was another two years before I made it through the wire again. Gary and I were loose for fifteen days before they caught up with us. Still, I was ready to try it again. But this last week in the isolator, a lot of things became clearer to me. Do you believe in a God, Paul?"

"Yes," I said.

"Has he ever spoken to you?"

"Not like you and I are talking right now, but at times I think he sends me a message, if that's what you mean."

"Well, I think he's spoken to me," he continued, watching my face closely.

I nodded respectfully and invited him to continue.

"My spirit was nearly broken after they brought me back here. I kept asking God what could possibly be the purpose of my being alive if it wasn't to escape and be with my family? What do I do now after losing them again? But then I heard a voice inside me say: 'There is only one question. What meaning will you give to the life you have remaining?'

"At that moment it dawned on me that I'd been doing nothing but escape from one tight spot after another ever since Khabarovsk. I realized that maybe my job at Kamas wasn't to escape but to lead toward something greater. And I got the strongest feeling that a test was coming. Now I think I know what it is. Yesterday's strike was the beginning.

"Yesterday Rocco outsmarted us but I think we learned something from it. What we need to do now is stay alert and be ready for the next challenge, then move quickly to seize the initiative. But to do that, we need the best and brightest men we can find. People like—"

At this point one of Reineke's aides interrupted us. It was Gary Toth, Reineke's escape partner and the man who had brought down the attack dog on our first night in Utah. Toth, a former Navy SEAL, had been taken prisoner by the Chinese during an unsuccessful raid on occupied Vladivostok. After the Armistice, he and his fellow POWs had been repatriated straight into a corrective labor camp north of Ogden, Utah. He was in his early thirties, six and a half feet tall, and powerfully muscled even after a week in the isolator. He was also rumored to be one of the enforcers who slit the throats of suspected stoolies.

"I have someone to see you, Major," Toth broke in. "He said he has information you might want about camp security. Would you like to see him or should I send him to Pete Murphy?"

"Have you debriefed him?" Reineke asked.

"He won't talk to anybody but you, Sir."

"Do you think he might be one of the Wart's people?"

"I doubt it. He doesn't seem at all the type for it. We've checked him for weapons--he's clean."

"Then bring him in."

Reineke turned to me again.

"Paul, excuse me, but long experience has taught me that it doesn't pay to keep informants waiting."

"Would you like me to step outside?" I asked.

"No, stay. Let's see if he's willing to talk to both of us."

Toth brought forward a young black man, tall and slender, with delicate features. He approached the bunk without any sign of fear or apprehension.

"Have a seat," Reineke offered. "This is my colleague, Paul. Whatever you'd like to tell me is safe with him."

"Thank you," the visitor said, sizing up each of us. "I don't know quite how to start this, Mr. Reineke, but my name is Ben Jackson and for three nights now I've been having some strange dreams about the camp. Every night it's the same and every night is clearer than the last. After hearing you talk to us yesterday, I thought you might be the man to bring it to."

"A few weeks ago I probably wouldn't have been the right man," Reineke replied. "But lately I've been picking up strange messages of my own, Ben, so I guess that puts us in the same boat. Go ahead. Tell me about yours."

"I haven't been at Kamas very long. I arrived with the last convoy. Before that, I used to work in a bank in Baltimore. One day a couple of the bank's officers asked me to generate some reports and make some accounting entries that were way outside the rules. So I reported it to the regulators and figured it was no more of my concern. I was a whistleblower and I thought I'd be protected. But the next thing I knew, U.S. marshals came and handcuffed me right in my office and dragged me off to jail. They used to beat me pretty hard in jail sometimes and since then I haven't been able to work very well without getting dizzy or fainting.

"When I faint I see strange things sometimes—things that haven't happened yet. Oftentimes I can tell when someone in the barracks isn't going to make it. That's happened five or six times now."

"I've known men who had visions like that just before combat," Reineke said. "Almost drove them nuts, trying to decide whether to say anything about it. I'm glad you came to talk to me."

"In the first dream I saw Kamas from way above, like I was in an airplane or something," Jackson continued. "Only there was no snow in the valley, just in the highest mountains, so I figure it must have been summer. And the walls between the divisions were torn down, and women were mingling with the men all over camp.

"On the second night I saw the same thing, except that the camp was surrounded by soldiers in trenches and sandbag bunkers with tanks and armored troop carriers all around. Bulldozers were digging up the ground and creating huge clouds of dust. And off in the hills there were security people watching through telescopes and binoculars and listening with big radar-like dishes. They were watching and listening day and night.

"On the third night, I saw the camp after dark, but the sky was bright because there were flares floating above all the yards and spot lights shining on the camp from every direction. But inside camp it was quiet and there were only a few people still awake. Then suddenly the bulldozers started moving in toward the fences, knocking them down and crashing into the barracks and the workshops. The tanks came right on their heels, doing the same thing. And as people started coming out of the buildings, troops with Tommy guns followed the tanks in and gunned them down. Some of the prisoners fought back and the killing went on and on until I thought I couldn't stand it any longer.

"But as I got closer I could see that the prisoners knew exactly what they were doing and that most of them expected to die. I looked into their faces and into the faces of the troops and it seemed clear to me that the prisoners were really the winners while the attackers had lost everything that mattered."

Ben Jackson stopped talking and looked at Reineke and at me for a sign that we had understood him. I nodded and did my best not to show either of them that I was shivering. For what Ben had described was uncannily similar to my vision the night of my arrival in Heber, except that Ben's dream extended into the future. And while I had dismissed my vision for lack of a conventional explanation, now it was back again, with corroboration.

"Quite a vision," Reineke replied. "I guess it means we may die with our boots on after all. If you ask me, an old soldier can't ask for much more."

"You'll die that way for sure, Major Reineke. But Paul won't. He'll be gone by then. And so will I. I believe I'll be dead before all this comes to pass."

I felt as if he had plugged my hand into an electric socket.

"Gone where?" I pressed. "Do you mean 'gone' as in 'away' or 'gone' as in 'dearly departed?'"

"All I know is you won't be in camp," he answered with a shrug. "You'll be somewhere; I just don't see where."

"Well, I just hope you have better luck at escaping than I've had, Paul," Reineke told me before offering Ben Jackson his hand.

"Ben, if there is anything at all that I can do for you, come back and let's talk some more. In the meantime, if you aren't feeling well enough to work, talk to Schuster in the infirmary and tell him I sent you. He'll give you a break, I promise."

Ben took Reineke's hand and held his gaze for several seconds before leaving. Reineke remained standing and turned his attention to me.

"You've probably figured out by now what I was about to ask you before Ben came along. Only now that I've had time to think about it, I've changed my mind. We still need good men to help us with counterintelligence, but I suspect that's not the reason we crossed paths last week in that railway car.

"Something is about to break loose here at Kamas. Whatever it is, I've stopped trying to escape it. But I think Ben is right about you, Paul. This is not the hill you were meant to die on. Before we're done here, I think we'll have more than enough martyrs to go around. What we need are more witnesses.

"So here's the offer I'd like to make to you. I want you to go all over this camp. Talk to people. Find out all you can about Kamas and what makes this place tick. People like Knopfler and Murphy can help you. Then remember it all. Write it down if you have to, but imprint the important details on that educated mind of yours. Then when the time comes, I'm going to find some way for you to get out of here and tell our story outside."

"Wow, that's a heck of an offer. I don't know what to say," I answered, unsure of all that acceptance might imply.

"Listen, Paul, you saved my life the night we arrived. I owe you one."

"But Glenn, my sentence is only a fiver and I have a family outside," I objected. "I'm not sure I have what it takes to be a spy."

"But I'm not asking you to be a spy," Reineke answered wearily. "Just a witness. And a survivor."

"That's it?" I asked, still wavering.

Reineke gave a solemn nod.

"Do it," he said. "For your family."

I hesitated a moment longer, then reached out and took Reineke's extended hand.

"It's a deal," I replied.

CHAPTER 13

"We who lived in concentration camps can remember the men who walked through the huts comforting others, giving away their last piece of bread. They may have been few in number, but they offer sufficient proof that everything can be taken from a man but one thing: the last of the human freedoms—to choose one's attitude in any given set of circumstances, to choose one's own way."

—Victor Frankl, Man's Search for Meaning

Monday, March 18

The worst of the frigid weather lasted four more days. But since the fourth day fell on a Sunday, we did not have to face it outdoors, except for our brief forays to the mess hall and the latrine.

An unnatural quiet pervaded the barracks that Sunday. After nearly two weeks at camp, we newcomers had adjusted to our new work, learned what to expect from the warders and work team leaders, and had settled down sufficiently to see that all we could expect for the indefinite future was more of the same. By now only the most doctrinaire Unionists among us expected the Warden to make good on his promises.

Our day of rest also gave us an opportunity to take our minds off immediate issues of work and survival long enough to contemplate our past and future and the meaning of our lives in camp. For the first time in months, I found myself unable to repress thoughts of my former life and, particularly, of my wife and children.

Fifteen months earlier, I had driven myself nearly mad with worry over how my they would survive after my arrest. My failed efforts to keep my business alive had left me jobless and nearly destitute. Now, having been arrested and charged with political crimes, my wife would be unemployable and my children disqualified from attending public school. As my months in prison dragged on, I imagined my wife selling all our possessions to pay the rent and keep the children clothed and fed.

The only hope for their future lay in collecting enough money to pay the emigration tax and join my wife's relatives abroad. But until I confessed, exit visas would be out of the question. So after refusing to budge through a year of nightly interrogations and beatings, I finally signed a plea bargain agreement on the condition that State Security would allow my wife and daughters to emigrate. A week later I was told that their exit visas were granted.

Then, on the eve of my departure west, I received a smuggled message that my in-laws had wired money for their emigration tax and that Juliet, Claire, and Louisa would be boarding a flight to London in a few days. At last they would be free. But I would be sent to the camps and might never see them again. How could I have let such a thing happen?

Around that time, an older inmate at Susquehanna had assured me that unconquerable feelings of guilt and regret were normal following a political prisoner's arrest. In fact, guilt tended to be strongest precisely among honest and principled people. He then pointed out that the State Security interrogators relied on such guilt to crush a prisoner's will and extract his confession. The only sensible course of action for a prisoner was to put aside longings for home and family, and start an entirely new life in the camps. Only by accepting the end of one's former life could a prisoner hope to preserve his sanity and have a reasonable chance to survive.

I had accepted the man's advice. Yet images of my wife and daughters continued to pass before my eyes whenever my mind was idle. In an instant I found myself reliving perfectly preserved moments from the days before my arrest, memories that had lain repressed for more than a year. It did not require much analysis to trace these thoughts back to my conversation with Glenn Reineke five days before, when my hopes of a new life beyond the camps were suddenly rekindled. Perhaps the time had come to use the hope of rejoining my family as an incentive to escape.

My thoughts were occupied with little else all day Sunday and into the night. When I awakened on Monday morning, I knew that I could no longer pursue a path of pessimism and self-denial. From that moment I nurtured the idea that my presence in Kamas really did have a larger purpose and that I might discover it by paying closer attention to events going on around me.

Apparently I had not been the only prisoner to have spent Sunday contemplating the meaning of life at Kamas. Others had brooded, too, and had reached different conclusions from mine. One young prisoner, a Cuban from Miami, had slit his wrists during the night. A middle-aged bachelor in Barracks B-8 had slipped away from the barracks and hanged himself from a lamppost. Between dawn and roll call, two other prisoners ran into the perimeter wire and were electrocuted before they could be shot. And, as was the usual pattern on Monday mornings, several Division 3 residents had simply given up hope and expired in their sleep.

An emaciated young prisoner who had been a college senior when he was arrested two years earlier appeared to have given up hope but not breath. He lay on his back in a lower bunk two rows from mine, staring open-mouthed at the ceiling of the bunk above him. A kind-hearted, white-haired prisoner whom I knew from the recycling site knelt by his side and held the youth's hand while doing his best to cajole him into rising for roll call. The older man was Al Gallucci, an aeronautical engineer from Georgia who for some unfathomable reason still worked as a common laborer, having refused repeated offers of promotion to foreman or team leader.

"Paul, could you help me lift him? He's not responding, but I think that if we could get him on his feet, he'd come along."

I grabbed an arm and the two of us raised the youth to his feet. At that moment, the warder Sam Renaud swaggered through the barracks door with a rubber truncheon in his hand and blood in his eye. Renaud spotted someone still in bed and delivered a vicious whack to his unprotected shins. He slashed another prisoner across the lower spine as the man rolled onto his stomach to flee. When he reached us, he searched for an exposed target zone, then brought the truncheon down on the youth's collarbone. When his victim failed to resist or even shrink from the blow, Renaud raised his weapon again.

Without thinking, I grabbed Renaud's wrist and drove my shoulder into his ribcage, shoving him back against the oak pillar of a bunk. His head connected with a heavy thunk and for a moment he was stunned. I used the opportunity to bring around my hand and tear the truncheon from his grip. But he recovered more quickly than I expected and shoved me away before lowering his head and coming at me like a crazed bull. Although I was taller by at least four inches and had once probably had a hefty weight advantage, Renaud now had the benefit of three square meals a day and the use of the guards' weight room to keep up his strength. I feared for my life if he succeeded in getting on top of me.

An instant before impact, I sidestepped Renaud's charge and grabbed his elbow, pushing him off-balance so that he sprawled forward onto a vacant bunk. With the desperation of an underdog, I leaped onto his back and wrapped my forearm around his throat, pulling with all my strength. I felt his body tense as his air passages closed and he could no longer scream for help. He tried to reach behind to grab my head but failed to connect. I felt his muscles tense and then slowly go slack. Running through my mind was the thought that, the bosses would probably not execute me for killing a warder, who was just another prisoner, but sparing Renaud's life would invite deadly revenge at a time and place of his choosing.

Before I knew what was happening, a hand gripped me under the chin while someone else wrested my left arm away so that I lost my leverage against Renaud's throat. I was being pulled from behind off the warder's back. Then I saw the rubber truncheon come down against Renaud's head.

Gary Toth unzipped his coveralls a few inches and slipped the rubber truncheon inside.

"Drag him into the corner and leave him," Toth barked to the man who had pulled me off Renaud's back. Then he turned to me.

"Come on, let's get out of here. It's not worth going to the isolator for killing this lowlife scum."

Having felt weakened for so long by hunger and cold, I had forgotten the superhuman strength that adrenaline provides in moments of desperation. I was shaking all over and gasping for air but I no longer felt cold or afraid.

I arrived at roll call just in time to be counted. As it turned out, Gallucci had managed to coax the student onto the parade ground after all. I saw the two of them after breakfast in the column heading out to the recycling site. But two days later the student ran into the wire.

By the time we lined up and marched out to the recycling site, the sky was a bright and cloudless blue. Despite the residual cold and the blanket of snow on the ground, the sun radiated warmth through our coveralls and gave us hope that spring would not be many more weeks away.

Our three days without noonday meal bars were now behind us. When the foreman's whistle announced the lunch break, I slipped my ration bar out of my coveralls and sat on a half-loaded pallet to savor my midday meal.

"Mind if I join you, Paul?" came a voice from behind me.

It was Al Gallucci.

"I admired what you did this morning, Paul," he began. "Maybe it wasn't the most sensible thing to do, but Renaud had it coming to him."

"I'm sure he did but why is it always up to the newcomers to draw the line on goons like him?"

"Too many of the older prisoners have lost their spirit. Especially the ones who've been up north."

"Have you been there?" I asked

"Only for a summer, thank God. In winter, I wouldn't have lasted more than a week. And wouldn't have wanted to."

"What do you mean?"

"I've watched what happens to men who have returned from the north," Gallucci explained. "I believe too much cold can kill a man's soul. Emotions disappear, too. No more love or hatred; no more anger or even pity. And the worst: no more friendship, either. I've seen friendship survive enormous adversity in the camps, but where life is too harsh, friendship can't take root and grow. And that's what State Security aims for, because that's what lets them rule the camps."

"So how do you fight it?" I asked. "You make it sound as if every prisoner eventually knuckles under."

Gallucci shook his head.

"Far from it. Hundreds of men in this camp have resisted the worst tortures imaginable and have never signed confessions or denounced another human being. But most men aren't made of such stern stuff. That's why the bosses are constantly seeding the camp with stooges to help them weed out the strong and keep the rest of us from uniting. Believe me, I'm not a violent man, Paul, but I'll grant the hard-liners this much: unless we eradicate the stoolies we'll be on our knees till the day we die."

"If you feel so strongly about the need to unite," I interrupted, "why aren't you out there leading the way? Men like Reineke and Quayle serve as barracks representatives. Knopfler leads a work team. You're an engineer, yet I've heard you've refused promotion to foreman. Why?"

"I refuse to bend another man to my will or the will of the bosses. I'll work to eat but I'll never let them use me to oppress another man. It's fundamentally wrong."

Gallucci pointed a finger toward the fence between the brickyard and the lumberyard, where I had seen Reineke in conversation with Ralph Knopfler the week before. Once again, Reineke and another prisoner were talking quietly with their heads bowed close together on opposite sides of the fence.

"Do you see that man talking to Glenn Reineke?" Gallucci asked. "He knows more about how to stay clean in the camps than any other man I know. Alec Sigler has been in the system for nearly eight years and he's still standing tall after everything they've thrown at him. His term is up this summer and he has a wife in Heber who's waited for him the whole time. If you want to learn how to get out of here with your spirit in one piece, talk to Alec."

"Do you mean that they actually let prisoners out of here when they've served their time?" I asked, having heard that releases were rare.

"Not many," Gallucci conceded, "and the ones I know of weren't politicals. But if Sigler can do it, I suppose there's hope for you and me if we live that long."

We finished our lunch break eating in silence. I watched Alec Sigler retreat from the fence and resume his work sorting good bricks from broken ones. As the afternoon wore on, from time to time my eyes returned to that spot, watching Sigler's slow measured movements, serene expression, and easygoing teamwork. I found myself thinking about how to approach him.

About an hour before quitting time, I glanced over at the sorting area one more time and spotted Sigler heading toward a tool shed near the perimeter fence. All at once the hairs on the back of my neck bristled and I thought of the ill-fated Lillian, shot during my first afternoon in camp. She, too, had strayed too close to the wire. I raised my eyes to find the nearest watchtower and saw a glint of light reflecting from the telescopic sight of a sniper's rifle. A flash leapt out of the gun's black muzzle and a moment later I heard the sharp crack of a rifle shot. Sigler fell.

I sunk to my knees, utterly deflated.

The men around me dropped their loads of bricks and faced the tower from which the fatal round had been fired. A second shot rang out—no doubt Sigler's belated warning shot. Beyond the outer perimeter wire I spotted Jack Whiting emerge from the cab of a canvas-topped troop truck.

At Whiting's command, a dozen black-uniformed guards leapt from the truck onto the snow-covered ground and trotted across the no-man's land into the brickyard. The guards, armed only with nightsticks and pepper-spray, surrounded Sigler's corpse while two of their men dragged it by the ankles toward the gate.

Suddenly a husky voice cried out from among Sigler's work team.

"Put him down!"

Others joined in.

"Let him be! Don't you dare take him away!" someone shouted at the circling guards.

"Let's get him back!"

In an instant men snatched up picks and shovels and loose bricks and converged on the guards. Two men grabbed each of Sigler's arms and held fast. The guards swung their nightsticks and discharged their pepper spray but could not dislodge the prisoners' grip. A pair of men in orange coveralls leveled their long-handled shovels like lances and jabbed at the guards holding Sigler's shoulders until they let go.

The guards were already in retreat when a burst of machine-gun fire raked the skirmish line. The shovelers fell backward. Instantly every prisoner in the brickyard hit the deck while the guards retreated empty-handed into the no-man's-land and swung the gate shut behind them.

Nearly a full minute elapsed before the first prisoner crawled slowly to his feet and advanced to the aid of the fallen shovelers. Others followed and soon scores of men arrived on the scene from every corner of the brickyard. Seething with suppressed rage, I joined them in hoisting Sigler's body onto our massed shoulders and hauling it toward the main gate. A minute or two later, others did the same with the remains of a dead shoveler.

It was not yet quitting time, but none of us lifted another brick that day. We had only one thing on our minds and that was to bear Sigler's body and that of the fallen shoveler back into camp for all to see.

CHAPTER 14

"In a state worthy of the name there is no liberty. The people want to exercise power but what on earth would they do with it if it were given to them?"
—V.I. Lenin

Tuesday, March 19

We did not succeed in carrying Sigler and the dead shoveler out of the recycling site on our shoulders. No sooner did we leave the site's main gate than we were surrounded by a detachment of Tommy gunners from Jack Whiting's security detail. While they trained their submachine guns on us, a squad of warders seized the corpses and made away with them in a jeep.

The march back to the barracks was as grim as the one a week before, when we had returned to work after our one-day strike. Once again, a troop truck with a rear-facing, .50-caliber machine gun headed the column, and once again the armed escort had been doubled. As before, an advance security detail met us outside the camp and led us within range of marksmen posted in the watchtowers. We viewed the firepower arrayed against us and asked ourselves whether such heavy security had been planned all along or whether it was just another example of the Wart's uncanny prescience.

I felt confused and demoralized by the setbacks we had suffered since the strike. The Warden's false promises, the increased quotas, the reduced rations, the murder of Sigler and of the man who tried to recover his body, and now the doubled escort. The bloody days of William Barry seemed back upon us.

The first whisperings about a new strike arose at dinner in the mess hall.

The consensus among the prisoners was that the Wart had singled out Sigler for assassination because he could not permit someone who had withstood the worst that the system could inflict to walk out of Kamas a free man. The Wart's assertion that Sigler had brought the shooting upon himself by threatening a guard was preposterous. Everyone even remotely acquainted with Sigler knew that he was a devout Christian, non-violent and respectful of camp authority and its rules. Being only a few months short of finishing his eight-year term, he had no conceivable motive to make trouble or escape.

In our eyes, the only acceptable response to Sigler's murder was to stop work until Whiting and the guards who fired on us were suspended or dismissed. This time promises would not be enough. We must reinstate the strike and hold firm until our original demands for suspension, investigation, punishment and compensation were met. Sentiment favoring another strike spread quickly. In Barracks C-14 we heard impassioned pleas from one visitor after another:

"Brothers! How much longer are we going to go on slaving away, taking our wages in bullets? No more! Tomorrow morning, nobody goes to work!"

Barracks after barracks, the message made the rounds. Some attached notes to rocks and threw them over the wall to Division 2, where political prisoners from Canada, Mexico, China, Russia, the Middle East, and a variety of other countries languished together with their American counterparts. Many of the foreigners still harbored hopes of being repatriated in bilateral prisoner exchanges, yet they, too, took the risk of supporting another strike.

The next morning's events unfolded identically to the events of Tuesday the week before. Prisoners reported for breakfast but stayed in their barracks when the time came to assemble for work. Again the bosses looked on in apparent frustration.

About an hour after work was to have started I was on my way to the latrines, and saw a phalanx of warders and armed escort troops massing outside the Division 3 gate. They wore helmets and light body armor but carried no weapons more lethal than nightsticks.

Suddenly the gate opened and the attackers fanned out, sending a ten-man squad to assault each of the barracks near the gate. I ran forward to watch. Their method was simple: they sent eight men into a barracks and kept two outside the door. Six of the inside men moved in pairs from bunk to bunk, grabbing prisoners and dragging them to the doorway, where the two remaining inside men shoved them into the waiting arms of the pair outside. Once outdoors, the prisoners were escorted to the parade ground and held there under armed guard. Having been unable to defeat our work stoppage the first time, it seemed that the bosses had developed new countermeasures to prevent us from striking again.

But the measures failed to give our oppressors the upper hand. While the prisoners offered only passive resistance, clinging to bedposts and going limp once dislodged, the work proved slow and tedious for the security men. With each barracks holding about a hundred prisoners, the warders and troops soon became exhausted. More than that, some of the prisoners they succeeded in evicting slipped away en route to the parade ground and took refuge in other barracks or the latrines.

The guards and warders kept up the eviction work for two hours but succeeded in emptying less than a third of the barracks in Division 3. By mid-morning they withdrew. For the balance of the day, we enjoyed the warmth of our bunks, coming out only to use the latrines and to visit the mess hall. Our methods had prevailed, we thought. Now the administration would have no choice but to deal with us in good faith.

On the second morning of the strike, the phalanx returned before dawn with reinforcements and with Colonel Tracy at their head. He and his squad leaders went as before from barracks to barracks, waking everyone with rough shouts from portable bullhorns.

Ours was one of the first barracks graced by a visit from the Colonel. He entered in his neatly pressed black uniform and peaked hat, unarmed but backed by a retinue of eight junior officers and guards. Even in the dim pre-dawn light, I could see that his face was flushed with anger and that he was hell-bent to have his way with us.

"Listen here!" he bellowed. "How long do you prisoners intend to go on with this slacking? The mess hall and these cozy bunks of yours are only for men who work!"

He pointed to a prisoner who sat on a nearby bunk while lacing his boots. Then he pointed in turn to several other prisoners who were not yet fully dressed.

"You there! Outside! And you, too! And you and you and you!"

He waved for his attendants to seize the men and take them outside. This time the captives were hustled onto a truck and held there at gunpoint.

Someone shouted from the back of the darkened room.

"Come and get us if you have the guts, you swine!"

"Find that man and make sure he spends the next week in the isolator, Lieutenant!" Tracy ordered. "Now which of you are going to work and which of you are going to the camp jail?"

No one moved.

"All right, Lieutenant, fill the truck!"

With that, Tracy turned on his heel and left. His men succeeded in dragging a few dozen more onto the truck but suffered a humiliating setback when most of them escaped in a rush when the truck door was left too lightly guarded. The guards dragged off just enough prisoners to refill the truck before giving up the battle for Barracks C-14.

Once they left us, I ran over to watch the evacuation of Pete Murphy's barracks. There Tracy and his henchmen were having more success, hustling one prisoner after another into the waiting truck.

But Murphy was not one to accept defeat lightly.

"If it's work or jail, I pick jail! Here, take me first!" he insisted.

Other voices cried out in support.

"I pick jail, too!" one exclaimed. "Save room on the truck for me!"

Within moments, the entire barracks exploded in a chant, "We want jail! We want jail!" and surged forward, overwhelming the doorkeepers.

Colonel Tracy, still blocking the doorway, was forced to scramble outside to avoid being crushed in the stampede. His face filled with disgust at being so close to the foul-smelling and disrespectful prisoners. As I watched him brush the soot off his uniform it seemed to me that the irony of Murphy's gesture had been utterly lost on him.

Barely an hour later, Tracy ordered the trucks to depart. The operation ended after making off with fewer than 200 prisoners. Our spirits soared as we watched the gate close behind the last of the guards. Within minutes, however, Tracy announced over the loudspeaker that those who were jailed would remain in jail until the rest of us went back to work. Then he added that all of us would be put on bread and water effective immediately. This crude attempt to divide us seemed to strike some of the men particularly hard. Within moments I felt an odd tingling at the back of my neck.

It was D'Amato glowering at me from the barracks door.

"Satisfied?" he snarled.

That night I received a summons to visit Glenn Reineke at his barracks just after lights out. When I arrived, Gary Toth met me at the door and took me back through the semi-darkness to Reineke's bunk. The Major was writing in a notebook by the light of a single stubby candle.

"Sorry for asking you to come over so late, Paul," Reineke began with a courtesy that seemed out of place, but, quite frankly, was endearing for precisely that reason. "But I thought it might be better for you if we met more discreetly."

"How can I help?" I asked, relieved that he had sensed my reluctance to stand out in the crowd.

"Something has come up and I need a hand from someone I can trust."

"Happy to oblige," I said uneasily. "As long as it doesn't involve any throat-slitting."

"Not this time," Reineke replied with a half-smile. "It's about Alec Sigler. Did you know Sigler left a widow in Heber?"

"I've heard."

"She doesn't know yet that he's dead. I'm looking for someone to tell her."

I didn't know whether he was joking or had lost his marbles.

"Would a letter do or should I visit her at home?"

Reineke chuckled.

"A letter will do just fine. And in case you're wondering how to send it to her, you'll be using the same method Sigler used to smuggle his own messages to her."

"I see. So you have ways to smuggle things out of here?"

"Yes," he answered.

"And you want me to risk everything to smuggle letters to a woman I've never met?"

"You could look at it that way. But having a connection to the outside might be valuable to someone who intends to get out of here soon. Which is why I thought of you."

"All right, now I'm hooked. Go on," I said, driven by a superstitious feeling that it would be unworthy of me not to help the widow of a man like Sigler when fate had singled me out for the task.

Reineke went on to reveal the details of how Alec Sigler would conceal a written message in the cylindrical hole of an ordinary brick fragment, seal each end of the hole with mud and drop it along the shoulder of the road on his way back from the recycling site. His wife did something similar by rolling her paper message into a spindle and tucking it into a hollowed stick of a certain size to be tossed over the fence into the brickyard. Reineke drew me a map of the spots in the brickyard and along the road to the recycling site where the messages were left. Some thirty minutes later, after learning these and other details, I was ready to begin a clandestine correspondence with the widow of a man I had admired but never met.

"I'll need some paper and something to write with," I told him.

He gave me a manila envelope with a dozen sheets of blank copy paper and a cheap ballpoint pen. I stuffed the envelope into my coveralls.

"Keep it in a safe place and return what you don't need. And don't let anybody see what you're doing. Whiting's stoolies are on high alert. If you suspect anybody is watching you, tell Gary or me, and stay clear of them."

Reineke rose from his bunk in a way that made clear he was ready for me to leave. But before I did, I couldn't resist asking him for news about the strike.

"Has the Warden responded to our demands yet?"

"There's not going to be a response," Reineke replied calmly. "They're out to crush us."

His words hit me like a blast of arctic air. Like many of the new prisoners, my decision to strike had been largely an emotional one without fully considering the consequences. From the beginning, I had assumed that the work stoppage would be settled quickly and that a settlement would bring some minor concessions from the camp bosses that would allow both sides to save face.

"What now?" I asked.

"Same as before. We refuse to work."

"That's it?"

Reineke was silent for a moment.

"Until someone comes up with a better idea."

The next morning, on the third day of the strike, I could sense that some of the weaker prisoners were wavering after hearing that they would no longer receive full rations. Even the hardiest of men could not maintain his strength on punishment rations. At roll call the word spread that the threat of jail and loss of rations had proven too onerous for our brothers in Division 2. Their section leaders had already capitulated to the Warden.

In Division 3, each prisoner watched his neighbor for signs of what was to come, much as we had when the first strike broke out just a week earlier. Anxious prisoners milled about the mess hall doors and the edges of the parade ground to catch any last-minute signs of flagging resolve. But, as before, when the siren blew, it was clear that Division 3 had decided to continue the strike. No one set foot on the parade ground.

I watched from the barracks door as I had the previous Tuesday and saw the normal complement of warders and escort troops waiting for us to line up by work group. As before, they waited for thirty minutes before they withdrew to the perimeter. But instead of leaving us in peace, within ten minutes the largest-ever phalanx of officers, guards, and escort troops massed outside the gates. At their head was a company of warders in plastic helmets and body armor.

I estimated the entire force at 300 men, which meant that the Warden must have drafted additional troops from State Security units all along the Wasatch Front. There were also at least two dozen empty troop trucks, each escorted by armed infantry. This time the bosses had come fully equipped to achieve their objective of breaking the strike once and for all.

The troops used the same tactics as the previous morning, moving against the barracks in squads of ten and removing anyone who did not agree to line up for work. The trucks filled quickly with strikers and carted them off to the camp jail in Division 4. There the trucks remained just long enough to unload before returning for more strikers. By my calculation, within an hour the jail must have exceeded its official capacity of 500.

By the time the shock troops reached Barracks C-14, they seemed to sense that they were winning the battle and moved at a more leisurely pace, pausing to bait and harass us as they went.

Colonel Tracy seemed to be in a particularly expansive mood. He entered our barracks in a fresh uniform and imposing peaked hat, backed by a retinue of nine or ten hulking guards. He sat down on one of the low bunks nearest the door, ignoring the gaunt and forlorn old prisoner who squatted next to him on the bed. Tracy elbowed the old man aside and sat with arms akimbo so that no space at all was left for the miserable prisoner.

"Come on, old friend, move over a bit, eh? Can't you see I'm a colonel?"

Three or four other black-uniformed officers followed his lead, displacing the occupants of nearby bunks and appearing every bit as uncomfortable with their proximity to the foul-smelling prisoners as the latter were with being shoved aside. Tracy then grabbed his quaking neighbor by the elbow and thrust him into the arms of waiting guards, who ran him out of the barracks as if on rails. The other officers followed suit, though gingerly, so as not to soil their uniforms.

When they reached my row of bunks, I saw no point in clinging to a bedpost or otherwise resisting the trip out to the truck. I rose as my captors approached and offered them both arms to escort me outside. It was an almost dignified journey down the aisle and out into the yard to join the other strikers.

But to my surprise no truck waited for us there. A load of prisoners roared by, then another, before I noticed that all the trucks were heading for the gate while none was returning. The camp jail, it seemed, was full.

The guards escorted the rest of us on foot to the parade ground. About 2,500 of us squatted side by side, the great majority of whom had surrendered rather than go to jail. Of the thousand or so who had refused to work, most were presumably behind bars.

The guards warned us to remain seated on the ground until the Warden addressed us over the loudspeaker system. Before long we heard his voice.

"This is the Warden speaking. Your elected leaders have now informed me that the illegal strike is at an end. All of you will report for work immediately. Guards, assemble the prisoners in columns for departure to their job sites. That is all."

The strike had lasted three days. We had gained nothing by it.

CHAPTER 15

"The task of Soviet corrective labor policy is the transformation of the nastiest human material into worthwhile, fully useful, active and conscientious builders of socialism."

—I.L. Averbakh, Stalinist-era penal theorist

Friday, March 22

After the Warden announced the end of the strike, the troops assembled those of us who remained on the parade ground into columns and marched us off to work. Guards with attack dogs harassed us all the way.

At the recycling site we worked slowly and steadily to avoid any pretext for the warders to harass us. With Alec Sigler's death still fresh in our minds, we also took pains not to approach the perimeter wire. When anyone stopped working or dropped a load, the warders showed no mercy with their truncheons.

Our team was lucky that we had Ralph Knopfler to guide us through these critical hours. Knopfler reorganized the brickyard crew around the absent workers and managed to turn out a respectable day's work despite our short-handed crew.

The march back to camp was tense but uneventful. The uppermost question in most minds was whether we would still receive our evening meal or would be dropped off at our barracks and locked up for the night. We all regarded this as a key indicator of how the camp authorities would treat us after the strike. I felt enormous relief at seeing the column head for the mess hall, where we were served an unusually meaty chicken stew.

Once back in the barracks, however, the rows of empty bunks left me anxious about how events would unfold once those in jail rejoined us. There was little of the customary storytelling or card playing that went on most nights after dinner. Nearly everyone lay quietly in his bed. As soon as the lights went out, I climbed down from my bunk and crossed the aisle to visit Knopfler.

"It's Paul," I said quietly. "I need to talk."

"Sure, climb up."

"You've been around here a while, Ralph. You've seen strikes before. What do you think they'll do to us?"

"These days it's not easy to say," Knopfler answered, sitting up. "A year ago, they never would have let us get this far. By the second day, they'd have taken a few dozen of us off to the gravel pit to be shot. And they'd have kept on doing it until the strike was broken or there was no one left to shoot. I haven't seen any trucks going from the jail to the gravel pit yet. That's a good sign."

"What will they do with the men they put in jail?" I asked. "By my count, there must be nearly a thousand."

"It all depends on what the bosses see as more important right now: meeting quotas or enforcing discipline. If it's work quotas, whoever's in jail will be left to stew for a few days on punishment rations. Then Whiting will throw a few of the ringleaders into the isolator and send the others back to work. If it's discipline they're after, they'll pack the entire thousand off to the northern camps and bring in a whole new crew to replace them."

"So what do you think it will be?"

"My money is on transfers," Knopfler replied. "We've been watching the stoolies closely ever since the strike started. Whiting has been working them like dogs to identify the strike leaders."

"You know who the stoolies are?" I asked in surprise.

"Most of them. They're not all that hard to spot. Usually it's the ones who ask too many questions." He stared at me hard.

I gulped.

"Don't worry, Paul, "Knopfler laughed. "You don't fit the profile. Usually stoolies have the softer jobs in the warehouse or the infirmary or the mess halls. Typically they transfer in from other camps within the district. As soon as we spot them, our people put them under 'round-the-clock surveillance. Before long, we usually catch them sneaking off to meet with Whiting's people. While they're making their hit lists, we make ours."

As we spoke, I had a growing sense of being watched. I didn't know whether it was simply the result of hearing Knopfler talk about stool pigeons, or whether someone's eyes were indeed following me in the dark. I thanked Knopfler and returned to my bunk, my heart pounding.

Having seen so many prisoners shot, beaten, worked to death, or driven to suicide over the past two weeks and hearing about impending mass transfers north brought home to me just how vulnerable I was. Even under the best conditions, the odds of outliving my sentence seemed poor.

Ever since my arrest, I had done my best to hold my temper and remain as inoffensive as possible. I had taken pains to avoid making controversial statements. I had refrained from provoking my interrogators or cellmates and, on all but a few occasions, had even declined to defend myself when challenged. But by helping Glenn Reineke in the railroad car, by attacking Renaud, and by associating with people like Reineke, Gary Toth and Knopfler, I had almost certainly identified myself to the Wart's informants as one of Reineke's diehard anti-Unionist clique.

I tried to console myself with the memory of Ben Jackson's dream, which had been so similar to mine in many ways. Ben had foretold that I would be out of Kamas by summer. I wanted to believe it, and sensed that there must be some truth to it because of my own vision. But perhaps the dream meant that I would leave Kamas under transfer to a northern logging camp and not under some parole or pardon. While I resolved not to let negative thinking carry me away, fear had already left its mark. I feared not only for myself but also for my wife and daughters, and for camp friends like Jerry Lee and D.J., who might be drawn into the abyss because of me.

I interrupted this tailspin of worry only when I heard someone moaning in a nearby bunk. I listened hard and through the gloom I saw John D'Amato's chest heave in rhythm with the sobs.

"Is that you, D'Amato?" I whispered.

No reply.

"If you don't want to talk about it, then how about keeping the noise level down? The rest of us need our sleep."

"Not me. I'm staying up," D'Amato answered through his sobs.

"Don't be an idiot," I told him.

"If I sleep, they'll come and kill me."

"The damned door is locked, D'Amato. Besides, they're not coming for anyone until morning. Go to sleep."

"Not the guards. The vigilantes."

"The who? Stop babbling."

"The ones who slit people's throats. You know them, Paul. They're your friends."

I did know, and, apparently, others could see that I knew.

After a few moments, D'Amato stopped whimpering. Not long afterward I fell asleep. But it was a troubled sleep. I dreamt of the nightly beatings at Susquehanna and the howling winds in the brickyard and of boarding a prison train for the Arctic Circle.

In the morning, I still had not shaken off a sense of impending doom. I looked across the aisle to D'Amato's bunk. It was empty.

At the latrines, I overheard prisoners talk knowingly about the coming prisoner transfer. Some expected the transferee count to go as high as a 500 or 1,000. Others vowed that they would run into the wire rather than be shipped off to the Yukon or Hudson Bay.

Not until I returned to the yard did I learn what had happened to D'Amato.

"There were two in our barracks," I heard someone say in the next row. "There's not a barracks that didn't lose at least one."

"Suicides?" I asked.

"Executions. The vigilantes must have been preparing a long time for this. I'd say they took out at least thirty stoolies. Knifed, strangled, smothered, garroted—you name it. Now we're really in for it."

"Keep an eye peeled for trucks parked outside the gates," someone said. "That's how you'll know a transfer is coming."

I thought of D'Amato's empty bunk and felt nausea overtake me. Even though roll call would begin in another minute or two, I ran back to the barracks and pulled the blankets off D'Amato's bed. One side of the mattress was soaked in dark, half-congealed blood. While I lay sleeping, someone had walked past me and cut his throat only a few feet away. I threw the blanket onto the floor in disgust and ran back to the yard for roll call.

An unusual silence reigned as the remaining 2,500 prisoners in Division 3 took their places on the parade ground. The guards and warders stood in their usual positions and eyed us warily.

Then the voice of one of the chief warders came through the loudspeaker.

"The following prisoners will rise and take two steps forward. Bravo-0638. Romeo-8996. Foxtrot-7334. Whiskey-0885..."

After the fourth number was called, I didn't need to listen anymore. I stood and took my two steps forward.

As soon as the last number was called, the columns were sent off to the worksites. A squad of warders led nine of us into a waiting van.

We sat opposite each other on two long wooden benches inside the windowless van. Some faces were familiar but the only man I recognized in the dim light was Gary Toth.

"Gary, they wouldn't be doing a transfer with just nine prisoners, would they?" I asked.

"This is no transfer, my friend. We're headed for the isolator. Count your blessings."

"Some blessing," I muttered.

"Don't be greedy," Toth snapped. "The bosses aren't going to let us off without at least some punishment. The only question is how much. What would you prefer? The isolator or a bullet in the back of the neck?"

"A bullet? For going on strike?" I asked in disbelief.

"For God's sake, Wagner, where have you been? For killing stoolies, man! Over thirty in one night! That's got to be some kind of record." Toth accepted a triumphant high-five from the prisoner across the aisle.

"But I had nothing to do with it!" I protested.

"Okay, maybe not stoolies, but a warder is close enough. They found your pal Renaud face-down on his bunk this morning with a wire around his neck."

The prisoner across the aisle from Toth gave a devilish laugh.

"You ever been in an isolator before, Wagner?"

I shook my head.

"They don't get much worse than the one here in Kamas," he warned, "but you can beat it if you keep the right mental attitude. Just remember, the guards are required to give you enough food and water to keep you alive. And even at this time of year, it won't get cold enough to kill you as long as you stay healthy. And as for the tricks your mind will play on you, don't pay any attention. You'll snap out of it soon enough once they turn you loose. Remember, it's only a week."

We heard someone unlock the padlock and then the van's rear doors flew open. We were parked at a loading dock in a bleak courtyard enclosed on all sides by sixteen-foot cinder block walls. A quartet of armed guards led us one by one across the loading dock, through a doorway and down a flight of stairs to a massive steel door. The moment the door opened, I felt a rifle butt slam between my shoulder blades.

I followed the two guards along a dank corridor down the middle of which ran an evil-smelling drainage trough. Beside the steel door to each cell stood a rusty steel gym locker. When we reached cell number 8, a guard instructed me to remove my hat, boots, and all my clothes except my underpants and undershirt. I stuffed the clothes into the locker.

The chill air induced shivering within seconds. I found myself wondering what the lice would do now that they no longer had any place to hide.

The guards opened the outer door to my cell. A steel inner door contained a recessed compartment at about knee height large enough to hold a daily ration of bread and water. Access to the compartment was controlled by a hinged metal flap that only the guard could lock and unlock. In the brief moment when the cell's inner door opened and I was shoved inside, I could see by the corridor's dim light that the cell was about eighteen feet deep by six feet wide with a rudimentary porcelain toilet just inside the door and a wooden bench at the far end. I had to step over a six-inch doorframe to enter.

When I set down my foot I discovered that the floor was covered with three inches of ice-cold water that quickly numbed my feet and made my ankles ache. The odor of mildew from the walls and ceiling and of sewage from the open toilet was overpowering.

The cell's inner door closed behind me, leaving only the faintest glow of light around the doorframe. I waded through the icy water, reaching out to the slime-covered walls to keep my balance. At last I stepped onto the bench and squatted with my back to the rear wall, my arms hugging my knees.

A few minutes later, having found it difficult to remain upright, I experimented with lying on my side and bringing my knees up to my chest in a sort of fetal position, with each hand tucked into the opposite armpit. But I couldn't hold that position, either. Finally, I sat with my back against the wall and stretched my legs out on the bench. Before long, I felt the circulation being cut off from my lower limbs. Still, I found the numbness preferable to the cold and closed my eyes to catch a few minutes of sleep.

As I might have expected, the chill air, the hard bench and the insidious dripping from the ceiling made sleep impossible. I dredged my memory for songs to sing but, after a few verses, I didn't like the sound of my own quavering voice, so I hummed instead. Soon I felt the need to urinate, which meant dipping my feet into the cold water again and wading back across the floor. The muscles on the soles of my feet cramped so severely on my return that I collapsed onto the bench with pain.

I tried to control my mounting irritation at the dripping sound by counting each drop in the vain hope that this would at least help me fall asleep. But the ploy was only partially successful and I drifted in and out of a shallow sleep, alternately soothed and agitated by the steady dribble.

This pattern went on for several hours before I heard a clanking behind the steel door and saw a dim glow coming from the food receptacle. Wading across the cell, I reached inside and found two foil-wrapped meal bars and a plastic pitcher of water. I downed a third of the pitcher in a single draft, then brought the meal bars back with me to the bench. For many minutes I weighed the alternatives of eating both bars at a single sitting or saving the second bar for later. Not certain whether the bar would remain available if I returned it to the food niche and having no other dry place to keep it until I was ready to eat, I decided to devour both bars at once and to wash them down with the water remaining in the pitcher.

After my meal, I lay down on my side across the bench and imagined myself lying in the warm sand of a sun-drenched Hawaiian beach with foaming waves lapping rhythmically at my feet until I drifted off to sleep.

CHAPTER 16

"The trouble with Eichmann was precisely that so many were like him, and that the many were neither perverted nor sadistic, that they were, and still are, terribly and terrifyingly normal. From the viewpoint of our legal institutions and of our moral standards of judgment, this normality was much more terrifying than all the atrocities put together."
—Hannah Arendt, *Eichmann in Jerusalem*

Friday, March 22

Claire led the way along the foot track to Helen's cabin. It was early afternoon and the sun was laboring hard to melt the two feet of snow that covered the hillside.

"Look, Claire, deer tracks," Martha called out. "It's a regular deer highway."

"Helen says she needs a dog to keep them away," Claire replied, "but she can't afford to feed one."

As they rounded a grove of pines, the cabin came into view.

"What a delightful setting!" Martha exclaimed. "Do you think she's in?"

"Helen's always here this time of day," Claire replied. "She's probably in the kitchen getting ready to meet the early train from Denver."

Helen beamed with pleasure at seeing Claire dressed in her newly cleaned and patched red parka.

"Don't be strangers, come on in!"

She led them into the kitchen where she was weighing out and packaging dried herbs as usual.

"I hope we aren't intruding," Martha began. "Claire and I needed your help so we decided to come up and ask for it in person."

"I'm glad you did," Helen replied. "Would you like some chamomile tea? I just made a pot."

"I'd love some," Martha answered as she surveyed the cabin's neat but austere interior.

At a nod from Helen, Claire set off for the kitchen. She came back a few moments later with the pot and three mugs.

"Tell me, Claire, have you started school yet?" Helen asked.

Claire lowered her eyes and said nothing while she filled Martha's mug.

"We've gone to register," Martha offered, "but I'm afraid we're still facing some administrative obstacles."

"Even in the federal school?"

Martha nodded.

"Without a national I.D. card, the principal insists on a full background check. Doug says that could take months. We were hoping perhaps Claire misplaced her documents while she was staying with you."

Helen shot a quick glance toward Claire.

"I truly wish I could help," Helen replied. "But as I've said, Claire seems to have lost her I.D. on the train. She told me it was in a special pouch and that all the papers she had were in it."

"That's what she told me, too," Martha remarked. "Odd that she could lose it if she wore the pouch around her neck."

"Considering the people you run into on the trains these days," Helen said calmly, "it doesn't surprise me at all."

Martha sighed and then turned her attention to Claire.

"Well, I suppose we'll just have to fill out those forms the best we can, won't we?"

"If you wouldn't mind my asking," Helen ventured, "might your husband know some way to overcome the school's objections?"

"Doug says it's best not to get their backs up," Martha replied. "His idea is to handle the paperwork through special channels if it comes to that."

"Well, if I can be of any help, let me know. You can't imagine how many government forms I've had to fill out over the years. I'm getting pretty good at it."

"Actually, that might be very helpful," Martha said, brightening. "For some reason, getting information from Claire hasn't been easy. Perhaps the three of us could sit down and give it a try."

Claire refilled both mugs, suddenly eager for an opportunity to interrupt.

"Helen, would you mind if I lie down? I don't feel so well."

Helen reached out to place her hand on Claire's forehead.

"You do seem a bit warm. Why don't you go to your old bedroom and take a short nap? Perhaps you'll feel better afterward."

"Don't worry about Claire's education," Martha said once Claire had closed the bedroom door. "We can use home schooling materials from the town schools till fall. By then I'm sure Doug can get Claire a new I.D. card. His office could get new papers for the Devil himself."

"The way you say it doesn't sound very flattering for his office. State Security, I presume?"

Martha flushed.

"Yes. I don't always approve of what they do, if that's what you mean."

"Isn't it difficult to be married to someone whose work you don't approve of?"

"I suppose that's true," Martha replied, staring down into her mug. "It was different when we lived in Washington. There was so much to do there that I hardly paid any attention to Doug's job or the people he worked with. In the beginning all I knew was that he was helping to bring back our POWs. I thought that was something we could be proud of."

"But now you don't feel that way?"

"They brought back the POWs all right. Only they never made it back to their hometowns. Unless their hometowns were in places like Kamas."

"I know," Helen said. "People out here aren't as ignorant about such things as they pretend to be back East."

"To be honest, Helen, I've been miserable ever since we got here. If it weren't for Claire and the baby, I doubt if I'd bother to get out of bed some mornings. The only people I see in town are from the government and the only ones who will have anything to do with us are from the Department. I feel like a leper sometimes when I go places with Doug in his uniform."

Martha looked at Helen for words of comfort, but when none came, she continued. "Doug's colleagues come over for dinner at least once a week now—more if visitors are in town. And they always end up drinking. Sometimes I see a side to Doug that I never knew. An ugly, mean side. When I married him, Doug was a good man—stubborn sometimes, but decent and kind. He's changed since he left the Army. The way he talks about the prisoners frightens me sometimes. I was just a teenager when the Events started, but I don't remember the government ever treating people the way they do now."

"You remember right," Helen said. "There were prisons then but nothing like Kamas."

"And now there's something else," Martha added softly. She stared at her hands and unconsciously twisted her wedding ring around her finger.

"I probably shouldn't say this, but I suspect Doug has been unfaithful."

"What makes you think so?" Helen asked. "Did he tell you?"

"No, of course not," Martha replied. "All I really have to go on are signs that wouldn't mean much to anyone but me. But I've heard the men talk about it when they don't think I can hear them. They brag about having their way with female prisoners in exchange for a better job or a warm jacket or a parcel of food. It turns my stomach to think that my husband works side by side with these men and that he brings them home to where Marie and I have to live. To think that Doug might be doing it..."

Tears welled in Martha's dark eyes.

"Now I have a child and a new baby coming and there's absolutely no one I can talk to!" she sobbed.

Helen took her hand and led her to a faded blue easy chair in the living room. She pulled another chair close alongside.

"Just sit and close your eyes," Helen soothed her. "If you want to talk, I'll be here. If you want to rest, I'm right beside you."

A little over an hour later, Claire emerged from the bedroom to find Martha and Helen still in the parlor. They were huddled close together and speaking to each other in low voices the way her parents had spoken the day they announced the family would have to sell the old stone house.

On seeing Claire, both women attempted to appear cheerful.

"Are you feeling better?" Martha inquired.

Claire nodded sleepily and smiled.

"Then it's best for us to head back into town. We still have some grocery shopping to do before our guests arrive for dinner."

"Can we go to the bakery first?" Claire asked eagerly.

"You bet."

Martha rose and gave Helen a hug before donning her coat and taking Claire back down the snowy footpath toward Heber.

****

Claire tucked the baby into bed early and descended the stairs into the living room. As usual when they expected dinner guests, she heard Martha and Doug moving about the kitchen. Doug set up the bar while Martha prepared dinner. Claire joined them and began assembling napkins, place mats, and silverware. Doug appeared not to notice her and continued talking.

"I know it's a pain in the neck to entertain so often, honey, but I really appreciate all the work you do to make it happen. When you're stuck in an outpost like Heber it's the only way to make the connections you need to move up."

"I know, Doug," Martha answered wearily. "I really don't mind having guests. With Claire taking care of the baby and Rosa cleaning up, it's not so much work. I'll get used to it."

"And don't forget the reimbursement," Doug added. "We come out ahead every time we entertain."

"It's all right, Doug. Really it is."

Martha was the first to hear knocking at the front door.

"Claire, dear, would you go quickly and answer that? Tell them we'll be right there."

Claire opened the door and recognized Warden Rocco, Major Whiting, and Colonel Tracy. With them was a somber little man in an elegant Russian fur hat and a navy blue overcoat like the one her father used to wear. The little man's solemn expression, neatly trimmed black mustache, and gold-rimmed glasses gave him the look of a doctor on a house call.

The Warden spoke first.

"Good evening to you, Claire. I'd like you to meet Director Cronin. He's been waiting all day to taste one of the delicious roasts that only you and Martha know how to make. May we come in?"

Claire smiled sweetly and shook the Director's hand, then held the door open for the others to enter. Before she could think of anything to say, she heard Martha and Doug coming up behind her.

"We're so pleased you came," Martha greeted them, shaking Cronin's hand and giving Rocco and Whiting each a polite kiss on the cheek. "It's been dreadfully quiet here all day. It's about time we had some company to liven things up."

The guests hung their coats in the front closet, then followed Doug into the dining room, where they congregated around the bar. Doug took drink orders while Claire delivered bowls of nuts, crackers, and chips before returning to the kitchen to help Martha prepare a salad.

Moments later Claire heard Fred Rocco tap a spoon against his tumbler to capture the other men's attention. She peeked through the doorway toward the bar.

"While Director Cronin is with us, I wanted to take a moment to congratulate all of you for your professionalism in putting down this week's strike. In all my years of government service I've rarely seen a better combination of intelligence work, planning, and seamless execution. So I'm delighted that we have with us tonight the director of the entire corrective labor system to see firsthand how we do things at Kamas."

Cronin acknowledged the warden with an indulgent smile and raised his glass of orange juice.

"You have a fine team, Warden. I'm sure your after-action report will meet with interest at Headquarters."

Jack Whiting spoke next.

"Thanks for the pat on the back, Fred, but if you don't mind my injecting a note of caution, you should know that if we had another strike tomorrow, I'd be hard pressed to deliver half the intelligence we had this time around."

"And why might that be?" Cronin interrupted.

"Because this morning, we lost nearly thirty of the informants whose reports guided us through this episode. Murdered overnight. Even before the strike, our crew of informants was dangerously thin. Now the few we have left are more afraid of the vigilantes than they are of us. Some went to jail rather than collaborate with us. Others have refused to go back to their barracks and are begging to be transferred."

"If your informants fear the vigilantes more than they fear you, you've got your work cut out for you, Jack," Colonel Tracy said without smiling.

"We know what needs to be done and we know how to do it," Whiting retorted. "I just want everyone here to know it's going to take time and a lot of support from Headquarters. Today I sent a request for some experienced informants from other camps. I also asked for an intelligence team to help us recruit more informants. Low-level agents aren't enough anymore. We need high-ranking types who can infiltrate the prisoners' leadership cadres and dig out their plans and intentions."

"I think Jack has the right approach," Rocco added. "If you agree, Director, perhaps you'd consider expediting his request when you get back to Washington."

"Send me a note, Warden, and I'll see that you get my full support," Cronin answered without enthusiasm.

"Jack is quite right about the need for more informants," Colonel Tracy pointed out. "But we also need to think about getting rid of the troublemakers. The way I see it, we ought to cull out a couple trainloads worth and send them up north where they can't cause any more trouble. But even transfers don't get to the heart of the matter with prisoners like these. It used to be that, when all means of correction were exhausted, we had the authority to terminate a certain number of incorrigibles at the local level. What might be the chance of getting back that authority, Director Cronin?"

Cronin raised his eyebrows slightly and took a sip of juice before answering.

"First of all, let me say that I have no objection to transfers of the kind you're talking about. But, as for local authority to terminate, I don't see a consensus for that quite yet.

"Still, you aren't left entirely without options. Look at your attrition rate. Has it ever been challenged? Of course not. You have always been completely free to exploit local conditions to overcome disciplinary problems. Nobody says you have to coddle these men. Medical care, heating, clothing, nutrition: all these can be adjusted to achieve your objectives. In my day, I found that a special diet often brought difficult prisoners around. I assume your people are no less resourceful."

Claire stepped away from the door. She recognized Doug's voice next and shot a glance at Martha, who stood motionless before the pork roast with carving knife in hand. Martha also appeared to be listening to the men but her face had grown ashen and she did not look well.

"Our staff is highly resourceful, Director, and we already use Kamas's natural advantages to help keep the prisoners in line," Doug explained. "All the same, Sir, we find ourselves facing a dilemma. Since Director Barry's departure, the extent of our discretionary authority over the prisoners has been unclear. On one hand, if we show too much zeal in putting down disturbances, we risk becoming scapegoats for people who accuse the Department of excess. On the other hand, if we show too little zeal, we could be accused of going soft on our enemies. How do we steer a safe course between the two extremes?"

"You probably can't," Cronin answered. "And to see why not, you have to understand the new generation of political leaders in Washington. Lately, a movement has arisen in some Party circles to, shall we say, expunge certain aspects of the President-for-Life's political legacy. With an aim to tarnish his reputation, this movement has drawn attention to false reports about the Department's so-called excesses.

"Having had the privilege to know the President-for-Life personally, I can assure you that we will never in our lifetimes see another leader like him. The Union needed a man like him to take us through the Events and to give the country a fresh start. He single-handedly transformed the old class-ridden system into a new single-class society that offers justice for everyone.

"Our job in State Security is to preserve and protect this new society from those who want to go back to the old ways. So, you see, there can never be an issue of too much zeal in pursuing the traitors who would tear it down."

After everyone had absorbed Cronin's remarks and each had duly registered an amen, the conversation languished momentarily. Martha filled the silence by announcing that dinner would be ready in five minutes. To Claire's relief, Martha's cheeks seemed to have regained their color.

Doug used his wife's interruption to change the subject.

"Director, I've heard that you spent some time in Utah early in your career. What are your impressions from those days?"

"I recall Utah as being a very odd sort of place," Cronin replied. "I don't know how much you all remember about the old Mormon Church, but Mormons dominated the state in those days. The Church of Latter Day Saints possessed enormous wealth and a vast infrastructure in the region.

"I happened to be regional director for FEMA before the Events. When refugees started pouring inland from California after the first big quakes, my job was to supply them with food and shelter along the major evacuation routes. At that time Utah was a major relief station. At first, the Mormon Church was a tremendous help to us, turning over vast quantities of stored foods and clothing and helping us provide emergency housing all over the state. But as our needs grew, and as the moment arrived to make greater sacrifices for the good of the country, their help began to dry up.

"One day the Mormon elders circled their wagons and refused to take in any more refugees. Before long, articles in the local press began featuring crimes committed by refugees and public health risks from the refugee camps and accusations that FEMA had taken sides with the refugees against Utahns.

"When the locals started arming themselves and organizing local militias, we had to take action. That's when the Utah governor gave his famous order to clear the refugee camps and expel the homeless to Colorado. Of course, at that point we had to move in and use force to restore order."

Cronin turned to Rocco.

"Warden, how many Mormons do you suppose are left in Utah?"

"Probably less than a hundred thousand. Not many will confess to being Mormon anymore, so it's hard to say. Their last temples were brought down or converted to civil use eight or ten years ago, when the President-for-Life declared the LDS church an illegal terrorist organization."

"We get a few Mormon prisoners by accident from time to time," Doug Chambers noted. "But as soon as we check their dossiers, we send them back north. There are special camps set up for them and the Muslims in the Northwest Territories."

"Which takes us back to what we were saying about the Department's mission," Cronin continued. "These Mormons, and for that matter, all other religious zealots and militiamen in this country, have stubbornly rejected the Unionist goal of a one-class society and have put themselves in direct defiance of the Party. The people who denied relief to the California refugees are the same who refused to send their sons and daughters for voluntary national service. They lorded their wealth and privileges over everyone but blocked the path for others to get ahead. These people have deliberately chosen to sit on the sidelines of nation building and snipe at us rather than join the team.

"As far as I am concerned, these people have had their day. History has passed them by and soon they will sink into oblivion. And when they're gone, we won't have a need for corrective labor camps anymore. The camps will be closed and before long no one will know that they ever existed. I'll tell you, that's the day I'm dreaming of."

Martha dropped the silver serving platter onto the sideboard with a clatter.

"Dinner is served," she said, and abruptly left the room.

CHAPTER 17

"You'll get used to it, and if you don't, you'll die."
—Soviet camp saying

Tuesday, March 26

I woke up so thirsty that my tongue stuck to the roof of my mouth. My lips were cracked and peeling, and my throat was too parched to swallow.

The cell was as dark and quiet as a mineshaft. I no longer knew whether it was day or night or how long I had been there and I feared I had slept through my daily feeding. When I waded across the cell to the door, the receptacle where the guards left my bread and water was locked.

I returned to the bench and lay on my side, my cheek pressed against its rough surface. I resolved to sort out my thoughts and to find some way to occupy my mind until my body was ready to sleep again. But thoughts kept darting about, passing back and forth through my head like actors crossing a stage. I tried to slow them down but they wouldn't respond.

Despite the cold and discomfort of the cell, my starved and overworked body still could not seem to get enough sleep. The constant shivering brought a new kind of exhaustion that made every muscle ache. I knew I couldn't afford to miss my daily rations and tried to stay alert for the sound of the receptacle's hinged flap swinging open. But I found myself drifting in and out of consciousness and lost the ability to distinguish minutes from hours.

Sleep was my only refuge. Sleep kept the incessant thirst and hunger away and stopped the lice from tormenting me. Sleep dispersed the palpable clouds of fear that hovered around my head. Sleep let me forget that at Kamas I was no longer Paul Wagner in the eyes of my government, but Prisoner W-0885, convicted under Title 18, Section 2384, for seditious conspiracy against the Unionist State of America, sentenced to five years of corrective labor and expected to die long before my release date.

After a while, the flashing images in my sensory-deprived brain became a source of entertainment. People, places, and events reappeared that I had not considered for years. Some brought momentary joy, some guilt or sorrow, but most were nothing more than images without emotional value. Many times I had to drop a foot into the water or reach for the wall to verify whether a particular vision was real or imaginary.

One vision that returned more times than I could count was that of a nine-foot by a twelve-foot interview room at Susquehanna. Gray cinder block walls, gray tiled floors, a high whitewashed ceiling with an overhanging globe lamp, and a pair of rusting steel chairs, both bolted to the floor on opposite sides of a steel table.

In the vision, I sat in the chair closest to the door in my filthy orange coveralls, flimsy rubber sandals on my feet, listening to the acne-scarred interrogator with the chipped front tooth and dirty slicked-back hair tell me once again that this was my last chance to sign a voluntary confession.

"It's no use, Wagner," he told me. "Your partners have already told us about your plans to assassinate the Party leadership in Pittsburgh. We know everything: how you selected your targets, how you tracked their movements, what weapons you planned to use, and how you planned to make your escape.

"Are you saying your co-conspirators are all liars? Your old friends, neighbors, and co-workers? Why on earth would they accuse you if you weren't guilty? Do you deny meeting with the persons who named you in their sworn statements? Do you deny that you owned the high-powered rifle and the large-caliber pistol that we found in your basement? You know it's a felony for civilians to keep firearms, don't you? You could be sentenced to ten years on those charges alone.

"Why not cooperate and give yourself the chance to lighten your sentence? Have pity on your family and spare them the burden of a lengthy trial. Believe me, Wagner, this is your last chance. You can start writing out your confession here at this table right now or I can send you back downstairs to Memory Recovery and let them pull it out of you bit by bit. What's it going to be?"

I felt every muscle fiber in my body tense into a knot while my throat constricted so tightly that I couldn't utter a word.

'No! Never!' I wanted to scream. But was that really what I intended to say? Wasn't it, 'No! Please no more isolation!' Hadn't I made up my mind to resist? Or had I changed it? I felt confused and needed more time to think but the interrogator awaited my answer.

I lost consciousness and regained it in a white tiled room with a grated drain in the center, strapped to a bare wooden table. By craning my neck, I could see a short, stocky figure with a shaved head facing the far wall, adjusting an instrument panel. He wore a black State Security uniform. It was Sam Renaud and his eyes smoldered with hatred. But Renaud had been killed by the vigilantes. It didn't make sense.

"You don't fool me for a minute, Wagner," Renaud sneered. "What a hypocrite! You make yourself out to be some kind of martyr, an innocent husband and father dragged off the street by government goons for no reason at all. What horseshit! You're as guilty as any of us. You'd have killed those Party big shots in Pittsburgh if we hadn't caught you first. You're not at all the solid citizen you make yourself out to be. You hate our guts as much as we hate yours! You'd love to kill me right now, wouldn't you? Well, think again, Wagner, the joke is on you."

I struggled against the straps and somehow managed to pull a foot loose and reach for the floor. Then I felt the shock of the frigid water around my ankle and the scene melted away. I was lying once again on the slippery wooden bench in the isolator cell. But my breathing was labored and my limbs tensed, as if I had actually strained against the canvas straps of Renaud's torture table.

I felt something warm and soft against my cheek and looked up to see a young woman squatting in the cell beside me as if to comfort me. For some reason I couldn't understand, there was a dim glow in the cell that offered enough light for me to see her and the rest of the cell quite clearly. The woman was about twenty-five years old and had a sweet round face with a flawless white complexion. Her hair was tied behind her head with a torn strip of cloth, camp-style, and she wore a fresh pair of orange camp coveralls.

I tried to speak to her but no words formed on my lips. Slowly she shook her head and smiled, as if words were unnecessary. When she peered into my eyes, I felt a flush of warmth pass from my head down through my trunk and into my extremities. At that moment I recognized the woman as Lillian, the work scheduler who was killed on my first day in camp, but it didn't matter to me anymore whether she was alive or dead. I just wanted her to stay and comfort me.

I don't know how long I lay there gazing into her liquid eyes before I lost my concentration and her image faded away. Then the usual torrent of random thoughts and emotions returned and I felt as if I were floating along a fast-moving stream with a flotilla of images moving alongside, some faster and some slower, but always drifting out of view eventually.

As I watched the pattern repeat itself with flashes of my pre-arrest life, I heard familiar voices and looked around me. The voices became louder and clearer until I recognized those of a woman and a young girl.

"Paul, we're so happy to reach you! We want you to know that we're fine and you don't need to worry about us. Just relax and let yourself get stronger. We want you to get well just as fast as you can."

The voices belonged to my wife and to my younger daughter, Louisa. I strained to catch sight of them at the outer edge of my vision. Before long I saw them emerge from behind a swirl of cloud or mist. They were holding hands and each wore the knee-length down parka that I had bought her shortly before my arrest. Each also wore a fleece hat and scarf and carried a small backpack and gave the impression of being dressed for a long journey. I reached out to embrace them but they were already out of reach. Suddenly I was overwhelmed by the joy of knowing that my wife and daughter were safe and that my confession had not been wasted. They must have made it to London, after all.

An instant later their images faded and slipped back into the darkness while the stream of motley scenes continued. Before long I caught sight of a bright light in the distance and, as I concentrated, it drew nearer and then shone directly into my eyes. I had a sensation of looking through a keyhole into a well-lit room. And as my eyes adjusted to the light, I saw that it was an L-shaped bedroom with beige wall-to-wall carpeting, a double bed with a white chenille bedspread and pink flannel sheets, art posters on the walls, and a young girl's clothing strewn carelessly across the floor.

A girl of eleven or twelve with long chestnut hair, sat at a white wooden desk writing out a homework assignment in a spiral notebook. Even without seeing her face, I knew it was my older daughter, Claire. I called out her name. She stopped writing and raised her head for a moment as if she had heard a distant voice, then went back to writing.

For a long time afterward I tried to hold the picture in my mind, but eventually it faded away and the stream of random images returned. I was so elated to have experienced such a lifelike vision of Claire that I didn't think to question why she appeared separately from her mother and sister.

From time to time when my thoughts cleared, I tried to look more closely at the visions I had of Renaud, Lillian, my wife, and daughters in an effort to uncover any hidden messages or meanings that might be there. But concentration was difficult and for a long time afterward I drifted in and out of sleep.

The next thing I remember was the clank of the cell's steel doors opening and a blinding white light pouring in. Two guards in khaki coveralls and knee-length rubber boots entered the cell and grasped me under the shoulders. Once we were in the hallway, they wrapped my semi-naked body in a thin white terry robe and led me down the corridor to an interview room. Immediately upon entering I felt the room's luxurious warmth. After spending days at a temperature somewhere in the 40s or 50s, it seemed as if my dream of the warm Hawaiian beach had come true. I wanted to stay there forever.

Across a rough oak table sat a lean and hard-muscled man of about forty with long graying sideburns, a trimmed mustache, and a wart on his left cheek. He wore khaki coveralls without any insignia of rank or unit, but I recognized the man at once as Jack Whiting. On the table before him were a plastic tray with a thermos pitcher, two coffee cups, and a pair of matching bowls filled with sugar and powdered creamer. Whiting poured coffee into one of the mugs, stirred in some sugar and creamer and took a long sip.

"Like some? Go ahead. It won't hurt you," he said.

My mouth was too dry to speak. I nodded and Whiting poured me a cup.

"Cream and sugar?"

He didn't even wait for my nod before ladling in two heaping teaspoons each of sugar and creamer. He handed over the cup and I drank greedily, totally unconcerned with whether the coffee might be hot enough to burn my mouth. I could feel the warmth of the coffee flow into my stomach and spread slowly all over my shivering body.

"It's a bit warm in here," Whiting said lazily. "Should I turn it down?"

"It's fine," I said, having wet my mouth and throat enough to speak.

"If you don't mind, I'll get right to the point," Whiting continued. "We know you had it in for Renaud. We haven't found any witnesses yet but we know you're the one who whacked him. Now, Renaud was one of our best warders and I hate to lose good men. Normally, when this kind of thing happens, we put the troublemaker in a maximum-security prison until he sees the error of his ways. Then we send him up north where the cold tends to keep even the most hard-edged bastards out of trouble, if you follow me.

"Now, in your case, since this is your first offense and there may have been some extenuating circumstances, I might be prepared to make an exception. But you see, we're kind of short on help these days, so what we'd like from you is to volunteer to take Renaud's place—one for one. Not as a warder, of course. Politicals don't qualify, I'm afraid. But we could definitely use your help as a source of information. Nothing special, just everyday happenings around the camp. We'd meet privately once a week and I'd ask you some questions and you'd try to find out the answers for me. Would you like some more coffee?"

I nodded.

"I didn't hear you," he said.

"Yes," I answered.

He emptied the thermos into my cup, then added sugar and creamer and set the cup down before me. I drank, enjoying the radiating warmth.

"I've prepared a simple plea bargain contract for you to consider. You're welcome to read it before signing, but the gist of it is that you confess to murdering Renaud. In return for your guilty plea we give you a suspended sentence for as long as you continue working for State Security."

I made no reply.

"Why not look it over?" Whiting suggested, pushing it across the table. "You may find our terms attractive, all things considered."

I finished the cup of coffee and set it back on the table before picking up the document and ripping it in half, then doubling it up and ripping it again.

Whiting stared at me without speaking. His cold eyes were devoid of any anger, sympathy, or pity. He called for the guards.

"Take him back," he said. He remained seated as they yanked me onto my feet. "This one seems to be a slow learner."

The coffee had worked wonders in clearing my mind, and as soon as I was back in the isolator after my interview with Whiting, I spent hours thinking carefully about my visions. Were they nothing more than my own subconscious mind wrestling with my guilt and grief? Or did the visions represent actual communication?

Having resolved for so long to think only of my own survival and to not torment myself over my wife and daughters, I realized that I had made a crucial mistake. Far from distracting me from my survival, love for my family gave me a reason to survive—even to escape. Since my arrest my strength had been in decline because I had stopped believing I would ever rejoin my family. Now, I resolved to find a way back to my wife and daughters or die trying. Within moments, I felt my strength return.

CHAPTER 18

"The most potent weapon in the hands of the oppressor is the mind of the oppressed."
—Steve Biko, South African dissident

Friday, March 29

The next time I heard the cell's steel doors open I was fully awake. At first I thought it was simply my ration bars and water being delivered and was startled when the door opened and the room filled with light.

Two guards waded across the dark waters to grasp me under the armpits and ferry me out to the corridor. Seeing that I might lack the strength to stand on my own, they set me down on a bench in the corridor while one of them closed the cell doors and the other removed my clothes and boots from the steel locker and ordered me to put them on. Desperate for warmth, my numbed fingers fumbled to remove my wet underwear before I stepped into my coveralls and boots. I stuffed the underwear into a pocket and grabbed my hat and gloves in time to be hustled down the hall toward a brightly lit holding cell. I sat shivering on the floor, eager for the warmth of the heated room to raise my temperature.

One by one, the other prisoners who had arrived with me at the isolator appeared. The first was Dennis Martino, a sharp-witted medical student from Atlanta in his mid-twenties, who had been convicted of harboring deserters from the armed forces. At the time of his arrest, he had been moonlighting as a bartender. His fatal error had been to turn away

State Security officers who had asked him to report on certain patrons of the bar. He later learned that among those patrons had been men wanted for desertion. For failing to denounce them he was sentenced to eight years of corrective labor under Title 18, Section 1381.

I had seen Martino around the camp from time to time and I recalled him as an amiable fellow with a wide range of acquaintances. But there was no trace of his sunny disposition when the guards brought him into the holding cell. His face was a deathly white, his lips a dull blue, and his shivering even more violent than mine. Without a word, he lay on his side in a fetal position and closed his eyes.

The next to join us was Brian Gaffney, a red-bearded giant from Portland, Oregon. Gaffney had been a commercial artist before the Events but, with the decline of marketing and advertising activity, had settled for work as a night shift supervisor in a Kansas City molding and extrusions plant. Gaffney had somehow managed to retain an air of cheerfulness at Kamas and could claim many friends in camp. But I barely recognized him when he shuffled into the room. His face was gaunt and his eyes seemed to have retreated back into his head. His breathing was so shallow and labored that I feared he had pneumonia. He returned my greeting with a feeble smile and then sank into sleep.

Some ten minutes later we were joined by J.J. Johns, a black taxicab owner from St. Louis, who had been convicted of economic sabotage for refusing to sell his cabs to the municipal taxi collective.

"How are you holding up, brother?" J.J. asked.

"Better than I expected," I replied. "Somebody once told me that solitary confinement is like going to the dentist. You always think that the worst is yet to come when it's really already behind you."

J.J. returned a thin smile.

"Don't I know you from somewhere?" he asked.

"We came in on the same transport," I said.

"Oh, yeah, one of Reineke's boys."

I winced.

"I didn't kill any of those stoolies, if that's what you mean."

"I don't mean nothing at all," J.J. replied. "You boys do what you got to do. I'm too damned worn out to think about that shit."

The door opened and Gary Toth limped into the center of the room. His entire face and neck were a mass of swollen and discolored bruises together with fresh cuts and scratches that had barely stopped bleeding. He nodded to us without a word, then took off his boots and began winding his footcloths around his feet in preparation for our release back into the frozen outdoors.

Moments after he finished the door opened again and eight guards stood outside.

"Into the truck. All of you."

All of us rose except for Martino.

The chief guard pointed at J.J. and me.

"You two, pick him up and bring him along. Move!"

When the double doors opened at the end of the corridor, the sunlight reflecting off the snow nearly blinded us. The four of us lifted Martino into the waiting van, climbed in after him and took our seats on the benches facing each other as we had the week before.

"We were nine on the way in," Gaffney pointed out as soon as the door was locked behind us. "What about the others?"

"Dead," Toth answered. "They check once a day and remove anybody who's gone cold."

Toth spoke with an odd lisp. Then I saw that the entire top row of his front teeth had been broken. Toth showed no embarrassment at the loss and continued to speak despite the pain his cut and swollen lips must have caused him.

"Let's see if we can wake him," Toth continued, pointing to Martino. "You hold him up. I'll try to shake him out of it."

As we lifted Martino's violently shivering body into a sitting position, he mumbled incoherently and pushed us away. After three or four minutes of vigorous rubbing on his back, arms, and thighs, Martino's eyes opened. Then Toth kept him propped up while we alternated massaging his back, legs, and arms.

"Can you talk?" Toth asked him.

"Leave me alone," came Martino's faint reply.

"He'll make it."

Toth then turned to me.

"Did Whiting bring you in for a talk?" he asked gruffly. "About halfway through the week? Give you hot coffee?"

I hesitated.

"Yeah, he called me in," I admitted.

"How about you, J.J.?" Toth went on.

"I saw him," J.J. said.

"Brian?"

"Me, too."

"Hey, Martino, listen up," Toth continued, speaking directly into Martino's ear. "Did the Wart take you out of the can for a talk?"

Why?" Martino asked, suddenly grown canny.

"Don't ask me why, Martino. Did he or didn't he?"

"Yeah."

"Okay, that makes it unanimous. Nobody gets to the isolator without the Wart bringing him in for a little java. See these teeth? That's how I paid for mine."

He drew back his bloodied lips and paused to make sure he had our attention.

"Unless Whiting has changed his M.O., he leaned on every one of you to become his stool pigeon and report on your buddies. No question, the isolator softens a man. So if you turned him down, good for you. It takes grit to say no when you're half crazy from the cold and the darkness and the goddamned dripping water and everything else that rips you apart in that stinking hole.

"But if you said yes, I'm telling you right now that you have nothing to be ashamed of. Nothing at all. That is, if you admit right now in front of all of us that you knuckled under. Nobody knows what you went through better than we do. The main thing is that you undo any promise you made in there and tell Whiting to pound salt when he tries to contact you. Believe me, if you turn back now, you have nothing to fear from him. He won't punish you because that might blow his chances to get to you later. It may be years before he gives up on you.

"But now, you may ask yourself, what if I don't admit to going along with the Wart? What if I just quietly meet his people now and then for a chat? Well, sooner or later we'll find out. And we'll come after you. And all the suffering you've gone through will have been wasted because you'll die a traitor."

Toth glared at each of us in turn and then faced me.

"You first, Paul. Did you accept Whiting's pitch?"

"I refused. He sent me away and that was it."

"J.J.?"

"I walked out before we got to the second mug. I could see it coming."

"Brian?"

"Turned it down."

"Dennis?"

Martino hung his head and didn't respond.

"What did you tell him, Martino? Yes or no?"

His answer could barely be heard above the sound of the van's engine. "Yes."

Martino's shoulders shook with silent sobbing. He drew a desperate breath and put his head between his knees. His sobs turned to dry heaves.

Toth put his arms around Martino and spoke softly to him.

"Dennis. What you've told us required more courage than most men find in a lifetime. Hold onto that courage. Hold on and try not to let it get away again."

The van stopped and Toth addressed the rest of us.

"Anybody want to change his story before we go back to work?"

I looked around the van. J.J. and I looked at each other and then at Toth and shook our heads. Gaffney wouldn't meet my gaze and jumped out of the van without speaking.

We were at the new wing of the camp infirmary in the Service Yard. I had been to the camp infirmary only once before, on a weekend when I had cut myself with a saw while stripping branches from a fallen tree. At the time the guards had taken me to the old wing, which was generally the only one that prisoners were permitted to enter. The new wing was used to treat camp staff and contract workers. It also housed the medical unit's administrative offices and laboratory.

The guards led the five of us into an empty waiting room that was connected to the treatment areas by a steel door. One by one, a pair of guards led each of us through the door into a vestibule and then through a second door, each controlled electrically by the receptionist inside. When my turn came, I passed through an open reception area staffed by a foursome of middle-aged nurses in white uniforms and went down a corridor lined with empty hospital beds. The infirmary smelled of disinfectant, alcohol and ether and was the cleanest, most civilized place I had seen since my arrest. I found myself scheming to find some way to stay there.

At the end of the corridor the guards turned right and stopped at a white curtained enclosure whose only furnishing was a stainless-steel examining table. The older of the two guards ordered me to sit on the table and be quiet. A few minutes later, a short, plump, dark-haired woman of about fifty entered the room wearing a knee-length laboratory coat. A balding, round-shouldered man in his mid-fifties followed behind. Both wore gold-rimmed spectacles and cold, dour expressions and carried clipboards under one arm. The name on the woman's badge was Dr. Renée Nagy while that on the man's badge was Dr. Ernest Fell.

"Prisoner W-0885," the guard announced to the doctors.

"How long ago was he released from the punishment block, Sergeant?"

"Less than an hour ago," the guard answered.

"W-0885, we are going to give you an examination and ask you some questions. You are to speak only when you are spoken to. Remain standing."

They told me to undress and began what seemed to be a routine physical exam. Then Dr. Nagy turned to the next form on her clipboard and started asking me questions from a standard medical questionnaire.

After the fourth or fifth question, I interrupted her.

"May I ask a question, Doctor?"

Dr. Nagy seemed surprised that I was capable of speech.

"What is it?" she asked impatiently.

"May I ask what is today's date and the time of day?"

"Friday, March 29th, about four in the afternoon."

"Can you also give me something to eat? I haven't eaten for twenty-four hours."

"This is not the mess hall," she retorted. "Dinner begins at six. You seem well enough to survive till then."

"You are a doctor, aren't you?"

"This is not a treatment session. This is an examination. Now please answer my questions. Have you ever been treated for...?"

Suddenly it became clear to me what they were doing, and I thought of Al Gallucci and the reason he gave for not becoming a foreman.

"I get it," I interrupted. "You're studying my reactions to the isolator so you can make it more effective in crushing the next poor slob you throw in there."

Trembling with rage, I reached out and grabbed the clipboard, tore off the entire set of forms and ripped them in half, then doubled them and ripped them again, and doubled them again until they were too thick for me to tear.

"Go to hell," I said to both doctors. "Get your stinking data from somebody else."

Nagy pursed her lips like a petulant child and glared. Fell was expressionless.

"Guards, take him out," he said.

Both physicians turned on their heels and left without bothering to draw the curtains behind them. I got dressed, and the guards led me back to the waiting room in handcuffs.

There I waited for an hour until the others completed their exams. When all had finished, the guards led us outside and around the building to the old infirmary wing, which was packed with prisoners in various states of distress, from high fever to exhaustion to crushed limbs to self-mutilation.

Apparently we had some sort of privileged status here because we were called ahead of more urgent cases. When my turn came, the guards led me through an examining area crammed with rows of long tables on which prisoners sat or lay awaiting treatment. The air was foul with the odors of unwashed prisoners and their untreated wounds. Trash bins brimmed with discarded bandages and dressings.

The nurses and orderlies, all prisoners themselves, wore dour expressions that spoke of long hours, unremitting stress, inadequate resources, and an abandonment of hope. I took the table next to J.J. Johns and waited for a nurse or orderly to appear. Unlike the new wing, here the guards dropped us off and withdrew promptly to the waiting room. Since the staff and doctors were all prisoners, there was apparently no need to protect them from us.

After a few moments, a compact man wearing a soiled white lab coat and a stethoscope around his neck appeared from a side office. I guessed he was in his mid-thirties, although the gray in his whisker stubble and the deep lines in his face made him appear older. He stopped at J.J.'s table, handed him a brown plastic prescription vial, and delivered some final instructions on the importance of drinking plenty of liquids, conserving energy, and doing whatever he could to obtain extra sources of food. As a parting gesture, he handed J.J. several supplemental meal vouchers good for extra ration bars or hot meals at the mess hall.

The clinician spoke with a Spanish accent that I guessed was from South America. On my previous visit to the infirmary, I had heard that the chief surgeon in the camp hospital was a young Argentinean named Schuster. As rumor had it, Schuster had been a resident in a leading Cleveland teaching hospital when border skirmishes flared up between the U.S. and Mexico. When Unionist forces launched a surprise attack along the Rio Grande, Schuster's native country had been one of the first Latin American nations to send troops and munitions to help repel the invaders. Within a few days, plainclothesmen arrested Schuster and took him to an internment camp for enemy nationals.

Eventually, most Latin American internees were deported, but a smaller number were charged with political crimes and transferred to corrective labor camps, possibly in order to have fodder for future prisoner exchanges. In any event, Schuster had been at Kamas for nearly six years. He had a reputation as a competent and caring physician who worked hard and demanded the same of his staff. Although most policy matters were referred to Fell and Nagy, Schuster maintained high professional standards among his staff and enforced a system of strict triage to ensure that the infirmary's heavy workload never overwhelmed them. A genuinely sick or injured prisoner who managed to reach the infirmary could be confident of receiving attention while malingerers were quickly exposed and returned to work.

Schuster sent J.J. back to the waiting room and turned to me.

"You are one of those released from the isolator?"

"Yes, Doctor. Prisoner W-0885. Five years. Seditious conspiracy." I recited the formula by which prisoners were required to identify themselves to camp officials.

"What is your name, my friend?"

"Paul Wagner."

"Mine is Georg. Georg Schuster."

He gave a perfunctory nod.

"So, may I assume that Dr. Nagy has already given you a complete physical examination?"

"No," I said. "I wouldn't let her finish."

"Ah, I see," the doctor replied. "Well, never mind. They never give us a record of their examinations, anyway. Their field is scientific research, you see. They prefer to leave treatment to us. Now, please open your mouth wide."

He examined my throat, then unzipped my coveralls and applied his stethoscope to my bare chest. I removed my coveralls and he went through an abbreviated form of the examination Dr. Nagy had attempted.

"How old are you and how long ago were you arrested?"

"Forty-five," I answered. "I was arrested sixteen months ago and arrived in Kamas early this month."

"For a forty-five year old, you have a remarkably strong constitution. The isolator is a rich storehouse of pathogens. Most men emerge with a variety of infections. You appear to have none. Other than hypothermia, exhaustion, and malnutrition, which are normal under the circumstances, your condition seems stable. Were you able to sleep?"

"The first day was difficult. After that, I think I slept most of the time. I was pretty fagged out from the brickyard, even after the strike."

"I see," Schuster noted. "What was your weight before your arrest?"

"About 220."

"You have lost a lot of weight."

"No kidding."

"The first month in a labor camp after a long interrogation, particularly when arriving during winter, is a violent shock to the system. But our bodies possess a remarkable ability to adjust to the most extreme conditions, given enough time. In my opinion, the isolator may have saved your life by giving you time to adjust and recover. Do you have any injuries or acute pains?"

I thought about it for a moment and shook my head.

"Nothing that isn't taking care of itself, I suppose."

"Then I shall have to release you," Schuster announced. "But remember that a short time ago, you were exposed to conditions that kill one of every three men. You must begin immediately to rebuild your strength. As I have told each of your fellows, you must seek to remain warm, avoid unnecessary exertion, sleep as much as possible, and eat as much nourishing food as you can find. You may take these extra meal vouchers. Tell me, can you make hot water in the barracks?"

"Sometimes."

"I will bring you some herbs that we obtain locally to help rebuild stamina. Wait one moment."

Schuster took a few steps toward his office, called out to someone inside to join him and returned to my side. A moment later, a tall young woman dressed in an immaculate white nurse's uniform followed him out of the office. She had a stunning figure and her ruddy, slightly bronzed complexion made her appear in the peak of physical condition, unlike the few haggard-looking, underfed female prisoners I had seen in work crews around camp. Even her shoulder-length brown hair was attractively cut and groomed, as if she were exempt from the harsh camp conditions that made it virtually impossible for female prisoners to maintain their good looks. I found myself wondering what special arrangement she might have made with the camp bosses.

"Gwen, could you find this patient some tonic herbs that might be useful to rebuild his stamina? I think some echinacea and Siberian ginseng would be good if we have any left."

"We may have given out the last packets. I'll check the drawer, Doctor."

She remained expressionless, spoke in a flat voice, and lowered her eyes when Schuster spoke to her. In less than a minute she returned with a brown paper lunch bag. Inside were three or four plastic baggies of dried herbs, all of a deep green hue and cut finely for making tea.

"These are the last. Shall I send for that woman in town to bring more?"

"Please. Tell her to double the amount she brought last time. And ask whether she can bring us any more of the wild honey and bee pollen. As much as she can lay her hands on."

"Yes, doctor."

"I am very sorry that we cannot admit any of you men as inpatients after your ordeal," Schuster continued. "Our orders strictly forbid it. Could you perhaps arrange for your foreman to shift you to lighter work for a few days?"

"I doubt it," I told him. "My team leader gets a hundred requests a day for that kind of thing. As far as I can see, Doctor, the only way to get easy duty around this camp is to make a deal with the bosses and I haven't come this far to do that."

Gwen's cheeks reddened as she handed Schuster the bag and retreated. It seemed I had struck a nerve.

Dr. Schuster called for an orderly to take me back to the waiting room. I was the last of the five to arrive. As soon as I did, the guards led us out to the van for the short trip back to Division 3.

Along the way, J.J. delivered the news that the mess hall would be closed for dinner. Someone had stolen a sack of rice from the kitchen storeroom and Jack Whiting had threatened to close the mess halls until the thief came forward. It was now nearly six o'clock and the culprit had not been found.

When I returned to Barracks C-14, nearly all the prisoners were lying silently on their bunks, hoping for a last-minute reprieve from a night without food. Only a few prisoners noticed me enter the barracks and take my bunk after a week's absence. Gallucci called out a greeting, as did Ralph Knopfler, Jerry Lee, and D.J. Schultz, who had recently transferred into our barracks. The others seemed lost in their own thoughts and troubles. Morale seemed lower even than when I had left.

"I heard about dinner," I said to Knopfler, who sat cross-legged on his bunk. "I was planning to use my extra ration coupons tonight to celebrate beating the isolator. Wrong night to celebrate, I guess."

"That's not all. Did anyone tell you about Monday's transfers?"

"No," I replied. "How many?"

"Maybe five hundred. Most of the men were taken straight from jail and put on a train headed north. It was a weird assortment, though. Not as many hard-liners as I expected. It's as if they couldn't tell the rebels from the Unionists. The Wart must really be low on stoolies if that's the best he could do."

"Any other fallout from the strike? How about work quotas?"

"They worked us hard all week. After losing so many men, making up lost output has been a stretch. If we don't get reinforcements soon, we'll be hurting."

"Any change in rations?" I asked.

"They docked us a meal a day to make up for what we ate during the strike. Not including today's double loss, we ought to be back on full rations by Monday. All in all, Paul, it looks to me like you didn't do so badly spending the week in the can. At the very least, it kept you out of the transfer."

"The doctor thinks the isolator saved my life. Still, once is enough for me."

"Some of the men seem to feel the same way about the strike," Knopfler said. "They're afraid. Some have given up. We may be in for another crop of suicides."

"Don't we have a priest or a rabbi or somebody?" I asked.

"I don't think we have any priests in C-14 but maybe we can get one of the old-timers to give a talk. We used to have Sigler do it."

"How about Gallucci?"

"Go ask him. I'll give him an introduction if he wants one."

A few minutes later I came back with Al Gallucci, who had been thinking along the same lines. Knopfler rose from his bunk, stood by the door, and clapped his hands to get the men's attention.

"Men, I think the time has come to spend a minute talking about morale. Over the past few weeks we've lost many good friends to starvation, sickness, and suicide. Many of these men didn't have to die. The real reason they aren't with us is that they gave up hope. We all reach moments when it seems easier to die than go on living. I've had those moments myself, but each time I just kept on going and it was the right decision every time. But my reasons to stay alive might not be the same as yours. All I can say is that tonight is a good time to take stock of those reasons—whatever they are—and to remember that you're not alone.

"That's all I have to say except that our friend Al Gallucci would like to add a few words of his own."

Knopfler returned to his bunk while Gallucci took his place at the door. He swept both his hands slowly back over his head and down his neck before clasping them in front of him as if he were about to pray. Then he looked down each row of bunks at his fellow prisoners and spoke.

"This year marks the twelfth year of the Unionist regime. This month marks a year since the death of the President-for-Life. To anyone who sees the situation objectively, our future must seem hopeless. I myself have finished eight years of a ten-year sentence and I put the chances of my release at less than ten percent. Still, I don't intend to give up on life. Who can know for certain what the future may bring? Even if the Unionist regime seems to have an unshakable grip on the country, who knows better than we do, after enduring anarchy, war, and the camps, how a great opening may sometimes present itself in a man's darkest hour?

"Think of all the joys in your past life and how their brightness still shines through today's darkness. Nothing can take these experiences away from you. Think of it: everything you have ever experienced, accomplished, suffered, or endured still exists and cannot be lost.

"Even here in Kamas your life can have its own special meaning. Regardless of the circumstances, human life always has a meaning, and this meaning also attaches to suffering, longing, deprivation, and death. We cannot deny the gravity of our present situation. But we must also recognize that this gravity—even hopelessness—need not rob life of its dignity.

"Consider also that someone looks down upon each of us in our time of trial. It may be a wife, a child, a parent, or friend—or a God, if you believe in one—and we would not want to disappoint him. He—or she—should find us proud in our suffering, not abject or miserable, but embracing the suffering that is life.

"No matter who we are or what our situation may be, our sacrifice has a meaning. It is essential to the very nature of this sacrifice that it must appear pointless to the world of material success. But there must be no doubt in anyone's mind that the meaning exists. Those of you who have held on to your religious faith will have no difficulty in recognizing this.

"No man wants to die for nothing. Rest assured, no matter how many days you have left in Kamas or on this earth, there is a meaning and purpose to the sacrifices that you make here every day."

Although we had no dinner that night, there were no more complaints.

CHAPTER 19

"In Germany, they first came for the Communists and I didn't speak up because I wasn't a Communist. Then they came for the Jews and I didn't speak up because I wasn't a Jew. Then they came for the trade unionists and I didn't speak up because I wasn't a trade unionist. Then they came for the Catholics and I didn't speak up because I wasn't a Catholic. Then they came for me— and by that time there was nobody left to speak up."
—Martin Niemöller

Saturday, March 30

My first day in the brickyard after returning from the isolator was probably the most miserable I had faced at Kamas. I was still shivering when I rose from bed and the shivering didn't stop until I had finished my oatmeal and three or four mugs of tea. After breakfast, we marched out to the recycling site under dark skies through driving sleet that turned to freezing rain and then to snow as a cold front blew in from the northwest. By the time we arrived for work my coveralls were sodden inside and out.

I prayed for the snow to stop long enough for my body temperature to overcome the chill of the wet coveralls.

Adding to my misery was the prospect that we would receive no ration bar for our midday meal to make up for the meals we had taken during the strike. I did my best to disconnect my conscious mind and let my body work on autopilot. But when I did, instead of slipping into a meditative trance that made time go by faster, by some paradox I found my mind focusing in minute detail on every action I took: selecting good bricks from the pile, placing them in the hod, carrying the hod to the pallet, and stacking them properly onto the pallet.

The disturbing images that had plagued my mind in the isolator returned to haunt me. The benign visions of my wife and children returned as well, not as vividly, but close enough to shake my grasp on reality. I decided once again to drive all thoughts of my pre-arrest life out of my mind, at least for the present.

Then I remembered Gallucci's speech and resolved to find the meaning in my current situation. What was the meaning to be grasped from declaring the old Paul Wagner dead and renouncing attachments to family, place, and profession? My original grounds for such detachment had been to boost my chances for survival. But why was it necessary to detach from my life in order to save it?

Once more I considered Ben Jackson's prediction that I would be out of Kamas by June. I dropped my hod before the brick pile and prayed for the strength to make it through the day. Tomorrow was Sunday. If I could hold out until then, I could spend the day in my bunk getting warm and regaining my strength. And on Monday, we would be back on full rations.

I felt someone come beside me and lay his hod on the ground alongside mine. It was D.J. Schultz. I had not seen him since leaving for the isolator. It took a moment for him to recognize me.

"Hey, Paul, you don't look so hot."

"You don't look so great, either, pal."

D.J. appeared to have lost another five pounds in the week or so since we had last seen each other. His eyes were dark and sunken, and his breath had the foul odor of decay. No trace remained of the careless, easygoing attitude that I had noticed about him on our first day in camp.

"Gary told me about your week in the isolator," he said.

I said nothing.

"Gary's with the vigilantes, you know," D.J. continued. "He's looking for some new men to replace the ones they lost in the transfer."

"And you're thinking of joining up?" I asked.

"I don't know. A couple of weeks ago I would have said no for sure. But after talking to Gary, I'm starting to see things differently. Listen, I'm only twenty-three and, at the rate I'm going, I'm lucky if I'll last another year. I don't deserve this! Who the hell are these people that they can do this to us?"

D.J.'s eyes began to glisten.

"D.J., don't do it. No matter what the bastards have done to you, it's not worth sinking to their level."

"Thanks for the sermon," he snapped, "but I don't feel like turning the other cheek anymore. Somebody has to stand up to these sons of bitches."

"How about Jerry Lee? Have you talked to him about it?"

"Jerry Lee says there's not a dime's worth of difference between Gary Toth and a serial killer. He won't have anything to do with the vigilantes."

D.J. looked at me with tired and angry eyes and said no more. We each filled our hods with bricks and carried them off to separate pallets.

The snow stopped and the clouds began to thin out and break up. By midday, the sun had penetrated through the cloud cover and I could feel my coveralls begin to dry. I sat alone during the lunch break, thinking about D.J. and the vigilantes. By any moral or ethical standard I knew their execution of stoolies was wrong. But from a practical viewpoint, the vigilantes were the only effective opposition we had. Was it wrong to side with the lesser of the two evils? No, I reasoned, so long as I didn't take a hand in the bloodshed.

For the rest of the afternoon I moved slowly between brick pile and pallet with my mind far away. From time to time I looked up at the fleets of fluffy white clouds and felt deeply grateful that I had the energy to continue and that the sunshine was making me warm and dry again. When the siren blew at quitting time, I realized that no prayer had ever been answered more directly or clearly than the one I had offered at the shift's start.

That night in the dining hall the soup, bread, and weak tea were no better or worse than any other night. Yet I savored each mouthful, confident that a day of rest lay ahead of me and that I was growing stronger.

After dinner, I settled into my bunk, as weary as I had ever been at Kamas, ready to sleep all the way through until Monday. I had barely closed my eyes when I felt someone shake my shoulder. It was Ralph Knopfler.

"I saw Glenn at dinner. He'd like to see you, if you're well enough to talk."

"I'll go," I said, rose and crossed the yard as the last glow of sunset faded behind the hills. Reineke was alone in his bunk. As I approached him, I sensed the gaze of prisoners watching me from both sides of the aisle. Though I might still think of myself as neutral, to others there could be little question whose side I was on.

"Welcome back to the land of the living, Paul." He examined me closely to assess how much damage the isolator had done. "Tell me, was there ever a time in there when you thought you wouldn't make it?"

"Actually, no," I said. "I was at the end of my rope the whole time, but never quite willing to let go."

"Good for you. Some old-timers say that a man with a clear conscience has nothing to fear from the isolator. I guess that means you're an honest man."

"I had my share of nightmares," I replied.

"Like Ben Jackson?" Reineke probed. "Did you see the future?"

"No," I replied distantly. "I saw my family. And it was real. But I don't know what I'm supposed to do about it."

"Give it time," he answered. "You'll figure it out. But right now what you need is rest. Knopfler told me you were pretty wobbly today. He said he offered you an easier work assignment but you wouldn't take it. Listen, Paul, why don't you take Sigler's old job for a few days until you're stronger?"

"Counting pallets and spotting defects?" I asked.

"Sure," he said. "You'd still have to hump bricks half the time but the rest of the day you'd just walk around with a clipboard. How about it?"

"I'll pass. I don't want to be the one to make someone miss his quota. Besides, with a cushy job like that some people might think I cut a deal with the bosses."

"Not this job. Knopfler controls work team assignments, not the Wart."

"All the same, I'll take a rain check."

"If that's what you want. Anyway, I still owe you one."

I asked Reineke about the final terms on which the strike had been settled and how he thought the camp authorities might treat us in the coming weeks.

"No matter what anybody says, having two strikes within a week was a black eye for Rocco. He bet wrong when he tried to sweep the first strike under the rug. Calling for outside help with the second one must have made him look even worse. My guess is that we'll see a quiet period while he plans his next move, then he'll be back to hammer us hard."

"How about the prisoner transfer? Was it what you expected?"

"Not at all," Reineke replied. "Whiting's intelligence was terrible. He had very little idea who the hard-liners were, so he selected his transferees on the basis of who opted for jail and who didn't. The problem was that many of the guys who chose jail were actually stoolies or closet Unionists—guys who feared spending another night in the barracks. And many of the men who went back to work were actually hard-liners who would have opted for jail except that it was already full. So, in the end, we didn't lose nearly as many of our people as I expected."

"When do you expect replacements to arrive?" I asked.

"A couple hundred have already rolled in from Denver. But it may be weeks before we're back up to full strength. What we need now is more ex-military types, veterans of the Manchurian War who will fight till their last breath.

"At the moment there's a Marine colonel in the camp jail who may be the kind of man we need. Until a few months ago he commanded a regiment in Texas. They arrested him along with several of his unit commanders when a squad of his men scooted across the DMZ to the Mexicans. If he's half the leader he's said to be, he could be a great asset to us. But if he's pro-Unionist underneath, he could be poison. When he gets out of the can in another week, I'd like you to get to know him and tell me what you think."

"There you go again, Glenn, trying to recruit me."

Reineke laughed.

"I'm not looking for a thumbs up or thumbs down on him. I'd just like your help in trying to figure him out. I sincerely hope Colonel Majors will turn out to be our friend."

"And if he doesn't..."

"We can't afford to be soft on Whiting's stooges. This is war."

"I'm not arguing, Glenn, but sometimes I have to wonder how much difference there is between a Gary Toth and a Jack Whiting."

"If you knew Gary better, I don't think you'd be so hard on him."

"It's not my intent to be hard on him," I insisted. "I admire Gary. Still, I find it unnerving to be around anyone who's so utterly implacable."

"Let me tell you a little story about Gary that may help you understand him. About two years ago, Gary was one of several hundred prisoners being transported up the Missouri River on a prison barge. During the night, the barge hit an underwater obstacle and began to sink in the cold water of the spring melt. Many of the prisoners were too weak to swim to shore. Gary, having been a Navy SEAL, is a powerful swimmer and saved scores of prisoners by pulling them to a boat that came to the rescue.

"But when it was his turn to get into the boat, no space was left. An old-timer who had watched Gary save the others quietly climbed overboard to give Gary his place. Before he let go of the rail he made one last request: that Gary dedicate whatever time he had left to destroying Unionism and liberating the camps. Gary gave the old man his word and has been on a holy war ever since."

I rose to leave.

"One last thing," I said. "You wouldn't have any more writing paper, would you? I'm afraid I lost what you gave me."

"No, you didn't," Reineke replied with a grin. "We retrieved it for you."

He returned to me the pen and paper that I had left in my bunk the morning I was sent to the isolator. Clearly Reineke did not intend to let me off the hook so easily.

"Thanks for remembering," he said. "It'll mean a lot to her."

On the way back to the barracks, I thought about what I would say in the letter that I had promised to send to Alec Sigler's widow. I was tired and wanted only to sleep, but it seemed wrong not to jot down a first draft before the day was over.

I took out a sheet of paper and printed the following message in block letters:

YOUR HUSBAND LEFT INSTRUCTIONS FOR CONTACTING YOU AFTER HIS DEATH. I REGRET HE IS NO LONGER ALIVE. ALL WHO KNEW HIM UNDERSTOOD THAT HE HONORED AND LOVED YOU ALWAYS. MY AIM IN WRITING IS TO GIVE YOU THIS NEWS AND OFFER TO CONTINUE THE WORK THE TWO OF YOU DID THROUGH YOUR LETTERS.

I WILL NOT MENTION MY NAME OR YOURS. IF YOU DESIRE TO CORRESPOND, WE SHOULD TAKE PRECAUTIONS. FIRST LET US ENCODE OUR MESSAGES USING THE BOOK CODE DESCRIBED ON THE ATTACHED SHEET. OTHER PRECAUTIONS WILL FOLLOW.

MY NEXT MESSAGE CAN BE FOUND ONE WEEK FROM NOW IN THE SAME PLACE. LEAVE YOUR MESSAGE WHERE YOU LEFT YOUR LAST. UNLESS I RECEIVE WORD FROM YOU WITHIN THREE WEEKS, I WILL ASSUME OUR CORRESPONDENCE HAS ENDED. I AWAIT YOUR DECISION.

CHAPTER 20

"Violence can only be concealed by a lie, and the lie can only be maintained by violence. Any man who has once proclaimed violence as his method is inevitably forced to take the lie as his principle."
—Aleksandr Solzhenitsyn

Tuesday, April 30

I remember April in Kamas as an eerily peaceful month. We mounted no strikes. The guards shot no prisoners. And no one was transferred north. The guards and warders even used their nightsticks sparingly. But prisoners who participated in the March strikes still lived under the cloud of further transfers. And my forty-sixth birthday came and went.

As many of us had expected, the promises the camp administration had made during March went largely unfulfilled. There was no joint investigating commission, no suspension of trigger-happy guards, no compensation for victims. Work quotas remained the same despite fewer men on each team. And food rations remained as before. The only promises the Warden kept were to show movies in the yards on Sunday evenings and to permit prisoners to petition for a case review by a three-judge special hearing panel.

Snow and freezing rain continued almost daily for most of the month, with the last big snowstorm taking us by surprise on April 24. Gradually temperatures rose, the snows thawed, and the mud deepened. In late April our heavy winter coveralls and insulated winter boots were exchanged for thinner summer coveralls and standard-issue army boots. For the first week after the switch, the frosty mountain nights made it more disagreeable than ever to crawl out of bed in the morning. But as always, we adjusted.

Although food rations had not changed, the milder temperatures meant that we needed less energy to stay warm. Yet none of us gained weight because the reduced numbers of men on each work team since the transfer meant that each of us had to work harder to meet our weekly quotas. The failure to improve living conditions and the fear of reprisals and the lack of hope led to another outbreak of suicides during the last week in April.

It was a time of intense vigilance among both Jack Whiting's stoolies and Gary Toth's stoolie hunters. Every day Whiting and his staff summoned selected prisoners from the barracks, the infirmary, worksites, mess halls, and bathhouses for discreet meetings. There they offered cash, food, tobacco, and easier work assignments to entice new informants to report on their fellow prisoners. Those who refused were threatened with the isolator, beatings, transfer north, and even reprisals against family members outside the camps.

At the same time, Toth's counter-intelligence squads followed these same prisoners wherever they went, interrogated them after each suspected contact, and warned them of dire consequences if they informed on their neighbors. Every week brought the discovery of another suspect whom the vigilantes had stabbed, smothered, or garroted. Among these was the genial medical student from Atlanta, Dennis Martino, who had left the isolator too weak to withstand the Wart's relentless pressure.

The strikes had further polarized the camp population along partisan lines. Those who pledged their loyalty to the Unionist Party went out of their way to distance themselves from the rebels in camp. Those who opposed the Party lost no opportunity to remind fence sitters of our sufferings at the Unionists' hands.

Many rookie prisoners joined the ranks of the hard-liners during April, having shed in March any remaining illusions about the nature of the labor camp system. D.J. Schultz was among the new converts. For this he sacrificed his close friendship with Jerry Lee. But even moderates like Pete Murphy and Chuck Quayle, who had belonged to the delegation that settled the first strike, hardened their stance after the second strike was crushed. Only devoutly religious prisoners from persecuted sects like the Amish, Mennonites, Hutterites, Jehovah's Witnesses, Orthodox Jews, and Seventh Day Adventists, together with a few New Agers and secular humanists like Al Gallucci, managed to steer a clear course between the opposing political camps.

One of the few post-strike events of common interest was the announcement that the Department of Justice had appointed a three-judge special hearing panel to review the cases of Kamas political prisoners. Each evening after the mid-April announcement, a queue formed in the mess hall to pick up petition forms and instructions at a table manned by the legal appeals clerks, judges Richardson and O'Rourke. From dinner until lights-out, prisoners of all ages and backgrounds could be seen toiling to prepare their petitions. It seemed that hope lingered in every man's breast that Washington would at last discover its errors and order his immediate release.

As for myself, I had no desire to line up for the privilege of consulting the judges. Nor did I believe that there was a chance that I would gain legal relief through such a petition. I saw the case reviews as nothing more than a cynical trick to distract the credulous by occupying their leisure time and sapping their will to resist.

I spent most of my spare hours trying to restore my health. On several follow-up visits to Georg Schuster at the infirmary, I came away with enough supplemental ration tickets to stabilize my weight and actually gain a few pounds. Schuster's nurse, Gwen, also resupplied me with tonic herbs and slipped me a bottle of expired multivitamins to speed my recovery. On Sundays, I napped, ate, read books from the camp library, visited with friends like D.J. and Jerry Lee, and went to bed thinking of my wife and daughters.

Early in the month I received my first clandestine message from Sigler's widow. It was an ordinary sheet of cheap copy paper twisted into a scroll to fit into a hollowed stick. I felt a special thrill on seeing a woman's handwriting in a note addressed only to me, and an even greater thrill when I read that she agreed to correspond.

In Helen Sigler's second letter, using the code I had proposed, she explained that she and Alec had used their letter exchange primarily to convey messages between women in Division 1 and men in Divisions 2 and 3. Helen visited the women's division regularly under the pretext of trading food, herbs, soaps, and skin lotions for prison handicrafts that she resold in town. As security measures in the women's camp were relatively flexible, and as she paid a portion of her revenues in bribes to the gate guards, Helen was able to meet scores of women prisoners, some of whom had brothers or husbands only a few hundred yards away on the other side of the Service Yard.

Nearly all the messages we exchanged during April were devoted to requests from female prisoners to locate their male relatives and to the men's responses. I soon found that the task of searching for these men was the easy part of the job. Since nearly all the women already knew that their loved ones had been arrested, finding them alive and in the same camp came as joyous news. Even to learn of a relative's ill health or death was preferable to knowing nothing.

Delivering the women's messages to the men, however, was not as simple. In most cases, the male relative had been the first family member arrested and, being denied the right to correspond, was unaware that any other family member was in custody. It was also natural for any prisoner who had agreed to cooperate with State Security to expect that such cooperation would spare his relatives. So the news that a man's wife or sister or daughter had landed in a labor camp almost always came as a crushing blow. It took me most of April to devise a method for preventing or cushioning these reactions.

On the last day of the month, rumors of an incoming prisoner transport began before roll call. According to several warders and guards, a convoy had arrived just before dawn and consisted of five or six hundred prisoners. But the new men were not politicals like us. They were common criminals convicted of crimes like murder, drug trafficking, extortion, kidnapping, rape, and armed robbery. Most of us had encountered this breed of prisoner in transit camps before our arrival at Kamas. But apart from the transit camps, which served political prisoners and common criminals alike, politicals and thieves had always been held in separate correctional facilities.

News of the incoming transfer sent a shockwave through the camp. Nearly every prisoner who had been thrown in with the thieves in the past dreaded facing them again. We remembered how the thieves had intimidated us, beaten us, cut us, stolen our food and belongings, raped the young and weak and murdered those who stood up to them, all without risk of punishment from the authorities. We remembered how our fellow politicals generally lacked the stomach to match the criminals blow for blow and how the thieves, who operated in gangs, easily dominated the independent and disorganized politicals.

As we marched off to our worksites on that last day in April, we fretted about how our lives would change when we returned from work. Mercifully, the thieves would be held in quarantine for their first full day. That would give us time to conceal treasured possessions and perhaps lay hands on a weapon. But what would happen when the thieves moved into our barracks?

At the worksites we talked of nothing else. How would we meet our production quotas when the thieves shirked their work and refused to contribute to the team effort? What if the thieves were appointed as warders, foremen, or work group leaders? And how could we keep the thieves from informing on us to the camp bosses as they invariably did?

Our work team returned to camp that evening more agitated and depressed than we had been in weeks. As we entered the mess hall, we watched the thieves as closely as they watched us. In the lead were simpering rat-faced punks, cocky gangsters, and sullen, slow-witted giants who served as their bodyguards and enforcers. Behind them were the capos and their lieutenants, resembling professional wrestlers in their exaggerated villainy and exuding an unmistakable brutality and animal cunning. The next day they would be our new barracks-mates.

The fact that the thieves were permitted in the mess hall at all was the first indication that the warders and guards were unwilling to enforce the rules against them. According to quarantine regulations, transferees were to remain separate from the regular camp population for twenty-four hours after their arrival.

We waited until the last of the thieves left the mess hall, and then filed in for dinner. Conversation was lackluster.

After we returned to our barracks, Ralph Knopfler called me outside to watch the spectacle of the thieves smashing their barracks windows and lighting bonfires on the parade ground. It was not until after lights-out that guards arrived with fire extinguishers to put out the fires. These stern disciplinarians now were seen chuckling at the audacious spirit of the young criminals. Unlike politicals, the thieves represented the underprivileged, whose foibles were tolerated in the new Unionist society.

If the thieves' arrival heralded a new tactic in the bosses' campaign to crush the political prisoners' will, it seemed off to a promising start. The threat of an alliance between the thieves and the camp bosses had caught us completely off guard. On the eve of the May Day holiday, none of us slept soundly.

CHAPTER 21

Tuesday, April 30

The late afternoon sun filled the Chambers living room through half-opened blinds. Claire sat at Martha's desk hunched over her math worksheet and concentrated hard on finishing her last few fractions problems before Marie stirred in the upstairs nursery. Once she heard the baby's cries, there would be no more time for homework until much later.

The doorbell rang. It was Helen Sigler.

"Hello, stranger."

Claire buried her face in Helen's brown wool jacket and squeezed her around the waist. A pair of covered straw baskets lay on the doorstep.

"I brought some herbs for Martha. Is she in?"

Claire welcomed Helen inside.

"She's in the kitchen. I'll go get her."

Marie let out a wail upstairs, and so Claire set off up the stairs the moment she came back with Martha Chambers.

"Helen, what a lovely surprise!" Martha said with genuine warmth. "How about a cup of tea? I have some Earl Gray that Doug just brought back from Denver."

"No thanks, I can only stay for a few minutes," Helen answered, removing her coat and accepting a seat on the sofa. "Your gate guard comes on duty at six. I'd prefer to be gone before he arrives."

"Six is when Doug comes back, too. He's bringing the Warden with him again," Martha said with a frown.

"All the more reason to be brief," Helen added. "But before I forget, please take these herbs. I brought them in case they questioned my reason for visiting at the gate."

Upstairs, Marie let out a piercing wail.

"Do you need to get that?" Helen asked.

"No, Claire knows what to do," Martha replied. "Tell me, Helen, do you have children of your own?"

"A daughter. She graduates from college next month."

"You must be very proud," Martha said. "Will she be coming back to Utah?"

Helen lowered her eyes.

"Lucy has never been to Utah. She lives with my sister and her husband in Virginia. They agreed to adopt her after Alec's arrest so that Lucy could stay enrolled in school."

"I'm sorry. I didn't realize—"

Helen continued as though she hadn't heard the apology.

"It was the only way I knew to give her a fair chance in life."

"What was Alec charged with?" Martha asked.

"The charge was merely a formality. The point was that Alec ran for the state legislature on a ticket that opposed the Unionists. When he lost, Alec presented evidence that the other side had stuffed the ballot boxes. A week later he was arrested. That was eight years ago this fall."

"Eight years in the camps for that?"

"They called it advocating overthrow of the government," Helen replied. "But at least Alec had the satisfaction of standing up and publicly opposing them. And of never giving in. This June he would have completed his sentence."

"Would have?" Martha repeated.

"Alec died last month."

"I'm so very sorry," Martha said, reaching out to touch Helen's hand.

"You had no way of knowing. Even I didn't find out until weeks later."

"What will you do now?" Martha asked.

"I don't know. I plan to stay in the cabin a while longer until I sort things out."

"Forgive me for being so naïve," Martha began gently. "There's so much I still don't understand."

Helen looked up at Martha with a sympathetic smile.

"You see, when we came back from Paris after the Events," Martha continued, "everything around me had completely changed. But nobody wanted to talk about it. Whenever I asked Doug what it was like during those years, he said he just wanted to forget."

"Then why on earth would he choose to join State Security?" Helen asked.

"Looking back, I think Doug knew very well what he was getting into when he joined the Department. I remember how desperately unhappy he was after being wounded and how he brooded that his Army career was over."

"And was he surprised at what State Security expected from him?"

"If he was," Martha replied, "I don't recall that he showed it. In fact, what worries me sometimes is how well Doug has adjusted. It doesn't seem to matter at all what they tell him to do as long as he can hold onto his rank, bonus pay, free house, and car. It's as if he's given up on himself and has let them take over his life."

"Have you told him how you feel about his work?" Helen asked.

"Not in as many words. I've told him how I think he's changed but he doesn't want to hear it."

"Do you love him?"

Martha took a deep breath.

"Frankly, I'm not sure I ever did."

"Then why on Earth did you marry him?"

"I ask myself that nearly every day. When I met Doug he was handsome, witty, affectionate, fun to be around—just about everything I wanted in a man. And he adored me. He was so dogged about asking me to marry him that I didn't know quite what to do. I told him I didn't think I was in love with him but he said not to worry—, that it would develop with time. Except it hasn't. I still care deeply about him, but I'm not in love with him. And then the business about the girl in camp had to come up..."

"Actually, that's one of the reasons I came here to see you," Helen said. "I asked my contacts in the women's camp about her. It hurts me to say it, Martha, but what they told me appears to agree with what you learned on your own. It seems that Doug has been seeing a young nurse's aide by the name of Gwen. They meet in a private examining room at the infirmary two or three times a week. My sources tell me Gwen has received special privileges that would be impossible without a high-level protector."

Helen paused for a moment

"Martha, what I'm saying here doesn't prove anything and I would be the first to tell you that it's not enough to support a decision to leave your husband. But I do know that the only way you're going to know if it's true, other than catching him in the act, is to ask him about it."

"These women you talked to…" Martha pressed. "Are you sure they have no ulterior motive?"

"I can't rule it out," Helen replied. "But they're decent, honest women who appear to pity Gwen more than they envy her. They're the ones I've relied on for years to distribute free herbs and vitamins in the women's camp. I trust them completely."

Martha stood up, paced back and forth several times, then crossed the room to her desk and returned with her purse.

"I don't know what to say, other than to thank you."

She removed all the money from her wallet and handed it to Helen.

"I'd like you to take this to buy more vitamins for your women. It's my own money, not Doug's. It would mean a lot to me if you could help someone with it."

When Helen didn't move, Martha tucked it into the pocket of Helen's coat.

Helen rose to leave.

"It's nearly six," she noted, glancing at the clock on Martha's desk. "I'd better say goodbye to Claire and be on my way."

"I'll call her," Martha said. "And thank you for all the help you've given me. After I've had time to think, I'd like to visit you again at your cabin some time to talk some more."

"Anytime," Helen answered.

Martha called up the stairway for Claire, who came down promptly with Marie in a fresh diaper. They conversed for a minute and then Helen gave Claire a hug and picked up her baskets to leave.

The moment she took a step toward the door the doorbell rang. Martha looked out the peephole.

"Oh, my God, it's the Warden," she said, panic rising in her voice. "What do we do now?"

"Let him in," Helen answered in a whisper. "I was delivering the herbs you bought, remember? And if anyone noticed how long I was here, it was because I showed you how to use them."

Martha opened the door. Helen stepped out as if she had been unaware that anyone was waiting on the doorstep.

"I'll have some new items in a few weeks, Mrs. Chambers," Helen announced in a businesslike voice as she walked past the Warden. "Come by the station some evening and I'll show them to you. Meanwhile, take good care of yourself and the baby. Good night."

Fred Rocco watched Helen step past him with the puzzled expression of someone who recalled having seen her face before but not quite remembering where. Before he could make the connection, Martha Chambers ushered him inside.

"Doug's not home yet. May I fix you something, Warden?"

"Please, call me Fred. I'm off duty."

"Of course, Fred. Bourbon?"

"I'd love some. Just a touch of water and lots of ice."

Martha led him into the kitchen and filled his glass with ice while he donned his bifocals to scan the newspaper lying open on the counter.

Not far away, in the breakfast nook, Claire spoon-fed Marie in her high chair.

"Do you know that woman well?" Rocco asked, fixing Martha with a sharp look over his spectacles.

"I buy homemade breads and herbs from her sometimes. Why do you ask?"

"She comes to the women's camp now and then to peddle her junk. Her husband used to be a prisoner. I've had a hunch for some time that she exchanged messages with him somehow but we were never able to prove it. At any rate, there's no chance of that happening anymore. Her husband was shot last month while attacking a guard. Good riddance, too. He wasn't the kind of prisoner we would ever want on the streets again, believe me."

Martha's hand shook as she topped off the bourbon with water and stirred it with a spoon.

The warden watched her closely and gave a contented smile.

CHAPTER 22

"Some [trade unionists] are crying that they were beaten. Yes, you will be thoroughly beaten!"
—Robert Mugabe, Zimbabwean dictator

Wednesday, May 1

The May Day holiday fell on a Wednesday. In keeping with tradition, even political prisoners were excused from work.

After roll call, the warders divided the newly arrived criminals into groups of fifteen or twenty and led them to their new barracks. The group assigned to Barracks C-14 consisted of young gang members and assorted delinquents between the ages of sixteen and twenty-five, with none over thirty. Nearly all were urban poor, evenly mixed among Hispanics, blacks, and whites.

The warders entered the barracks ahead of their charges, announcing that our new barracks-mates were genuine Americans, not traitors like us, and that we should treat them with respect.

"Watch how they live and follow their example," Grady lectured us with his usual sneer. "Maybe you'll learn something about how real men handle themselves."

And to the young criminals: "It's about time we had some red-blooded macho men like you to keep these traitors in line. You can count on us to back you to the hilt."

The criminals stayed close together as they made their way down the aisles toward the rear of the barracks, ignoring vacant bunks as they went. When they could go no further, they gestured for the existing occupants to vacate the last three rows of beds. There was a moment of uncertainty while the occupants considered whether to defend their bunks and the thieves considered whether to take them by force. Then the confident voice of an older prisoner spoke up.

"Come on, let's show these men some hospitality. Let them have their own area in back if they want it. You guys in back, come on up here with us. There's plenty of empty billets to go around since the transfers."

And rather than begrudge the newcomers the bunks they coveted, the politicals at the rear of the barracks gathered their belongings quietly and moved to vacant bunks closer to the entrance. An uneasy quiet prevailed as the new arrivals took their places.

But the quiet was quickly broken. On a bunk adjacent to those of the criminals, an emaciated political used a homemade knife to whittle a tiny bear from a block of wood. A slender youth with a wispy mustache and goatee crept up behind him and snatched the knife away.

"Go make yourself another one, old man," he said as he retreated with his prize to a third-tier bunk.

Not far away, a compact, muscular youth eyed a bespectacled prisoner reading a paperback novel and made a beeline for it.

"Let me see that," he said, but only after he had already torn it from the startled man's grip. He glanced impatiently at the cover, then tore a handful of pages from of the middle and tossed it on the floor.

"What kind of bullshit book is this, anyway? Who's got some porn around here? Come on, you limpdicks, hand it over!" He scanned the other bunks within range for more reading material.

The political prisoners turned their backs on their new neighbors. Most had learned in the transit camps that when the thieves crossed the room to torment and plunder, it was best to surrender whatever they wanted and offer no resistance. If it came to blows, the thieves would defend each other to the death while the politicals cowered and left their fellows to meet their fate alone.

To the thieves, fighting was a way of life and an essential survival skill. No blow or trick was too foul or underhanded if it offered a tactical advantage. The thieves flaunted their brutality to intimidate the politicals, who abhorred violence both in principle and in practice and lacked the stomach to hit below the belt, bite, stomp, gouge an eye or break a nose, even to save their own life or that of a close friend. The result was that, whenever politicals mixed with thieves, any sense of unity or camaraderie among the politicals broke down and every man was left to fend for himself.

In Barracks C-14, however, we politicals outnumbered the thieves by a margin of at least five to one. Like many of my neighbors, I was prepared to fight if I had to. But I was not inclined to start the fight and risk facing the thieves alone if no one joined me. Before I could decide what to do if one of them attacked me, a scuffle broke out two rows away.

A pair of thieves in their late twenties sat down on either side of the youngest political prisoner in the barracks, an eighteen-year-old high school student who had been arrested for publishing an article in his school newspaper critical of Unionist officials in his town. The student looked panic-stricken. My instincts told me that they were sizing him up for rape. I looked around to determine whether anyone else had noticed and whether I would be alone if I came to his defense.

To my surprise, Brian Gaffney was already on his way. At six feet three inches and nearly two hundred pounds, he was one of the strongest men in the barracks even after his stay in the isolator. Before starting his career as a commercial artist, Gaffney had once worked as a lumberjack and had also crewed on commercial fishing vessels off the Alaska coast. Gaffney faced the two thieves and spoke to them in a low voice.

In an instant, both thieves jumped him. I hesitated for a moment, then rushed to his aid, grabbing one of the attackers around the throat and tossing him back into the thieves' corner. Two politicals blocked his return while Gaffney dispatched the other thief with rapid-fire punches to the face. The rest of the thieves were ready to fight but were held in check by a handful of politicals separating them from Gaffney and his opponents.

Gaffney stood, flushed with anger and dripping blood from his nose and mouth. He looked around the barracks and saw how few of his fellow politicals had supported him.

"You people are pathetic! Here we are, seventy-five against fifteen, and you're willing to stand by and let these punks humiliate us? When are you finally going to stand up for yourselves?"

Before anyone could speak, I heard the hard rap of a wooden nightstick swinging against a bunk. It was Grady. He and Mills had watched the entire fight without intervening. Now the two warders swaggered down the aisle toward Gaffney.

"It's back to the isolator for you, pal," Grady declared.

Mills circled behind Gaffney and pushed him toward the door while Grady raised his stick to strike. Suddenly a hand darted out from a top bunk and snatched Mills's hat from his head. Another pair of hands reached out from beneath a bunk and untied his bootlaces. Mills didn't know which one to attack first. Another hand reached out from a mid-level bunk and slipped Grady's pepper spray out of his breast pocket.

"Hey, give that back or I'll..."

There was a faint hiss and Grady screamed as he raised his hands to his eyes. The next spray hit Mills. Both men fell writhing to the floor. The thieves instantly went to work stripping the warders of their boots and coveralls and dragged them out of the barracks into the yard. Their hats, nightsticks, boots, pepper spray, and the contents of their pockets disappeared.

The thieves tossed the empty coveralls back to the disabled warders and disappeared into the crowd that had gathered outside. Nothing like this had ever been seen in Kamas. Before long, a squad of guards came along and carried Grady and Mills off to the infirmary. But the prisoners who had seen the attack on the two warders talked about it all day long, wondering aloud why the thieves would have come to the aid of a political whom they had battled only moments before.

At lunch I fell into line behind Jerry Lee and Steve Bernstein, the Long Island drug salesman I had met on my first day in camp. As a four-year veteran of the camp system, Bernstein had lived among thieves in a variety of transit camps. He also had an ear for gossip. We took our seats at a table at the rear of the mess hall. Bernstein pointed out the table where the thieves sat.

Their senior capo, Bernstein told us, was Frank Brancato, a thirty-five-year-old brute who stood six feet six inches tall and weighed nearly three hundred pounds. According to Bernstein, Brancato had once competed as a professional wrestler and was still known by his wrestling name, "The Beast," which some said referred to the mat of black fur that grew on his back, chest, and limbs. After leaving the ring, he had joined a narcotics-distribution ring in western Massachusetts and had served three years of a five-year sentence for drug trafficking.

Two seats away sat Brancato's chief deputy, Randy Skinner, a one-time motorcycle gang leader and methamphetamine entrepreneur. Bernstein explained how, during the Events, Skinner's network of mobile meth labs had delivered drugs to fighters on both sides of the battles that raged across the Plains States. Skinner's paranoia and raging temper fueled speculation that he himself was a speed freak but those who knew him claimed that these were simply the natural traits of a born psychopath.

The head table of the thieves' contingent also included various sycophants and personal attendants. Among those were Ramon Sanchez, a Mexican-American drug smuggler who spoke for Hispanic gang members at Kamas, and Jabril, a Harlem-born master burglar whose specialty was looting retail stores by night and reselling the wares by day to an army of sidewalk peddlers.

Bernstein painted a bleak picture of what was in store for us once the thieves gained a foothold at Kamas.

"You've got to remember, people like Brancato and Skinner buy and sell small-time government schmucks every day of the week. Labor camp trusties are no different. Before you know it, Brancato's men will show up as warders, then in the mess halls, and then even as foremen and team leaders. After a while they'll be running the whole goddamned camp. Believe me, all you can do is to stay out of their way and give them what they want."

"Come on, Steve," I argued. "Most of the thieves I've seen are just ignorant kids. They can't be very bright or they wouldn't be criminals in the first place. For heaven's sake, we've got hundreds of combat veterans among us. It would be absurd for us to surrender to a handful of delinquents."

"Not as long as Rocco and Whiting run the show," Bernstein countered. "Look, if Whiting can grind us into the dirt the way he's doing now, how bad do you think it can get with six hundred criminals on his side? And who's to stop him from shipping in a thousand more? No, this time Whiting's really got our number."

Jerry Lee and I looked at each other and finished our meals in silence. There was no point in arguing with someone like Bernstein. He had already accepted defeat.

We were about to leave when we saw Reineke, Knopfler, Perkins, and Murphy coming our way. They passed behind us in single file and continued in the direction of Brancato's table. Approaching the table from the left and right were two other groups, one led by Gary Toth and the other by one of Toth's lieutenants. As they came nearer, everyone at Brancato's table stood except Brancato and Skinner.

Jerry Lee and I followed a few paces behind in a show of support.

"We've heard you're the leaders of the new transferees," Reineke began, speaking directly to Brancato. "The four of us were elected a while back to represent the prisoners here. Now that your men and ours are going to be living together, we thought it might be a good idea to have a talk. Can you bring together your top men and meet us outside? We'll be waiting."

Brancato acknowledged Reineke with a slight nod.

Reineke headed for the door with his team in tow. Jerry Lee and I joined them outside and waited for Brancato. A few minutes later he came out with an entourage of more than a dozen. They glared at us from the porch.

"Let's talk four on four," Reineke called out to Brancato. "Follow us behind the mess hall. Leave everybody else here."

"There will be six of us," Brancato replied.

"Fine," Reineke called back. Then he pointed in our direction. "I need two more men: Wagner, Quayle, come on over."

I swallowed hard and set off to catch up with them.

When I reached the back of the mess hall, Reineke and the others were already seated cross-legged on the ground. I took a seat next to George Perkins as Brancato arrived with his team. I recognized Skinner, Ramon, Jabril, and two of Brancato's enforcers.

Reineke introduced himself and then followed the camp custom of stating the section of Title 18 under which he had been convicted, along with the number of years in his term. The other five of us did the same. Brancato and his team followed by naming their own crimes and sentences.

Then Reineke went straight to the point.

"In case you haven't heard about Kamas, let me give you some highlights. Over the last year we've executed over fifty stool pigeons. Last month we held two strikes and a thousand of us went to jail for it, some to the isolator. Five hundred more were sent north. We're not the same breed of politicals you're used to seeing in the transit camps. We know how to enforce our rules and you'll live by them or suffer the consequences."

"You know how my boys are," Brancato replied with a crooked smile. "They aren't used to rules. I'm not sure I can help you much there."

"Then let me make it even clearer," Reineke continued. "There are six hundred of you in this division, three thousand of us. Nearly a thousand of us have seen combat during the Events or against the Chinese. We can make knives as good as yours but we can also kill with our bare hands if we have to.

"We're offering you a choice: war or alliance. If you want war, we'll start today and we won't stop until you're on your knees or dead. If you agree to be our allies, we'll expect you to side with us against the bosses each and every time. And your men won't be permitted to work as stoolies or warders or accept any special privileges without my express permission. It's as simple as that: war or alliance. What will it be?"

Brancato looked at Skinner and then at Ramon and Jabril and was silent for nearly half a minute before he replied.

"Perhaps there has been a misunderstanding here. My men are no friends of the bosses. The way I see it, it's a very natural thing for my men to work with yours. Count us in."

CHAPTER 23

"Revolution is not a dinner party, not an essay, nor a painting, nor a piece of embroidery; it cannot be advanced softly, gradually, carefully, considerately, respectfully, politely, plainly and modestly. A revolution is an insurrection, an act of violence by which one class overthrows another."

—Mao Zedong

Sunday, May 19
Day 1

To nearly everyone's surprise, three weeks after the May Day truce between politicals and thieves in Division 3, the peace was still intact. In every barracks, the criminals obeyed Brancato's command to refrain from their usual habit of extorting our food, stealing our pitiful belongings, bullying us around, picking fights, raping the weak, and colluding with guards and warders to subvert our rules. At the same time, the Wart and his minions were perplexed by the thieves' refusal to accept positions as warders, foremen, kitchen workers, and orderlies.

At the worksites, the thieves cast aside their usual disdain for manual labor and pitched in as best they could despite their poor work habits and shortage of useful skills. Even the incorrigible slackers showed marked improvement after having their rations docked. And the stool pigeons among them came to have second thoughts about being seen with security officers when two of their number were found hanged outside the mess hall on their second Saturday at Kamas.

The criminals became acutely aware of their numerical inferiority and stayed close to their fellow thieves at worksites, barracks, mess halls, and latrines. Observing their leaders meeting daily with leaders of the politicals, they were cautious not to do anything that might provoke a confrontation. Some whispered that a faction of malcontents was coalescing under Randy Skinner with the aim of ousting Brancato and abrogating the truce with the politicals; however, most saw this as a move that could only lead to disaster for Skinner and his followers.

The younger thieves seemed to have the most difficult time observing the truce and playing the role of dutiful camp citizens. They expressed their high level of nervous energy and lack of self-control daily through stunts, pranks, and silly antics directed primarily at the warders and guards, since politicals were off limits. The juvenile thieves, or vandals, as we called them, amused themselves by hooting, whistling, heckling, snatching warders' caps, hiding during roll call, climbing the high wall separating Divisions 2 and 3, shooting out floodlights with slingshots and even teasing the sharpshooters in their watchtowers. They badgered the guards and warders incessantly to give them a peek at the women in Division 1 and would have clambered over the wall to see for themselves had armed sentries in the Service Yard not stood in their way.

The third Sunday after the thieves' arrival was heavily overcast with a bitter and penetrating wind. Division 3 was characteristically quiet before lunch. Most of us, politicals and thieves alike, had gone back to our bunks to sleep after breakfast. I joined Ralph Knopfler, Jerry Lee, and Brian Gaffney in the mess hall for lunch.

"It goes against nature," Knopfler remarked as I took my seat and stirred my oatmeal. "Politicals and criminals are like oil and water. The bosses brought in the thieves for only one reason: to torment us. Sooner or later they'll find a way to drive a wedge between us and we'll be at war."

"Ralph has it right," Gaffney added. "The Unionists have always had a soft spot for criminals. No matter how bad the crime, they get plea bargains and paroles while we get shot or sent to the mines. I can understand why the Unionists hate politicals but I've never quite understood why they're so fond of the thieves."

"It's a class thing, like the ant and the grasshopper," Jerry Lee suggested. "The Unionists identify with the grasshopper. They sing and dance all summer long and then, come winter, they hate being lectured about thrift and hard work by the damned ants who've stored up all the grain. A Unionist will always sympathize with the bum, the blowhard, and the black sheep and blame all his troubles on the mean, humorless uncaring ant. Remember how the Events started out here? Doesn't it all come down to the President-for-Life deciding to bleed the greedy Mormons white to care for the needy California refugees?"

"That may be so," Gaffney responded. "But from what I've seen, the criminals aren't nearly as fond of the Unionists as they are of the criminals. It's their nature to bite the hand that feeds them."

"Frankly, I think the Warden made a colossal mistake in bringing the thieves here," Knopfler concluded. "Once they came, it was inevitable that we would offer them a choice between war and alliance; that they would choose alliance; and that the alliance would turn the thieves back against the bosses. The only question is how long before the bosses catch on."

After lunch, I returned to the barracks for more sleep. For me, no amount of slumber was enough, given the long workdays. I had slept soundly for several hours when loud hoots and whistles outside awakened me. Then I heard shouts and cheers and noticed that the barracks had emptied.

Outside I found hundreds of prisoners on the barracks roofs watching a troop of young vandals climbing over the twelve-foot wall into the Division 2 yard. Some climbers used homemade ropes made from blankets and bed sheets while others stacked crates and furniture to make it to the top.

I spotted some makeshift wooden handholds someone had nailed onto the sides of Barracks C-14 and used them to climb onto the roof. From there I could see vandals and young politicals forming a loose skirmish line under the direction of leaders still perched atop the wall. On the leaders' command, the line charged across the Division 2 parade ground toward the far wall, beyond which lay the Service Yard. Most of the 2,000 prisoners in Division 2, which included many foreign-born politicals and POWs, watched cautiously from the edges of the parade ground. But a few of the younger and bolder prisoners from Division 2 joined the column and followed it toward the gate.

I asked some men on the roof what the vandals expected to accomplish. Some believed it was to plunder the food warehouses, while others were convinced that the attackers would not stop until they had reached the women's camp and satisfied their long-denied lust for the opposite sex.

The column came to a halt outside the sliding metal gate to the Service Yard and dissolved into small squads that searched for tools and materials with which to force the gate or create a breach in the wall.

Meanwhile, the warders of Division 2 had been alerted and were assembling outside the division's eastern gate, outfitted with helmets, plexiglass shields, and long wooden staves. At the same time, warders were circulating among the barracks in Division 3, urging politicals to rally to their aid.

I watched Grady and Mills approach Barracks C-14, run inside to deliver their appeal, then re-emerge crestfallen to address those of us on the roof.

"Listen up!" Grady barked. "The thieves are on their way to break into the women's camp! It could be your wife or sister they're after! Come on, we've got to stop them!"

"Go to hell! Can't you see we're busy!" shouted a thief who watched the events from the edge of the roof.

"Go there yourself and bend over for them if you're so worried about saving the women, you lousy prick!" another yelled.

Several naïve politicals stepped forward to aid the warders but were quickly pulled back by others who reminded them that a treaty was a treaty.

A few minutes later the eastern gate of Division 2 slid open and a platoon of warders and security troops in riot gear swarmed into the yard. Jack Whiting directed them from behind, shouting orders through a bullhorn. The troops advanced on a squad of prisoners who had found a steel I-beam and were ramming it rhythmically against a portion of the wall in an attempt to force a breach. As soon as the troops closed within a few paces, the prisoners dropped the beam and fled back toward the Division 3 wall.

The warders then intercepted the remnants of the original column. The vandals dispersed without attempting to defend themselves, relying on the rear guard sitting atop the dividing wall to cover their withdrawal with volleys of stones and brick fragments. The riot-clad troops and warders seemed content to stay beyond missile range and let the thieves clamber back over the wall.

The entire spectacle lasted little more than a half-hour before the last vandal was safely back in Division 3. As soon as the skirmish was over, the exterior gate of Division 2 reopened to discharge the security troops, leaving the division back in the hands of the warders and prisoners. But to our surprise, none of the warders made any attempt to punish those who had scaled the wall.

Never before at Kamas had prisoners attempted so audacious an act without paying dearly for the attempt. Since the attackers were thieves rather than politicals, the authorities seemed prepared to dismiss the episode as high-spirited mischief. Or perhaps they feared antagonizing the criminals and cementing their shaky alliance with the politicals. In keeping with this restraint, the warders maintained a low profile and dinner was served in the mess halls on time.

After dark the administration had scheduled a feature film to be shown in each of the two men's divisions, as had been the custom every Sunday during April and May. In Division 3, the film was to be the Depression-era classic, *The Grapes of Wrath*. We all assembled at the south end of the parade ground near a section of the wall that had been whitewashed to serve as a projection screen. The Joad family had scarcely made it across the border into California, however, when the distinctive hoots and shrill whistles of the vandals sounded behind us. One by one, we saw the flood lamps at the northern end of the yard wink out. I followed a rush of prisoners across the yard to find out what was afoot and decided to watch the events, as before, from the roof of Barracks C-14.

Now the sound of broken glass could be heard along the perimeter fence as the thieves used homemade slingshots to put out the floodlights that illuminated our end of the camp. From my rooftop I could see swarms of thieves and young politicals climb the stone wall and drop into Division 2 to resume their attack on the Service Yard. With no riot troops stationed in either of the men's divisions, the warders seemed to have calculated that the odds ran against them and remained on the sidelines. Seeing they were unopposed, one group of vandals took up steel rails and crowbars to force open the gate from Division 2 to the Service Yard while others used an I-beam as a battering ram to create a new breach in the wall. As soon as the vandals penetrated the Service Yard, their lead group went to work on the gate to the women's camp while others broke into food warehouses.

A small band of prisoners actually succeeded in breaking through to the women's division by the time we saw the sky light up with flares. Within moments after the first flare, a detachment of shock troops in helmets and body armor entered the Service Yard firing long bursts from their submachine guns, then shorter bursts as they pursued their quarry at shorter range. Strobe-like muzzle flashes erupted all over the yard. As fast as the troops drove the prisoners back toward Division 2, the prisoners scrambled through the wall carrying or dragging their wounded comrades behind them.

As soon as the guns fell silent, an orange signal flare soared into the sky and gave the cue for the shock troops to fan out in pursuit of any remaining prisoners. We watched with horror as they stopped to finish off every orange-clad figure they found. Then they opened the gate to let in a pair of flatbed trucks laden with sandbags. With the shooters standing watch, a dozen warders stacked sandbags into waist-high bunkers opposite the breaches in the wall. When their work was done, they withdrew and the gate closed behind them, leaving the troops in the Service Yard with the bodies of more than twenty fallen prisoners.

While the warders busied themselves building sandbag bunkers in the Service Yard, the vandals lost no time constructing their own barricades in Division 2, set back a few yards from the breaches they had created. They brought cinder blocks, stones, lumber, sheet metal, and whatever else they could find that might stop or deflect the submachine guns' small-caliber bullets. By the time the warders' sandbag bunkers were complete, so were the prisoners' barricades.

Divisions 2 and 3 were now interconnected. No warders remained in either division, having fled earlier to the safety of the Service Yard. As for any thieves who might have succeeded in making their way into the women's camp, their fate remained unknown to us. The wall separating Division 2 from the Service Yard had become the new confrontation line.

As the hours wore on, the camp slowly fell silent. Any prisoners not manning the barricades returned to their bunks. One after another the lights of each barracks blinked out except for the barracks in Division 2 where Georg Schuster set up an impromptu surgical theater that operated throughout the night.

CHAPTER 24

"Never, never, in a single instance, have our soldiers resorted to physical violence. Never have our revolutionaries resorted to torture."
—Fidel Castro, Cuban dictator

Monday, May 20 (Morning)
Day 2

Despite having remained on the roof until well after midnight to watch the standoff at the Service Yard wall, I was wide awake the next morning at the usual hour of five o'clock. There was a palpable excitement in the air. Had we really taken over the Service Yard? Had the guards actually opened fire on their working-class allies? We were now on strike for a third time—how would the warders respond to such a colossal provocation? I made my way to the latrines past huddled prisoners sitting on barracks doorsteps, posing the same questions to each other in low tones.

I decided to visit the barricades to see for myself. Entering Division 2 through the gap where the sliding iron gate had been torn off its tracks, I moved along the perimeter toward the wall that divided Division 2 from the Service Yard. As I passed the last row of barracks, I could see the shadowy outlines of barricades that the prisoners had erected opposite the gate to the Service Yard, now manned by squads of drowsy youths wielding picks and shovels and axe handles.

A few dozen prisoners still kept vigil on the rooftops. I climbed a makeshift ladder onto one of the barracks and found several acquaintances there, among them D.J. Schultz and Kevin Gaffney. Schultz was peering at the women's camp through binoculars—booty liberated from the guards the night before.

The submachine-gunners remained at their posts in the Service Yard, the tops of their helmets barely visible in the darkness behind sandbag bunkers. I counted twenty-seven orange-clad bodies sprawled throughout the yard amid dozens of orange caps with sewn-on number patches. In the watchtowers at each corner of the yard, guards glared at us from behind belt-fed machine guns.

From time to time a prisoner would shout a curse or an insult at a guard on the other side of the wall. Sometimes the guards shouted back. As the darkness slowly turned to dawn, more prisoners joined us on the rooftops and the taunts grew more heated. Several of the prisoners flung stones over the fence or sniped at the submachine-gunners with slingshots. One gunman, narrowly missing being struck in the face, fired a warning burst over our heads.

A few feet away from me, a toothless prisoner with silvery stubble covering his cheeks rose and waved his cap at the soldier who had fired the shots.

"Come on, you butcher! Shoot an old man! Come on, shoot your fathers and uncles! Finish us off!" He unzipped his coveralls to the waist and pulled up his filthy gray undershirt to reveal his emaciated ribs.

A younger man popped up from behind the barricade and repeated the old man's gesture. Someone else lobbed a brick over the wall and another submachine-gunner fired a warning burst into the air. I heard a shouted command behind me and spotted a squad of vandals moving forward to reinforce the barricades. Tension was building on both sides of the wall.

I heard the sound of hammering and sawing somewhere behind me and noticed a team of prisoners dismantling bunks to create shields from the mattresses and boards. At a maintenance shed along the western wall other prisoners fashioned spears from rakes and long-handled shovels.

As I watched them, I felt a hand on my shoulder. It was D.J. offering me his binoculars.

"Paul, take these and check out the action by the eastern gate of the women's camp. Zoom in on the men in orange and tell me what you see."

I adjusted the focus and saw four tall, strongly built men in orange caps and coveralls being led through the gate into the women's camp along with the same number of civilians carrying what looked like cameras and camera bags. Not far away was a line of six women prisoners, also in orange coveralls, seated cross-legged on the ground while a squad of black-helmeted warders stood over them with truncheons at the ready.

As if on command, the warders retreated behind the cameramen, leaving the women to their fate, while the men in orange approached the women at a trot and started pulling them about, ripping open their coveralls and dragging them toward the barracks. Moments later, while the civilian photographers took flash pictures from every angle, the warders swooped down inexplicably with raised nightsticks to defend the women.

"Here, you take them," I said, handing D.J. the binoculars. "I've seen enough."

It did not take long to apprehend that the beefy men in coveralls were not prisoners at all, but State Security apes dressed up as prisoners so that the camp authorities could stage photographs showing warders defending the women from assault. What better way for Jack Whiting and the Warden to justify firing at defenseless prisoners than to show how they turned back a raid on the women's camp by a mob of crazed rapists?

I watched the rest of the cynical set piece without binoculars. The impostors delivered real slaps, kicks, and punches to the women, while the warders pulled their punches against the impostors. The episode lasted two or three minutes and was over the moment the last camera flashed. While the warders and impostors congratulated each other with high fives and hearty slaps on the back, the six women lay motionless on the ground, too dazed, bruised, and terrified to move.

The warders escorted the photographers and phony prisoners out of the women's camp to a waiting van at the Division 2 gate. No sooner had they resealed the door to the women's camp and watched the van depart than they began dragging the bodies of prisoners killed the night before out the same gate and onto a waiting truck. Within a few minutes, the yard was cleared of bodies and the warders and submachine-gunners followed the truck outside, leaving only a pair of sandbag bunkers and dozens of orange caps behind.

None of us who observed this odd retreat could understand it. Was it a trick or a blunder? We held our breath while, one by one, as the remaining jeeps and vans parked outside the Service Yard's eastern gate started their engines and departed. The shock troops were gone. The Service Yard was ours.

For about five minutes, the vandals remained silent and distrustful behind their barricades. Then the first handful of curious prisoners approached the gate and peered cautiously into the yard. They saw the same thing we saw from the barracks roof: the darkened patches of dirt where prisoners had spilled their blood, the gaping doors to the food warehouses, the abandoned sandbag bunkers, and the scattered caps with number patches stitched front and back.

Then came the shouted hurrahs, ecstatic embraces, and crazed victory dances of the young vandals who reclaimed the territory they had abandoned the night before. Soon prisoners poured into the Service Yard from Division 2. Many headed straight for the food warehouses and re-emerged carrying entire cases of canned meats and vegetables. Others picked up crowbars and went to work on the chains and padlocks that resealed the gate to the women's camp.

Moments later that gate yielded. On the other side the prisoners found not only the throngs of women they had so long dreamed about, but also eight missing vandals who had entered the women's camp the night before. Apparently the female prisoners had given them shelter and held off the riot troops, even though the troops struck the women with rifle butts and dragged many of them off to the women's jail. But the troops had been forced to withdraw without capturing a single one of the men.

The liberation of the women's camp was like a miracle. Some still balked at the gate and before the breach in the stone wall, afraid to enter this forbidden place. At first only a few women ventured out toward the men's camp. Yet all three residential divisions were now in the prisoners' hands. No guards or warders were left anywhere in the Kamas camp save for the jail compound in Division 4.

The camp was still surrounded by electrified perimeter fences, of course, and by hundreds of armed troops brought in to reinforce the camp's warders and guards. The tower guards still trained their machine guns upon us. Escape remained out of the question. But there were no gunshots now, even when we hurled taunts and insults at our captors.

Within the boundaries of the camp, we were in control.

The euphoria of victory and the rush of freedom that swept over us at that moment cannot be understood by anyone who has not experienced the hopelessness of a corrective labor camp. In an instant, eight thousand slaves who had no sense of fellowship or unity became a single body, united by the act of seizing freedom for themselves and for each other. After being reduced to the crudest animal selfishness, the brotherhood of man had broken through.

Opinions varied widely on what we should do next. But none of us raised any objections to having seized our freedom. We had cast off our chains and, whatever happened, there could be no regrets. One day of freedom had somehow made all the suffering worthwhile.

CHAPTER 25

"The victor will never be asked if he told the truth."
—Adolph Hitler

Monday, May 20 (Evening)
Day 2

The mess hall stayed open continuously from breakfast through dinner. We went through the line as many times as it took to get our fill. Banners crafted from bed sheets proclaiming our newfound freedom unfurled from the mess hall rafters. Spirits remained high into the evening.

Around seven o'clock, Jerry Lee and I sat talking outside the old infirmary in the Service Yard when we heard a static crackle emerge from the government-controlled loudspeakers above us. The yard fell silent as we all awaited an announcement.

Warden Rocco declared a cease-fire and announced that a delegation from State Security would hold an open meeting in the Division 3 mess hall in exactly one hour. All were urged to attend. It was a bold stroke, as had been Rocco's offer to resolve the first strike. Though the warden's promises on that occasion had been broken and the next strike ended by force, many prisoners still hoped that his better side might prevail. That Rocco was willing to face the prisoners on their own turf also showed boldness, though not as much as a non-inmate might suppose. For, unlike ordinary convicts, political prisoners in the labor camps tended to be non-violent and a savvy warden like Rocco knew that we responded more favorably to persuasion than to ultimatums. If so, this might be his last chance to regain control before his superiors intervened.

Jerry Lee and I started for the mess hall right away, as the building could hold only about 2,000 prisoners. Along the way we saw Glenn Reineke and a half dozen barracks representatives approach the exterior gate of Division 2. My thoughts went back to our original one-day strike some two months before and how our representatives had been duped into accepting the Warden's empty promises in exchange for ending the strike. The stakes were far higher this time and it was vital that our representatives be less gullible. Reineke and his team of representatives would have to be firm with the Warden or face a backlash, not only from hard-liners among the politicals, but also from the thieves.

Three visitors entered the gates promptly at eight o'clock as the sun was sinking behind the western hills. Two wore black State Security uniforms and the third a business suit. None was armed and, by prior agreement, no bodyguards attended them. Instead, a mixed escort of unarmed politicals and thieves accompanied them to the seldom-used speaker's dais at the east end of the mess hall. George Perkins, an elected barracks representative with a centrist reputation, introduced the three visitors and announced that he would be moderator for a question-and-answer session.

The first of the visitors to be introduced was Brigadier General Jake Boscov, Director of the Corrective Labor Administration's Western Region, based in Denver. He was a short, deep-chested man in his mid-fifties with a square jaw and a ferocious demeanor. The second was Major General Gil Hardesty, from the Operations Division at State Security Department Headquarters in Washington. He was tall and lean, rigid of posture, and had chilling blue eyes set in a hatchet-like face. The third visitor was a small, owlish man with a neatly trimmed black mustache and gold-rimmed glasses dressed in a well-tailored charcoal suit. He was introduced as Kenneth Cronin, Director of the Corrective Labor

Administration. All were said to be former devotees of the late William Barry who had somehow escaped the anti-Barry purge.

Perkins opened the session by commenting that our visitors had come to Kamas to conduct a fact-finding mission into prisoner grievances and camp conditions.

Perkins posed the first question.

"How much do you gentlemen know about Kamas? I mean, have you been here before? Do you receive periodic reports about what happens here?"

Boscov took the microphone and answered the question in a surprisingly civil tone.

"Of course we do. I've visited your camp several times. Since I'm based in Denver, I stay in close touch with Warden Rocco and I'm well aware of the incidents that have taken place over the past few months. We've made it a top priority to find out what's been going on at Kamas."

An angry voice boomed out from the back without waiting to be recognized.

"If you knew about the strikes, then why have our demands been ignored? And why did the Warden go back on his promises once we returned to work?"

Cronin took the microphone and gazed calmly out at the unfriendly audience of shaven-headed prisoners.

"I, for one, have read your list of demands and find them quite reasonable."

Uneasy shuffling of feet and mumbling among the audience made it quite clear that the prisoners were not ready to accept this.

Perkins recognized an agitated prisoner in the front ranks.

"What about the shootings? What will you do to punish the guards who've been murdering our men?"

"Those found responsible will be held to account, I can assure you," Cronin answered. "Unprovoked shootings will not be tolerated."

A full-figured woman of about forty with a round, tomboyish face stood to speak. Jerry Lee whispered to me that this was Libby Bertrand, chief representative of the women's camp. She had been arrested for writing a letter to the President-for-Life objecting to his ruinous education reforms. Not long after her arrest her husband suffered a fatal heart attack and her four young sons were dispatched to a state orphanage.

"Why did the troops beat our women last night?" she demanded. "Do your regulations permit guards to bash unarmed women with rifle butts and clubs?"

General Hardesty leaned over to speak to Cronin and the microphone picked up his words.

"That can't be true," he insisted.

"Then please allow me to show you their injuries, General," Bertrand rejoined. She turned around and gestured for a group of her fellow prisoners to rise. Six women found their way to the dais. As they passed close by I could see the bruises on their faces, necks, and exposed arms.

The visitors examined each woman in turn and exchanged grave looks.

"I assure you this will be investigated," Cronin promised.

"Investigated, my eye!" Bertrand retorted. "The men who did this are beasts and ought to be fired immediately. You can easily find out who they are. Your own men photographed the whole thing as it happened. Just do it and tell us when it's done!"

Cronin ignored her outburst. Perkins called for more questions.

"How about taking the locks off the barracks doors?" an older man proposed.

"Fair enough," Boscov answered amiably. "We've done it in other camps. They may take a while to remove, but in the meantime I'll tell the warders to stop locking them."

"Take the numbers off our uniforms! Call us by our names, for God's sake!" a hollow-eyed skeleton proclaimed.

"I believe we can do that. Jake, that's doable, isn't it?" Hardesty inquired.

Boscov nodded agreeably.

"Let the gates between camp divisions stay open," a young man shouted from the rear of the mess hall. "We ought to be able to mix with each other."

Boscov and Cronin exchanged amused looks.

"Okay, my friend, mix as much as you like!" Cronin agreed. "Let the interior gates stay open."

There was a pause as we prisoners struggled to comprehend all that the visiting officials had conceded.

Jerry Lee said under his breath, "Quick, Paul, think of something else while we've got them on the run."

A sonorous voice demanded attention from the back.

"Yo! Perkins! We've got a brother here who wants to say something."

The speaker and another young black prisoner raised a third man by his shoulders. It was Ben Jackson, even weaker and thinner than I had seen him in March when he had told Reineke and me about his dreams. The prisoners fell silent as if in deference to his delicate condition.

"You've made us a slew of promises tonight," Ben said in a high clear voice upon gaining his feet. "General Hardesty, are you fully empowered to speak for your Department and to see to it that these promises are kept?"

Hardesty leaned over and spoke into the microphone.

"Absolutely. Among the three of us, we have full authority to carry out all of the changes we've talked about."

"Well, so far this year, including last night, I've counted over sixty unarmed prisoners shot in cold blood by your men. Tell me, General, if the Department, in its great wisdom, ordered you to shoot another sixty of us tomorrow, would you carry out that order?"

Hardesty was silent. Having risen to the rank of general officer under William Barry, he understood that no order from Headquarters could be ignored. If he said yes, there could be little doubt that his answer would find its way back to Washington and would be waiting in his personnel file for the day when someone wanted his head on a platter. But if he said no, he would destroy his credibility with the prisoners.

"Ken, would you like to take that one?" Hardesty asked.

"I make it a rule not to answer hypothetical questions, Mr....."

"Jackson. Ben Jackson," Ben replied boldly. "I kind of figured you'd want to know my name. But I'm not worried about that. I'm pretty much a goner already. Besides, Mr. Cronin, I think I know your answer."

The visitors made no reply. They'd shoot again and we all knew it.

Perkins called for more questions. There were none.

"So what if they're lying?" one man commented heedlessly as we were leaving the mess hall. "We got what we wanted. We raised hell for a couple days and now we'll have to pay for it. Let's take our lumps and get on with it."

Another dismissed the meeting as a diversionary tactic and expected a full-scale attack in the morning.

But most of the prisoners, I sensed, lacked the heart and mind to question their well-dressed, well-spoken superiors. As they had when the President-for-Life seized power, most seemed to accept at face value whatever the bosses told them.

On our way back to the barracks I griped to Jerry Lee about the credulous majority. How could they fall for the same trick time after time?

"Don't be hard on the weak-minded, Paul," Jerry Lee answered. "Blind faith is the only thing that keeps them going. After every disappointment they've got to raise a fresh batch of it or they'll soon be goners."

"Yeah, but if they keep putting their faith in men like Cronin and Boscov, we'll all be goners," I replied.

CHAPTER 26

"Sometimes democracy must be bathed in blood."
—Augusto Pinochet, Chilean dictator

Tuesday, May 21
Day 3

By morning my pessimism seemed amply justified. The conversations I overheard outside the mess hall indicated that most prisoners favored an immediate return to work. The fact that nearly everyone went back to his barracks that night instead of manning the barricades confirmed it. Though many of us doubted the visitors' promises, our misgivings were not sufficient to outweigh our need to believe that things might somehow get better.

My fellow politicals in Division 3 appeared nervous at roll call, just as we had been before the two earlier strikes. Through the open gate we could see that the men in Division 2 looked equally on guard. The unusually high number of men lining up for sick bay was a further sign of tension. Then George Perkins arrived to announce that our elected representatives had reached a settlement in a closed session with Director Cronin and generals Hardesty and Boscov that called for all prisoners to return to work. Since I was not an elected representative, I had no right to attend. Still, I felt disappointed that Reineke had not found a way to include me and resorted to rationalizing that he had not wanted to put anyone at risk who had not consented to it by standing for election.

With Perkins's announcement, tension among the prisoners slowly drained away and the usual submissive mask reappeared on most faces. Except for the hard-liners, who clenched their teeth and quietly vowed to resist.

Any palpable signs that we might have made a terrible mistake by caving in to authority did not appear until we began our march out the camp gate to the recycling site. Following not far behind was a column of three or four hundred female prisoners, a rare appearance. Additional columns of women were led toward the other worksites, as well. With the apparent exceptions of the jails and dispensaries, it seemed the entire camp was being evacuated. Later, as we climbed a hill that gave us an overview of the camp, we spotted a procession of heavy trucks waiting to enter Kamas from the opposite gate.

At the time, I didn't give much thought to the trucks because I was fast approaching the spot along the roadside where I was to leave a brick fragment with a concealed message for Helen Sigler. From the moment we left the camp gate, my attention had been focused on the guards, warders, and attack dogs that marched alongside us. Today the guards were positioned at close intervals of twenty yards along the column. As luck would have it, the cloud of dust we kicked up as we trudged along the dirt road hampered their vision.

I unzipped my coveralls a few inches, inserted my hand as if to scratch my chest and palmed the brick. The nearest guard was fifteen yards ahead of me. I faked a stumble over an imaginary rock and, as I bent down, let the brick roll off to the edge of the road as I had practiced dozens of times before. If anyone had been watching, I doubted he would have seen a thing.

Our arrival at the recycling site was uneventful except for the close attention we paid to the approaching women. Our spirits soared at the prospect that they might be assigned to work with us. Our hopes were quickly dashed, however, when a warder announced that the women would be doing cleanup duty in areas emptied in advance of all male prisoners.

The moment we arrived at the brickyard, I scanned the strip along the perimeter fence where Sigler's widow had agreed to toss a hollowed-out stick overnight with her coded message. As I carried my load between the brick pile and the pallet yard, I looked for a stick of a particular size and shape. I found it on my third trip to the pallets, tossed it into my hod and a few moments later slipped it inside my coveralls. The rest of the morning went by slowly as I speculated about what I might learn when I decoded the message secreted inside.

After lunch, the work team in the neighboring section of the brickyard withdrew and was replaced by a platoon of women who set about gathering trash. At the time, I was teamed up with a young Mexican-American car thief named Jimmy Vega to strap clay bricks into bundles using a steel banding device. As it happened, both of us were paying more attention to the women than to our work and failed to notice a defective fastener that caused the steel band to snap open, slicing into both my hands and tearing a deep gash in Jimmy's cheek and temple. The foreman, seeing blood gushing from our wounds, called for guards to drive us to the camp infirmary.

I have always reacted badly to the sight of my own blood. As I watched the bloodstain soak through the rag the foreman had given me to wrap around my hands, I felt increasingly light-headed and had to take deep breaths to keep from passing out. While Vega held his rolled-up undershirt against his bloody face and waited stoically for our ride to end, I gazed out the window to find something—anything—that would take my mind off my wounds. By the time we came within a few hundred yards of camp I had found it and suddenly understood why I had seen trucks entering the camp the moment we left.

For during our brief absence the camp had become a beehive of activity. The clever officials of the Corrective Labor Administration apparently had spared no pains to restore the damage we had done to the camp the night before. Every officer, guard, warder, and contract worker must have been pressed into service to prepare the camp for our return. As we learned later, security men who had lost the habit of manual labor years ago pushed wheelbarrows and carried hods. The more skilled among them took up trowels or hammers. Skilled tradesmen arrived from nearby military units and civilian workshops to repair metal gates and to change locks. Men in hydraulic cherry pickers replaced bulbs in broken flood lamps and covered them with wire cages.

As we drove the short distance from the camp's outer perimeter into the Service Yard the extent of their work became more impressive. The breaches in the walls were largely bricked shut. Prohibited zones were being marked with lime twenty feet from each wall. Precast concrete fence posts had been installed along the perimeters of the prohibited zones and barbed wire strung between them. Sandbag bunkers were being built at strategic spots around the yard. It was remarkable what wonders these men could achieve when they knew the brass was watching.

The guards who had driven Vega and me into camp paid no attention to the construction and made no attempt to conceal any of it from us. They led us into the crowded waiting room of the old infirmary, stayed long enough for the receptionist to sign us in, and then left. After a while the nurses admitted us into the treatment area and directed each of us to take a seat on an examining table.

Paramedics appeared a few minutes later to disinfect our wounds and stitch them up—without the luxury of anesthesia. I marveled at Jimmy's fortitude as he endured painful stitches to his face. By the time my own wounds had been stitched and dressed, I was a nervous wreck. Once they finished, however, I had the consolation of knowing that, for many days to come, my injured hands would exempt me from virtually all manual labor. Jimmy would be lucky if he didn't have to return to the brickyard the same afternoon.

Back in the waiting room we learned that no one would be admitted back into the yard until after dinner. Since dinner was at least three hours away, Vega and I looked for a place to sit. We found two chairs near the admitting desk.

"You boys waiting to be treated?" asked the raw-boned man in his mid-fifties seated next to me. He had the suntanned, leathery face of a cowboy and a drawl to match.

"Nope. Done already," I answered. "How about you?"

"They worked on me this morning."

He had gauze dressings on his forehead, nose, and neck.

"Melanomas," he continued, anticipating my question. "Malignant. I don't even want to know where they've spread. I suppose I'll feel a lump somewhere one of these days and then it'll be downhill fast."

"Well, if you don't want to die of cancer, there are plenty of other possibilities around here," I replied. "I'm Paul Wagner. This is my partner, Jimmy."

"Earl Cunningham. What are you in for?"

"Seditious conspiracy," I replied. "A fiver. And you?"

"Insurrection, treason, conspiracy, serving a foreign power. Take your pick. I've got a lifetime, no-cut contract."

"What did you do to get them so pissed off at you?"

"I emigrated," Cunningham answered. "Then I came back and fought with the partisans. There's more, but I won't bore you."

"Wow. How long have you been here?" I asked.

"Four years. My wife and I and my oldest son were in Mexico for a meeting when the Mexicans signed their secret treaty with the Unionists. We never knew what hit us. The Federales arrested us at our hotel. The next day I was in chains on a rendition flight to Denver."

"What about your wife and son?"

"The last I saw my wife she was on the same plane, drugged out of her mind. My son died during our first week in Colorado."

"I'm sorry," I said.

"You know, Paul, you're the only person who's said 'sorry' to me in years. I'd almost forgotten the word existed."

"It must be the effects of being a free man for a day. Funny how civilization starts to creep back in."

We both fell silent for a moment as we thought of the extraordinary events of the past two days.

"I don't know about you, Paul, but I want it back real bad," Cunningham went on. "Now that I've tasted freedom again, I'd rather die than go back to the mines."

"You might just get your wish," I told him. "The next time we take them on they're likely to turn this place into a free fire zone."

"I don't care. Watching those kids bust into the Service Yard taught me something important. By God, the next time they head for the wall, I'm going with them. I don't care how far I get. So long as I'm facing the enemy I'll feel like I died a free man."

Earl looked past me toward Jimmy Vega, who had started paying attention to Earl when his speech became impassioned.

"So, Jimmy boy, what do you say?" he asked the Mexican. "Do we go again?"

"You bet," Jimmy replied. "We took them twice. We can take them again."

Little more was said among the three of us until they brought us our soup, bread, and tea at about seven o'clock. When we had finished our food and were waiting to be released, Earl turned to me one more time.

"Do you think this country can ever go back to what it was before?"

"Someday," I replied. "It may take a generation or two, but I think we can get over Unionism, given enough time."

Earl shook his head and pressed his lips together.

"Well, I don't. I used to think so, but not anymore."

"Fortunately, civilization is a renewable resource," I said. "It just doesn't look that way right now because there's such a shortage of it."

"And the Unionists are doing their best to stamp it out," he countered.

"Let them try," I said. "They're not that strong."

I was already back in my bunk when the rest of the prisoners returned from work. They had been held at their worksites a half-hour longer than usual and had not objected to being herded straight to the mess hall for dinner. Nor did they appear to have given it much thought when they were escorted straight from the mess hall to their barracks, where the doors were promptly padlocked.

But word about the repairs traveled fast. The meeting, the concessions, the cajoling, had all been a ruse to enable the DSS to get us out of the camp long enough to beef up its physical security. The crackdown had already begun.

Ironically, it was the thieves who expressed the greatest outrage at the treachery. For the next two hours the vandals huddled in their corner of the barracks plotting their counteroffensive. Some of the more hotheaded young politicals joined them. As soon as the time came for lights out, the group sprang into action.

The vandals' first act was to remove our barracks door from its hinges. Within moments we heard the thieves' long-drawn whistles shrilling throughout Division 3. Whistles from Division 2 came in response. Before long the whistling turned into a blood-chilling chorus. The warders who patrolled the camp in threes or fours took fright and ran for the gates. At first the guards refused to let them out, but when they noticed the warders being pursued by packs of savage prisoners, they relented. Within an hour after lights-out, all warders or guards had left Divisions 2 or 3. The prisoners swarmed into the camp yards but this time it wasn't just the thieves who raised the battle cry.

Still the vandals faced the same problem they had faced on Sunday: a wall divided their forces in two. The first time they scaled the wall, the guards had tolerated it. But this time, when the first wave of rebels approached the newly marked prohibited zone, the tower guards loosed a torrent of machine-gun fire upon them. The gunfire killed a half dozen vandals and left at least as many wounded.

The vandals wasted no time. They aimed their slingshots at the floodlights as before. With better planning and more practice, they needed even less time to knock out all the floodlights within their range, despite the protective cages. The towers responded by releasing illumination flares. The tower gunners had also taken the precaution of alternating one tracer round with every five conventional machine-gun rounds to better guide their aim.

But the prisoners had an answer to this as well. They had discovered a pair of uniformed escort guards left behind in Division 3 and tied them to a mess hall table as hostages. They then pushed the table toward the wall flanked by other mess tables while the guards screamed to their comrades not to shoot. The firing ceased.

Meanwhile, the prisoners breached the barbed wire surrounding the boundary zone and used shovels that they had concealed about the camp the night before to dig a trench under the wall. Working both sides of the wall at once and using hostages for cover, they shoveled in relays, then formed teams to scrape away the loose dirt and stone with kitchen knives and mess tins. By the time the guards had sought and received permission to resume firing, the trenches were deep enough and enough tables were stacked around those who were digging to shield them from view. By now, the prisoners also had the advantage of enlisting scores of seasoned combat veterans who were accustomed to digging trenches even under heavy fire.

In little more than an hour, the first trench connecting Divisions 2 and 3 was complete and a second was underway in the semi-darkness. Both entrenching teams now began the task of burrowing their way into the Service Yard, which was held once again by a platoon of Tommy gunners with support from machine-gun crews in the watchtowers. To help cover their mates, the prisoners kept up a barrage of slingshot fire against the towers as well as a hail of stones and bricks tossed over the wall at the Tommy gunners. Before long, the prisoners had three separate trenches in progress along the wall and were distributing knives to those who waited to attack the submachine-gunners from the completed trenches. A staff team of experienced infantry officers and non-coms planned the assault while the troops deepened the trenches.

As it happened, no assault was required to dislodge the Tommy gunners. The bosses, apparently having weighed the likelihood that prisoners might overrun the troops and turn their captured weapons against the watchtowers, ordered the tower guards to hold their fire while the armed troops withdrew from the Service Yard.

I watched all this from the same barracks roof in Division 2 where I had sat two nights before. As soon as the east gate shut behind the submachine-gunners, we let out a great shout that spread throughout the compound. For there was hardly a man or woman in the Kamas camp who was not involved somehow in supporting the action or who did not cheer it on from the sidelines. A single orange cap tossed into the air became a swarm of caps. When the caps hit the ground, we tore off the number patches from front and back and trampled them in the dust.

As soon as the trenches into the Service Yard were complete, slingshot marksmen and an archer with an improvised bow and arrows sprinted to the safety of the sandbag bunkers to complete the extinction of the surrounding floodlights. Then the vanguard of the entrenching team moved forward yet again and burrowed under the wall to the women's camp while other prisoners set about dismantling the interior gates. Still others broke into the tool sheds and took up picks and crowbars to help finish the job of dismantling boundary fences, reopening aboveground breaches in the interior walls, and deepening the trenches. Within a few short hours, the entire day's labor by the camp authorities and their collaborators had been nearly undone.

The second liberation of the women's camp was no less triumphant than the first. Men and women embraced and searched for loved ones as they had two days before. I saw many couples come together across the division boundaries and linger in the Service Yard as if to prolong that initial sense of reunion.

But this time the women's camp was not the last section of the camp remaining to be liberated. At the opposite end of the compound, in Division 4, the men's jail was still in government hands. The leaders of the assault on the Service Yard reassembled their men and called on them to follow to the Division 4 gate. After taking the precaution of erecting a barrier of mess hall tables to protect them against machine-gun fire from the watchtowers, they set to work dismantling the gate and opening a breach in the wall using steel girders as battering rams.

Seeing the prisoners on the way and concluding that resistance would not be worth the risk, the warders and guards in Division 4 fled out the east gate, leaving the jailed prisoners in their cells. I was among the first non-combatants to follow the assault team into the jail compound and witness the release of the prisoners held there. Among them was Colonel Mitchell Majors, the man Glenn Reineke had mentioned to me some days before. Several Marines who had once served with Majors embraced the Colonel and shared the honor of leading him out of captivity.

Before leaving the jail compound, I also took the opportunity to visit the isolator cell where I had spent the longest week of my life and the interrogation room where Jack Whiting had attempted to recruit me as an informant. Depression and fear engulfed me and I was sure I could not keep my sanity if I were ever sent there again. Later I heard that several former denizens of the isolator went on a rampage that night and wrecked what little could be destroyed in that accursed building.

I stayed outdoors until sunrise, wandering from one end of the camp to the other, enjoying this unparalleled fourth uprising in ten weeks. Three times we had turned our backs on freedom and returned voluntarily to captivity. Why had we treated this rare privilege so casually? And having cast it aside, why had we continued to rebel?

What were we to do now that we had recaptured our prize? Place our faith in the empty promises of authority and be cheated yet again? Or surrender and take our punishment bravely?

One thing was clear: whether we accepted it today or after enjoying a week or a month of freedom, the punishment would be equally cruel. So why not wait and enjoy our freedom a while longer?

CHAPTER 27

"Power gradually extirpates from the mind every humane and gentle virtue."
—Edmund Burke

Wednesday, May 22
Day 4

Dawn broke over a sleepless and feverish camp. Like many, I stayed outdoors until breakfast and then returned to my bunk for a few hours of sleep. When I awoke, I saw a Kamas that scarcely resembled the painstakingly reconditioned camp of the evening before.

The parade grounds were littered with stones, bricks, number patches, and shards of glass from shattered flood lamps. Overturned mess tables lay scattered on both sides of the interior walls, hiding the tangled strands of barbed wire that only hours before had spanned concrete fence posts. Makeshift banners hung from barracks roofs proclaiming the Kamas Free State.

Prisoners no longer marched in formation or even followed marked paths as they moved freely from one division to another. Some independent-minded souls, having discovered storerooms where the civilian clothes of past and present prisoners were kept, selected colorful new outfits. The dusty brown camp with its overtones of coverall orange took on entirely new colors. Some of the grim faces softened into kind smiles.

I watched men who had been last-leggers only days earlier approach the breaches in the interior walls, look around timidly, and cast questioning glances at those nearby. How could it be that nobody shouted at them and they no longer needed to duck blows or dodge kicks? The sudden changes felt unreal, as if perceived in a daydream. How often we had been tricked by brittle dreams that shattered when the camp siren wailed or the warder's whistle blew. We repeated the word—*freedom*—again and again without grasping its meaning and without realizing how little of it we had wrested from our captors.

The sudden relaxation of tension after years of the most extreme suspense made us go slack with relief. Through the outer perimeter wire I could see early wildflowers in bloom. Yet in the moment I had only the faintest appreciation of them. Not long after, I overheard two middle-aged politicals in conversation along the path to the latrines. One took the other aide and said discreetly, 'Tell me, were you pleased this morning?' The other, with an expression of shame, replied, 'To be honest, no!'

It seemed that those of us who had spent any appreciable time in the camps had lost the ability to feel pleased and would have to relearn it slowly. Few dared dream then that our peculiar blend of liberty and bondage would last for weeks rather than days. But others still saw only the machine-gunners, the barbed wire and the walls and denied that we had won any freedom at all.

It is man's good fortune that the body has fewer inhibitions than the mind. What prisoners wanted to do most on the first day of their self-proclaimed liberation was to eat, sleep, and talk. It is remarkable what prodigious quantities a person can eat when his diet has been kept at or below the subsistence level for months on end. Now that prisoners ran the mess hall with no official supervision, they set no limits on how many times a man could pass through the line. Limits also no longer existed on what one could say without fear of betrayal by stool pigeons. On this first day of comparative freedom, some prisoners, feeling an irresistible urge to speak, talked for hours at a time. And, of course, we all slept as much as we possibly could.

Except for prisoners who had spent only a brief time in captivity, the sexual urge was generally absent due to exhaustion. Even among the thieves, there had been relatively little sexual activity at Kamas. But now women looked at men and men looked at women and they took each other by the hand. Some couples, both married and unmarried, who had corresponded inside the camp through ingenious and surreptitious methods, met at last. Religious girls whose weddings *in absentia* had been solemnized by priests and rabbis on other side of the wall now saw their lawfully wedded husbands for the first time.

For the spiritually inclined, our newly won freedom was particularly significant. For first time in years, no one sought to prevent the faithful from meeting in prayer. The sects most heavily represented in camp felt themselves singularly blessed: Catholics, Orthodox Jews, Seventh Day Adventists, Jehovah's Witnesses, Amish, and the various born-again Pentecostal groups that burgeoned during the Events until the President-for-Life began his campaigns of religious persecution. Meanwhile, Buddhists, New Age mystics, and yoga practitioners caught up on their meditation.

It is a paradox of repressive dictatorships and totalitarian regimes that the one place where honest political debate can truly thrive is the penal camp. Kamas was no different. Evenings in any barracks offered continuous discussion of politics, economics, military strategy, and foreign affairs. The only element lacking was campaigning for elective office.

By late morning we no longer lacked for that, either. Colonel Mitchell Majors and his campaign team appeared in Barracks C-14 shortly before lunch while I sat talking with Pete Murphy. We heard the sound of boots on the doorstep, then a loud knock on the door. Majors entered first, followed by George Perkins, Chuck Quayle, and two younger men whom I recognized from among the Colonel's liberators the night before.

Majors started down the center row of the barracks and reached out to shake hands with each man there.

"Mitch Majors, U.S. Marines," he announced as he fixed each man with a stern gaze from his bold blue eyes.

Majors was a thick-necked bulldog of a man who exuded determination and self-assurance. When my turn came to shake his hand and look him in the eye, my intuitive sense was of a forceful but one-dimensional personality. By now in his mid-50s, he seemed to be one of those men for whom being in charge is more important than the mission itself and for whom being a big man takes precedence over doing big things.

When he had shaken hands with each of us, he stood in the exact spot where Colonel Tracy of State Security had stood two months earlier to evict us.

"For the moment," Majors began in a ringing voice that carried easily to the far corners of the barracks, "last night's revolt has won us certain limited freedoms along with an opportunity to achieve limited reform. But we risk wasting this opportunity unless we decide very quickly on the direction our revolt should take.

"In my view, we can improve our lot only if we negotiate with the legitimate authorities to exchange our return to work for their meeting our demands. What should those demands be? That's for all of you to decide.

"But let me make one thing clear: the undercurrent of anti-Unionism running through this camp will be our undoing. If we adopt anti-Unionist slogans we'll be crushed without mercy. If we raise banners and broadcast speeches that reject the regime's authority over us, the regime will justify itself in shooting us like dogs. Our only chance lies in loyalty to the Union whether we like it or not."

Majors was adopting the political doctrine of the camp's orthodox Unionists, who condemned any attempts by prisoners to fight for our basic human rights, whether though strikes, revolts, petitions, or reprisals against government informants. They condoned virtually any form of repression, provided that it came from above, and rejected any use of force from below. The distinction seems to arise from the loyalists' unconditional acceptance of state power and their rejection of any power residing in the people themselves.

After the Colonel's brief speech, George Perkins announced that elections would be held after lunch for a new prisoners' commission. The commission would be charged with negotiating a return to work in exchange for reforms and would govern the camp until state authority was restored. Perkins urged us all to vote. Although he didn't say whether elections would be held for a chief commissioner, it was obvious that this was the real reason behind his and the Colonel's visit.

As soon as Majors and Perkins moved on to the next barracks I asked Pete Murphy to come outside for a walk.

"You're a military man, Pete. Do you know anything about Majors?"

"Not much," Murphy replied. "We both fought in Mexico for a while, but that's about all. We didn't cross paths very often when I was at the Pentagon."

"Reineke seems to think Majors could help us. Now that you've seen him in action, what do you think?"

"He's got drive, all right," Murphy replied. "But from what I hear, Majors was known more as a ticket-puncher than a combat leader. He's the kind of guy who does whatever his commanding officer asks, says whatever the brass wants to hear, and never lets his principles get in the way of a promotion."

"So who do you think he'll take his cues from now?" I asked. "Us or the Warden?"

"We may not know for a while. In public, I expect he'll make all the right moves. But if you're asking me if Majors is capable of selling us down the river, I wouldn't rule it out."

"I wonder if he himself knows."

We continued walking and arrived at the mess hall just as it opened for lunch. After downing a triple helping of stew I retired to the barracks to sleep. At about three o'clock I awoke to the sound of a voice on the camp loudspeaker system summoning all prisoners to elections for the new commission.

When I arrived, George Perkins was already at the microphone at the center of the dais, flanked by four other elected barracks representatives: Glenn Reineke, Pete Murphy, Chuck Quayle, and Ralph Knopfler. Perkins called for discussion, after which he said he would accept nominations for chief commissioner and for members of the commission at large.

Many prisoners rose to give their views about the goals of our revolt and the demands the commission should make, but the first speech of any real significance was the one that Colonel Majors delivered. His remarks repeated the stump speech he gave in the barracks but placed even greater weight on the dangers of pursuing an anti-Unionist line.

Majors was heckled by men expressing outrage against the regime that had trodden their lives into the mud, but each time someone interrupted him, the colonel grew more insistent:

"Anti-Unionism will be our death knell!" he declared. "State Security is out looking for an excuse to crush us, and anti-Unionist rhetoric gives them exactly what they want. We must not allow anyone to take advantage of this revolt to serve an extremist political agenda!"

Majors closed on a line of reasoning that, while reminiscent of the regime's determinist doctrines, was perceived as being so sensible that it helped win over many undecided prisoners.

"When a train takes you in the wrong direction," Majors explained, "the reasonable thing to do is to jump off, isn't it? But everyone knows you have to jump with the momentum of the train and not against it or you'll get hurt. The same principle applies to the momentum of history, which right now favors the Unionists. We have to move with the authorities and not against them if we want to achieve meaningful reforms."

After Majors, a number of rank-and-file prisoners took turns and then it was Reineke's time to speak.

"Just as each of us decides individually whether to participate in a strike or a revolt, each of us has to consider the principles he wants to be governed by. Now that we've thrown out the Unionist bosses, what sense is there in endorsing their discredited ideology? Why compromise our principled opposition to the Unionist dictatorship at the moment when we are strongest?

"Let's not forget why we rebelled in the first place. It's because we belong to a race of pioneers who must forever be opposed to any authoritarian system. We and the Unionists represent two irreconcilable classes, one representing the common right of humanity and the other the divine right of kings. Can we allow the State, under the false guise of democracy, to trample on the rights of its citizens to life, liberty, and the pursuit of happiness?

"For our own sake and that of our families, and for the sake of men and women in other labor camps across America, we must stand fast against the bosses. Though we may gain little by our resistance, we have already given up everything to gain this small measure of freedom. To stop resisting now would be to deny the very essence of who we are."

The prisoners fell silent and no one raised his hand to speak. Perkins took it upon himself to respond:

"Those are very high-sounding words, Glenn. But who will pay the price for them? The last time we went on strike, hundreds were sent off to the northern camps. Since Sunday we have lost dozens more in the fighting. We are still the ones behind the barbed wire, unarmed and at the mercy of the Warden's troops. Unless we compromise, what possible hope do we have of winning any reforms at all?

"It seems to me that the unreasoning hatred and obstructionism of men like you has been just as responsible for the nation's ruin as the Unionist regime's blunders. In today's society there is no place left for lone wolves and mavericks. We all depend on each other and have to work together to survive.

"I appeal to you and to those who support you: stop letting your vendetta against the Unionist Party stand in the way of a fair settlement of our grievances. This is our last chance; let's not squander it."

Perkins paused to make eye contact with Colonel Majors in the front row.

"Now, if there is no more discussion," he concluded, "let's move on to the elections."

Ralph Knopfler, Al Gallucci, and several others stood and raised their hands to speak but Perkins refused to recognize them.

Instead, he launched into a detailed explanation of how the elections would be conducted, as determined by the five representatives now seated at the dais. There were to be three elections: one to elect the chief commissioner; one to elect three commissioners representing each of the three camp divisions; and one to elect eight members at large, each assuming a distinct functional role. Nominations, including self-nominations, would be accepted from the floor.

As I had expected, few prisoners wanted to take on the risk or responsibility of serving on the commission. With few exceptions, only one candidate stepped forward for each office and, where more than one stepped forward, one candidate almost always declined in favor of the other. Each person who volunteered was someone already prominent in camp affairs and thus well known to the camp administration. Every prisoner knew that, when the time came for reprisals, the commissioners would be first to get the chop.

Some two hours later, every office was filled and the office holders approved by acclamation. The commission consisted of the following members:

Chief Commissioner: Mitchell Majors
Division 1 Representative: Libby Bertrand
Division 2 Representative: Georg Schuster
Division 3 Representative: Chuck Quayle
At-large representatives:
Security: Glenn Reineke
Defense: Pete Murphy
Information: Ralph Knopfler
Government Relations: George Perkins

Technical: Terry McIntyre

Food: Betty Shipley

When the voting was finished, Perkins formally relinquished his chairperson's duties to the new chief commissioner, whose first official act was to convene the commission at eight the next morning.

As soon as the general meeting was adjourned, I made my way to the dais to congratulate Reineke, Knopfler, and Murphy. By the time I reached Reineke, he was already tied up in a lively conversation with Knopfler and Gary Toth.

"It's high time you got some credit for the work you've been doing, Glenn," Toth remarked amiably. "But Security Commissioner sounds far too bland. Chief Vigilante would be more to my liking."

"Watch your step," Knopfler replied, only half in jest. "The Wart is going to be mighty jealous over this. He's not going to think Kamas is big enough for two security chiefs."

"Maybe if we tried another escape, he'd look the other way this time just to be rid of us," Toth joked.

Reineke and Knopfler smiled. But Toth suddenly turned pensive.

"You realize, Glenn," he cautioned, "that by accepting this position you have signed your own death warrant..."

"Maybe so," Reineke relied. "But the idea of dying doesn't bother me quite the way it used to."

"Now that doesn't sound like you at all," Toth replied with a skeptical look. "You've always had a stronger grip on life than anybody I know."

"It all depends what you mean by dying. If by dying you mean the loss of everything you love in life, I've already experienced that death. If you mean extreme physical pain, I've been there, too. If you mean banishment from society and consignment to oblivion, I don't see how I can be any deader than I am now. So let the bosses do their worst. I have nothing more to lose."

Reineke seemed totally at peace with himself at that moment. I allowed him to savor it before stepping forward to congratulate him on his election and shake his hand. Then I left him to confer with the other commissioners and headed back to the barracks to await dinner. It wasn't until I lay down in my bunk and closed my eyes that I remembered the coded message I had picked up the day before from Sigler's widow. It was still tucked in the lining of my boot. I reached under my mattress, found the paperback volume of the President-for-Life's memoirs that was the key to our book code and began deciphering.

The message began as follows:

MESSAGE SIX RECEIVED. HAVE PASSED YOUR INFORMATION TO FEMALE RELATIVES OF MALE PRISONERS. SPECIAL REQUESTS FOLLOW. FIRST IS TO LOCATE PRISONER PAUL CURTIN WAGNER, AGE 46. BORN PITTSBURGH PA. ARRESTED NOVEMBER 2022. REQUESTER IS WAGNER OLDER DAUGHTER LOCATED UTAH. WIFE AND YOUNGER DAUGHTER TAKEN INTO STATE CUSTODY. PLEASE LOCATE WAGNER BUT DO NOT NOTIFY HIM. SPECIAL CIRCUMSTANCES APPLY. SECOND IS...

I read no further.

CHAPTER 28

"It is true that liberty is precious...so precious that it must be rationed."
—V.I. Lenin

Wednesday, May 22
Day 4

The afternoon sun emerged from behind a blue-gray cloud and scattered its reflection across the wet pavement. Claire extended the stroller's gaily striped canopy to shade little Marie's eyes.

Martha and Claire and the stroller continued down the hill toward Reservoir Road until they passed the compound's guardhouse, then stopped at the crossing. .

"Keep this envelope in your backpack until you reach Helen's cabin," Martha instructed her as she handed Claire a sealed envelope. "If you're stopped at a security checkpoint along the way and someone makes you open it, tell them it's payment for some things Helen sold to me."

She gave Claire an affectionate smile and a quick hug before setting off with the stroller back up the hill.

It was not uncommon since the Events to encounter checkpoints along Heber's streets and surrounding highways. The entire Wasatch Front was still a Restricted Zone, studded with military installations and corrective labor camps. In addition to the town police, drivers were obliged to pull over for military police and State Security patrols.

Claire first spotted the checkpoint as she rounded a bend in Reservoir Road and came out from behind a row of poplar trees. Two jeeps were parked diagonally across the road where deep drainage ditches left the shoulders impassable, allowing room for only one car or small truck to pass down the center.

Claire kept walking. Two soldiers in red berets and camouflage dress watched her from beside the jeeps while two others waited behind them. As she approached she saw that all four had submachine guns slung over their shoulders.

The two soldiers standing beside the jeeps came forward to meet her. The taller of the two, a slim, dark-eyed youth with a neatly trimmed black mustache, asked her to remove her backpack for inspection. She handed it to him and he unzipped it on the open tailgate of one of the jeeps. He called out the identity of each item to his partner: water bottle, candy bar, cookies, plastic raincoat, folding umbrella, sealed white envelope.

"Where are you going, Miss?" the dark-eyed youth asked.

"To visit a friend of mine. Her cabin is in the woods up ahead."

"What's your friend's name?"

"Helen Sigler."

"Jeff, check the list," the dark-eyed soldier ordered his partner.

"Bingo. We have a hit," the shorter soldier declared excitedly after flipping through the dog-eared pages on his clipboard.

"May I inspect the letter?"

"Do you really have to?" Claire asked.

"Not unless you want us to take you to the command post."

"Okay, go ahead. Just don't lose anything," Claire replied anxiously. "I don't want to get in any trouble with Mrs. Chambers."

The soldier opened the envelope using a sinister-looking black dagger that he pulled from a sheath hanging upside down from his shoulder harness. He unfolded the letter, counted the money inside and described the contents of the envelope aloud.

"Envelope is addressed to 'Helen.' Contains a three-page letter, written on one side only. A pair of folded twenties inside. Nothing else unusual about it, as far as I can tell."

"Hand it back," his partner replied. "But take down her name and address."

With Claire watching, the dark-eyed soldier folded the money into the letter, tucked it all back inside the envelope and returned it to Claire's backpack.

"See, that wasn't so bad, now, was it?" the dark-eyed soldier teased.

"I guess not," Claire admitted. "May I leave now?"

"Go right ahead."

She took a step forward and stopped.

"Just what were you looking for, anyway?"

"Just doing our job, Miss. You'd be surprised what we find sometimes."

Claire felt a chill as the soldier gave her a closer look. She stepped past him, then quickened her pace for the rest of the trip to Helen's, as if crossing a graveyard after dark.

She arrived at Helen's door fifteen minutes later. Helen could see immediately that Claire was shaken and listened patiently while she told the story.

"Did the soldier keep anything that was in the envelope?" Helen asked after Claire had finished talking.

Claire shook her head.

"Did he hold the letter up to the light to look at it?"

"Nope. Didn't even read it."

"That's all there was to it?"

"Well, your name was on some kind of list they had on a clipboard. That's why they decided to open it in the first place. They wrote down my name, too."

Helen frowned and turned around abruptly to boil water for tea.

"Did I do something wrong?" Claire asked, sensing the change in Helen.

"No, dearest," Helen replied, still facing the stove. "You did just fine."

As soon as the tea was ready to pour, Helen carried the tray out to the living room and the two of them sat down to talk.

"So tell me, how is Marie doing?" Helen began with forced cheer.

"Marie's doing fine," Claire answered. "But Martha seems sad all the time. I catch her crying sometimes when I go to her room."

"Why do you think she's sad?"

"I hear her arguing with Doug often. And sometimes when he comes home at night he looks drunk. I stay out of his way when I see him like that. Martha avoids him, too. I know because the next morning I usually find her sleeping in the baby's room."

"Grown-ups go through tough stretches for a while and still manage to pull out of it okay. Do you think you can hang on a while longer?"

"I guess so," Claire answered. "But I miss my real family a whole lot. I'd give anything to see Mom and Dad and Louisa again."

Helen held out her arms for Claire to sit on her lap. Claire cried tears of longing for her family, tears she had not allowed herself to shed in front of Martha and Doug. Helen stroked her head and rocked her softly until the sobs let up, then took a handkerchief from her jacket pocket and wiped Claire's moist cheeks.

"Maybe it's time we talk about that, Claire. You see, I haven't been idle these last two and a half months. You may not recall, but the night you came to the cabin I found some papers in your jacket. I hid them because I was afraid they might cause problems for you. But one of them had your grandparents' address in England. I wrote to them and told them you were safe. I also told them what happened when you and your mother and sister tried to leave the country. I'm hoping we'll hear from them soon."

Claire tried to thank Helen, but the sobs came too quickly.

"I've also made some inquiries about your father. I expect to find out very soon whether he's at one of the camps in Utah. If he is, maybe your grandparents can do something to get your family back together again.

I know others have done it. The Unionists will break almost any rule of theirs if you're willing to pay in cash. But in the meantime, Claire, you need to be a good girl and keep working hard for Mrs. Chambers."

****

Claire took a different route home, one that Helen showed her along a deer path that crossed hillsides thick with scrub oak. She arrived shortly after five o'clock, just in time to start her evening chores.

"Claire, I have a special job for you tonight," Martha told her. "I'd like you to set the dining room table for five, using the good china and silver. I'll also need your help in serving and clearing."

"Sure, but how about Marie?" Claire asked.

"I'll have Rosa take care of her tonight. Serving dinner for Doug's guests is something only you and I can do. Now as soon as you finish setting the table, I'd like you to go upstairs and take a shower and put on that pretty long blue dress you picked out last week. I'll have an apron waiting for you in the kitchen when you're dressed."

When Doug came home with his guests, Claire recognized all but one. Apart from the Warden, she remembered General Boscov from Colorado and the odd little man with the Russian hat from Washington, Mr. Cronin. Doug introduced the last guest as Howard Barger from the Department of Justice. He was a short, stout, unhealthy-looking man whose pasty complexion and gray hair made him appear the oldest man in the room. His slightly confused expression, together with his off-center bow tie, frayed collar, and baggy corduroy suit, reminded Claire of an absent-minded professor she once saw in a movie.

The five men went directly to the dining room and served themselves drinks from the bar before taking their places at the table. After they had seated themselves, Doug suggested they go ahead and start eating since they all needed to retire early.

"We've been keeping heightened surveillance on all four camp divisions since last night," Doug began, in a brief situation report on the day's events in the camp. "At the moment it's still a stalemate. They can't get out but we can't get in without mounting a full-scale assault. The warehouses in the Service Yard contain enough food to keep the prisoners going for thirty to sixty days. We can cut off their power, but not their water, which comes from wells beneath the camp."

At this point General Boscov broke in.

"There are obviously some serious design problems with Kamas and other camps of the same vintage. This was clearly a disaster waiting to happen."

"I would agree with Jake on that," Doug continued. "But today, our focus has to be on the prisoners' plans and intentions. My personal assessment is that, the longer we wait to go in, the messier it will be. If the prisoners get accustomed to running loose, experience tells us that their resistance will stiffen. Delay will also give them time to analyze their situation and organize defenses. We have to force the issue quickly."

Boscov looked across the table at his boss, Kenneth Cronin, and drummed his forefinger on the linen tablecloth.

Boscov agreed. "If we let it go on, we'll face a nightmare of copycat mutinies."

"I assure you," Fred Rocco broke in, turning to Kenneth Cronin, "that from the moment the prisoners breached the walls we have done all we could with the limited resources on hand, starting with a complete overhaul of the perimeter. And for the past three days we've been requesting the resources and authority to cope with this mess. But until your arrival this afternoon, Director, Headquarters has been oddly silent."

"There's no need to be defensive, Warden," Cronin replied smoothly. "You're not on trial here."

Fred Rocco looked away and slowly laid down his fork.

"What the devil do you expect from Washington these days, Fred?" Howard Barger interrupted, throwing up his hands. "I can tell you right now the Attorney General won't want anything to do with this crazy revolt of yours, particularly now that you've brought non-political prisoners into the camp. Nor will anyone on the seventh floor at State Security. And don't even think of pulling strings with the Party Central Committee."

"That's all fine, Howard," the Warden replied, "but while we wait for Washington to untie our hands, we lose production days and risk defaulting on our contractual obligations to recycling customers."

The men looked up as Martha and Claire entered the dining room to clear their appetizer plates. Conversation stopped while the plates were removed and the men refilled their glasses.

"As I've said before, Warden," Boscov continued after the women had left the room, "why on earth do we need a decision from Washington before we act? When Bill Barry was Director, we faced this kind of thing dozens of times. We never let regulations hold us back then and we shouldn't now."

"Not so fast, General," Howard Barger broke in. "We're up to our ears in legal work with Kamas already. Somebody has to justify each and every one of the fatal shootings. Our people are having a devil of a time these days figuring out how to make it all appear legal."

"Gentlemen," Cronin interrupted. "What I would suggest is that you meet with the prisoners again tomorrow and do whatever is necessary to bring them back to work. Call up the Department's experts on hostage negotiations and find out how they do it. There's absolutely nothing original about any of this. What we need at the moment is determined action, delivered swiftly."

"That's precisely my point!" Boscov insisted. "If the President-for-Life were alive, we would have shot all 8,000 by now, just for fear he'd find out what had happened and accuse us of shirking! Now, I ask you, what if those days were to come back again? Which is better: to act and get a slap on the wrist or not act and get a bullet in the neck?"

"Jake, the days you describe are long gone and I don't see them coming back," Cronin replied calmly. "I can't authorize you to shoot a prisoner unless he attacks your men or attempts to escape or threatens the safety of the other prisoners."

Boscov was about to interrupt when Cronin continued.

"Now, as to the issue of an assault, begin planning for it in case all other methods fail. But, as I've said, let's try negotiating first. Put together a plan and a timetable. If Doug is correct, it may be weeks before you get all the action approvals you'll need. If you haven't jawboned the prisoners back to work by then, come back to me and I'll sign the order myself."

"Colonel Tracy and I have already done some preliminary planning," Doug volunteered. "The way I see it, the prime objective of the assault should be to subdue the prisoners quickly, with a minimum number of friendly casualties, and then to swap out the surviving prisoners for fresh ones so this won't happen again. Fred, would you agree?"

Fred Rocco swirled the red wine in his glass before answering.

"Nothing would make me happier than to ship all 8,000 to the Arctic Circle tomorrow," Rocco began. "But this is a production facility as well as a penal camp. If we ship out our foremen and our skilled craftsmen and our best workers in exchange for an entirely new crew, production will plummet.

"Now, if we do that, is someone going to lower our output quotas for us? And who's going to pay for the extra guards and the transport charges and the cost of the assault, not to mention the expense of rebuilding the camp? These things cost money."

"As I said, Warden, you aren't on trial here," Cronin repeated ominously.

"Ken, go easy on the Warden," Howard Barger interrupted with a forced smile. "Fred and his staff have had a perfectly miserable three days since this all started. If I'd gone through what they have, I'd be homicidal by now."

Cronin smiled coolly at both Barger and Rocco.

"The longer this revolt drags on, the harder our task will be. Which is why I've decided to set up a special task force here in Kamas with the sole objective of putting down the revolt. The leader of that task force, effective immediately, will be Doug Chambers."

Cronin nodded to Doug.

"From now on, Doug, I want you to report your plans and progress directly to me every week. What I'm looking for is one or two pages, as clear as possible, as vague as necessary. Request whatever resources you need and I'll back you up. Just get the job done."

Someone tapped a spoon against a wineglass.

"Let's all drink to Doug's success," Cronin proposed. "From now on, I'm going to hold Doug personally responsible for ending the revolt on the best possible terms."

Martha re-entered the dining room as the men held up their glasses to drink. She caught sight of Doug just as he reached across the table to shake Director Cronin's hand. In his eyes she detected a peculiar mixture of exhilaration and fear.

CHAPTER 29

"It is not rebellion itself which is noble but the demands it makes upon us."

—Albert Camus, The Plague

Thursday, May 23
Day 5

I lay on my bunk with eyes wide open through most of the night, listening to the sound of raindrops on the thin tarpaper roof. A constant stream of disturbing thoughts and feelings about my wife and daughters raced through my mind. For a long time I had assumed that all three would have succeeded in joining my wife's parents in England once their exit visas had been approved and the emigration tax paid. There had always been a risk that State Security might go back on their promises and revoke the exit visas, but as the weeks went by, I ceased to dwell on that and chose instead to believe that my wife and children were safe abroad.

The message from Helen Sigler filled my mind with the worst sorts of speculation that my wife might have landed in a camp and my children in a state orphanage or even a juvenile detention facility. The prospect of their being thrown in with criminals as brutal as the ones I had seen in the transit camps haunted me no matter how many times I tried to reason it away.

I sat on the doorstep outside the entrance to the mess hall and gazed at the sunrise. The early morning rain shower had moved on, leaving the sky clear and blue over the Kamas Valley. But above the mountains to the east, the horizon was alive with clouds of ever-changing shapes and colors, from bright orange to deep purple. The muddy camp yards, weather-beaten watchtowers, and rusty wire fences offered a stark contrast to the luminous sky and the puddles of rainwater reflecting the clouds' colors from below.

I sensed someone sit down quietly beside me.

"How beautiful the world can be," said a familiar voice. It was Al Gallucci.

I made no reply.

"I noticed you staring off into space yesterday, too," Gallucci continued. "I've never seen you so lost to the world. Is it something you'd like to talk about?"

"I had a message from the outside," I told him. "I thought my girls had left the country a year ago. Now looks like they never made it."

"Do you know that for sure?"

"No," I said. "But with the revolt, I won't be able to get any more messages in or out."

"Is there any way I can help?"

"Who knows," I said in despair. "I can't even think straight. One moment I feel guilty for leaving them behind; the next moment I want to bust out of here to find them. But I wouldn't know where to look for them if I could. I've even thought of running into the wire, though I know that would be stupid and wrong. It's driving me crazy thinking that my wife might be in some camp all because of me. And to think of my little girls..."

I couldn't bear to say aloud what I feared for them.

"I know what you mean, Paul. I've been there myself. I wish I could say the pain goes away, but it didn't for me."

"You're married?"

"Yes," Gallucci replied.

"Children?"

"Three teenagers," he said.

"Where are they?"

"The last I saw them, we were all in a police van on our way to an interrogation camp outside Atlanta."

"I'm terribly sorry," I said. "How do you manage to stay sane…?"

"Each man's destiny is different, Paul," Gallucci continued. "Sometimes it calls for action, sometimes a change in attitude, and sometimes simply suffering and acceptance. When it's suffering, you have to remember that your own pain is totally unique in the universe. Nobody can relieve you of it or suffer it in your place. It's the way you bear it that gives your life its special meaning.

"Dostoyevsky once wrote that there was only one thing that he dreaded: not to be worthy of his sufferings. The way I see it, what determines whether a man is worthy or not are the choices he makes. No matter how desperate the conditions, no matter how great the suffering, no one can deprive you of that last inner freedom to choose your attitude toward life."

Gallucci and I waited on the mess hall doorstep until it opened and we ate breakfast together. Afterward, I walked around the inner perimeter, observing the other prisoners and their adjustment to our new circumstances.

I soon discovered that freedom did not bring instant happiness to all the prisoners nor make them all better people. Some were unable to shake off the brutalizing influences of the warders even after the warders had been removed. These men became petty oppressors, instigating fights and bullying others and justifying their behavior by the punishments they themselves had endured.

Others became greedy, demanding more food, more space, more privileges than their rightful share, all to make up for past deprivations. One man was caught stealing cans of soup from a storeroom.

"Why are you denying me this?" he protested. "Hasn't enough been taken away from me? Arrested for no reason, my life ruined, and you would keep me from taking a few cans of soup?"

Still others became consumed with revenge. One prisoner rolled up his sleeve, thrust his right hand under a man's nose and swore to cut off the hand if he didn't drench it in blood the day the guards came back to attack us.

I was on my way back to the barracks when I came across Ralph Knopfler, who urged me to come with him to the first meeting of the camp commission at eight o'clock. The commission, he said, would face a formidable array of tasks and would need people with managerial experience to help them.

When we arrived at the mess hall, members of the commission were seated at two adjoining tables. Colonel Majors stood at the end of one of the tables, clipboard in hand, requesting a brief status report from each commissioner.

He called on several before turning to Pete Murphy.

"Major Murphy, how are your defenses coming along?" he asked.

"Fine, Sir. The improvements we proposed to the camp's fortifications are already underway."

Perkins raised his hand to speak.

"If I may speak to that, Colonel," Perkins interrupted, "I object strongly to the building of new fortifications. The camp authorities are almost certain to see them as a deliberate provocation. I propose that we defer building any new barricades at least until after Monday's negotiating session."

"Negotiations?" Reineke broke in. "I'm not aware of any negotiations between us and the administration. Are you, Colonel?"

"My apologies, but George is right," Majors replied sheepishly. "The Deputy Warden called me first thing this morning and asked that we receive a delegation Monday at ten. I was going to mention this later, but now that it's been brought to the floor, do I hear any objections?"

"No objections to hosting the delegation," Murphy broke in. "But Perkins is out of his cotton-picking mind if he wants to delay our fortifications by even one day. We need time to train our troops and prepare our weapons. Fortifications are our best deterrent to an early attack."

"I agree," Reineke replied. "Perhaps George wouldn't mind sticking to negotiating strategy and leave military strategy to us."

"Now that we've heard from both sides, Colonel," Perkins replied coolly, "what's your decision?"

"I'm going to give Major Murphy the benefit of the doubt on this one. The fortifications continue. But before we go on, George, is there anything else you'd like to add about the agenda for Monday's session?"

"There's no agenda," Perkins replied. "The other side plans on sending Doug Chambers, Jake Boscov, and one other. We can bring whomever we like. Ten o'clock Monday in the women's mess."

"Thank you, George," Majors continued. "I hope all of you will find time to attend. Major Murphy, do you have anything else to add on military matters?"

Murphy declined.

"Anything else on security?"

"No, Sir," Reineke answered.

"Technical is next. What do you have for us, Terry?"

Terry McIntyre was a brilliant and very good-natured man of about fifty who had been a prominent consulting engineer before his arrest. At Kamas he had made the Service Yard workshops a haven for the brightest technical minds in the camp.

"Our top priority right now is to figure out how to produce weaponry that the Military Department can use," McIntyre explained. "The problem is that our electrical current comes from outside. If the Warden cuts off our juice, most of the equipment in the workshops won't function. I've put a task force to work on alternatives, but at this point, I can't be terribly optimistic."

"Give it all you've got," Colonel Majors urged. "And keep me posted. Now, how about medical? Dr. Schuster?"

"We will continue to operate the infirmary as before," the surgeon began. "But the administration has stopped delivering any new medical supplies. I expect this to create shortages within a matter of days. We will adjust our triage rules accordingly."

"Betty, what about the food supply?"

Betty Shipley was an elegant woman in her mid-forties who had been a senior administrator at a large Philadelphia hospital before she was arrested for refusing to dismiss a group of prominent surgeons who had publicly criticized the deterioration in medical care under the Unionist regime.

"Fortunately for us, the warehouses in the Service Yard contain enough food to keep us all fed for another thirty to sixty days at our current rate of consumption," Shipley reported. "Unless the commission objects, I've decided to leave the standard rations unchanged. Now that we're using an honest measure and the warders aren't around to pilfer, portions will be noticeably larger."

"Excellent," Majors said. "I propose we adjourn until tomorrow at eight so that I can meet individually with as many of you as possible. George, why don't you come first?"

While Majors and Perkins returned to their offices in the women's camp, I accompanied Reineke, Knopfler, and Quayle on a brief tour of barricades and fortifications. At Pete Murphy's direction, work crews were busy recycling the bricks removed from breaches in the interior walls and using them to reinforce the barricades that faced all exterior gates. These gates remained in the hands of the guards and could open at a moment's notice to admit an assault force.

Other crews strung out coils of barbed wire to create entanglements blocking likely avenues of approach. Wherever the barricades or entanglements went up, women from the Technical Department dropped off boxes of ground glass that could be thrown into the eyes of attacking Tommy gunners.

We stopped by a metalworking shop to inspect the progress on converting iron fence posts and concrete reinforcing bars into pikes by grinding and sharpening their ends. Nearby, smiths were busy forging knives, sabers, and even halberds that sported axe-like cutting blades and dagger-like spikes. Although the weapons were primitive, the prisoners carried them with dignity. Some vandals went a step further and created elaborate leather sheaths and scabbards for their newly forged blades.

Pairs of roving sentries passed us as we returned to the barracks. With the puritanical air of revolutionary springtime, the male and female guards treated each other with deference and respect. To the prisoners, the presence of women at the barricades was a sort of weapon in itself, since it demonstrated our unconditional will to resist.

"How long can all this last?" I asked Reineke, pointing at the proud young sentries. "What possible chance do we have with pikes have against machine guns?"

"Probably more than you think," Reineke replied. "But what's important from now on is not how long we last, or even whether we survive, but how we handle ourselves in the time we have."

CHAPTER 30

"History will absolve me."
—Fidel Castro, Cuban dictator

Monday, May 27
Day 9

On Monday at ten o'clock, Doug Chambers, Colonel Jim Tracy, and General Jake Boscov appeared at the gate of the women's camp and called across the no-man's-land to request permission to enter. All three were dressed in their black State Security uniforms. I stood on our side of the no-man's-land with Ralph Knopfler and Glenn Reineke, who had invited me to attend in Terry McIntyre's place, as McIntyre could not be spared from the laboratory.

The prisoners manning the barricades cleared the visitors to enter and led them to the women's mess hall, where the commission was waiting for them.

Along the way, Boscov and Tracy inspected every feature of the compound, with the close attention that one might expect of professional military officers reconnoitering enemy territory. Boscov took the lead, being highest in rank, and all three men walked through the camp with the confident air of proprietors rather than visitors.

The commission members sat at two mess hall tables forming the opposite sides of a horseshoe, while the State Security men sat at a third table facing the horseshoe's open side. No bodyguards were present.

Colonel Majors greeted the three visitors at the mess hall door and led them past a long row of black vinyl body bags lying in a row on the floor. The bags contained the remains of prisoners killed while attempting to capture the Service Yard. The moment the visitors entered the hall, the camp commissioners rose while the visitors filed past the line of cadavers with evident discomfort. I found it heartening that, before negotiations had even started, Majors had seized the high moral ground and put the State Security men on the defensive.

When all had taken seats, Majors introduced everyone around the table.

"Before we go any further," he continued, "I'd like to assure you and Warden Rocco that the election of this commission was in no way intended to show disrespect for the government's authority. We simply thought it would be useful to have…"

Boscov accepted the colonel's assurances with a perfunctory nod.

"We fully understand the need for representatives," he said. "One can't hold a conversation with a mob, after all."

"Yes," Majors answered curtly. "I now yield the floor to your side to tell us why you called for this session."

Boscov appeared to be taken off balance.

"Ah, well, we wanted to get a dialogue going right away. To let cooler heads prevail, so to speak. After all, we don't want bloodshed any more than you do."

"A laudable goal, General," Majors agreed. "But on the substantive side, what new proposals do you bring?"

"None, for the moment," Boscov replied. "We came more to listen than propose."

Even Majors appeared puzzled by this remark.

"Excuse me, General," Ralph Knopfler broke in. "But isn't that exactly what you told us a week ago when you sat up on the speaker's platform? As far as I'm concerned, if you aren't going to bring any proposals to the table we might as well adjourn until you do."

"Isn't there anything you can offer to keep discussions moving?" Majors proposed. "It would be a pity to disappoint Director Cronin by sending you away as soon as you arrive."

"Perhaps there is one area to discuss," Doug Chambers suggested. "You may be aware of the progress we've made lately in the area of case reviews. This week we've brought a senior Justice Department official with us to select some cases for expedited treatment before a special hearing panel. Would this be the kind of thing your men might be looking for?"

"It might be a good place to start," Majors replied. "You know as well as I do that most of us here had our confessions beaten out of us. In my own case, I've filed a sheaf of review petitions but they never seem to get to first base."

Chambers listened attentively to the colonel's complaints and made sympathetic noises. I sensed he had something up his sleeve.

"It sounds to me like yours is just the kind of case our colleague from Justice could help with. Perhaps we could talk later about arranging a private conference for you. Is anyone else here in a similar situation?"

Reineke objected.

"This is a blatant attempt to identify sympathizers among us and buy them off with special treatment. If there's to be any review of a commissioner's case, it should be conducted within ordinary channels. I hereby propose that all case reviews for commission members be suspended until we reach a final settlement."

"Seconded," Pete Murphy declared.

"We'll have to think about that one, Major Reineke," Chief Commissioner Majors answered. "Let's table it and move on. General, do you have anything else for us?"

"Well, as I said before," Boscov resumed, "we did want to take some time to hear any grievances or suggestions..."

But Chuck Quayle stepped in before Boscov could complete his sentence.

"Is this going to be a re-run of last Monday's pointless...?"

"Please don't interrupt," Boscov demanded.

Quayle bristled and looked to Majors for guidance. Majors shrugged.

"I beg your pardon," Quayle offered, barely holding back his anger.

"You may rephrase your question if you like," Boscov replied, having reasserted control.

Quayle started over.

"As I was saying, is this going to be a repeat of last Monday's exercise? What about the commitments your side has already made to us?"

"Investigations are underway and Washington is reviewing your proposals," Chambers assured him. "These things take time."

I looked at the lineup of commissioners and saw folded arms, bored expressions, and eyes rolled upward.

A moment later a woman's voice spoke out. It was Libby Bertrand.

"I represent the women's camp and I'll tell you right now that we don't buy your stalling for one minute. For starters, the rules segregating female and male prisoners must end. We demand—"

Colonel Tracy cut her off.

"Just a moment," he snapped. "Prisoners do not demand. They request. This is still a labor camp, whether you like it or not."

"Why, you, miserable little black-shirted—" Bertrand fumed.

Again Colonel Majors played referee.

"No, Libby, the Colonel is right. We don't govern here. Rephrase, please."

Bertrand regarded Majors and Tracy with cold fury but continued.

"We request that male and female prisoners no longer be segregated in separate divisions and that women be permitted to work alongside men in all job categories. Is that clear enough?"

"Clearly absurd," Tracy shot back. "Do you think we can rewrite departmental regulations just like that? Don't hold your breath."

General Boscov rapped his knuckles on the table to curb muttered objections from some of the commissioners. The hardened expressions on both sides held out little hope for reaching a consensus on anything.

"All right, all right," Majors ordered. "Enough of this bickering. Unless someone objects," he announced over the voices of several others in the room, "I propose that we suspend any further discussion of our demands..."—here Majors corrected himself—"requests until we've had time to boil them down to a single comprehensive list. For that, I expect we'll need to hold further meetings at the barracks level and perhaps a camp-wide town meeting. We'll need time."

"Time for your defense teams to complete their fortifications?" Tracy asked sarcastically. "We weren't born yesterday."

"If you'd like us to speed things up, Colonel," Majors answered, "I'd be happy to move our town meeting up to tomorrow night for you. You may even attend if you'd like."

"Actually, we'd like that very much," Doug Chambers responded quickly.

That was something I had not expected at all.

"But tomorrow's not good for us," he added. "How about Wednesday?"

"Done," Majors agreed, apparently surprised at the Deputy Warden's willingness to appear before two thousand or more hostile prisoners.

"Wednesday at seven in the Division 3 mess. Now that we've settled that, I suggest we reconvene one week from today. We now stand adjourned. Major Reineke, would you mind escorting our guests to the gate?"

"But what about the inspection tour your man Perkins offered us?" Tracy broke in. "You're not going back on your promise, are you?"

Again Reineke objected.

"Colonel Majors, it would be lunacy to let these men inspect our alterations. Perkins has no authority to make an offer like that..."

But it was clear from the look on the colonel's face that he sided with Perkins.

"Give them their damned tour," Majors growled.

"No," Reineke answered defiantly. "With all due respect, Colonel, I request a vote of the full commission."

The tension between Reineke and Majors became palpable.

"All right, have it your way, Major Reineke. All those in favor of giving General Boscov his inspection tour, raise your hands."

Six hands went up, representing Majors, Perkins, Quayle, Schuster, and the two women.

"All opposed?"

Four hands went up, representing Reineke, Murphy, Knopfler, and me.

"The ayes have it," Majors announced with a triumphant smile. Then he appointed the four of us who opposed the inspection to lead it.

We started immediately, maintaining a brisk pace and making few stops. For the most part, we stayed on the north-south road leading through the center of camp and kept away from fortifications and barricades.

We usually sensed when our visitors came across something they found useful. General Boscov was the first to notice from the sound of machines in one of the workshops and from the overhead lights in a food warehouse that the camp still had a source of electric power. I heard him ask Doug Chambers about it when he thought no one was paying attention. Chambers pledged to cut us off from the power grid at once.

****

On my way back to the barracks I was surprised to find Pete Murphy racing to catch up with me. For weeks Murphy had seemed distant and ill at ease. Now he seemed intent on striking up a conversation.

"Glenn told me that you sometimes get dreams about the future," he volunteered after making small talk for a minute or two.

"I hate to disappoint you, Pete," I replied, "but I don't know any more about the future than anyone else around here."

"Oh, I'm not looking for predictions," he said apologetically. "It's just that I've been having dreams, too, and I don't know quite what to make of them."

"Is it the same dream again and again or is each one different?"

"They're mostly different," Murphy explained. "But there's one dream in particular that I can't seem to shake."

We continued walking as he spoke.

"I couldn't see who was talking," Murphy began, " but a voice told me that I could ask any question in the entire world and it would give me the answer. No exceptions. Anything."

"What did you ask?"

"What do you think?" he said. "I said I wanted to know when I'd be done with the camps. Not just when my sentence was up, but when I'd actually be free."

"Did it give you an answer?"

Murphy slowed his pace and came close enough to speak softly into my ear.

"Yes. It said very clearly, 'The eighteenth of June.'"

"When did you have the dream?" I asked.

"On the thirtieth of March."

"Well, are you excited about getting out?" I asked, half in jest.

"I don't know," Murphy said without humor. "I still don't know if I can believe it. After all, it's just a dream. But at the same time, I'm kind of anxious about how I might take it if we get to June 18 and it looks like nothing is going to happen. My hopes are set so high, I don't know how I'd handle the letdown."

"Frankly, Pete, I think the real miracle would be that we're not all mucking for gold in the Yukon by the middle of June. Would you do me a favor? Remind me the day before. Meanwhile, I'll keep my eyes open. Who knows, maybe it will be a lucky day for both of us."

CHAPTER 31

"You only have power over people so long as you don't take everything away from them. But when you've robbed a man of everything, he's no longer in your power—he's free again."

—Alexander Solzhenitsyn, The First Circle

Wednesday, May 29

Day 11

On Wednesday evening, I found myself waiting at the gate once again for visitors from the Department of State Security. Glenn Reineke, Pete Murphy, Colonel Majors, George Perkins, and I watched in silence as a pair of black government sedans pulled up outside the gate to Division 3. Across the no-man's-land we saw a pair of plainclothes bodyguards hop out of each car and look around before opening doors for their high-ranking passengers. Doug Chambers and General Jake Boscov emerged from the first car while Kenneth Cronin and an older man with tousled gray hair emerged from the second. Colonel Majors called across the buffer zone to invite them in.

Once inside the inner perimeter, General Boscov introduced the new man as Howard Barger of the Justice Department. We headed toward the Division 3 mess hall, where some 2,000 prisoners were packed together on benches and against the walls, waiting to hear what our captors were prepared to offer.

Just before we entered, Colonel Majors took Director Cronin aside and told the rest of us to proceed onto the speakers' platform. Reineke looked at Murphy and me with alarm. It wasn't lost on us that Majors might be floating a private settlement proposal or requesting special treatment for himself.

Boscov, Chambers, and Barger stood to the side of the dais while they waited for Cronin and Majors to catch up.

Colonel Majors mounted the dais, tapped the microphone twice to test it and called for silence. He then invited the visitors to take their places on the platform while he sat off to the side to act as moderator. After introducing each guest he addressed the prisoners.

"A little more than a week ago, many of you met here with two of the officials seated before you tonight. I was in the camp jail at the time, but I've been told that the meeting was not a happy one. Since then, fortunately, our circumstances have improved."

Laughter broke out at the rear of the hall.

"Tonight, I understand that our visitors are prepared to speak about what they expect from us and what we can expect from them going forward. As before, once they have had an opportunity to speak, the floor will be open for questions."

Majors turned to Cronin.

"Director Cronin, it's all yours."

Kenneth Cronin gazed upon his audience with perfect serenity. He appeared to be fully aware that most prisoners ranked him at the top of their enemies list. Yet this nondescript little man did not hesitate to sit before them, unarmed, without a bodyguard, for what the President-for-Life had been fond of calling 'a full and frank exchange of views.' Certainly, Kenneth Cronin was made of very special stuff and he seemed to know it.

"The purpose of the corrective labor system," Cronin began, "is not revenge or punishment or even deterrence. Camps like Kamas were created for rehabilitation and correction, to help prisoners prepare for their return to Unionist society. Putting a citizen in a corrective labor camp is a measure of social defense: it removes the dangerous element from society while it works to correct the thoughts and behaviors that created the danger in the first place.

"As Director of Corrective Labor, what I expect from you is hard work, responsible behavior, and a proper respect for the Party and the State. I expect you to show that respect by your willingness to learn and your readiness to contribute to Unionist society, starting here in the camp.

"From what I have seen in my visits here, what is most lacking at Kamas is an understanding that the highest good is what's good for society, not what's good for you or me as individuals. Once a person accepts this principle and begins serving society rather than himself, he is on the road toward rehabilitation. But the harder he persists in a pattern of selfish behavior, the greater the need for strictness of the kind most commonly associated with camps much further to the north.

"What I can offer you today is a path back toward rehabilitation into Unionist society by way of your immediate and unconditional return to work. If you accept, I can also offer you my personal assurance that I will follow through on each and every promise made to you—whether by me, by the Warden, or the officers on his staff. I plan to meet with your elected representatives tomorrow morning to work out the details. These include a prompt review of cases; a thorough investigation of all accusations of official wrongdoing; improved working and living conditions; enhanced nutrition; and the opportunity to earn additional privileges through productive labor.

"There you have it. That's my offer to you. To accept it, you need only return to work. Now, do any of you have questions?"

A rumbling rose from the audience. Though the prisoners had shown Cronin the courtesy of listening to him without interruption, many were restive.

A heckler bellowed from the back.

"I have a question. What kind of idiots do you think we are?"

Cronin ignored him.

Chuck Quayle rose. Colonel Majors gestured for him to speak.

"Some of my men have petitioned many times to have their cases reviewed, but nothing ever seems to happen," Quayle said. "Yesterday you told the Commission that our case reviews will get fast-track treatment. Could you or Mr. Barger tell us when that's going to start and how we'll know when it does?"

Howard Barger leaned forward to pick up the microphone.

"I have scheduled a meeting tomorrow morning with your case review clerks, Judges Richardson and O'Rourke, to discuss how we can carry out an expedited review like the one Director Cronin mentioned. Afterward I would like to hold a separate gathering for everyone who has filed or is interested in filing a petition for review. Whatever may have happened in the past with this, we're going to cut through the red tape and act promptly on every petition we get."

"Yeah, yeah, yeah," a woman exclaimed from the far side of the room. "How many times do you think you can fool us with that one?"

"Next question," Majors shouted over hoots and whistles.

Kevin Gaffney stood up next and was recognized to speak.

"How are we supposed to believe a word you say as long as we see the same trigger-happy guards every day looking down their gun barrels at us? What's to investigate? Every one of them is a hardened killer. If you people had the slightest intention to punish any of them, it could have been done years ago. So don't bother us anymore with your phony promises to investigate. It'll never happen."

"What you say is unfair and simply untrue," Cronin replied calmly. "An investigation is underway as we speak."

A tall, painfully thin woman in her mid-forties rose from the crowd.

"Look at me," she demanded. "And look at the prisoners around you, women and men both. Is a single one of us overweight? We work outdoors in summer and winter, eleven hours a day plus marching time, six days a week. Our rations aren't anywhere near enough to keep us going. What you see before you is worse than malnutrition—it's execution by hunger. And it ought to shame even a bloody Unionist butcher like you!"

The woman's speech brought forth a rousing cheer. General Boscov looked as if he were about to have a stroke. Doug Chambers signaled he would respond.

"Prisoners' rations are calculated according to scientifically determined tables," Chambers began calmly. "The law requires us to follow these tables, which are used in every federal prison, detention facility, and military stockade in the country. I might point out that these tables were worked out long before the Unionist Party came to Washington. Last year, Warden Rocco requested a recalculation of the base ration for Kamas, based on the higher altitude and colder winters here. I've been told unofficially that you can expect a ration increase in the next month or so. So please bear with us."

A short, dark-eyed woman with a New England accent spoke up without waiting for the moderator's permission.

"How dare you treat our basic human rights as privileges! How dare you take away our rights without even a trial and offer them back to us in bits and pieces for a lifetime of servitude!"

This brought forth another round of cheering.

Suddenly Boscov grabbed the microphone and raised his voice above the din.

"You want to know how you lost your rights?" Boscov challenged. "I'll tell you how! You were convicted of treason! Traitors and public enemies don't have rights!"

An uproar broke out among the prisoners. Colonel Majors reached for the mike but could not make himself heard.

Glenn Reineke jumped to his feet in the front row, where he sat with the other commission members. He turned toward the audience and waved both arms until the uproar subsided.

"General Boscov!" he called out. "Tell me, how many of your own kind have turned out to be public enemies? The last two chiefs of State Security were arrested under Title 18 just like us! How do we know that you're any better than they were?"

Kenneth Cronin clenched his teeth but did not reach for the microphone. The other visitors followed his lead and remained silent.

Colonel Majors pounded on the table and called the audience to order.

"Presidential appointments are not the subject of this meeting," Majors proclaimed. "We are here to discuss conditions here at Kamas. Who else would like to speak to our conditions here?"

"I would," Libby Bertrand declared from her front-row seat. "What about the investigation you promised us into the beatings your troops handed out in the women's camp? You've had a week now to investigate; what have you found?"

"It's too early to say," Cronin replied. "We'll let you know when we have something definite to report."

A chorus of groans rose from the prisoners. Majors shouted above the noise to restore order.

"Ladies and gentlemen, let's be reasonable. Tonight we have been promised a review of our cases, an increase in our rations, and an investigation of official wrongdoing. Our visitors have been patient, but some of you seem to interpret this as a sign of weakness. Why attack these men? They're here to help us."

"Wake up, Majors, for God's sake!" Ralph Knopfler roared, rising from his seat. We're way past giving State Security the benefit of the doubt. What they deserve isn't our support, it's resistance—to the last drop of our blood! And theirs!"

The prisoners cheered and whistled and stomped their feet wildly.

The three visitors faced the unruly prisoners with grim resolve though their foreheads gleamed with nervous perspiration.

George Perkins stood to speak next but the prisoners would not let the noise settle down. He waited, then climbed onto the dais and grabbed the microphone from Majors. Soon the roar diminished enough for him to be heard.

"Look here, people, tonight the government has offered us a chance to redeem ourselves. They've offered a compromise that would let us go back to work without reprisals and improve our living conditions at the same time. Why do you diehards always have to demand more? If we refuse, they'll bring in tanks and hammer us to dust. Believe me, the Party will get its way no matter what."

Perkins's words had an oddly sobering effect on the crowd. With each sentence, the noise lessened. Judging from the lack of applause, Perkins did not seem to have many supporters but his arguments had made an impression.

Knopfler mounted the dais next and seized a microphone from the table.

"We're not against redeeming ourselves, George," Knopfler replied. "We just refuse to do it your way. For you, redemption can only be granted by a state that monopolizes all power in its own hands. The idea of someone determining his own fate is anathema to you.

"You talk of our duty to build a new Unionist society. I reject that duty! Our duty is to build a free society and we're already succeeding at it! We're demonstrating how it ought to work right here in Kamas. And by comparison your Unionist society is oppressive and false.

"Whether we defeat Unionism or it defeats us is not what's important. Our task is to do our duty as we understand it and accept the consequences. That will be redemption enough for me."

For a moment after Knopfler stopped speaking, the mess hall remained silent. Then suddenly the air was filled with whistles and cheers and stomping and deafening pounding on tables while the men on the dais cast grave looks at one other. From that moment, there could no longer be any doubt of our determination to pursue the revolt to the end—or likewise of State Security's determination to crush it. There would be no more mess hall meetings or negotiations.

CHAPTER 32

"Criminals and their victims cannot live together."
—Francisco Franco, Spanish dictator

Monday, June 3
Day 16

After the final mess hall meeting with the representatives of State Security, talk of compromise ended on both sides. We drew up defensive plans, erected barricades, and armed ourselves the best we could. Outside the perimeter, the guards, warders, technical specialists, and visiting brass poured their efforts into surveillance.

Day and night, specialists from the Department's Technical Services Directorate kept vigil in the high watchtowers, crowding the machine-gunners aside with their audio and video monitoring equipment.

At the most basic level, guards monitored our fortification-building and troop movements through high-powered binoculars. Visiting experts kept surveillance logs for key locations while the guards helped them identify and track specific prisoners. After dark, the tower guards peered down on us through night-vision goggles, never seen before at Kamas and reported to be on loan from the military.

An audio surveillance team arrived from Washington to take on the mission of tapping internal camp phone lines and eavesdropping on any wireless communications that might be emanating from the camp. To pick up ordinary conversations inside the yards, the audio team installed directional dish amplifiers and employed trained lip-readers from a regional school for the deaf. To monitor conversations inside camp offices, they used special infrared detection equipment that directed beams of invisible light against the offices' closed windows, and read as sound the minute vibrations on the outside surface of the glass. Consequently, our own technicians warned us at every opportunity not to hold important discussions where we could be overheard.

The most important job of the audio surveillance team was to operate radio-monitoring equipment to pick up any wireless transmissions that prisoners might use to communicate with outside allies. In theory, it should not even have been possible for prisoners at Kamas to receive or transmit radio messages. Camp regulations banned radios, walkie-talkies, mobile phones, and other wireless devices in any area frequented by prisoners. A prisoner caught with any kind of electronic device risked summary execution. And since the Events, electronic circuitry was subject to tight government control and was far from being as cheap and widely available to the public as before.

Nonetheless, on the first day after we had taken over the camp, Jerry McIntyre made an appeal over the loudspeaker system to offer the Technical Department any electronic components that we prisoners might possess. As the camp population included dozens of electrical engineers, communications technicians, and computer experts, our fondest dream was that McIntyre's techs might find parts sufficient to assemble a transmitter that could broadcast our pleas for help to Europe or South America. Failing that, we hoped that our scientists might at least be able to intercept the government's telecommunications and warn us against imminent attack.

The Technical Department's very existence gave us comfort. The constant rumors about exotic projects that our scientists had underway— chemical weapons, improvised explosive devices, strobe-like sound and light weapons to disorient attacking troops, and even psychic remote viewing to spy on the camp bosses—offered reason for optimism as the rest of us carried out mundane tasks like sentry duty, fortifications building, and trench digging.

One of the most serious challenges the Technical Department faced early in the revolt was the loss of electricity. Most affected by the power cutoff were the workshops where weapons were made, the commission's offices and the mess halls. Fortunately, McIntyre's staff had already anticipated a power outage and had converted a portable generator from gasoline to propane fuel, of which we had an abundance. They placed the generator in a conspicuous place, as if to boast to the bosses how little time we had needed to recover from the cutoff. What most of us didn't know at the time was that the Technical Department was diverting even more power from the electrified perimeter fences and from other electrical lines that ran close by.

****

On the day after the town meeting, I made my way after lunch to the infirmary to have the dressings changed on my cut hands. Far fewer prisoners filled the waiting room than when I had been wounded two weeks earlier.

I approached the reception window and asked for a nurse.

"Take a seat and I'll call you in a few minutes," the receptionist said.

To my surprise, she was as good as her word. An orderly escorted me into the examining area, which looked far tidier than on my previous visits.

The first person to come by was Georg Schuster. The diminutive chief surgeon was unshaven and wore a soiled lab coat but, when he smiled, the lines in his careworn face seemed less deep than the last time we had met.

Schuster went to work immediately inspecting my cuts, cleaning around the stitches, and applying disinfectant.

"I'd like to let the wound dry for a few minutes before we apply a new dressing. Would you mind if I send a nurse to complete the job?" he asked.

"Not all," I replied, pleased to have escaped with so little pain. "Do I get a choice? How about Gwen, the good-looking one?"

Schuster turned his head to look for her. I spotted Gwen sitting at the room's far end filling out a stack of forms at a cluttered desk.

"Actually, Gwen isn't a nurse," he confessed. "She's only an orderly."

"I don't care, as long as she knows what she's doing," I replied.

Schuster brightened.

"Then Gwen it will be," he answered. "Unfortunately, I've had to be careful about Gwen's assignments lately because some of the other nurses have refused to work with her. You see, she was the Deputy Warden protégé. Now that he's no longer here to protect her..."

"She wasn't a stoolie, was she?" I asked.

"No, just a confused young girl who could not refuse a powerful man," Schuster said wearily. "But please, come this way. It will be less awkward if Gwen tends to you in the chronic care ward, away from the other nurses."

Schuster caught Gwen's eye and gestured for her to follow us into the next room. As she rose to join us, I noticed that she looked plainer than when I had last seen her. She no longer wore makeup and her hair was straight and tied behind her neck with a bow made of white gauze. Even her athletic figure seemed to have grown more fragile. But the plainness was offset by a look of humility in her eyes. I was curious to learn more.

I took a seat on an examining table at the end of a row of ten hospital beds, each one filled with a severely ill patient. Every prisoner knew that the chronic care ward was generally filled with last-leggers and my nearest neighbor appeared to qualify. I was surprised when Gwen greeted him with a hearty pat on the shoulder and his response was to open his eyes and break out in a broad grin.

"Wake up, Jon, we have a visitor."

She examined both my hands and then wrapped the right one with fresh gauze while she spoke.

"Paul, meet Jon Merrill. Jon used to work in the silver mines before they brought him here," she continued. "You think he's skinny now? You should have seen him a month ago. I could practically see through him."

She finished bandaging my right hand and took up the other.

"I like to tell everyone how I brought Jon back to life. He was a goner when he got here but in another week or two he'll be back on his feet. All because he loves me so."

"I'll agree with anything you say as long as you don't send me back to the mine," Jon replied in a sleepy voice.

Gwen finished taping my left hand.

"You're done," she told me as she turned to leave. "But why don't you stay and chat a while. It'd be good for Jon. He sleeps far too much, anyway."

"Isn't she marvelous?" Jon said dreamily as soon as Gwen was out of earshot. "When I came here, nobody thought I'd last more than a day. Even I thought it was over. But Gwen fed me and massaged me and talked to me for hours and hours. After she had invested so much time in me, it would have been ungrateful of me to die, so I hung on. And before I knew quite what happened, I wasn't a goner anymore."

"How long have you been in Kamas?" I asked.

"A little short of nine months. I arrived just before the first snowfall and it was all downhill from there. I kept missing my quota and they kept docking my rations. As the weather got colder I got weaker. I thought to myself: sixteen years of school and this is how it ends?

"At the interrogation center, I told myself that, if I could only make it through the beatings, I could handle anything. Then, in the transit camp, all I wanted was to get away from the thieves. Then, when I finally made it to Kamas, it dawned on me that this might be the last home I'd ever see."

"It still might. What's your sentence?" I asked.

"Eight years. Sedition," he replied. "Do you want to know what I did to deserve that? I refused to rake leaves in the admissions director's yard! Can you believe it? Just because I was on a government scholarship, he thought I was his indentured servant. When I threatened to report him, he had my scholarship canceled. A week later State Security came to take me away."

"What would you say if they offered you back the leaf-raking job?" I asked.

"Until a couple weeks ago, I would have agreed to rake those leaves every day for the rest of my life."

"I can't blame you. Anything would beat the mines."

"That's what I kept telling myself," Jon replied. "Somewhere in the back of my mind I still hoped that it was all a big mistake and that before long they'd let me go. But when my twenty-first birthday came around without any sign that things would get better, it was me who let go. One morning I refused to get out of my bunk. No threats or blows from the orderly could get me to move. They had to carry me to the infirmary."

"What made you change your mind?" I asked.

"I came down with a fever. I still have no idea what it was, but for two days I hovered between life and death and was out of my mind most of the time. The second night I became lucid again and listened to Gwen pray for me to stay alive. She said I was the only friend she had and she couldn't bear being left alone.

"Suddenly it dawned on me. Even though I no longer expected anything from life, perhaps it was time to start thinking about what life might expect from me. Here was a beautiful woman who had done everything in her power to bring me back from the grave and now she was the one in need.

"As I got stronger, I realized that each day brought new responsibilities. I started paying attention to the strikes and thinking about what I could do to help. I started to think that maybe my arrest wasn't some sort of cosmic joke, after all. Now I'm hoping that the revolt will go on long enough for me to get out of this bed and lend a hand, even if it's to grind knife blades or be a lookout."

At that moment Gwen came back through the curtain from the treatment ward and took Jon by the hand.

"You're not talking about joining the revolt again, now, are you?" she scolded. "I thought we agreed that you wouldn't be ready to return to the barracks for at least another two weeks. Why, you can barely walk. What good could you possibly be to the revolt as an invalid?"

"I'm sure you could land a job at one of the observation posts when you're up to it," I said. "All it requires is a good eye and an alert mind."

"See?" Jon teased. "I think the time has come to step up my physical therapy. Gwen, could you bring me that walker over there? I'm going to see how many laps I can do before mealtime."

Gwen beamed at him and I understood how the kindness in those dewy brown eyes could have brought any last-legger back to life.

CHAPTER 33

"Power corrupts. The beast hidden in the soul of man and released from its chain lusts to satisfy its age-old natural instinct—to beat, to murder. I don't know if it's possible to receive satisfaction from signing a death sentence, but in this, too, there is doubtless some dark pleasure, some fantasy, which seeks no justification."

—Varlam Shalamov, Kolyma Tales

Monday, June 3
Day 16

Little Marie Chambers squatted on the living room floor and stared with rapt attention as Claire Wagner stacked wooden blocks, layer upon layer, until they towered over Marie's head. Claire then sat back and waited.

Marie reached out with her pudgy hand, slowly at first, watching for a reaction from Claire, who feigned open-mouthed horror. Then the little hand gave a backhand sweep that knocked the foundation out from under the blocks and sent them crashing to the floor. Marie looked up with a mischievous grin.

"Oh, no! You terrible, terrible girl!" Claire exclaimed melodramatically. "You're a wrecker! And a public enemy, too!"

Claire crawled slowly toward the toddler on her hands and knees, pretending to stalk her. Marie backed away, giggling with excitement.

"Now we're coming to get you! He-e-e-re we come!" Marie turned and fled, stopping every few steps to make sure Claire was still behind her, a ferocious make-believe beast nipping at her tiny heels.

"Claire?" Martha Chambers called from the kitchen. "Could you bring Marie? It's time for lunch."

"Yes, Martha," Claire called out and scooped up the child with a roar that delighted her.

"And would you be a dear and set the table on the deck? There will be five for lunch. You and I will eat in the kitchen."

Claire handed Marie to Martha and continued onto the deck. Today was Heroes & Martyrs Day and it would have been a perfect day for a picnic lunch. But with so many visiting officials in town to help Doug put down the revolt, the Chambers family would have little time to enjoy it until evening. The working lunch for Doug and his new task force was Martha's way of keeping him at home for at least some of the holiday.

Claire set out the place mats, then the napkins and silverware, then the water glasses, and the pitchers of ice water and iced tea. The salads and chips were already laid out on the serving table and the bar was set up in the kitchen. As usual, Martha would carry out the sandwiches at the last moment. If Doug were bringing home the usual foursome—Warden Rocco, Major Whiting, Colonel Tracy, and General Boscov—Claire doubted that the men would be drinking iced tea.

"I'm finished," Claire reported. "Would you like me to handle Marie again?"

"You're a mind reader," Martha replied.

Claire sat opposite the high chair until Marie had finished eating, then led her up the stairs for a nap. Marie was still standing in her crib and crooning through the wooden slats when Doug's car pulled into the driveway.

By the time Claire returned to the kitchen, the men were already gathered around the bar to pour their drinks. The Warden and Doug drank bourbon and water, while Colonel Tracy and Major Whiting drank beer from long-necked bottles and the General topped off his orange juice with vodka. Having brought refills to each of them on numerous occasions, Claire knew their drink preferences by heart.

Claire listened to the men's conversations while she waited for Martha to finish preparing the sandwich tray.

"I had a message from Ken Cronin over the weekend," Doug remarked. Claire noticed that Doug's voice seemed husky and he slurred certain words.

"He wants us to set a date for retaking the camp. How's the timeline coming?"

"I saw an updated version this morning," Colonel Tracy replied. "Other than getting approvals, the critical item seems to be finding enough armored vehicles. I'd say we're looking at another three weeks, at least."

As Tracy spoke, Martha Chambers looked up from placing the final garnish on the sandwich tray.

"Lunch is out on the deck," Martha announced coolly. "If you need anything, Claire and I will be here in the kitchen."

The men freshened their drinks and followed Doug onto the deck.

"Intelligence is another key piece," General Boscov continued as they lined up at the serving table. "We'll need to identify all the ringleaders and track their movements on a twenty-four-hour basis or we'll run into the same problems we had in March, when we lost our informants. Now that the technical teams are in place, we ought to be in better shape."

"But not as good as we need," Whiting cautioned. "We still need better coverage of their leadership. Several of the prisoners we've been cultivating are pretty senior. The trick is getting one of them alone long enough to make a pitch."

"We need a high-level informant badly," Doug replied. "What would be the downside if you pitched one of them and failed?"

"One botched recruitment could blow all the others," Whiting warned. "But considering what's at stake, I think it's a risk we may have to take."

"Have you given any thought to using lower-level agents to get rid of the most dangerous of their leaders?" Tracy asked casually as he loaded his plate with potato salad and club sandwiches.

"If you ask me, the last thing we want right now is to create more martyrs," the Warden observed as he filled his own plate. "Martyrs are what got us into this mess in the first place."

The Colonel's cheeks flushed but the Warden paid no attention.

"There's another problem with your idea, Jim," Boscov joined in. "With Headquarters so concerned about legal niceties these days, we're in enough hot water as it is. I don't want to give them any more cause to make a scapegoat out of me."

"You and me both," the Warden agreed as he took a seat at the table next to Boscov. "Look, I'm eligible for retirement in July. When it's time for me to ride into the sunset, I don't want to lose any sleep over what happened at some god-forsaken labor camp in Utah. The more times Ken Cronin tells me I'm not the one on trial, the more I wonder whether I am."

****

It was nearly four o'clock in the afternoon when Doug and his friends left the house. By the time Martha and Claire finished cleaning, the baby had already risen from her nap. Claire brought Marie into the living room and sat with her on the carpet. Martha put her fashion magazine aside and looked down from the sofa at the two children.

"Claire, darling, there's something I've been meaning to ask you. I've been thinking about going back east this summer to have the new baby. Would you be interested in coming along to help?"

Claire sat bolt upright.

"Would it be anywhere near Pittsburgh?" she asked.

"Close enough for us to stop there, if you'd like."

"I'd like that a lot," Claire said eagerly.

"Good. But there's something you have to decide before making the trip. You see, I can't say for sure when we'll come back. I know you've been hoping to find your father out here, but Helen tells me the chances of doing that very soon aren't so good. She thinks you'd have a better chance of finding your mother back in Pennsylvania. I want you to think it over."

A thoughtful expression came over Claire's face.

"If I don't go, could I stay here with Helen?"

"I don't know," Martha replied. "You'd have to talk to Helen. But here's an idea. Why don't you go visit her this afternoon and ask? I have a note I'd like you to take to her when you go. Then we can talk again tonight, if you like."

"Does Doug know you're not coming back?"

Martha beckoned Claire to come closer and hugged her tightly so the child would not see the tears welling in her eyes.

"I've told him, sweetheart, but I don't think he's heard it just yet."

CHAPTER 34

"To choose one's victims, to prepare one's plans minutely, to slake an implacable vengeance, and then to go to bed...there is nothing sweeter in the world."

—Joseph Stalin

Friday, June 7
Day 20

Several days after my visit to the infirmary, Jon Merrill and I were scheduled for observation post duty together. It was Jon's second night on duty and only his third out of the infirmary. We sat side by side on the roof of a warehouse near the Service Yard's eastern wall and took turns using liberated binoculars to scan the no-man's land, the perimeter fence, and the road for enemy activity.

We were about halfway through our four-hour watch when we heard dull thuds coming from behind the wall in several places along the perimeter. It was a moonless night, without a glimmer of light except for the flood lamps mounted on the watchtowers and on the outer perimeter fence.

"Did you hear that?" Merrill asked.

"Sounds like someone hacking at the wall," I answered.

We listened closely for another minute or two to what sounded like attempts to breach the wall with picks and sledgehammers.

"Should we sound the alarm?" Merrill asked.

"I think we'd better," I replied. At that, Merrill pulled a pack of matches from his pocket and lit one of the kerosene-soaked signal torches stored at every observation post. I blew hard on the police whistle hanging around my neck.

A clatter erupted at the sentry posts and barricades nearby as prisoners took up their pikes and sabers. A shift leader called up to ask what we had seen.

"Sounds like somebody is trying to break through," we shouted back, and indeed now the clatter of hammers, picks, and shovels was very distinct. The shift leader summoned reinforcements, who waited behind the barricades while breaches appeared in the wall and grew larger by the minute. Before long, four gaps appeared in the Service Yard's exterior wall, each large enough to admit three or four men abreast. As dawn broke, we waited nervously for hordes of heavily armed attackers to pour through the breaches. But dawn came and the sun rose over the eastern hills without a single Tommy gunner showing his face.

By the time our shift ended, the Security Department had counted more than a dozen such breaches along the entire length of the camp's perimeter wall. Peering through the breaches at ground level, we could see that State Security troops had erected their own sandbag barricades opposite ours, complete with machine-gun emplacements. None of us had any doubt that the main purpose of these breaches was to facilitate an assault on the camp.

For several hours that morning, our military and security people deliberated over countermeasures. By noon, they had decided to dismantle the remaining sections of interior wall separating the camp divisions from one another and to use the materials to erect a second perimeter wall of lower height just inside the main wall. As soon as Colonel Majors approved the plan, construction crews set to work. For the Colonel, having seen the prisoner sentiment surge in favor of the revolt, had abruptly stopped talking of compromise and repositioned himself as a hard-liner.

While the crews built the new wall, the Military Department dispatched additional defense platoons to protect them while the Security Department assigned extra sentries to watch for signs of trouble. At each security post and defensive position hung a short length of steel rail to ring like a gong in case of attack. Men assigned to defend the breaches were keenly aware that they would be the camp's first line of defense and would confront automatic weapons with little more than swords, pikes, and stones. Even those who initially balked at such a matchup, however, soon adjusted to it and before long took perverse pride in the long odds they faced.

I left the Service Yard at midday to eat lunch, then made my visit to the infirmary to change the dressings on my hands. On my way to the reception window, I noticed a middle-aged couple sitting quietly in a corner. I recognized the man as Earl Cunningham, the Montana rancher and insurgent whom I had met in the same waiting room nearly three weeks before. Beside him was a frail-looking woman of about sixty, with a gaunt, angular face and limp black hair streaked with gray that fell loose to her shoulders.

I walked over to Cunningham and greeted him.

Cunningham rose to shake my hand, then introduced me to his wife, Irene. I held out my hand and she took it without speaking or making eye contact. Her hand was cold and her grip was feeble.

"Irene's not quite herself," Earl explained. "I found her in a section of the women's camp set aside for invalids. It seems she had a stroke right before Christmas. She doesn't even know who I am."

His voice thickened and he choked back tears.

We sat in silence a few moments longer before the receptionist called my name. I entered the treatment area and in a few minutes Gwen appeared through the curtain that marked off the chronic care ward. Her eyes were red and puffy and her hair unkempt without the gauze bow that usually held it in place. She seemed preoccupied and sat down across from me without saying a word.

"Jon sends his greetings," I told her as she reached out to take my bandaged right hand. "He's doing great."

"I'm happy for him," she answered without enthusiasm. She picked up a pair of scissors and cut away the bandage.

"Is there something wrong?" I asked. "You don't seem well."

"Just tired. I've been on the night shift and haven't had much sleep." She examined the wound and began cleaning it with alcohol.

"Are you sure that's all it is?"

"I'm not sure of anything anymore," she answered dully.

She gave me back my right hand and reached out to take the left.

"Is it Jon?" I asked. "Has he visited you since he moved into the barracks?"

"He's visited," Gwen replied irritably as she cut away the bandage on my left hand. "It's just that his leaving made me see what a mess I've made of my life. For years it's been one stupid mistake after another. I don't see any way out of it."

"There's always a way, Gwen. But first you have to decide where you want to be."

"Right now, anyplace would be better than where I am," she said.

Her eyes met mine for an instant and then she looked down again at her lap, where she finished disinfecting my hand and wrapped it with gauze.

"If you want to leave the infirmary, I'm sure they could use your help in one of the other departments..."

She shook her head.

"I don't give a flying hoot about your revolt. I just want to get out of Kamas and start over."

Gwen applied the final piece of adhesive tape to my bandage. Before I could think of anything to say, Gwen's eyes told me she was beyond reach.

After leaving the infirmary I returned to the barracks for a nap before dinner. I had just risen and was preparing to leave for the mess hall when I heard distant shouts and whistles and the banging of steel on steel that signified an attack had begun. I ran toward the Service Yard and climbed to the roof of the warehouse that was my observation post.

Jon Merrill was already there, watching the gaps in the wall and giving a detailed description of the action to a messenger from the command post. He explained to me that the enemy had moved a platoon of Tommy gunners into two of the four gaps in the perimeter wall.

Through the gaps I could see a training facility that lay just outside the camp perimeter. Its second-floor verandah was packed with high-ranking police, military, and State Security officers spying on us through binoculars, telescopes, and enormous telephoto lenses. I borrowed a pair of binoculars from Jon Merrill and stared back at them, spotting Fred Rocco, Doug Chambers, General Boscov, and Colonel Tracy among the crowd. They appeared to be watching our defenders' reactions to their side's probing. Their men would advance just far enough through the breach to lure our men out from behind their barricades and then theirs would retreat behind the wall.

Meanwhile, the video cameras rolled and the still cameras captured the fierce postures of our primitively armed fighters. The officers laughed heartily from the safety of their distant balcony, delighting in the bizarre spectacle of impassioned savages confronting their civilized and well-armed opponents.

Suddenly Jon Merrill tugged at my sleeve and pointed to the gate at the far left of the Service Yard. There a squad of Tommy gunners charged from behind the gap in the wall and held their ground as a squad of warders rushed in from behind them to storm our barricades. The Tommy gunners leveled their weapons, ready to offer covering fire to the warders, who used hooks, nets, and lassos to capture our defenders as if they were hunting wild animals.

If the warders were counting on taking a few defenders back for interrogation, however, they were thwarted in this and nearly lost a few men of their own. As it happened, our defenders included elite troops skilled in hand-to-hand combat. Seeing the warders advance without firearms, our troops charged them, whirling and kicking and punching furiously and inflicting worse damage than the attackers had expected. The Tommy gunners resorted to firing over the heads of our men to cover the warders' escape. They continued to play a game of cat and mouse this way for nearly another hour.

During this final hour of probing, the enemy introduced another tactic that they would use repeatedly in the days to come. They broadcast an appeal for deserters, using loudspeakers mounted on the watchtowers to the east and west of the Service Yard.

"Prisoners, come to your senses! Don't let the mutineers use you to put off their day of reckoning. Leave the camp now. No unarmed prisoner who approaches the gates will be fired upon. If you come out now you will be treated fairly and will not be charged with mutiny. Drop your weapons and walk past the barricades to the gaps..."

At first many of the prisoners who heard this message were confused. A few closet Unionists seemed sorely tempted to run for the gates but hesitated for fear of being cut down from behind. Within twenty minutes of the first appeal for deserters, however, Glenn Reineke announced over our own loudspeakers that anyone who trusted State Security to make good on its pledge was more than free to leave. He ordered our defenders to hold no one back from deserting. Once we knew we could leave at any time, any sense of urgency disappeared. Not a single prisoner deserted that day.

Seeing that the gambit had failed, the Tommy gunners withdrew and the high-ranking spectators packed their cameras and departed in their vans. But we knew they would be back. The conflict had simply entered a new phase.

CHAPTER 35

"One day Larisa Fedorovna went out and did not come back. She must have been arrested in the street at that time. She vanished without a trace and probably died somewhere, forgotten as a nameless number on a list that afterwards got mislaid, in one of the innumerable mixed or women's concentration camps in the north."

—Boris Pasternak, *Doctor Zhivago*

Monday, June 7
Day 23

Over the weekend every able-bodied supporter of the revolt turned out to work on the massive project of tearing down the interior walls between the camp divisions and using the rubble to build a new inner perimeter wall. The new wall was set back about fifteen yards from the original and was given added height and thickness where it faced breaches exposing us to gunfire from outside.

All day long the camp bosses broadcast propaganda messages from their network of loudspeakers surrounding the camp. They broadcast live speeches by the Warden and by visiting brass hats. They broadcast recorded speeches from the late President-for-Life and other Unionist leaders. They even broadcast prerecorded interviews with ordinary citizens of Heber and the Kamas Valley, apparently to impress upon us that we could expect no sympathy from the local population.

In response, Ralph Knopfler's Information Department redirected our own loudspeakers outward to tell our side of the story to the guards and to the troops surrounding the camp. Before long, each side resorted to jamming the other side's messages through simultaneous broadcasting, with the result that the air was filled with unintelligible noise played at earsplitting volume, sometimes well into the night.

On Sunday our Information Department tried a new trick: tying bundles of crude propaganda leaflets to kites and releasing the leaflets as soon as they were over enemy positions. After the first few bundles hit their targets, State Security officers rode across the hills on motorcycles to intercept the leaflets the moment a kite soared above the perimeter wall. We never learned whether the leaflets persuaded any guards or troops to soften their attitudes toward us but we could be sure that the leaflets threatened the bosses when the guards began firing machine guns at the kites. When bullets did not succeed in bringing down the kites, security officers sent up attack kites to tangle strings with ours and bring them down the old-fashioned way.

At breakfast on Monday morning, Ralph Knopfler predicted that the Technical Department would soon have a radio transmitter with sufficient power to reach Mexico City. Texan Jerry Lee, who worked in Knopfler's Information Department, added that writers from that outfit were already busy drafting radio scripts aimed at attracting international attention to Kamas.

D.J. Schultz scoffed at the idea of publicizing the Kamas revolt.

"You could reach every country in the world and raise protests from all of them without making the slightest dent in the bosses' thick skulls," D.J. declared. "The Unionists don't respect public opinion. All they respect is force. And who's going to send troops or planes against Washington over the likes of us?"

Jerry Lee held his tongue and let his boss respond.

"There are other ways of getting to them besides force," Knopfler explained. "There's economic pressure and diplomatic pressure. The

Unionists need plenty of things from overseas that the free countries could cut off through economic sanctions."

"I'll believe it when I see it," D.J. replied. "Which countries stood up to those bastards when they bombed civilian targets during the Events? Who stood in their way when they invaded Mexico and Canada? Who raised hell when the Unionists executed politicals by the thousands and sent their families to death camps at Hudson Bay?"

"My Lord, D.J., where did you suddenly pick up so much history?" Jerry Lee asked in mock surprise.

"I'll admit that I was too young to understand what went on in those days," D.J. said defensively. "But Gary's been holding classes…"

"Don't take everything Gary Toth tells you at face value, D.J.," Knopfler warned. "Gary has his own axes to grind and sometimes he grinds them pretty hard."

As we dropped off our dirty dishes at the kitchen I mentioned that I was on my way to the security offices. D.J. said he was going that way, too.

" Jerry Lee and I haven't been seeing eye to eye lately," he volunteered as soon as we were alone. "I told him this morning that I'm moving out of the barracks."

"I'm sorry to hear that, D.J. I thought you two were pretty close friends."

"We were. But since I signed up with Gary's outfit, we've been arguing a lot. Jerry Lee says they're filling me with hate. I say I'm fighting for what I believe in. I guess the best thing we can do is to go our separate ways."

"Where will you bunk now?"

"With my martial arts team in Barracks A-7. We start training this week to learn how to use the new weapons the workshops are making for us. Believe me, when the goons enter this camp, they're going to get the surprise of their lives."

"Is fighting something you enjoy, D.J.?" I was surprised at his transformation, having always seen him as friendly and easygoing—hardly the kind of person who enjoyed inflicting pain.

"Not exactly," D.J. replied. "I hardly fought at all until prison. Oh, I had a few years of karate during high school but I never took it seriously. It wasn't until I got banged around during interrogation and in the transit camps that I learned how to dish it out. When I came here and the warders smacked me every day, I felt like I had to pick a fight sometimes just to get the poison out of my system."

"Are you sure you're ready to go up against troops with assault rifles? How will you even get close enough to land a punch?"

"I probably shouldn't tell you this, Paul, but soon we're going to have a lot more than punches to throw around. The techs are making us high-powered crossbows, super slingshots, poisoned throwing darts, and all kinds of standoff weapons that we can use to hit the enemy at a distance. We're also learning how to capture their assault rifles and body armor to use against them. I think it's going to be more of an even match than anyone expects."

"Honestly, D.J., what chance do you think you have of living through the first assault?"

"Less than one in ten is my guess," he replied easily, looking me straight in the eye. "Paul, I realize that State Security will never give in to our demands and that the only way out of here is in a body bag. I just want to go down swinging."

"You're sure of that?"

"Dead sure," he replied with his boyish smile.

D.J. and I arrived at the entrance to the women's jail compound and presented ourselves to the guard on duty. D.J. was waved in right away. I told the guard that I had an appointment with Glenn Reineke and waited while he scanned his clipboard for my name. At last he waved me in, too.

I made my way to the one-story brick outbuilding that served as the Security Commissioner's offices. The duty officer led me to one of the rear offices that had been converted to a conference room.

"Come on in, Paul; we were just getting started," Reineke greeted me when he spotted me outside the door. With him were Pete Murphy and Gary Toth. Ralph Knopfler arrived a moment later and took a seat beside me.

"Lieutenant," he told the duty officer as soon as Knopfler was seated. "Please shut the door and don't let anyone in until I tell you."

"Yes, Sir," the lieutenant replied before closing the door.

"The reason I called you," Reineke began, "is that I need your advice on a situation that arose over the weekend. Last Thursday after Colonel Majors and I held our weekly truce conference at the east gate with the Warden and General Boscov, the General pulled me aside for a private talk. He started off by praising my war record. Then he said he had read my security file from cover to cover and thought I had been wrongly convicted on the desertion charge. He offered me what Doug Chambers offered Colonel Majors two weeks ago: expedited review before a special hearing panel. I reminded him that I didn't think any commissioner should get a rehearing until after the revolt was settled. When he finally got it through his head that I wouldn't take the bait, he backpedaled to erase the impression he'd been trying to recruit me.

"When Boscov left, I caught up with Colonel Majors, told him what Boscov had offered me and asked what Rocco had said to him when they were alone. Majors became extremely defensive. He told me he didn't think expedited case reviews were at all improper for commission members and that if I wanted to exclude myself, fine. But others had waited a long time for wrongs to be righted and it would be unfair to deny them their moment before a panel. In the meantime, he said he intended to exercise his privilege as chief commissioner to meet with his counterpart in State Security to keep the truce whenever and wherever he saw fit, without consulting me or anyone else. Then he turned on his heel and left."

"It seems to me that Colonel Majors cares more about getting his career back than he does about the revolt," Knopfler remarked.

"I don't like the sound of it, either," Pete Murphy agreed. "I think he's made up his mind to do what's best for Mitch Majors and to hell with everyone else."

"Ditto that," Toth said. "I wouldn't trust him, regardless. It all adds up. Start with his public and private statements: rarely anti-Unionist, usually sympathetic to the bosses. Then look at who he hangs out with: Perkins, a die-hard Unionist; Quayle, a fellow traveler; and the crooked judges, Richardson and O'Rourke. Then there's his personal life: right from the start, he set up a private suite for himself and has had special meals delivered to him from the mess hall. He plays favorites in doling out privileges and generally throws his weight around like he's cock-of-the-roost. The latest is that he's installed a mistress on his clerical staff. It all comes down to a question of character. If he'll cheat in small things, what's to hold him back from the big ones?"

"What do you think, Paul?" Reineke asked.

"I've had an intuitive suspicion of the Colonel for some time," I told him. "But I've kept it on hold until I had facts to justify it. For me, the central issue is whether the Colonel has put himself at the head of the revolt because he genuinely believes in it or because he thinks he can manipulate it to his own advantage. If he believes in the revolt but has some flaw that makes him act high-handedly, perhaps he can be forgiven. But if he deliberately sought the post of leader for the purpose of selling us out, then we need to move him aside before he can do any more harm."

"What kind of harm do you expect?" Murphy asked. "We're the ones who control the security and defense forces. He can't do much without us knowing about it first."

"He could create a pretext for the other side to attack," Reineke suggested. "Or fail to respond when they do. Or he could try to dismiss us and order our men to surrender. Paul is right: we need to be ready in case he steps out of line."

"And we need to keep Perkins, Quayle, and the judges under twenty-four-hour surveillance," Toth added. "If they do anything suspicious, I think we ought to bring them in for questioning or maybe even put them on ice for a while."

"We've already got four or five in custody for Unionist agitation, don't we?" Murphy pointed out. "What's a few more?"

"They might even welcome it," Reineke observed. "You couldn't ask for a better alibi when the revolt is over."

****

Late that afternoon another appeal for defections began blaring from the loudspeakers:

"Prisoners, vote with your feet! Show them what you really think of the revolt. Leave the camp now. We will not fire at any unarmed prisoner who crosses our lines. Your own commission has ordered its troops not to prevent you from leaving. So why hesitate? Leave today and you will not be punished...."

Over the weekend the Information Department had recorded a response to this speech similar to the response Glenn Reineke had delivered spontaneously the previous Friday. The recording assured prisoners that anyone who wished to leave the camp and surrender to State Security was free to do so without fear of reprisals. The defenders at the barricades were ordered to prevent no one from deserting.

Unlike Friday, today a small number of prisoners seemed ready to bolt. I watched them from a nearby roof. They joined the throng of prisoners watching from a distance, jostled their way to the front, and finally the first of them broke free and ran for the gate.

As the first defector passed between two of our barricades, every spectator held his breath. In an instant, a prisoner ran out from behind a barricade in hot pursuit but halted when his commanding officer bellowed for him to stop. The defector gained speed, vaulted over the waist-high new inner wall to a chorus of catcalls and escaped through the eastern gate, where warders pulled him to safety.

Seeing the first defector reach the gate without harm, two more bolted from the cordon of spectators toward the gate and encountered no interference, except for shouts of "Traitor!" from their fellow prisoners.

Then I saw a familiar figure break free from the crowd and start off at a brisk walk along the same path. It was George Perkins, crossing the yard without fear or shame as if he had business with his masters on the other side. Within moments, dozens of prisoners recognized him and cursed him roundly for his duplicity.

While Perkins disappeared through the gate, another familiar figure caught my eye at the far end of Division 2. It was a slender young woman in a white nurse's uniform whom I recognized even at a distance as Gwen. Like Perkins, she walked rather boldly across the yard, attracting a chorus of insults, particularly from the female prisoners. She never turned back, even when struck on the shoulder by a stone sharp enough to draw blood through her blouse. I pitied Gwen at that moment. But she had made her choice, even if she might add it later to the list of mistakes that she would claim had ruined her young life.

By the time Gwen reached the main gate, the insults were so impassioned that I expected the crowd to tear the next defector limb from limb. As it happened, Gwen was the last prisoner to desert us that night.

The bosses' idea had been a clever one: open the gates and lure out enough of the rats inside that only a few stubborn ones remained inside to be crushed. But the idea ultimately failed because the bosses' mentality remained so firmly rooted at the level of the rats they assumed us to be. Over the next two weeks, fewer than a half dozen prisoners would make the trip past the barricades.

CHAPTER 36

"Throughout history, it has been the inaction of those who could have acted, the indifference of those who should have known better, the silence of the voice of justice when it mattered most, that has made it possible for evil to triumph."
—Haile Selassie, former Emperor of Ethiopia

Friday, June 14
Day 27

The jeep climbed the narrow road that followed the southern shore of the Jordanelle Reservoir before starting the descent through the Upper Provo Canyon toward Kamas. Barely more than a decade earlier, the tranquil shoreline had been rimmed with vacation homes, picnic grounds, and manmade beaches. On the shimmering water, twenty-somethings had windsurfed while young children learned to swim and teenagers raced each other on the backs of noisy jet skis.

Now the beaches were empty and only a few half-destroyed houses remained standing within a mile of the reservoir's southern shore. These were the sturdier structures, generally made of cinder block or stone or poured concrete, usually located at strategic points flanking the road where local militias had ambushed attacking Army and National Guard units a decade before. In some places the remains of sandbag bunkers and barricades still stood out among the weeds and scrub oak. Elsewhere, flat concrete foundations dotted the barren landscape where wood-frame houses had burned to the ground or had been dismantled by Kamas recycling crews. The road through this wasteland was washed out in places by the spring runoff and marred by deep potholes.

"Why do the houses have so many holes in them?" Claire asked after she had passed yet another pockmarked wall, riddled with fist-sized apertures left by anti-tank shells and rocket-propelled grenades.

"Those are from gunfire," Martha replied. "When you were a baby people fought a war here."

"Who won?"

"The government did."

"Isn't it over yet?" Claire asked.

"It's been over for years," Martha replied. "Why?"

"Then where are all the people?"

"Most of them left or were sent far away."

"To camps?" Claire asked.

Martha hesitated before replying. "Mostly."

"Kids, too?"

"Some."

"Are the camps okay places to live in?"

"I haven't seen any place where they keep children, so I don't really know," Martha replied uneasily. "But, Claire, it's not a very good idea to talk about the camps. It's kind of unlucky—like walking under a ladder or breaking a mirror."

"My mom broke a mirror once and stayed in a bad mood for a week. She said it brought seven years of bad luck. Is it like that?"

"Sort of. Only sometimes it's forever. So what do you say we change the subject, just to be on the safe side, eh?"

The road straightened and a vista opened down a shallow canyon toward the Kamas Valley. To the north, Claire spotted the sprawling compound of the Kamas Corrective Labor Camp.

"Is that it?" she asked. This was her first visit over the hills to the Kamas Valley and she was eager to catch a glimpse of the camp.

"That's it. The town of Kamas is straight ahead," Martha answered, pointing to some commercial buildings and a few hundred houses clustered in the distance at the intersection of two state highways.

"Do you see the big stone house on the hill to our left?" Martha continued. "That's the administration building where Doug and the Warden have their offices. We'll be there in a few minutes."

But Claire could not take her eyes off the vast labor camp, with its walls and fences, watchtowers, parade grounds, and its multitudes toiling outdoors under the glare of the midday sun. As they came closer, she noticed that the camp was divided into five sections, three of which contained mostly one-story buildings of uniform size, while the other two held an assortment of structures resembling garages or workshops. A few minutes later she caught sight of tents nestled among the hills around the camp. Not far from each encampment, soldiers watched the camp from behind mounds of bulldozed earth.

Martha turned off the state highway onto a dirt road that led over a hill beyond which sat the three-story white house Martha had pointed out from a distance. Claire could now see that it was part of a compound that included a central yard the size of a football field. Behind the stone house Claire saw a pair of two-story cinder block bunkhouses, while to the right of the house was a sort of barn whose vast front door was raised to reveal a pair of tilt-cab trucks undergoing repair. In front of the barn-like repair shop was a gravel parking lot filled with jeeps, vans, pick-ups, and canvas-canopied trucks, all painted in various combinations of black, gray, olive drab, and desert tan.

The stone house had once been the vacation retreat of a Silicon Valley billionaire who enjoyed trout fishing and deer hunting in the nearby Uinta Mountains and who skied and partied at Deer Valley, some twenty miles to the west. Later, after serving as command post for an Army counterinsurgency unit charged with eradicating Mormon partisans in the Uinta Mountains, the Army had turned the house over to the Corrective Labor Administration.

It was built in the rustic Deer Valley style, with a half-timbered, stone-and-stucco exterior, steeply pitched copper roof, and vast tiled verandahs on the first and second floors overlooking the Kamas Valley. From either of the verandahs one could see nearly every acre of the camp.

Martha stopped the jeep at the compound's front gate and presented her identification and parking pass.

"I'm Martha Chambers. We're here to deliver some lunch to my husband and his staff. They're expecting us."

The guard, who wore a red beret and a desert camouflage uniform, glanced quickly at the documents, returned them and waved Martha through.

"Park anywhere you like, Mrs. Chambers."

Martha pulled up directly in front of the stone house. She and Claire removed the baskets from the rear of the jeep and carried them up the front steps.

Inside, Martha again presented her identification, this time to a black-uniformed duty officer. He led her and Claire past the half-open door of a conference room where a meeting was underway to an adjacent room whose rough-hewn oak table had been cleared for lunch. Martha and Claire placed their baskets on the sideboard and began to unpack. Through the thin plasterboard wall and the half-open door, they recognized the voices of Doug Chambers and Fred Rocco. Martha and Claire cocked their ears to listen.

"Give it some time," Jim Tracy said impatiently. "We've only been at it a week, for God's sake."

"And during that entire week the total number of prisoners who came out to us was what, twelve? Fourteen?" the Warden demanded. "And, Jack, how many of those were stoolies who were supposed to stay put?"

"About half of them," Jack Whiting replied. "The longer we open the gates, the more informants I expect we'll lose."

"How about the others who came out?" Doug Chambers asked. "Did we draw off any of their young fighters?"

"Not a one," Whiting said with evident frustration. "Which is a damned shame, because they could use more labor up in the Yukon. But, if it's any consolation, Doug, the medic at Yellowknife was mighty pleased to hear we're sending him a nurse, and a good-looking one at that."

Claire noticed Martha suddenly stop unwrapping the food she had taken from the wicker basket. Her face was ashen. When she saw Claire staring at her she turned away and began straightening the place settings.

Doug Chambers spoke next.

"It's good you're getting a head start lining up prisoner transfers," he said. "We'll need to make a clean sweep when this is all over. We also need to figure out a way to dispose of casualties in a way that won't alarm the local population. How is that part coming, Jack?"

"We've identified locations in the Kamas Valley where bulldozers can dig trenches deep enough to handle more than the estimated number of prisoner casualties. Since the valley is already sealed off to outsiders, I don't expect any problems with the locals. It's a matter of camouflage and speed.

"The only catch is that we don't have many bulldozers," Whiting continued. "And our brothers in the military haven't been very cooperative. You may recall that the National Guard turned us down when we requested backup last month. 'Not our kind of fighting,' their liaison officer told me. Frankly, Doug, I'm getting tired of being sneered at by those bureaucrats in uniform. Just because our work disturbs their precious peace of mind, they sit by and snipe at us, accusing us of being sadists and barbarians. They won't even lend us a damned bulldozer without a detailed accounting of what we plan to use it for. You know, I'm just trying to do my job. I don't see why I have to put up with their mudslinging."

The Warden addressed Whiting sympathetically.

"Let them say what they want. So what if they ask how we'll use their bulldozers? Go ahead and tell them—they'll still have to fork the things over. Cronin will see to that. Besides, a little knowledge will be good for our brethren in the military. Shared knowledge means shared responsibility. And shared responsibility means shared liability. There's the rub—once you say A and B, you can't stop at C."

"Fred's right," Boscov agreed. "The Department has faced this problem for years. The government is still clogged with bureaucrats and careerists from former administrations. We have to bring these backward types along with us and force them to become accountable."

"We're running out of time before lunch and there are still a couple of items on the agenda," Doug Chambers broke in. "Jack, do you have any progress to report from your informant inside the camp?"

"We're still talking and he's still promising us the moon," Whiting replied. "He's also upped his demands to full rehabilitation with back salary and allowances and a promotion to the next grade in rank. We told him we can consider it, but first he needs to show us what he can deliver. And fast."

"You didn't tell him anything about our timetable, did you?" Doug asked.

"Absolutely not," Whiting replied. "Surprise is essential."

He paused before speaking again.

"As for your other prospect, the one that General Boscov talked to recently," Doug continued, "I think it's fair to say that we've struck out. So, unless anyone objects, I would propose that we take an entirely different tack with him. Jack, do you still have any agents in camp who are willing to get their hands dirty?"

A few minutes later, the meeting broke up and the men came around the corner to the room where lunch was waiting. Having expected soup from the staff kitchen, Doug's colleagues seemed delighted to see the variety of sandwiches, salads, breads, and cookies that Martha and Claire had brought.

The men were also pleased to have female company for a change. The Warden was particularly attentive toward Claire, whom he said for the hundredth time reminded him of his granddaughter. At first, the conversation kept to innocuous topics like the weather, local flora and fauna, and the history of Heber and the Kamas Valley. But by the time the men had settled back for dessert and coffee, they reverted to talk about the camp.

"It seems to me," General Boscov suggested to Doug, "that we ought to be looking harder at ways to deflate the prisoners' fighting morale. Again and again we hear that the hard-line prisoners are hoping for some kind of sympathetic reaction from the other camps. They know that strikes have occurred elsewhere in the past and I think they still believe that, if only they could spread the word this time, unrest could infect the entire camp system."

"Of course, they're wrong. But how do we convince the prisoners of that?" Colonel Tracy asked while stuffing a chocolate chip cookie into his mouth.

"Why not take some of them on a tour?" Doug suggested. "After all, we brought people from the Department to visit Kamas. Why not take some prisoners to a camp or two in Orem or Provo and let them see for themselves?"

"We could also plant the rumor that deserters from Kamas will be transferred locally to Provo instead of being sent up to Yellowknife," Jack Whiting added. "Once they see that Provo isn't so bad, we might get more to desert."

"Let's discuss it again tomorrow," Doug agreed. "Unless anyone can think of some good reasons not to, I'm inclined to give it a try."

When everyone had finished eating, Doug and the Warden stayed behind to help clean the table and pack the leftovers for the return to Heber. For the first time in weeks, Doug was attentive toward Martha and seemed eager to please her. The Warden appeared to notice this and offered to take Claire for a short tour of the compound while Doug helped Martha carry the baskets to the jeep.

"That's kind of you, Fred," Martha said. "Claire, would you like to have a look around before we go?"

"Sure," Claire replied. "Could we go out on the balcony first? I'd like to look at the valley if that's okay."

"Come along with me," Fred Rocco offered cheerfully, taking Claire by the hand. "Your Uncle Fred will show you whatever you want to see."

With that, the Warden and the junior au pair set out for the verandah.

As soon as Doug and Martha were left alone, Martha gestured for Doug to take the chair beside her.

"Doug, don't you suppose I could help you more in your career if you talked to me more? Today's outing was nice, but it made me see just how little I know about what you do all day."

"That's not by accident, Martha," Doug replied. "You're better off not knowing. Believe me."

"Are you afraid to show me or ashamed?"

"Neither," Doug answered firmly. "First, this is a Restricted Zone. Just about everything we do here is classified. Second, what we do isn't as simple as it looks. You can't judge it on the basis of an occasional visit."

"So why don't you explain it to me? I'm your wife. I want to know what you're going through. I see how unhappy you are and I want to help."

"You're a wonderful wife, Martha, and I appreciate your wanting to help me. But there really isn't much you can do right now. The problem is the revolt, not anything between you and me."

"But don't you see, Doug, your work and this camp have been a problem between us ever since we came here. And it's getting to the point where I don't know what to do about it anymore. You won't let me get close enough."

"I'm sorry," Doug said. "I promise things will be better as soon as the revolt is over. It won't be long now. We're getting close to the end."

"If it's not the revolt, it's bound to be something else. Sometimes I think I hardly know you."

Doug sighed deeply and looked down at his hands as if they were weighed down by a terrible burden.

"So what do you want me to do?"

"Let me go with you when you take the prisoners to Provo. Show me the same things you show them. Let me watch you talk to them."

"I don't see what good it would do," Doug replied. "But I'll think about it."

"Thanks," Martha replied, kissing him on the cheek. "It would mean a great deal to me if we could get closer again, even for only a few days, before I go back east to have our baby."

"Oh, my God, I've completely lost track of when you planned to travel," Doug declared. "How late in the pregnancy can you go and still be allowed to fly?"

"It's already past that time. I've been planning to take the train and bring Claire with me. But Claire still has no travel papers. We're going to need your help with that."

"Her I.D. is already in the works. I'll ask them to expedite it," he promised.

"And I want you to be with me when the baby is born. Can you promise me you'll fly out before the due date and stay with us a while?"

"I will, Martha. I promise," Doug said. But his eyes were already looking out the door as his hands reached for the baskets.

****

When they returned to the house, Martha left Claire with Rosa, then headed east from the compound on Reservoir Road. After about a mile, she turned onto a dirt track and parked the car where a deer trail led up a hillside through scrub oak toward Helen Sigler's cabin.

CHAPTER 37

"Every revolution evaporates and leaves behind only the slime of a new bureaucracy."
—Franz Kafka

Saturday, June 15
Day 28

Every day saw new skirmishes at the barricades, new loudspeaker appeals for surrender, and new opportunities to defect. Adding to the tension were rumors, based on fragmentary local radio reports, that strikes had broken out in labor camps near Provo and Orem. Hopes arose among the prisoners that such revolts might spread to camps near Ogden, Logan, Price, and Green River. Some predicted that, before long, camps in Idaho and Colorado would rise and the whole Utah Security District would erupt and spread its choking gray ash over the entire camp system.

It was when these hopes rose to their highest level that the Kamas authorities offered Colonel Majors and the commission an opportunity to send a delegation of prisoners to camps at Provo and Orem. The offer was made at a truce conference late on a Friday afternoon with departure planned for early the next morning. Ralph Knopfler came to my bunk late Friday evening and asked if I would be interested in going. The delegation would consist of up to ten prisoners, including four from the commission: Chuck Quayle, Georg Schuster, Libby Bertrand, and Betty Shipley. Knopfler would not be going, nor Reineke, Murphy, or anyone from the Security, Military, or Technical Departments, out of concern that the bosses might not release them afterward. The primary objective of the delegation would be to assess first hand the likelihood of the Kamas revolt spreading to other camps in the region.

I reported to the barricades opposite the Service Yard's east gate promptly at eight the next morning. In addition to the other delegates, I also spotted Majors, Reineke, and Knopfler waiting behind a sandbag bunker. They were huddled together, deep in conversation.

At last a crackle of static emerged from loudspeakers outside the wall.

"Stand by for visitors," came the announcement. "Guard escort crossing the boundary zone."

Through the open gate I could see two black-uniformed officers crossing the no-man's-land, followed by several escort troops in desert camouflage. As they came nearer, I recognized the pair as General Boscov and Colonel Tracy. They stepped through the gate and stopped within a few yards of the barricade.

"Good morning," Boscov began cordially. "Are your people ready to go?"

"We are,'" Majors replied. "I have the roster if you'd like to check the names."

"We can do that on the bus," Boscov answered.

With that, Colonel Majors strode out from behind the bunker and handed Boscov the list. As he did, he leaned forward and spoke softly into the general's ear. The two men then stepped aside and conversed quietly for two or three minutes while the rest of us waited out of earshot. This was the moment that Glenn Reineke had been waiting for. Dish microphones installed on the second floor of a warehouse inside the Service Yard were at capturing the two men's conversation. If Majors were betraying us, we would know very soon.

At last Majors gestured for the rest of us to follow the escort troops across the no-man's-land. As I took my place in the single-file line heading toward the outer perimeter fence, I thought about how ironic it was to be leaving the camp this way: not slogging back to the worksite, not boarding a train for some northern camp, but joining a sightseeing tour to another camp as a special guest of the bosses. It seemed impossible, but could this be the exit that Ben Jackson had foretold?

As soon as we passed through the outer perimeter a squad of submachine-gunners led us across the road to our vehicle, a vintage orange school bus with steel anti-grenade mesh covering the windows. This was luxury compared to the boxcars, trucks, and police vans in which we usually traveled. As I inspected the doors and windows of the old bus, I wondered if I was the only prisoner aboard whose thoughts had turned to the possibility of escape.

Each of us gave his or her name as we spread our arms and legs for a weapons search. Then we boarded the bus and took our seats. Every few minutes the chief escort guard repeated the ground rules: only one person per bench, no talking, no lying down, keep your hands in your lap, no passing notes to anyone outside, no papers or writing materials allowed. Violators would be removed from the bus and returned to Kamas. Not wanting to miss the fun, I sat silently, hands folded in my lap, and looked out the window.

A late-model jeep approached from the direction of Heber, stirring a cloud of reddish brown dust as it parked behind a half-dozen other jeeps across the road. The doors opened and Doug Chambers climbed down from the driver's seat. Exiting from the passenger side were Fred Rocco and an attractive but unhappy-looking woman of about thirty. Chambers stopped to speak with one of the guards while the woman gave a farewell hug to a pretty brown-haired girl who jumped down from a rear seat. Judging from her body language and that of the Deputy Warden as they entered a waiting van, I inferred that they were a couple.

Something about the girl, however, compelled me to look more closely. She had the same round face, pale complexion, and soft brown eyes as my daughter Claire and even the same hairstyle, complete with long dark bangs falling over her eyes. When she turned to walk around the front of the jeep to the open passenger door, I could see that she even had the same loping gait. Unbelievable as it was, here was an exact double of my daughter riding in the same car with Warden Rocco and his Deputy. I summoned all my mental powers to will the girl to stop and turn toward me one more time.

She passed behind the jeep and then, as if she had sensed my intent, stopped and looked straight past me. I drew a sharp breath. It had to be Claire, though I knew it couldn't be. I gazed into the girl's eyes, seeking some glimmer of recognition. But there was none. She climbed back into the jeep, closed the door, and smiled sweetly at Fred Rocco as he took the driver's seat. A moment later the jeep made a U-turn and stirred up a second cloud of dust as it set off toward Heber. I had never hated the Warden more.

Before setting out that morning I had resolved to imprint into my memory every feature of the landscape between Kamas and Provo. But as I traveled across the hills into the Heber Valley and then south along the shores of the Deer Creek Reservoir into the Provo River Canyon, I barely noticed the landmarks that passed before me.

My mind was still comparing the face of the girl I had seen to that of the daughter I remembered. If it had been Claire, why didn't she notice me? Had I changed that much? I looked at my reflection in the bus window and suddenly realized how different I looked from my appearance a year and a half before. My thick crop of graying brown hair was shaven nearly bald, my whisker stubble now largely gray, my ruddy complexion weather-beaten and marred by deep wrinkles, my strong neck now as scrawny as a chicken's. Would even my wife have recognized me?

And if it was indeed Claire, what did that mean? She looked healthy, reasonably happy, and well cared for, apparently not confined to an orphanage or a juvenile detention home. If under the care of Rocco or Chambers, she would be relatively close by and not impossible to find if by some miracle I succeeded in escaping. And neither Claire nor the Department of State Security seemed aware of any connection between her and the prisoner Paul Wagner, Number W-0885.

My mind would not leave it alone. As we drove across the top of the Deer Creek Dam and began our descent down the Provo River Canyon toward Orem, I thought of nothing else.

We reached the Vineyard camp, located to the east of Orem near the shores of Utah Lake, around nine. The camp was slightly smaller than Kamas, holding about 6,000 male prisoners. It was rectangular in shape and consisted of five sections, following the same basic plan as Kamas. A major difference between the two camps lay in the type of work performed by the prisoners. While most prisoners at Kamas were occupied with recycling and mining, most prisoners at the Vineyard camp served the rail yards and rail lines along the Wasatch Front or operated the antiquated steel mill on the shores of Utah Lake.

Our visit to the Vineyard camp was so brief as to be perfunctory. The bus followed the procession of State Security SUVs into the camp's Service Yard and then through a sliding steel barrier to the rear entrance of a cramped mess hall. Once inside the mess hall, we were seated in a side room set up classroom-style with some forty chairs facing a lectern at the front. Within moments of taking our seats, the camp's Deputy Warden appeared at the lectern and summoned a panel of five prisoners who were instantly identifiable by their sleek, well-fed appearance as stool pigeons or warders.

The Deputy Warden led them through a catechism of questions and answers about camp conditions, recent strike activity, and prisoner attitudes toward events at Kamas. The answers were completely in line with Corrective Labor Administration policy. In short, the prisoners described conditions at Vineyard as utopian; they claimed no strikes had occurred there in living memory; and they thoroughly deplored the recent hooliganism at Kamas. Judging from the expressions of boredom on everyone's faces, including Doug Chambers and his wife, it appeared that even our captors found the session a complete waste of time.

Less than an hour later, we were led into a similar room at the South Provo labor camp. This camp, holding about 7,500 male prisoners, supplied the labor force for a series of state-run factories that produced prefabricated housing and building materials for government installations throughout the Utah Security District. It was in the South Provo camp that a strike had allegedly broken out in early June after an eagerly anticipated review of cases had produced early releases for only a handful of prisoners, all of them warders or Unionist Party members.

This time there was no welcoming speech by the Deputy Warden and no pre-rehearsed script for the panel of prisoners. A few minutes after we arrived in the briefing room, a door opened and five shuffling scarecrows in faded coveralls, looking very much like our own mirror images, entered the room. They moved slowly and spoke softly, but their eyes looked straight into ours and we did not doubt for a moment that they told the truth. Without any of their own camp bosses in the room, they told us familiar tales of overwork, malnutrition, exposure to the elements, extreme occupational hazards, and brutal camp discipline. They also told us of hunger strikes, work stoppages, and suicide pacts to protest camp conditions.

The most recent work stoppage had occurred in May but it had taken hold in only one of the camp's three residential divisions, lasted only two days, and had brought about the transfer of no fewer than a thousand striking prisoners to Yellowknife on its third day. What did the Upper Provo prisoners think of the revolt at Kamas? They wished us well, but they judged our revolt hopeless and had no intention of following suit, now or at any time in the future. The present generation of prisoners at Upper Provo had lost their will to resist. When and if a new generation of leaders emerged, they, too, would be spotted promptly and culled. To oppose the bosses, they warned, was futile.

I looked across the aisle at Doug Chambers, Jack Whiting, and the other turnkeys from Kamas. They were making an effort not to gloat, but there was no mistaking the satisfaction they derived from hearing defeat in the feeble voices of the Upper Provo prisoners and seeing discouragement in our eyes. By contrast, Doug Chambers's wife looked as if she had stared into the gates of hell.

As soon as the meeting was over, the escort guards called for those who needed to use the toilets to line up at the door. Since Upper Provo was an all-male facility, the women, including Mrs. Chambers, were escorted to a separate facility on the opposite side of the mess hall. After they returned, the guards whisked the visiting prisoners through the cafeteria line and back to the meeting room to eat. The visiting bosses and Mrs. Chambers were taken to the officer's mess to dine with their Upper Provo counterparts.

I took a seat at the end of the table and was surprised when Libby Bertrand sat beside me. "Something very odd happened in the restroom," she said in a low voice. "Have you ever met Martha Chambers?"

"How could I have?" I replied.

"Well, she seems to know you. She approached me in the ladies' room and said she had a humanitarian message for Paul Wagner. But she said she didn't dare use official channels because her husband didn't know what she was doing. She asked me to tell you she has a message from your friend's widow about your wife and daughters. If you want to hear what it is, I'm supposed to meet her again in the restroom after lunch."

Libby looked at me expectantly.

"Well, what do think?" she asked.

"I don't quite know," I replied, my mind racing to sort through all the possibilities. "On the one hand, State Security knows perfectly well what's become of my wife and daughters. So it would be easy enough for Chambers to use them as bait. It's a lot less likely that they would know about my friend's widow. What I don't understand is why State Security would go to such lengths to set a trap for either of us when they could have taken us the moment we left the camp this morning."

I fell silent and thought back to Helen Sigler's message about Claire being in Utah, to my vision of Claire while I was in the isolator, and to the girl I saw this morning who looked uncannily like her. If Helen Sigler believed that Claire was in Utah and if Martha Chambers claimed to have a message from Helen about Claire, wasn't it likely that the two women knew each other and that Martha Chambers was telling Libby Bertrand the truth now?

"Call me a fool, but I'm inclined to believe her," I said. "How about you?"

Libby nodded.

"But even if I didn't," she added, "as a mother, I'd never forgive myself for not trying to help your girls. And if I'm wrong—well, we can argue about that on the train to Yellowknife."

After lunch, Libby approached the senior escort officer and requested another visit to the toilets before boarding the bus. Martha Chambers waited a discreet interval before asking to do the same.

The moment the women returned, the escort troops led us back to the bus and counted heads one more time. When they allowed us to board, I took the seat directly behind Libby's.

"What was the message?" I asked a short while later.

"We didn't have much time. First, she said your wife and younger daughter are still in detention in Pennsylvania for attempting to emigrate on canceled exit visas. Your older daughter escaped and is close by in Utah. Then she gave me a blank sheet of paper from your friend's widow that contains a concealed message. She said you would know how to read it."

I recall virtually nothing about the rest of the trip back to Kamas. All I could think of was Claire and deciphering Helen Sigler's message.

But when we arrived at the barracks, it didn't take long to realize that other events might get in the way. The first sign that something was amiss was the delay in letting us off the bus. Then I saw the surveillance experts on the balcony of the training building peer at us through their telescopes. At the gate to the Service Yard I could sense heightened vigilance in our troops manning the barricades.

Before I could inquire about the increased tension, Glenn Reineke and Ralph Knopfler hustled the entire delegation off to the commission offices for a debriefing. There we reported what we had learned on our trip: that no strike or revolt was currently underway at either the

Vineyard or the South Provo camp and that little sympathy existed for the Kamas revolt in either place. We were therefore very much alone in our resistance and seemed likely to remain that way. The commissioners listened politely but asked few questions. It seemed as if they already knew what we would report. Colonel Majors thanked us for our efforts and adjourned the meeting without further comment.

One by one, the commissioners filed out except for Reineke and Knopfler.

"How long do I have to wait before somebody lets me in on the secret?" I asked as soon as we were alone. "Why is everybody here walking on eggshells?"

"Come on over to my office," Reineke answered. "I've got something to show you."

We walked in silence to the outbuilding where the Security Department had its command post. But instead of going to Reineke's office, we went to cellblocks at the rear of the building. There Reineke unlocked a sliding door and led Knopfler and me down a flight of stairs into a place that looked much like the isolation block. Down the center of a concrete-floored corridor ran an evil-smelling drainage channel while to either side were rows of steel doors resembling those of isolator cells. At the end of the corridor were four interrogation rooms with eye-level peepholes. Reineke gestured for me to look through the peephole of the first such room on the left.

Through the hole I could see two of Reineke's security officers standing on either side of a middle-aged prisoner whose wrists were manacled behind his back to a steel chair bolted to the floor. I recognized the prisoner's long face and sad, sleepy eyes immediately as those of Steve Bernstein, the pharmaceutical salesman from Manhasset who regaled us on our first day at Kamas. Now I listened through the hole in the door as Reineke's men badgered him into confirming the points of a confession they had written out for him.

"So it was at Green River that State Security recruited you as an informant?" the senior interrogator prompted.

"Yes," Bernstein answered wearily.

"And after your transfer to Kamas, you continued informing on other prisoners through Jack Whiting and members of his security detail?"

"Yes."

"And after the revolt broke out last month, you re-established contact with members of State Security and were issued an electronic device that you used to submit reports about camp defenses and security arrangements?"

"Yes."

Reineke tapped me softly on the shoulder and led me to the next window. Through the peephole I recognized the bruised and bloodied face of Brian Gaffney. From the condition of his face as well as the threatening posture of his interrogator, it appeared that Gaffney had not given them his fullest cooperation.

"Let me get this straight," the interrogator told him. "You admit that the Wart recruited you as an informant while you were in the isolator. And you admit to giving sensitive information about camp defenses to Bernstein when he recontacted you. And you admit attacking Glenn Reineke with a knife this morning. But you don't admit being part of any conspiracy?"

"That's right," Gaffney lisped, barely moving his grotesquely swollen lips.

"And you never had contact with Randy Skinner or Ramon?"

"Never."

"You didn't receive instructions from them or anyone else about attacking black or Hispanic prisoners?"

"Never."

"And you aren't aware of any plan to incite racial violence so State Security would have a pretext to storm the camp?"

"No way," Gaffney replied. "The only one I went after was Reineke."

I turned away from the peephole and looked at Reineke in disbelief.

"Gaffney jumped you with a knife?"

"He missed my neck by less than an inch," Reineke answered. "I sensed somebody coming at me from behind and ducked. One of Gary's men pulled him off me and took some bad cuts before we got Gaffney under control."

Then he led me to the door of the third cell, where the gangster, Randy Skinner, maintained a sullen silence.

"There's no point in denying it, Skinner," the interrogator pressed. "Before he died, Ramon told us all about how the two of you killed Jabril and tried to nail Frank Brancato. The only thing we don't know is who else was working with you. You could make it a lot easier on yourself if you'd just tell us."

No response.

"There's no point in counting on your thieves' code of silence, Skinner. Brancato has already washed his hands of you and has told us who he suspects was working with you. Do you want us to read you their names?"

Silence.

"All right, let's put aside the question of who else was involved. Why not tell us what the Wart promised you? We know he wanted you to start a race riot so that he'd have a cover for storming the camp. What was the bait? Transfer? Early release? Letting you take over Brancato's position as capo?"

More silence.

"That's too bad, Skinner. Because we're prepared to do whatever it takes to find out what deal the Wart offered you. So think about it. You have five minutes until kickoff."

I turned away from the door with a sinking feeling in my stomach and a confusion I had never felt before about the ends and means of our revolt. It would be naïve to think that our newborn camp government, unlike all other governments in all ages, could have survived without an effective internal security service. But, having seen the depths to which the State Security Department had sunk, how far along this path were we willing to follow? Did our taking of the moral high ground against the Unionists tighten the moral constraints we operated under or relieve us of them? The answers were no longer as clear as I had thought them to be.

I left the security offices under a promise to return after dinner. As troubling and absorbing as the day's events had been, my thoughts returned immediately to the folded sheet of paper that Libby Bertrand had given me on our return from Provo. I removed it from inside my coveralls and held it up to the light. It appeared to be the same kind of ordinary notepaper that Helen Sigler had used for her earlier messages. As usual, I could not detect any impressions left by pen or pencil.

The moment I returned to my bunk, I gathered my materials for developing the message chemically and deciphering its contents. Then I set to work. Some two hours later I scrawled the following message on a separate sheet of paper:

MESSAGE SEVEN (7). WIFE AND YOUNGER DAUGHTER REMAIN IN DETENTION NEAR PHILADELPHIA AFTER ATTEMPTING DEPARTURE ON CANCELED EXIT VISAS. OLDER DAUGHTER SAFE IN UTAH AND RETURNING EAST SOON. PLAN UNDERWAY VIA INLAWS TO REINSTATE FAMILY EXIT VISAS INCLUDING YOURS. YOUR RELEASE INTO EXILE LIKELY BUT ONLY REPEAT ONLY IF YOU EXIT CAMP BEFORE REVOLT CRUSHED. RELIABLE INFO SAYS ATTACK COMING IN SEVEN (7) TO TEN (10) DAYS WHEN ARMOR ARRIVES BY RAIL. TROOP DISPOSITIONS AND ORDER OF BATTLE FOLLOW. PLEASE PASS TO OUR MUTUAL FRIEND....

CHAPTER 38

"The Party denied the free will of the individual—and at the same time it exacted his willing self-sacrifice. It denied his capacity to choose between two alternatives—and at the same time it demanded that he should constantly choose the right one. It denied his power to distinguish good and evil—and at the same time it spoke pathetically of guilt and treachery... There was somewhere an error in the calculation; the equation did not work out."
—Arthur Koestler, Darkness at Noon

Monday, June 17
Day 30

Reineke never appeared at his office Saturday evening. Nor could I find him on Sunday. Three months earlier, Ben Jackson had told Reineke and me his dream of a Kamas camp under siege. His dream had foreseen an assault against the camp and had also predicted that I would be out of Kamas before the assault began. After hearing Jackson's prediction, Reineke had promised to help me find a way out if I would use my freedom to tell the outside world about Kamas. Would he remember his promise?

Late Sunday evening, Ralph Knopfler passed the word that Reineke wanted me to attend a short meeting the next morning to discuss camp security in the wake of Saturday's assaults on him and the gangster Jabril and the assailants' interrogations. After breakfast Knopfler, Pete Murphy, Gary Toth, and I appeared in Reineke's office. Reineke's eyes were bloodshot, his cheeks hollow, and his voice low and monotone. He thanked us all for coming and launched directly into an account of what he had learned from the questioning of Bernstein, Gaffney, and Skinner.

"As of this morning, Bernstein and Gaffney have made what amount to full confessions. Skinner still refuses to cooperate and is getting around-the-clock attention until he changes his mind.

"Right now we're fairly confident that there were three separate operations going on, one centered on Bernstein, one on Gaffney, and the third on Skinner and Ramon Sanchez. Bernstein's role was that of a conventional stay-behind informant. He picked up what he could about our defenses and security measures and reported it to Whiting wirelessly.

"But since Whiting and his people couldn't easily reach their other informants inside camp, they also had to use Bernstein as a go-between. They must have been desperate to take that risk. Any one of the informants could have compromised all the others, as Gaffney eventually did. As it turned out, our technical people knew early on that someone in camp was using a clandestine transceiver but they had no means of finding it until Gaffney led us to Bernstein.

"The Wart must have been crossing his fingers that Gaffney would be able to kill me off quickly and escape through the deserter's gate without his link to Bernstein ever coming to light. All the knife attacks were timed to coincide with the daily call for deserters.

"So why were the bosses willing to risk their entire informant network just to have Gaffney get rid of me? Several reasons, but I think the main one is that I rejected their recruitment approach. Because, at the same time they pitched me, they also pitched Majors, and I have reason to believe that he took the bait. They must have calculated that, with me out of the way, nobody else would have been able to stand up to Majors when he finally sold us out.

"Which brings me to the operation centered on Ramon and Skinner. On one level, it seems to have been a crude attempt to instigate a brawl between the politicals and the thieves. Or maybe it started with Skinner wanting a green light from the bosses to take Brancato's place as capo of thieves. In any case, the bet didn't pay off. Instead, we've shut down the Wart's entire network and Mitch Majors is under more of a cloud than ever."

"How bad is the case against Majors?" I asked. "I saw his *tête-à-tête* with Boscov in the no-man's-land Saturday morning before we left for Provo. Did the long-range dish microphones pick up any of their conversation?"

"We got the gist of it," Reineke replied. "Majors pressed for more concessions to help him persuade us to go back to work. There's nothing particularly damning in that. What troubled me more was his insistence on seeing the results of his own case review. They even dickered over what rank and pay he would be entitled to if he were released."

"Asking for a case review doesn't make him a traitor," Knopfler said. "Just about everybody in camp has a petition in the works, including most of the commission. Is there something else that leads you to think he intends to sell us down the river?"

"There is, but I can't talk about it quite yet," Reineke told us. "In the meantime, we'll need to keep a close eye on him."

For a moment no one spoke, then Gary Toth raised his hand.

"I've got a question," he said. "When their interrogations end, what are we supposed to do with Bernstein, Gaffney, and the others? Put them on trial, execute them, or just hold onto them? If we don't make an example of them now, we may regret it later when things get hot."

"I wouldn't want to risk making martyrs out of them," Knopfler replied. "Let's keep them on ice."

"Ralph is right," Reineke agreed. "If there's a settlement, we might be able to trade them for something useful. If the bosses storm the place, all bets are off, anyway."

Toth looked around the table before speaking again.

"Just tell me one thing: why did we ever go to the trouble of chopping every stool pigeon we could lay our hands on if we don't care who survives us? If we leave these bastards alive, the moment they're free they'll spread their poison among a whole new generation of prisoners. Say what you want, Glenn, but unless you're here in the cellblock with me when the tanks come rolling in, these stoolies are going to go down with us."

Reineke gave Toth a reproachful look but said nothing.

Our discussion went on for another half-hour, mainly about the chances for some kind of high-level intervention and, if none occurred, how soon government forces might attack us. Based on Helen Sigler's coded message and information from other sources, we were inclined to agree that prospects for a miraculous intervention were dim and that an attack would likely come within the week.

When the meeting ended, Knopfler and Reineke set off for the other side of the women's camp to attend the commission's scheduled weekly meeting. Reineke suggested that I come along because he wanted to nominate me to replace George Perkins as a commissioner. I thanked him for his confidence in me but declined.

"Nonsense, Paul, you're just the kind of person we need. Besides, you're practically a commissioner already after attending so many of our sessions."

"Glenn, can I have a moment with you privately?"

"Fine, let's get out of the sun," Reineke suggested, pointing toward the nearest barracks. But before we reached the barracks, Mitch Majors and Chuck Quayle overtook us from behind and urged us not to be late for the weekly meeting. Reineke shrugged and suggested we resume our conversation in his office after the meeting. At his insistence, I agreed to attend the session but only as an observer.

When we arrived, Colonel Mitch Majors stood at the head of the conference table and gazed out confidently upon his fellow commissioners. He looked commanding in the neatly pressed desert camouflage fatigues that he had borrowed from the camp storeroom. During the two weeks since the fateful open meeting in the mess hall with the visiting DSS bosses, Majors had done a masterful job of repositioning himself as the resolute leader of resistance despite his previous penchant for compromise. He was a gifted actor but his vanity and frequent high-handedness had not escaped notice among his fellow commissioners. I saw several of them exchange disapproving looks as Majors flashed a self-important smile at his personal secretary, a petite dark-haired woman of about thirty-five who sat along the wall with her stenographic pad at the ready.

"Did any of you notice that today marks the thirtieth day of the revolt?" the Colonel asked. "What do you suppose the enemy is doing to mark the occasion over in the other compound?"

The remark elicited smiles but no laughter.

"All right then," Majors continued, "Let's start around the table with the Military Department."

Pete Murphy looked unwell. His hair was disheveled, his face unshaven, and the gray circles under his eyes added to the unhealthy pallor of his complexion. He didn't even glance up from his notes as he spoke.

"Over the past five days, the enemy has added two more battalion-strength infantry units to the forces outside the camp. Training exercises and maneuvers have become more frequent, with many exercises occurring at night. Intelligence indicates that the enemy may have constructed a mockup of the camp nearby to train for an assault.

"To date, we have not seen any evidence that the enemy has brought in the kind of armor that one would expect to be part of an all-out assault on a camp the size of Kamas. Once it has arrived, I predict an assault within twenty-four to forty-eight hours.

"As I reported to you last week, our defensive preparations are complete and we continue to improve our training and readiness. But no one here should be under any illusions about the imbalance between the enemy's forces and our own. If they attack, our losses will be catastrophic."

The moment he finished speaking, Pete Murphy raised his head and looked around the table with an expression of palpable relief. It seemed to me that nothing in his Army career had prepared him for a battle like the one he had been asked to fight.

Glenn Reineke offered a summary of what he had learned from the interrogations of Bernstein, Skinner, and Gaffney, leaving out any speculation about Majors's possible disloyalty. Reineke also explained the reasons behind the policy of permitting disaffected prisoners to leave the camp through the deserters' gates. As long as the stalemate continued, he declared, those who opted not to fight would be free to use the gates. But once fighting broke out, anyone who attempted to leave would be considered a deserter and dealt with accordingly.

A moment of awkward silence followed.

Then it was Dr. Schuster's turn to report on medical matters. To illustrate how few drugs or medical supplies were left on hand, Schuster pointed out that Glenn Reineke's bodyguard was now near death from infection of the knife wounds he received while attempting to disarm Brian Gaffney. The knife blade, Schuster discovered, had been smeared with human feces to bring on sepsis. The faces around the table registered disgust but not surprise.

Next in line was Terry McIntyre, the Technical Department chief who ventured only rarely from his secret laboratory to attend commission meetings.

"I must say, you technical people certainly do a good job of keeping the lid on your secrets," Majors told him. "What encouraging news do you bring us today, Terry?"

McIntyre peered down his thick, horn-rimmed glasses at his notes.

"Well, if you're looking for breakthroughs, Colonel, I expect I may disappoint you," McIntyre replied. "Lately we've had to scale back expectations considerably."

"Perhaps then you could start with some of the things you *have* accomplished..." Majors pressed.

"At the moment, every project we've completed has already been passed along to the Military Department and the workshops. The gas masks, for instance, and the crossbows and the compound longbows, as well as some low-yield incendiary devices. But we've been rather stymied in the area of explosives. Given the shortage of raw materials—"

"You mean to say you haven't come up with the anti-tank weapons we talked about?" Majors interrupted. "How about electronic warfare?"

McIntyre shook his head.

"We scoured the camp for electronics and microcircuitry the very first week of the revolt. Not much turned up."

"So all the hype and rumor about secret weapons was nothing more than... hype and rumor?"

Beads of sweat formed on McIntyre's upper lip.

"Excuse me, Colonel, but you led us to believe that rumors were to be encouraged to keep up morale. If there's been a misunderstanding..."

The news came as a crushing blow. We had all wanted desperately to believe the rumors. The techs were our best and brightest. Surely, we thought, they would come up with something ingenious to help even the odds.

"No, there's no misunderstanding," Majors answered wearily. "Just try to wrap up whatever you're working on by the end of the week. And be sure to destroy your paperwork."

Majors continued around the table until all the Department heads had spoken but by now we were all on the edge of depression. Time was running out and we knew it.

"So, now we come to the question of questions," Majors continued. "Do we fight or do we surrender? You all know the terms State Security has extended to us. If they had offered us even the most minimal concessions, things might have taken a very different turn. But they always revert to the same old mantra: 'First go back to work and then we'll see...'

Majors turned to Ralph Knopfler.

"Ralph, I understand your people have done some opinion polling to track camp morale. Last week when you asked the prisoners if they wanted to fight or surrender, what did they tell you?"

"Nine out of ten wanted to hold out till we're attacked," Knopfler reported. "They won't go back to work unless the bosses meet all our baseline demands and offer credible guarantees."

"What sort of guarantees would they need?" Majors asked. "Would bringing in a member of the Party Central Committee be enough?"

"We asked that in the last poll," Knopfler replied. "Bringing in a couple well-known Central Committee men might help but only if they accepted our demands unconditionally."

Majors sat up and his eyes took on a look of renewed hope.

"That's what I proposed the last time I talked to Boscov," he said. "They're still non-committal about it but I still think a visit from somebody like Sturgis or Cook could be the key."

Knopfler and I exchanged puzzled looks. Why did Majors so often bring the discussion back to what sort of government promises might be sufficient to entice the prisoners back to work? While the Colonel had not advocated outright capitulation or disparaged those prisoners who favored holding out to the end, time after time he held out hope for the kind of negotiated settlement that the prisoners had clearly rejected. Did this reflect a fundamental respect for human life or an equally profound disrespect for human rights and values?

For the next half-hour our discussion continued without bringing us any closer to resolution. I left the commission offices more confused than ever. At the same time, I was eager to talk to Reineke about whether the time had come for me to leave Kamas as we had discussed three months before.

On the way out, Pete Murphy took my arm and gestured for me to sit down with him. "Paul, do you remember the conversation we had a few weeks ago about dreams?"

"Sure," I said. "You dreamed you were getting out. When's the big day?"

"Tomorrow, the eighteenth," Murphy replied with a worried look.

"Are you ready to go?"

"That's just it," Murphy replied. "I'm not. For the past two and a half months I've been thinking that if only I can last to June 18, I'll have it made. But now that it's almost here, I don't know what to do."

"Would it be so awful if your dream turned out to be wrong?"

"Not really. What spooks me is that it may turn out to be right. Because if it is, I can't imagine getting out of Kamas tomorrow any other way but by dying."

"If you're that spooked, why not stay in your bunk or check into the infirmary for the day. Let it blow over. Nobody deserves a rest more than you."

Murphy's face brightened.

"My God, Paul, I don't know why I didn't think of that before. That's exactly what I ought to do."

And without another word, he set off toward the infirmary.

When I arrived a short while later at Glenn Reineke's office I saw the deciphered message from Helen Sigler that I had brought back from Provo spread before him on the desk.

"Paul, do you remember what I said to you that night when Ben Jackson came to see me about his dreams?"

"I remember you tried to recruit me to hunt stoolies," I said with a smile.

"I did, didn't I? But then our relationship went off in a different direction and I'm glad it did."

"So am I," I said.

"Back then I told you we had enough martyrs in Kamas. I still believe that."

"Then you think I should leave?"

"You have a chance to live, Paul. Take it."

"Yes, but how?" I asked. "Stroll out the deserters' gate, just like that?"

"I wish I knew another way," he replied quietly.

"I'm going to have to think long and hard about that one, Glenn. You don't really expect the bosses to attack in the next couple days, do you?"

Reineke looked me straight in the eye as he spoke.

"Don't wait a day longer. And don't tell anybody about it. Just go."

CHAPTER 39

"A single death is a tragedy. A million deaths is a statistic."
—Joseph Stalin

Tuesday, June 18
Day 31

The blazing June sun was already high above the eastern hills when I spotted the dust cloud approaching from the direction of Heber. It crept steadily down from the heights of Upper Provo Canyon, trailing distant plumes of reddish brown dust.

"Bulldozers," Jon Merrill reported as he watched their progress through his field binoculars. "Seems the bosses are finally getting serious."

"Let me borrow those," I replied. I focused the glasses on the lead bulldozer and then on the second and third.

"They have Army markings," I said. "If the Warden can borrow a half-dozen dozers from the military, I expect tanks and APCs won't be far behind. It doesn't look good for the home team, Jon."

I gave Merrill the binoculars and gazed out from the barracks roof across the perimeter wall toward the enemy troop encampments three or four hundred yards away. Before long the bulldozers would be piling up new earthworks that would cut off our view of enemy positions. If and when the tanks and APCs arrived, almost certainly by night, we probably wouldn't see them coming.

Merrill reported our sighting to the messenger posted at the corner of the barracks and directed him to convey the news to the command post. Merrill returned a few moments later.

"Shift's almost over. Will I see you for the four o'clock watch?" I asked.

"No," Merrill replied. "I've been promoted to a desk job at the command post. I'll still handle the morning watch every day, but afternoons I'll be doing paperwork for Pete Murphy. The Doc says I'm fit to put in a full workday now."

"Congratulations. You certainly look stronger. Too bad Gwen isn't here to see it."

Merrill gazed out at the horizon.

"Yeah," he sighed. "I never expected her to bolt the way she did."

I sensed the hurt in his voice.

"I talked to her a couple days before she left. I didn't expect it, either," I said.

"She let a lot of people down when she walked out," Merrill added. "I still love her and feel deeply sorry for her but what she did was just plain wrong."

I opened my mouth to speak but thought better of it. What could I say that wouldn't become a lie if I, too, walked out of camp? For I had been thinking of nothing else since my conversation with Reineke the day before.

Merrill gave me a penetrating look.

"Let's be honest with each other, Paul," he said. "Nobody I know expects to get out of Kamas alive. When the bosses are ready to shut us down, they'll cut through here like a knife through butter. And there isn't a damned thing we can do about it."

Our watch ended a short while later. I made my way back to the barracks to rest until the mess hall opened for lunch.

I rose when the noon bell rang and followed the stream of prisoners toward the Division 3 mess. The first thing I noticed as we approached was the swarm of men at the bulletin board. A gray-bearded prisoner emerged slowly from the crowd with head hung low to join the flow of those entering the hall.

"What's posted up there?" I asked him.

"The first batch of case reviews," he replied gloomily.

"Does it show which petitions were approved?" I asked.

He shook his head.

"Only the ones that were reviewed. To find out if yours was approved you have to wait in line."

We entered the mess hall. Along the west wall of the building a hundred or more prisoners stood single-file before a mess table manned by our case review clerks, the judges Richardson and O'Rourke. While Richardson, a tall patrician with darting eyes, searched through a series of cardboard boxes for the next petitioner's file jacket, the short bespectacled O'Rourke notified each prisoner of the action that the special hearing panel had taken on his petition. I concluded at once that Colonel Majors must have acted unilaterally in permitting the authorities to deliver the panel's decisions to the clerks. If the commission had approved the action, surely I would have learned of it. And, from the looks on the men's faces, the whole exercise had been pointless, for very few petitions seemed to have been approved.

The lanky young prisoner at the head of the line listened to Judge O'Rourke silently for a minute or more before slamming his fist on the table and turning on his heel to leave. It was Jerry Lee.

I grabbed his arm as he passed me on the way to the door.

"Setback?" I asked.

"Setback, hell," Jerry Lee snorted. "The whole system is a fraud. No matter what grounds you have for appeal, they have a dozen reasons to turn you down. Nothing you could say could ever be enough to win."

"On what grounds did you appeal?"

"Lack of evidence," he replied. "As a fallback, I asked for a reduction in sentence."

"So how did you make out?"

"Zero for two. O'Rourke said if I didn't like it, I could wait a year and try again. The old farts are using that line on everybody. What idiots."

"Come on, let's have some lunch."

After lunch I returned to the barracks. There I gathered my toothbrush, razor, and spare set of underwear and the few belongings that would fit unobtrusively inside my coveralls and headed to the bathhouse for a shower. When I had finished, instead of returning to the barracks, I went to the Service Yard and sat in the shade near one of the warehouses located closest to the main gate.

Of all the places along the camp's perimeter, this point was closest to where the enemy loudspeakers most often directed would-be deserters to make their exit. If I was to make a break for it, I wanted to draw the least possible attention by slipping out in the first moments after the gate opened. So I sat back under the broad eaves of the warehouse and waited for the loudspeakers to crackle into life.

The afternoon was dry and warm and a fresh breeze stirred across my face. Occasionally I dozed off and then awoke when someone passed nearby. I lost track of time. It was probably after three o'clock when I heard the first sputter of static from the loudspeakers. The static served as prelude to a medley of Sousa marches that faded into a recorded speech by the late President-for-Life. But it wasn't until I heard the voice of George Perkins, former commissioner and highest-ranking Kamas deserter, that I came fully to my senses.

Perkins had become the government's Tokyo Rose, regaling us with reasons to be discouraged about our plight and excuses to throw in the towel. For the first three weeks of the revolt, Perkins had kept up his pretense of support for our cause. For another week after deserting us, he had held his tongue. Now, at last, he could give free rein to his defeatism and could reproach the hard-liners for seizing the freedom he never valued for himself. As if torn between vindicating his principles or his actions, Perkins's speech called both for collective surrender and individual desertion.

"Some of your leaders," he began after making his introductory remarks, "have decided that freedom can be won only with the help of sabers, pikes, and Bowie knives. In their arrogance and lust for revenge, they would doom all of you to a violent death.

"There is still time to bring the hard-liners back to their senses. But the way is not by preparing for violence. Let there be no mistake: if fighting breaks out, this camp will be wiped off the face of the earth, and any prisoner who survives the event will spend his last days digging in the frozen tundra.

"Why should you pay for the sins of these gangsters? Remove them now and elect new leaders who will negotiate in good faith! And if they refuse to step down, then why not take steps to save yourselves?

"This afternoon the camp authorities will again receive any prisoner who wants to leave camp. If you want to surrender, go now to the east gate of Division 2. The gate will remain open for the next thirty minutes. When the time has expired, anyone approaching the perimeter will be shot on sight…"

While Perkins delivered his speech, I watched the faces of prisoners in the yard. All listened with rapt attention and quite a few seemed on edge, as if weighing the pros and cons of taking up the offer. But on most faces I saw distaste, then anger, and then fury at this brazen attempt to talk us into discarding our hard-won freedom and trading it in for a well-worn yoke.

Suddenly there was a rush of prisoners into Division 2. Within seconds, a semicircular cordon formed some ten meters behind the barricades. I took a place as close to the front as I could reach. Across the buffer zone that separated the barricades from the perimeter wall, scores of black-helmeted troops in plastic riot armor massed behind the east gate as it swung open. On both sides of the buffer zone, all appeared to be waiting for the first deserter to step into the open.

My mind was in turmoil. On one hand, I had resolved today to leave at the first opportunity. Reineke had urged me not to delay and Perkins had left no doubt that this thirty-minute window would be the last chance to escape. If I didn't seize it, I might not ever see my family again.

But to be the first one to take up Perkins's odious challenge—to flee under the baleful gaze of hundreds of fellow prisoners—would be high treason and a mortal disgrace. Even if I succeeded in escaping from Kamas and bearing witness to what went on there, what credence would my testimony have after betraying principles and friends? My mind was paralyzed and my feet would not budge.

Seconds went by while I confronted this appalling dilemma. Suddenly a pair of vandals shot out from the right side of the cordon, vaulted over the low inner wall and sprinted to freedom. An angry murmur rose from the crowd and a handful of men leapt forward to intercept them, but without success. The riot troops fanned out now in front of the gate and stood motionless while the vandals ran between them and through the open portal. Neither a cheer nor a curse was heard.

A few seconds later, another vandal made his break, followed a fraction of a second later by a limping political, and then by a stoutly built thief. But this time a pack of vigilantes set off to intercept the deserters and a melee broke out just short of the wall. Our defense troops, crouching behind sandbag bunkers, watched the brawl but obeyed their standing orders not to intervene.

While the three deserters struggled to break free from their pursuers, a half dozen others stepped out from the line and made a run for the gate. Now scores of pursuers ran after them, dragging them down and beating them senseless. And as they did, two more deserters shot out of the crowd and called upon the government troops to protect them. Only when the runners were overtaken from behind and tackled to the ground halfway across the buffer zone did the black-helmeted troops step forward with batons in hand to rescue them.

These few steps forward were all it took to spur our defense forces into action. An attack upon non-deserting prisoners had now occurred inside the perimeter wall. Such an attack released our fighters from their orders not to intervene. They began by hurling a volley of fist-sized stones and brick fragments at the helmeted troops, then charging at the ones located furthest forward, wielding heavy wooden fighting staves whose massive impact knocked the armor-clad troops clean off their feet. Over the next few moments, rebels succeeded in dragging most of the would-be deserters back behind the barricades for additional punishment.

Thus the battle escalated to an ever-higher pitch, driven by passion and pride. With rocks and bricks flying, I took shelter behind the nearest barricade. At this stage in the skirmish, it might still have been possible for each side to withdraw from the buffer zone with its pride intact. But this was the moment when Pete Murphy arrived with a company of reinforcements from the Service Yard, where he had been spending the day secluded in an infirmary bed. It was June 18th, the day he had dreamed would be his last in camp.

Still a bit disoriented, Murphy assumed that the enemy's objective was to capture our defenders, as they had tried to do in many earlier probes. Accordingly, he led his entire company of fifty men in a ferocious charge across the buffer zone. Unencumbered by helmets or armor, they quickly overtook the government troops, pushed them back, and forced them to release their grip on prisoners still within the buffer zone. The government troops were now vastly outnumbered and their nightsticks were no match for the swords, spears, and fighting staves of the attacking prisoners.

The commander of the government troops, apparently fearing that Murphy's reinforcements might cut off his own men's retreat, ordered the watchtowers to open fire with .30-caliber machine guns on any prisoners remaining in the buffer zone. In an instant, Murphy's company was trapped in a ferocious crossfire from the two eastern watchtowers. Any fighters who found themselves within reach of the barricades now jumped back to seek cover. Those in the open crawled toward shelter. But their movements soon drew the attention of the machine-gunners, who fired at anything orange that stirred inside the buffer zone. As the seconds ticked by, the machine-gunners found their targets and, one by one, the orange fighters lay still.

I watched Pete Murphy crawl on his stomach through the dust, dragging behind him the inert body of a slim teenage fighter. A .30-caliber round hit Murphy in the leg but he kept on crawling. Another round grazed his wrist. He writhed in pain for a moment, then maneuvered his legs to the other side of the boy's body, grasped the boy's collar with his good hand, and continued to crawl. He was still crawling when the firing stopped and the black-helmeted troops re-emerged to rescue their injured comrades from the yard and take them back to safety. While they moved about, Murphy lay still. A few minutes later, the government had evacuated its casualties and left the orange-clad prisoners for dead. The buffer zone was silent. Our own men still dared not venture out again for fear of the machine guns.

I ran to the sandbag bunker closest to where Murphy lay. Our platoon and squad leaders were calling out from behind the barricade to find out if any of their men remained alive. I peered over the sandbags and thought I heard a low voice as Murphy's head rolled slightly onto its side.

"Did you hear that?" I asked the man next to me.

"I did," he replied. It was the rancher, Earl Cunningham.

"Will you help me bring him out?"

"Let's do it," he said.

We each rose slowly behind the wall of sandbags, raised our hands over our heads to show that we were unarmed and, with our hearts in our mouths, edged slowly around the sandbag wall into the open. Murphy lay on the ground no more than five yards away. His eyes were open and he was looking straight at us, but his life appeared to be ebbing away.

As we advanced, both of us pointed toward Murphy's body to show enemy sharpshooters that our sole aim was to bring him back to safety.

"Can you hear me, Pete?" I asked.

No reply.

"Do you hear me?" I asked again, louder.

"Don't let them take me," was his reply. "Not today. Please, not today."

"It's Paul and Earl," I replied. "You'll be safe with us."

We approached to within a foot of him and slowly bent down to grasp him under the shoulders. The moment we reached for him was the moment the machine gun opened fire. The first three-round burst landed in Murphy's upper back and the second burst sent a slug into the back of Earl Cunningham's head. I didn't wait to see whether either man was still alive. Without thinking, I jumped back and scrambled over the sandbags to safety. There I lay, gasping for air and trembling from an excess of adrenaline, thinking that Pete Murphy's dream had finally come true.

After a while, Jerry Lee appeared at my side, took my arm, and told me it was safe to stand up now. He led me to a bench where Libby Bertrand sat with a frail-looking woman of about sixty whose pale, angular face I recognized as that of Irene Cunningham.

"Does she know?" I asked Jerry Lee before sitting down between him and Earl Cunningham's widow.

"We haven't told her," he replied.

But when I took her hand and saw the tears fall from her tired eyes, it was clear that Irene Cunningham knew her husband was gone.

CHAPTER 40

"What luck for the rulers that men do not think."
—Adolph Hitler

Wednesday, June 26
Day 37

After the massacre in the Division 2 buffer zone the gates no longer opened in the afternoon for deserters. Perkins's voice was not heard again from the loudspeakers. An hour after our attempt to rescue Pete Murphy, government troops allowed us to retrieve our casualties from the blood-soaked yard. Once more, Georg Schuster's surgical team operated on the wounded far into the night. Eighteen prisoners were buried the next day in a newly consecrated graveyard near the Division 4 jail.

The next evening, General Boscov read aloud an order he had received from Corrective Labor Administration headquarters in Washington:

"For illegal striking, for destruction of state property, for sabotage, for use of deadly force against government officials, for advocating the overthrow of government, for armed mutiny, and for treason against the government of the Unionist State of America, the Director of the Corrective Labor Administration has ordered that its labor camp at Kamas shall be dissolved and evacuated and all the prisoners presently assigned there shall be transferred at the earliest opportunity to the Yellowknife transit facility for onward assignments within the Northwest Territories. End of Order."

Many prisoners kept a silent vigil for the rest of the night, expecting an attack and fearing that they might not live to see the dawn. Colonel Majors ordered our military and security forces on full alert. Yet the sun rose the next morning as before and all remained quiet for the next seven days. Though the very existence of Kamas's 8,000 prisoners hung suspended in mid-air, each new dawn was projected against the backdrop of normal camp routine: bunks made each morning; meals in the mess halls; changing of the guards and sentries; and the daily duty roster.

Why did the bosses let it drag on for so long? What could they have been waiting for? For the food to run short? They knew we had enough for another month. For more time to work out their plan of attack? It would be like shooting ducks in a barrel. For final approval from Washington? It could never have been in doubt. For a sampling of public opinion? They need hardly have bothered.

Throughout this week of stagnation, we sought solace in more training, further fortifications, and additional preparation for the coming assault. But our minds would not rest and the camp became a hotbed of rumors. Rumors of mass graves being dug outside the camp, of an empty prison train waiting for us on a siding in Heber, of chemical weapons exercises being conducted a few miles away—all these rumors and more weighed heavily on our nerves.

At least once a day a gate opened or a machine gun fired or an enemy platoon entered the buffer zone to probe our defenses. Within seconds, the nearest sentry sounded the alarm and squads of archers, pike men, and swordsmen took up positions behind the barricades. This war of nerves took a toll on our defense troops, particularly the greener recruits. But the officers, non-coms, and seasoned veterans took pains to reassure the younger men and to maintain their fighting edge.

Day and night the Warden's bulldozers drove in circles around the camp, stirring up perpetual clouds of reddish-brown dust. Was it construction or harassment? Or was it a cover for the sound of heavy tractor-trailers ferrying in tanks and armored personnel carriers from the Heber railhead? The nocturnal operations were as annoying as they were baffling and their unfriendly roar made the starless night appear all the blacker. With each succeeding day the cumulative loss of sleep took its toll on us, making us more listless, edgy, and morose.

Ever since our dreary visits to the camps at Orem and Provo, we had come to accept the fact that we were utterly alone in our revolt against the Unionist regime. We had cast aside any illusions that someone would come to our aid, be they fellow rebels from other camps, the voice of domestic or foreign opinion, or any of the officials who had made so many high-sounding promises to us. Nor was there any hope now of escape, with the gates closed to deserters and the military noose drawn tight around the camp.

The only glimmer of hope that remained for those who sought it was for some angel of mercy on the Unionist Party Central Committee to intervene on our behalf. A small number of prisoners, mainly Unionist sympathizers, still dreamed that the stately, white-haired Sturgis or the florid, garrulous Cook would drop out of the sky just outside the main gate in a shining white helicopter and demand to meet with our duly elected commission. He would come, that kind and righteous man, inspect the camp from top to bottom, and marvel at our stoicism for having survived such intolerable conditions. Then he would call for the murderers to be put on trial, for Rocco and Chambers to be placed under arrest, and for all our oppressors, civilian and military, to be dismissed on the spot. But such glimmers grew fainter by the day and looked more and more like a mirage.

Yet such minute quantities of hope were sufficient for some, particularly the camp newlyweds, who came forward nearly every day to be married and in most cases with a religious ceremony. Despite years of anti-religious agitation, most Catholics, Evangelicals, and Orthodox Jews in camp would not marry without one. For those who were wedded at Kamas, the bliss and the sadness normally encountered in marriage succeeded one another with a swiftness that ordinary people seldom experience in their orderly, slow-paced lives. The newlyweds at Kamas treated each day as their last and each delay in the government's assault as a wedding gift from heaven.

To the believers, it was never a question of hope. These prisoners prayed and meditated and were content to leave the outcome in God's hands without asking for a particular result. As in every camp, spiritual men and women were the calmest of souls and took earthly events in stride. By their example, they attracted more than a few converts as the weeks wore on.

Two days after the buffer zone massacre, a self-proclaimed prophet went around the camp calling for repentance and predicting the end of the world. As our entire world was the Kamas camp, his message seemed plausible enough to many and his credibility was helped along by an unseasonable, three-day cold spell that arrived the day after he received his call to preach. His followers sat cross-legged on the chilly ground, shivering as they called out to their Maker, and extended their arms to the thundering storm clouds that swept in from the north.

There are always some hearts that will not bear the strain of an impending doom. As we could no longer reasonably expect pardon or leniency, all we could do was live out our last days of freedom and either resist or submit as the will of the majority might dictate. But this was harder for some than for others.

Some behaved like ostriches, assuring themselves that they were not implicated in the revolt and need not be considered rebels if they stood apart. Others blamed their fate on the hard-liners. Still others, having been crushed mentally, begged secretly for the physical crushing to begin. Finally, some knew that they were fatally compromised and had only a few days left to savor life. These prisoners focused on how to squeeze more out of their remaining days and were not the unhappiest people in camp. The unhappiest were those who prayed for the end to come swiftly.

One of the oddest phenomena of the revolt was that, when all these people gathered at meetings in their barracks or mess halls and were asked whether we should surrender or hold out, the supercharged moral and political atmosphere caused their instinct for self-preservation to melt away. When it came to a vote for or against our continued defiance, the majority invariably voted in favor.

Such a vote was held in Division 3 the Saturday night after the buffer-zone battle. The occasion brought out strong expressions of resolve even from those who had not been the revolt's staunchest supporters. Colonel Majors, for example, now spoke with unsurpassed confidence in the revolt, as though he were privy to many secrets, and all of them to our advantage.

"We have more defensive firepower than we have talked about, and I tell you right now that the enemy will suffer at least 50 percent of our own losses or I am no soldier.... Even if we are destroyed, our destruction will not be cheap..."

Chuck Quayle added his own prediction that the bosses would think twice before launching an assault and that they would swerve rather than collide with us. He urged us not to give up hope for a settlement on good terms.

Then Glenn Reineke poured cold water on their optimism by repeating the warning that he and Gary Toth had given before:

"Just remember this," he said, looking slowly over the audience. "If anyone feels luck is on his side today but decides to cash in his chips tomorrow, we will settle accounts the moment he heads for the gate!"

He did not have to pull the Bowie knife from his belt for everyone to know what he meant.

****

On the following Wednesday my afternoon watch at the rooftop observation post ended uneventfully. The continuous roar of bulldozers offered welcome relief from the droning of nearby loudspeakers. I handed my binoculars to Jimmy Vega as soon as he climbed onto the roof to relieve me. Behind him came Al Gallucci, my old brickyard teammate, of whom I had seen little in recent days.

"Since when are you pulling O.P. duty, Al?" I asked him. "I thought you worked in the Technical Department."

"I did," Gallucci replied. "All my projects are completed or canceled."

"Tell me, Al, was the Technical Department as big a bust as people are saying? Did you guys come up with anything at all that you could honestly describe as a secret weapon?"

"Not that I ever saw," Gallucci replied. "The closest thing I can think of was the long-range radio transmitter we built. If we had ever been able to cut through the jamming we might have created enough of a stir to make the Unionists back off a bit. But it never happened."

"Couldn't you have beamed your message up to a communications satellite and made it through that way?"

"What satellite?" Gallucci protested. "The only communications satellites left in the sky are military, and all of those belong either to the Unionists or the Chinese. It's not like before the Events, when the heavens were filled with them."

"How about electronic warfare, then? With all those computer experts you couldn't hack into the enemy's computer system?"

Gallucci regarded me with puzzlement.

"Hack with what, Paul? You can't whittle a microchip out of a block of wood. We never had a chance."

****

I made my way back to the barracks more depressed than ever. I had missed my opportunity to sneak out the gate with the deserters and now it appeared that my next stop would be the Yellowknife transit facility and a camp somewhere in the Arctic. I lay in my bunk awaiting dinner, feeling angry with myself and wondering if I would ever get a second chance. I closed my eyes and caught glimpses of my wife and daughters recalled from my visions in the isolator. Claire held out her hand to me. I reached out to her but before we could touch she evaporated.

After dinner, the loudspeaker fell silent for nearly a half-hour, and then crackled back to life. I was tired of hearing the government's dreary propaganda and thought of stuffing bits of cloth into my ears to keep out the noise, but for some reason decided to listen. What I heard was a surprise so hard to accept that I called out to Knopfler and Gallucci to make sure I wasn't hallucinating.

It was the Warden's voice announcing that, at the direction of the Central Committee of the Unionist Party, Director Cronin had vacated his order of the previous Wednesday and had agreed to grant the principal requests that the Kamas commission had made in late May. To ensure that the Central Committee's order was carried out, two of its ranking members had departed Washington that evening and would appear in Kamas the next day for an official meeting with us and with our elected representatives.

As soon as the Warden completed his announcement, the loudspeaker fell silent. Moments later, the prisoner-controlled loudspeakers carried a brief but emotion-filled statement from Colonel Majors, confirming what the Warden had said. There would be no assault. Our voices had been heard, after all.

Although many prisoners had not heard or paid attention to the two loudspeaker announcements, news of Director Cronin's reversal spread rapidly throughout the camp. Despite initial skepticism, the news released an enormous reservoir of nervous tension among the prisoners. The credulous among us talked excitedly about what the news meant for our future. While skeptics and hard-liners reserved judgment, a vocal minority of Unionist sympathizers declared themselves vindicated and urged those who still longed for deliverance to let the Warden's statement sweep aside any lingering doubts.

Word arrived by messenger that the Warden, General Boscov, and Colonel Tracy were already on their way to the camp for an impromptu meeting with members of the commission. Ralph Knopfler and I set out at once for the commission offices. But, by the time we crossed the length of the camp and arrived in Division 1, the three State Security men were already emerging from the conference room, the session apparently having been completed. Majors and Quayle openly embraced their former oppressors and shook their hands, leaving the impression that all had been forgiven.

Yet, as I gazed upon these heartless jailers in their black uniforms, they appeared not an iota different than they had been on previous occasions when they had voiced the most outrageous lies to us without blinking. Why did they insist on coming here tonight? What really lay behind the Warden's announcement that the government had reversed its stance?

I spotted Reineke across the room with Gary Toth. He sent me a stern look that told me that he gave no credence to the announcement. Toth's downturned mouth and clenched jaws said much the same. I waited until Colonel Majors had led his guests out of the crowded offices and into the yard before I approached Reineke. He had put some distance between himself and the crowd and was watching the joyous throng march off toward the Service Yard.

"Is it for real?" I asked. "Shouldn't we be on guard in case it's a trick?"

"More than ever," Reineke replied. "But Majors has ordered me not to spoil the party by voicing my suspicions. So I suppose I had better not tell you what the lying bastard is up to, should I?"

"Let me guess," I said. "An attack at dawn?"

"Not quite that soon," Reineke replied. "Listen, Paul, I'm still working on a way to get you out of here. But first, I have a little job for you. I want you to go to my office, lock the door behind you, and open the bottom right drawer of my desk. Take the black telephone out of the drawer, pick up the receiver, and listen for the sound of my voice. Then just keep on listening. I'll tell you what comes next later."

"You bet, Glenn," I replied. "But don't worry about getting me out of here. I know you did what you could."

I set out at a run for the Security offices, checked in at the front desk, and did as I had been told. I held the black telephone receiver to my ear and waited. For ten minutes I heard nothing but footsteps, distant voices and slamming doors. Then I made out Reineke's voice and one I didn't recognize immediately. A door closed and the second man spoke again unobscured by background noise.

"What more do you want, Reineke? It seems to me that we've given you people just about everything you could ask for."

The voice belonged to Warden Fred Rocco.

"I'm not quite as easy to convince as Mitch Majors, I'm afraid," Reineke replied. "I'd like to ask you for a token of your good faith."

"What sort of token?" the Warden asked with an undertone of suspicion.

"There are some prisoners who opposed the revolt from the start but never got around to leaving camp when the deserters' gate was still open. The irony of it is, they never wanted to be lumped together with us rebels, anyway. And we aren't so keen on having them around any more, either. What I'd like to propose is that you and General Boscov take these men with you tonight and treat them on the same terms as the other deserters. I'll draw up a list for you. If you're agreeable, I'll bring them to you at the gate."

The Warden paused and I could imagine Reineke's cold unblinking eyes waiting for his response.

"Have you cleared your proposal with Colonel Majors?"

"Not yet, but I will," Reineke said. "He'll agree to it."

"Show me the list."

There was another pause and I thought I heard the rustling of paper before the Warden spoke again.

"Paul Wagner? Is this the same guy who sat in on the settlement talks? Quiet, middle-aged, business type?"

"That's him," Reineke replied.

"Well, if he's a Unionist, I'm a bloody Chinese," the Warden snapped. "We received a message about him from Headquarters yesterday. It seems his wife's rich relatives have pulled some kind of strings in Washington to get him released into exile. I told Chambers to say no. The guy is a rebel. Let him rot."

"Really, Warden, what difference is it to you if he rots on your side of the wire or ours? Letting him leave the camp doesn't mean you have to set him free."

"I don't plan on doing either," Rocco declared. "He stays."

"Perhaps I can make you an offer that would change your mind."

"And what might that be?" the Warden asked skeptically.

"Skinner, Gaffney, and Bernstein. Do the names ring a bell?"

The Warden fell silent.

"Maybe," he said. "What's your offer?"

"Take Wagner with the others and I'll give you Skinner, Gaffney, and Bernstein to do with as you please."

It took only a moment for the Warden to decide.

"I think you overrate their importance, Reineke, but it might be convenient for us to take them off your hands. All right…send them over."

"Thank you, Warden. You're doing the right thing."

"Hogwash. And tell Wagner not to get his hopes up," Rocco added. "He can come over to our side of the wire but he'll still be a rebel to us."

CHAPTER 41

"God does exist after all. From the Boss I deserved nothing but gratitude for loyal service. From God I must have earned the severest possible punishment. Look where I am now, and judge for yourself whether there is a God."
—Genrikh Yagoda, Chief of Soviet NKVD, in prison after his arrest

Wednesday, June 26
Day 37

It was early afternoon when Martha Chambers left Claire and Marie in Rosa's care and drove to Helen Sigler's cabin. Martha pulled off the road at a different spot this time, a hundred yards from the overgrown driveway and invisible from the main road, before starting on foot through the trees.

Helen met Martha at the door of the cabin and offered her a chair on the porch facing south across the Heber Valley. A cooling breeze riffled through the aspens and scrub oak. A thriving kitchen garden with lettuce, parsley, basil and other greens spread at their feet.

"I got your message last night. Sorry I couldn't make it here sooner," Martha began.

"You came in plenty of time," Helen assured her. "The news didn't come until yesterday and I'm not sure there's much we can do now, anyway."

"Was it from Claire's family?"

Helen nodded.

"Claire's grandparents have put up the money to renew all four of the family's exit visas and have arranged through a Washington lawyer to have Claire's father's sentence commuted to deportation, loss of citizenship and exile. They expect her mother and sister to be released as early as next week."

"But that's wonderful!" Martha exclaimed. "You mean, Claire might be able to leave the country after all?"

"So it would seem," Helen replied. "Of course, she'll have to get back to Philadelphia somehow, but that shouldn't be so hard. The sticky part is whether Claire's father will be released in time. Getting his sentence commuted won't do him much good if he's still in camp when the troops move in."

"How soon does he have to get out?"

"All signs point to an attack by morning."

"Oh, my God," Martha muttered. "Isn't there any way out before then?"

"Deserters were getting out until a week ago," Helen said. "But now both sides appear to have sealed the exits."

"But if Washington has already commuted his sentence, why would anyone hold him back?"

Helen shrugged.

"What about Doug?" Helen asked. "Is there any chance he might help?"

The question took Martha by surprise.

"I doubt it, but I suppose I could try," she replied, as if considering the idea for the first time. "He's going to stop by the house this afternoon."

"If there's anything I can do, just tell me," Helen offered. "I'd be happy to take Claire back east if that would be useful. Who knows, I might even stay there."

"But I thought Heber was your home…"

Helen shook her head.

"Only because of Alec. My sister and daughter live in Virginia. Susan is out of college now and is planning to get married this fall. I'd like to have a go at being my daughter's mother again."

"How soon do you think you might leave?"

"As soon as they launch the assault. Tonight I plan to camp out in the hills overlooking Kamas. If I'm right, they'll attack before daybreak. Once they do, there'll be nothing left for me here. That's when I'll go."

"Why not make the trip together? I was planning to leave tomorrow, too. We'll have a car as far as Provo and then we're planning to take the train to Denver and catch a sleeper to Philadelphia. We could share a compartment."

"You think there would be enough room?"

"Of course. Besides, traveling together will make the time pass twice as fast. Claire will be beside herself when she hears you'll be with us. How about if we pick you up on Reservoir Road by, say, nine?"

"I'll be there by half past eight. If I'm not, go on without me and I'll catch up to you in Provo."

****

Claire Wagner stood outside the doorway to Martha Chambers's bedroom and watched Martha fasten the zipper around her suitcase. Two other matching canvas bags lay on the floor at Martha's feet. Claire looked up at the clock on the dresser and saw that it was nearly four.

Marie's bag was next. Claire stepped quietly down the hall into the nursery, where Marie was asleep in her crib, and began opening dresser drawers. One after another, she withdrew the contents without a sound and laid out neat piles of toddler outfits on the floor.

Through the open door Claire heard a noise from downstairs and raised her head to listen. Next she heard the sound of keys dropping onto the marble-topped table near the front door.

"Martha?"

It was Doug's voice, which surprised Claire, because Doug usually didn't come home until six. She heard Martha's muffled steps descending the carpeted stairs and took up a position out of sight at the top of the stairway.

"I'm afraid I won't be staying for dinner tonight," she heard Doug say as he tossed the newspaper onto the table. "There's a big exercise tonight at camp. I stopped by to pick up a few things."

"But, Doug, this was going to be our last night together before the trip!" Martha exclaimed irritably.

"Yes. And I was all set to come home early. But something has come up. We'll be working all night. There's no way I can get out of it."

"I suppose not," Martha replied, her voice now drained of feeling. "It could mean a lot for your career. And compared to that, what's important about being with your wife and daughter?"

"Come on, Martha, we've been through this a hundred times. You know perfectly well that I can't set my own hours in this business. When there's a fight, we're expected to drop everything and pitch in."

"Some fight. A sneak attack on a camp full of unarmed prisoners..." Martha said before catching herself.

"Martha, stop it! What's done at the camp is none of your business."

"I used to believe that, Doug, but not anymore," Martha said. "This morning I paid a visit to Helen Sigler. She told me that she's managed to locate Claire's father. He's a prisoner at your precious camp..."

"She must be mistaken," Doug asserted.

"Paul Wagner is his name," she persisted. "Have you come across him?"

"There are nearly 8,000 prisoners at Kamas, Martha. I can't be expected to know each of them by name."

"Helen told me that Washington has issued exit permits to Claire's entire family, including her father. They even commuted his sentence from hard labor to exile so he could leave with them. The trouble is, he's stuck in Kamas. Tell me, Doug: If Claire's father can't find a way out before you attack, he'll be killed, won't he?"

"I can't answer that, Martha."

"Can't you help him?" Martha implored.

"You have no idea what you're asking. There's no way in hell to get anyone out of that camp tonight."

"But, Doug, he's Claire's father! And the Department has already approved it. All he needs is for you to go along with what's already been worked out in Washington."

"I can't," Doug insisted. "It's against the rules. If anyone ever found out I'd broken the rules to help him, I'd be finished."

"Would it be any different if they found out that you took his daughter into your household?"

For a moment, Doug seemed at a loss to reply.

"When she came here I had no idea who her father was. How could anyone say...?"

"Why couldn't they?" Martha asked. "From what I've seen, all State Security needs to arrest someone is an anonymous tip."

"Surely you're not implying that you would report it..."

Martha met his gaze with a look of cold defiance.

"Martha, this isn't like you at all. You have no idea what you're asking."

"Yes, I do, Doug, and so do you. If you were still the man I married, you wouldn't even blink at letting Paul Wagner go. What's happened to you? Ever since you joined up with these black-shirted thugs, it's as though you traded your self-respect for your title and now you're afraid to speak up for fear they might take it all back."

"That's not true, Martha," Doug protested. "My career in the Army was dead when I joined State Security. No other door was open. I took the job because it was the only way I knew to support my family. Where's the crime in that?"

"Neither of us knew then what they would ask of you. But now we do and we both know it's wrong."

"Breaking the rules to help Claire's father is wrong, too, and on top of that it's dangerous. If you have any sense at all you'll drop the idea right now."

"I can't," Martha said. "You can go on wearing that black uniform as long as you want, but I refuse to take my food and shelter one more day from someone who makes a living enslaving and tormenting innocent people. I've made my choice, Doug. Now you'll have to make yours."

There was a pause before Doug replied, now in a more conciliatory tone.

"I apologize for how I've been acting lately, Martha," he said gently. "But it's not as bad as you think. Go ahead, visit your parents and get some rest. I'll come out as soon as things settle down. We'll make it work. I know we will."

"This is not about my needing a rest, Doug. It's about our leading a decent life that we're not ashamed of. Sure, come see us at my parents' house when you when you get free. But don't expect us to come back with you if you're still wearing that uniform."

"I can't make that promise, Martha. Try to understand—"

"I do," she replied. "Now I hope you understand me."

Claire listened for Doug's response but there was none. A moment later she heard his steps across the parquet floor toward the staircase and realized suddenly that he was on his way up to the master bedroom. Claire scurried across the hall into the nursery and swung the door shut. Then she listened through the thin plasterboard walls while Doug opened the drawers of his dresser and began filling his overnight bag. A few minutes later he made a noisy descent to the front hall and slammed the door behind him.

Claire remained in the nursery a minute or two longer before following him down. She didn't want Martha to think she had been eavesdropping but her ears were burning with the news she had heard about her family's exit visas and the danger her father was in.

She came out of the nursery and peeked down the stairs into the living room, where Martha sat before an empty fireplace. Seeing Martha, she descended cautiously and stood beside Martha's chair. Martha looked neither happy nor sad, merely lost in thought.

"Martha?" she asked tentatively.

"Oh, Claire, come closer," Martha replied, reaching out to embrace her. Claire squeezed in next to Martha on the easy chair.

"Is my dad really at Kamas?"

Martha pressed her lips together tightly and looked at the floor.

"I believe so." She took Claire's hand and pressed it to her cheek.

"Will they let him out now?"

"I hope so," Martha replied. "But I have no idea when."

"Do we really have to leave tomorrow? Can't we wait for my dad?"

Martha shook her head.

"It's all arranged, sweetheart. We have to leave first thing in the morning. Your mother and your little sister will be waiting for us in Philadelphia. If all goes well, maybe your father will be able to follow along."

"Will I be coming back here again, Martha? To Utah, I mean?"

"Do you want to?"

"Not unless you're here."

"Don't worry, then, sweetheart. Come, let's finish packing, shall we?"

CHAPTER 42

"You die now. I'll die later."
—Soviet camp saying

Wednesday, June 26
Day 37

When the conversation between Glenn Reineke and the Warden ended, I hung up the receiver on Reineke's telephone and returned it quietly to his desk drawer. I heard footsteps and muffled voices outside the conference room but these soon faded away. Several minutes passed before I ventured to open the office door. No one was outside. Even the duty officer's desk was vacant.

Unsure whether Reineke would expect me to remain in his office or search for him outside, I went to the rear of the building to see if he might have gone to the cellblocks. I found the sliding door unlocked and descended the stairs into the central corridor of the former women's jail. At its end, Reineke, the duty officer, and two jailers were busy unlocking cells, handcuffing each prisoner to a heavy chain and arranging them in single-file.

"Need any help?" I called out.

"No, we'll be up in a minute," he called back. "Go on ahead to the main gate and tell the Warden we'll be there soon with the rest of his deserters."

"Will do," I replied, and set out at a trot for the Service Yard.

I no sooner rounded the corner of the building than I spotted Colonel Majors walking slowly toward the Service Yard with General Boscov and Colonel Tracy. Majors spoke with agitation as he went, jabbing his finger at Boscov's chest for emphasis. The General kept moving, his face a rigid mask. Then he stopped suddenly and faced Majors to deliver a cold rebuff whose words I could not hear. Before Majors could reply, Boscov had turned his back on him with an air of finality and moved on. Majors was left standing alone in the center of the road squinting into the harsh yellow glare of the evening sun.

A moment later, Majors resumed his walk toward the Service Yard but more slowly, as if lost in thought. I waited until a trio of other commissioners caught up with him on the road then followed behind. By the time they reached the sandbag bunker that faced the eastern gate, I was only a few steps behind. I overheard the other commissioners pepper Majors with questions about the Central Committee members' impending visit and how to handle the camp's transition back to government authority. Judging by his monosyllabic responses, it seemed to me that Majors was still reeling from Boscov's rebuff.

I approached Majors and told him that Reineke would be along shortly with one last batch of deserters for the Warden to take with him.

"Nobody told me about any more deserters," he grumbled.

"The Warden has already approved it," I said. "Glenn will be along in a minute with the list."

"He'd better make it quick. Our visitors seem eager to leave."

At that moment, Reineke and the two jailers came within view with eleven manacled prisoners in tow, including Gaffney, Bernstein, and Skinner. I stepped aside as Reineke handed Colonel Majors a handwritten list. By now, Majors was busy conversing again with General Boscov and gave the list only a cursory glance before signing it and handing it back. Reineke took up the list with a barely suppressed smile and carried it to the Warden, who made a quick count of the manacled deserters. Then Rocco ran his finger slowly down the list, folded it, and stuffed it in his pocket.

In the confusion of the moment, I joined my handcuffed companions without attracting undue attention and followed them across the buffer zone to the main gate and out into the no-man's-land. Judging from the absence of catcalls, no one behind the barricades seemed to have noticed that I was among the deserters. As relieved as I was to have escaped their attention, I felt ashamed to have become, officially and undeniably, Paul Wagner the turncoat, the deserter...the rat.

Even with Boscov, Tracy, and Rocco leading the way, never in my life had I felt as exposed and vulnerable as I did that evening traversing the ploughed earth between the camp's exterior wall and the perimeter fence. We marched in the long shadow of the wall under the menacing stare of machine-gunners, who kept their sights trained on us every step of the way. Before us the hills were still awash with the warm yellow glow of the setting sun. But between us and the hills was a forbidding series of obstacles: barbed wire, electrified fences, deep trenches, massive berms, and a cordon of troops and armor sufficient to destroy the camp many times over.

At last we passed through a gate in the electrified perimeter fence and were told to stop before the open doors of a waiting prison van. There a familiar squad of warders herded us into the van with a flurry of curses and a hail of blows from their fists, boots, and truncheons. I recognized Grady and Mills among them and they recognized me. That entitled me to extra slashes of the truncheon against my buttocks and back.

Once the doors slammed shut behind us, the van drove for only a few minutes over the bumpy dirt roads before turning us loose again inside a corral-like enclosure, some fifty yards on a side and twelve feet high, constructed of barbed wire and concrete stanchions. After a few moments, the same squad of warders pulled up behind us in a jeep, tossed a jerry can of water and pile of army blankets at us, and warned us to get some sleep. They promised to be back before dawn to put us to work.

Now that the sun was below the horizon, the dry air cooled rapidly and I shivered in my thin blanket as I tried in vain to sleep. Not only was the ground hard and rocky, but the incessant roar of the bulldozers on the other side of the berm made rest impossible.

As I lay on my back and looked up into the clear moonlit sky, I thought about what the dawn would bring, both for our small squad of deserters and for the nearly 8,000 prisoners left inside the camp. Those who accepted the Warden's glib lies at face value and expected Central Committee members to arrive the next morning to usher in a new dawn for Kamas and the entire corrective labor system doubtless slept better than those who expected tanks to roll through camp before breakfast. As for the latter, Reineke, Knopfler, and Gary Toth were no doubt already circulating among the sentries, pickets, and front-line fighters, warning them that their moment of trial would soon be upon them and encouraging them to live up to the trust of their fellow prisoners.

I imagined Terry McIntyre and his scientists burning their notes and sketches in open oil drums to keep them from falling into enemy hands. And I imagined more oil drums blazing outside the bathhouse where the Military Department kept its office and at the Security Department in the old women's jail. All the weapons the Technical Department had designed were deployed by now, all the Military Department's war plans had been implemented, and all the Security Department's secret intelligence taken into account.

I formed a mental picture of the mess halls where the camp's various religious congregations would be gathered to pray on the eve of what was to become their own special Judgment Day. Some would be praying for deliverance, some for forgiveness, and others for strength to endure whatever might come. There would be hymns and chants and responsive readings by the light of homemade candles along with silent meditation in the dark.

I thought of the sick and the wounded and the mentally ill, lying in their infirmary beds, some aware that their lives might change entirely by morning, others blissfully unaware. And I thought of Georg Schuster and his nurses and the responsibility they bore, not only for their current patients, but for the many hundreds who might become casualties the next day.

I thought of the newlyweds and the newly joined lovers who had already received far more joy in their short time together than they had ever allowed themselves to hope for once the dark curtain of arrest had fallen upon their lives. I wondered what plans they were making to remain united once the revolt was over, whether in Kamas, Orem, Provo, Yellowknife, or the peaceful land beyond the grave.

I thought of my fellow observation post watchers, including Jon Merrill, who would be the first to see the flares go up, the machine guns open fire from the watchtowers, and the tanks tear through the perimeter walls and fences. Would they sound the alarm when they realized that an attack was at hand or would they be paralyzed with fear? During their long vigil, would any of them remember me as a friend or would they curse me roundly as a traitor?

After all the thoughts and images had collided into one another and joined to spin around in my head, I thought of my family. I thought of my wife, Juliet, and daughter, Louisa, still captives in Philadelphia but who might soon be free to leave America and begin a new life in exile. I thought of Claire, who had enjoyed relative freedom over the last few months but had been forced to learn more about life and fate than any twelve-year-old should have to.

I even dared to imagine myself reunited with my wife and daughters to spend the rest of our lives overseas. But I also dared to peer down into the abyss, where I saw myself half-frozen, working a pick and shovel in a northern mine, determined to survive my sentence against all odds and to reclaim what remained of my life if and when the nightmare ever came to an end.

The frightful image of the northern mine jolted me to attention. With a mental clarity I had not experienced since the isolator, I realized that I could hear the somber whisperings of Brian Gaffney and Steve Bernstein, lying many yards to my right, as well as the yipping of coyotes in the far hills.

Suddenly I realized that the reason I could hear the coyotes was that the bulldozers had stopped roaring. The night was totally still. Before long even the whispering stopped as the other prisoners dropped off to sleep. I felt the muscles in my neck and shoulders relax as the accumulated tension of the day slowly loosened its grip. I imagined the same sense of relaxation passing over every barracks in camp, as those who had been kept awake night after night by the clatter of the earthmovers sank into sleep. And then I slipped into a deep, if not entirely blissful, slumber of my own.

CHAPTER 43

"You don't put an enemy down with sermons. You have to burn him."
—Nicolai Ceausescu, Romanian dictator

Thursday, June 27
Day 38

I felt a sharp pain in my ribs and emerged from a heavy and dreamless sleep. A dark figure loomed over me poised to kick again. I rolled onto my side and missed the full impact of the blow.

"Get up, vermin," came a shout from one of the black-helmeted warders who surrounded us. "You're late for work."

A faint moonglow penetrated through the clouds, enough to make out the shapes of the other men within the barbed-wire pen. With kicks, shoves, and whacks from their nightsticks, the warders herded us in a single-file line toward a two-ton truck. While we waited, a short, sallow-cheeked lieutenant in a neatly pressed desert camouflage uniform handed us each a rough poly-fiber sack of the kind used to make sandbags.

"Get into the back of the truck and pull the sack over your head so that it bunches up around your neck," the lieutenant instructed. "I'll be watching you out the back window. Go!"

With that, he pulled a .45-caliber automatic pistol from his holster and waited for us to obey his command.

We slipped the bags over our heads and in a moment the truck lurched forward. Despite the loose weave of my sack, within moments

I felt that I would suffocate. After the longest four or five minutes of driving in my life, the truck slowed, crossed a shallow ditch, and came to a lumbering stop.

"Pull off the sacks and leave them in the truck," the lieutenant ordered.

When my eyes adjusted to the light I saw that the truck was parked behind a row of a dozen or more heavy battle tanks, lined up ten yards apart behind the berm that rose between the camp's outer wire and us. The tanks' cannon barrels tilted over the edge of the berm as if to fire point-blank into the camp. Several turret hatches were propped open for the tank drivers to perform last-minute checks. A .50-caliber heavy machine gun protruded from each turret.

Arrayed twenty yards behind the tanks was a similar row of armored personnel carriers. In the APC closest to me, a crewmember poked his head out the forward hatch to gaze down upon us with disdain.

Our young escort officer waited a few more moments for our eyes to adjust before he spoke.

"Okay, hop down, hustle over to the tent on the double, and form a single rank three paces behind the other prisoners."

About fifty yards away, well to the rear of the APCs, stood a spacious, straight-sided tent of the kind used for Army field headquarters. Not far from the tent, some twenty prisoners were lined up at arm's length from one another. We formed a new rank behind the other prisoners as we had been told.

In the semi-darkness I could see three uniformed men emerge from the tent. They looked older and stockier than the lieutenant who had accompanied us on the truck, and I guessed it was they who were in command here.

"Stand at attention," the lieutenant ordered us. "Colonel Tracy will address you now."

We stood and waited for the colonel to speak. I glanced down the line and saw many familiar faces among these Unionist sympathizers and agents. They held their heads up proudly now, as if to proclaim their undying loyalty to the Party. But it was hard not to see in them the sniveling naysayers they had been in the days and weeks before. And here I was, just as much a deserter, but unable to call either side my own.

Colonel Jim Tracy paced deliberately back and forth before us in camouflage battle dress, his chest puffed up with a thorough appreciation of his own importance, then stopped to fix us with a solemn gaze.

"In a few minutes the punitive force gathered here will advance to crush the mutiny that has festered in this camp for the past forty days. A key objective of our mission is to identify the mutiny's ringleaders and bring them to justice.

"Each of you volunteers will be assigned to one of the armored vehicles that will enter the camp in the second wave. Once your assigned sector has been brought under control, your job will be to assist the security detail in identifying prisoners and in checking their names against our watch list.

"You will be unarmed and are not to take part in any fighting. Once you cross the outer perimeter, anyone who attempts to desert or refuses to carry out an order will be shot without warning. Do I make myself clear?"

The prisoners in the front rank remained at attention. Those of us in the back row looked at each other in quiet bewilderment. We had not volunteered for any of this.

Tracy seemed to sense our confusion.

"Are there any questions about what you are expected to do?" he asked, searching our faces with his penetrating stare.

"Yeah," someone called out not far to my right.

"What is it?" the colonel barked.

"I never volunteered for anything," the speaker declared angrily. "No way in hell I'm riding back into camp on one of your damned tanks!"

The voice belonged to the former deputy capo of the camp's thieves, Randy Skinner.

Colonel Tracy stepped aside to confer with our young lieutenant. A minute later he addressed us again.

"I stand corrected. Those of you who came over last night were not asked to volunteer. Never mind, I'm asking you now. If you volunteer, you'll receive the same reward as the others: a one-half reduction in your remaining sentence. If you refuse, you'll be sent north. So there you have it. All those in the second rank who volunteer, step forward two paces."

Everyone stepped forward except for Skinner, Brian Gaffney, and me.

"Very well, Lieutenant," Tracy concluded with a self-satisfied nod, "Deliver the volunteers to their assigned vehicles for the assault. Bring the others to me."

The prisoners who volunteered were loaded onto the troop truck and dispatched down the line of APCs, one prisoner to each armored vehicle.

Next the lieutenant summoned the waiting squad of warders to bring Skinner, Gaffney, and me to Colonel Tracy's command tent. As we approached I recognized Tracy's two colleagues as Doug Chambers and Jack Whiting. Both seemed agitated and restless. It occurred to me that Skinner, Gaffney, and I were not the only ones whose futures were in jeopardy should events go the wrong way.

"Do you know these men, Major Whiting?" Tracy asked.

"I certainly do," the Wart replied with a sardonic laugh.

"What do you propose we do with them?"

"Let's give them one last chance to cooperate," Whiting suggested. He unbuttoned the flap on his black leather military holster and turned to Skinner.

"You, Skinner, are you going to help us or not?"

"Go to hell," Skinner replied.

Without a moment's hesitation, Whiting drew his pistol from its holster, pointed it at Skinner's chest and fired twice. Skinner's body fell backward and hit the ground with a thud. The speed and utter cold-bloodedness of the shooting took my breath away.

"Now, let's see about the others. You, Gaffney," he called out, still holding the pistol. "Are you going to help?"

Gaffney opened his mouth but seemed too stunned to speak. Whiting raised the pistol.

"Hold your fire!" Doug Chambers called out suddenly and brought his hand down on Whiting's extended arm. "Not here. We don't want our fingerprints on this. Wait and let it happen inside the perimeter, in the heat of battle. Handcuff him to the turret, if you have to. The same with Wagner here. Warders!"

When he said my name I thought I saw a look of sadistic pleasure in his eyes.

At that moment, two of the warders who had marched us to the tent pulled plastic strip fasteners from their belts and grabbed Gaffney's wrists to tie them behind his back. At first Gaffney seemed to submit, but in a flash he broke free. He flattened the first warder with a punch to the jaw and lowered his head to charge the other.

"Don't shoot!" Chambers shouted once more to Whiting. "Take him alive!" The warder who was the target of Gaffney's charge grabbed hold of his attacker's coveralls with both hands and held on tenaciously until Gaffney slowed, lost his balance, and fell heavily onto his side. In an instant the other warders piled on, flailing away with their nightsticks and wrenching Gaffney's wrists behind his back.

From the moment Whiting unbuttoned the flap on his holster my mind had been racing. Having shot Skinner, would he shoot all three of us? What if I agreed to help? Would they chain me to a tank turret, anyway, and kill me inside the wire looking like a traitor after all? My spirits sank and I regretted ever having left the camp.

Just then it became clear to me that, above all else, I must not let the bosses take me back inside the wire. I accepted now that my life was over. All that remained was to avoid doing harm to my friends and showing further disloyalty to the revolt. I felt bitter disappointment at not being able to rejoin my family but I had long ago come to terms with the possibility of dying in captivity. My bitterness was more for my daughters' loss of a father and my wife's bereavement than for my own life coming to an end.

I saw Grady and Mills finish with Gaffney and start toward me with plastic wrist fasteners in hand. I felt an instantaneous surge of strength and vowed that they would not take me alive. My eyes fixed on the earthen berm and the row of tanks before me. Beyond them stretched the electrified perimeter wire. All at once I realized that, if I ran for the wire, death would be certain, either by electrocution or by gunfire. All I had to do was outrun a pair of hulking thugs long enough for one of their trigger-happy comrades to fire on me. It would be so sudden I probably wouldn't feel a thing.

With the other warders still swarming over Gaffney, I dodged Grady and Mills, sprinted past the tanks to the edge of the berm, and clambered up the rock-strewn slope. At the top, outlined against the horizon, I fully expected to die. But when I remained unharmed I lurched down the other side and, despite fatigue and lightheadedness, poured on every bit of speed to cross the remaining fifty yards to the perimeter fence.

I heard pistol shots and commands for me to stop but kept on running. As the fence loomed nearer, I thought momentarily about whether I should grab the wire or run straight into it like a sprinter breaking the finish line tape. Then the frightening thought came that someone may have turned off the electricity in anticipation of the attack. Never mind, I thought, I'll crawl under the fence and keep going until they shoot me.

Less than ten yards separated me from the wire when I felt hands grasp me around the hips and tackle me to the ground. A moment later, a second pursuer slammed onto my chest and knocked the wind out of me. I heard their breathless shouts and curses and recognized them as Grady and Mills. Their well-aimed truncheon blows came next, first on my head, then on my back. I curled into a ball with my hands clasped behind my neck and let them pound away while I set my mind free. I barely felt the pain until a crushing blow struck my lower back at a spot where I had been injured twice before.

The blow sent a column of pain roaring up my spine into my head with such force that it seemed to burst out the top of my skull and soar into the night sky. Like the ball of glowing fire that carried me through the roof of the prison car the night I arrived at Kamas, the surging pain took me high above the valley to an altitude where I saw the sun's spreading glow of the sun just below the distant rim of the Uinta Mountains. Far below, scrub-covered foothills spread out in all directions.

I turned my attention toward camp and instantly found myself hovering over it. Peering inside its walls, I saw huddled defenders waiting nervously behind the barricades, observers scanning the horizon from barracks roofs, and sentries marching in pairs along the inner perimeter wall.

Outside the wall I saw platoons of expectant shock troops looking to the skies as if for a sign and machine-gunners in their watchtowers fingering belts of shiny brass cartridges. Beyond the no-man's-land I saw tanks and APCs lurking behind the berm and felt the throbbing of their engines as they awaited the command to attack. And nestled among the hills overlooking the camp, I saw a brightly lit administration building whose broad balconies stirred with restless generals and bureaucrats eager to view the spectacle that was about to begin.

A steady wind swept across the valley from the northwest, creating swirls of dust on the open range. As I hovered above the camp, I felt buffeted, not by the winds, but by waves of emotion similar to those I had sensed when looking down from the sky the night I arrived. Once more I felt the prisoners' hatred, resentment, despair, and outrage rising up in a cloud soon to burst upon those below in a storm of catharsis. And as I had done before, I turned my face away from the camp and climbed higher.

I looked down again in time to see signal flares ignite over the camp with the brilliance of several full moons. This was the sign that the attackers had been awaiting. Suddenly the mighty engines of the tanks and APCs roared into action. Across the berm, pre-set explosive charges ripped massive gaps in the perimeter walls and fences through which the tanks could enter. Behind the tanks, helmeted troops in full body armor and gas masks boarded APCs that would carry them into battle.

And from low bunkers scattered to the north and south, mortars lobbed round after round of tear gas canisters from one end of the camp to the other.

I saw the canisters bounce and roll, burning with a white-hot heat and spewing clouds of choking gas across the open yards and among the barracks. I saw the snipers in the watchtowers, taking aim through night-vision scopes at forward observers, sentries, and defenders inside the wall. And in the same watchtowers, I saw machine-gun crews lay down interlocking fields of tracer fire across the women's camp and the Service Yard. The defenders who had been issued Terry McIntyre's primitive gas masks wore them, while others covered their faces with moistened undershirts or whatever scraps of cloth they could find.

Al Gallucci and Jon Merrill looked up from their observation post on a barracks roof in Division 2 the moment they heard the pop of the first flare being launched. It was Al Gallucci's last moment of life. The sniper who took aim at him from a tower at the northwest corner of Division 2 sent a single round straight through Gallucci's generous and ever-cheerful heart. Seeing Gallucci slump forward, Jon Merrill scurried to the edge of the roof and dropped to the ground. There he sounded the alarm before crawling into a hole under the barracks's cement foundation to hide from the machine guns' raking fire.

A burst of gunfire caught Judge Richardson unawares while he made his way to the latrine. At about the same time, a tear-gas canister plummeting through the thin roof of the judge's Division 2 barracks drove his colleague O'Rourke outside, where he, too, was brought down by sharp-eyed gunners. And all across the camp, snipers and machine-gunners kept the camp's defenders pinned down in their bunkers and trenches while non-combatants cowered within their flimsy barracks.

An orange flare rocketed skyward. A few seconds later the gunfire stopped. For a moment all was still. Then the clanking of treads and the throbbing of titanic tank engines grew louder outside the walls. Suddenly explosions rocked the northern edge of the women's camp where sappers demolished the exterior wall. A half dozen heavy battle tanks waded through the smoking rubble, lining up abreast into an unstoppable phalanx as they swept southward through the women's camp and into the Service Yard, their machine guns blazing at anyone who crossed their path.

The tanks no sooner passed from the women's camp into the Service Yard when some fifteen armored personnel carriers swarmed in from the north behind the tanks and pulled up opposite key buildings in Division 1, including the commission offices and the Security Department offices in the old women's jail. The armored vehicles raked these buildings with gunfire before disgorging shock troops to take the buildings. But the invaders found all the offices abandoned and nearly all documents destroyed, their ashes still smoldering in blackened oil drums outside.

Having expected a massive opening attack, the defenders had left only a token force to defend the women's camp. The force retreated quickly in the face of the tanks' advance. So instead of seizing the ringleaders of the mutiny and documents to establish their guilt, the shock troops of the invasion's first wave had to content themselves with evacuating captured women.

They assembled the terrified females—and in some cases their live-in male companions—in the yard and marched them north into the no-man's-land. Having heard fantastic tales of orgies and debauchery among the prisoners, the troops singled out the male captives for brutal beatings, knocking many of them senseless with blows from rifle butts before commission member Betty Shipley interposed herself between the attackers and their victims. But Shipley's selfless intervention merely infuriated the attackers; a moment later, one of the rifle butts smashed into her skull, killing her on the spot.

Meanwhile, in the Service Yard, defenders torched the Technical Department's offices and workshops. They were making an orderly retreat to trenches and bunkers along the edges of the yard when tanks entered from the women's camp. Now the snipers and machine-gun crews fired again from the watchtowers, picking off any defender who did not enjoy perfect cover. A sniper took off the top of Chuck Quayle's head when he peeked out from his bunker with Molotov cocktail in hand. J.J. Johns was nearly cut in two while scrambling from one barricade to another in search of better cover. And then a new volley of tear gas canisters rained down upon the Service Yard and upon Divisions 2 and 3.

The defense forces held their positions while they waited for the tanks to advance further into the Service Yard. Most of them were well protected in a network of deep slit trenches, while others occupied two-man foxholes scattered throughout the yard. All the digging had been carried out at night and remained carefully concealed by day. Here was where the defenders positioned their best and most experienced fighters. Glenn Reineke was there with fellow veterans of Vladivostok and the evacuation from Vanino. Hundreds of Russian, Chinese, Mexican, and Canadian POWs waited with them. Gary Toth was nearby with a company of picked men, including D.J. Schultz and other martial arts devotees in their dyed-black coveralls. And Colonel Majors, ever conscious of appearances, stood by gripping a cavalry saber he had checked out from the storeroom, cutting a bold figure in front of the men he had attempted to sell out. For the sale had not gone through, and General Boscov had left him inside the camp to die.

The most highly trained defenders were entrusted with the best arms and equipment, including makeshift gas masks, Molotov cocktails, and improvised weapons designed to disable a tank or APC by breaking a tread or stopping an engine. Some were armed with longbows, crossbows, spears, and throwing darts to engage attacking infantry at a distance so that others could close in for hand-to-hand combat. Rookie fighters carried pikes, swords, fighting axes, and machetes.

While the defenders waited for the attack to penetrate further into the Service Yard, the tanks slowed to a crawl, then stopped. For a moment the defenders seemed puzzled. Then, as enemy sappers suddenly brought down a lengthy section of the camp's perimeter wall, their plan revealed itself.

Behind the cloud of dust that rose from where the wall had been, a line of ten or twelve tanks advanced westward along a front extending from the northern end of the Service Yard to the southern edge of Division 2. The enormous vehicles punched straight through the walls of warehouses and barracks and came out the other side trailing bricks, barrels, and boxes.

One of the buildings that the tanks demolished was the old infirmary. A tank entered the building through the mental ward, crushing Libby Bertrand and Irene Cunningham under its treads before burying them and a dozen other helpless inmates under a pile of rubble. The same tank fired an inert cannon round into the infirmary's operating room, blasting Georg Schuster and his entire operating team to vapor as they prepared for surgery.

In Division 2, each tank struck out for a separate row of barracks, crushing one after another of these flimsy structures and sending the panicked inhabitants into the maw of the machine guns. Terry McIntyre met his end when a tank rumbled over his barracks and crushed him underneath. Colonel Majors's pretty young stenographer caught a sniper's bullet attempting to flee from the mess hall as the tanks closed in. And Jon Merrill, having been first to sound the alarm, met death when a tank's tread collapsed the corner burrow that had saved him from the machine guns.

When the tanks crashed in from the east, the remaining defenders in the Service Yard seemed to sense that the moment to expend themselves against the enemy had come. The veterans saw this first and leapt out of their trenches with a fury that impressed the raw recruits, who gamely stuffed back their fears and followed.

The defenders hurled themselves upon the approaching tanks, smashing their Molotov cocktails and incendiary grenades in the precise spots where they had learned to do so in practice. Anti-tank squads rushed forward carrying steel rails and other tread-busting tools and thrust them between the tanks' wheels. And one young vandal, having found a turret hatch unlocked, crammed his Molotov cocktail down the cockpit and ignited a fire that forced the wounded crew members into the open, where they became easy prey for the defenders' arrows and spears. But for every defender who made his mark that way, gunfire mowed down scores of others.

As soon as the tanks reached the camp's western wall they turned south and regrouped along the southern boundary of Division 2 for a sweep into Division 3. Until now prisoners of the camp's largest residential division had been pinned down by tear gas and gunfire. When they heard the tanks approaching, most of the non-combatants in Division 3 flocked south to seek refuge in the concrete cellblocks of the camp jail. To make their neutrality clear, one prisoner fashioned a white flag from a torn bed sheet and flew it from the flagpole outside the isolator.

But the surviving defenders in Divisions 2 and 3 did not yet consider themselves defeated. They hunkered down in their trenches and waited. By now their leaders had communicated with each other and had agreed that the best time to inflict serious damage would come after the APCs had entered the camp and disgorged their troops. In their initial confusion, the enemy infantry would be vulnerable to a sudden and overwhelming counterattack.

The cue for the APCs to enter the camp was a red flare fired overhead. Once it came into view, the APCs swept in along the southern edge of the Service Yard and headed south, moving slowly enough for their dismounted infantry to follow. As soon as the infantry came within close range of the defenders' slit trenches, the defenders let fly with arrows, bolts, and spears. Then platoon after platoon charged the enemy infantry and closed in for hand-to-hand combat.

But as the arrows and spears bounced harmlessly off the attackers' body armor the defenders' valiant charges into the hail of gunfire became nothing short of suicidal. Still the defenders fought on with the determination of men who had nothing to lose. Every casualty inflicted upon the Unionist enemy brought forth cheers from their surviving comrades and every captured firearm paid dividends in blood.

At one point during the battle, a platoon of fleet-footed vandals overwhelmed a squad of government troops as they emerged from their APC, seized some of their assault rifles, and carried the rifles off into the hands of experienced rebel marksmen. The marksmen set up covering fire against the closest two watchtowers while a squad of Gary Toth's commandos made their way with homemade incendiaries to the base of the towers. Within minutes, the towers were ablaze and their machine guns silenced.

The invaders, however, had firepower to spare. As soon as they caught on to the defenders' hit-and-run tactics, they learned to use the machine guns and firing ports of their APCs to better advantage and began mowing down the defenders the moment they emerged from their trenches and foxholes. The trailing infantry then wiped out remaining pockets of resistance to the rear of the APCs. As more infantry poured in and more defenders perished trying to halt their advance, the surviving commanders of the defense passed word to abandon Division 2 and regroup in Division 3.

Little more than half the original defense force was left now and the rate of attrition was horrific. But the survivors included some of the fiercest fighters in the camp, sworn enemies of Unionism who preferred death to surrender. Their superior military training and combat experience enabled them to adapt and evolve their tactics far more swiftly than the less experienced government troops. The survivors withdrew with as much weaponry as they could carry and prepared to make their last stand.

By now the government forces must have recognized that the tide of battle still ran overwhelmingly in their favor. Bodies in orange coveralls lay in heaps all across the Service Yard and the open spaces of Division 2. The defenders' hit-and-run attacks were far less frequent now, though no less ferocious than before, and by this time attacks on tanks and APCs had largely ceased. Having impregnable machines like these to lead the advance gave the attackers supreme confidence, as did their bullet-resistant helmets and body armor. For the first time in the battle, crewmen began opening hatches and raising their heads to view the carnage. Infantrymen clambered aboard tanks and hitched rides rather than walk.

By the time the invaders finished their sweep through Division 2, dawn was already approaching and the prisoners' occasional pop-up ambushes rarely succeeded in drawing blood. Tank commanders congratulated each other over the din while ground troops exchanged high-fives. As they approached the rows of flattened barracks in Division 3, the terrain looked all but deserted and the silence was eerie. The deeper the armored vehicles penetrated into the grid of destroyed buildings the less they could see of one another through the dusty haze. When the tanks reached the southernmost row of barracks and emerged onto the parade ground, they gained speed as if suddenly relieved to be in the open again.

The APCs followed the tanks down the same alleys, with the infantry creeping along behind. The troops walked more gingerly now, peering over and around the flattened barracks but often failing to see their comrades in the adjacent alleys. It was a highly vulnerable spot for the invaders, which is why Pete Murphy and his Military Department staff had worked so hard to plan the ambush that the defenders now unleashed upon the unsuspecting foot soldiers.

From their places of concealment in slit trenches, foxholes, and burrows dug beneath barracks foundations, the remaining defenders fell upon the enemy within a narrow corridor between two rows of barracks, attacking from front and rear and on both sides along a fifty-yard stretch. The ambush was so swift, the space so confined, and the audacity of the prisoners so great that the attack succeeded in killing or disabling five or six invaders for every prisoner lost. The surviving prisoners immediately turned their slain enemies' weapons against the invaders in adjacent alleys, proving more than an even match for them.

But by now the defenders were few and the invaders many. All available government reinforcements were rushed to the ambush site, including APCs that had initially run too far ahead of the ambushed troops to support them. Once again, the prisoners saw them coming and detected an opportunity.

The hitchhiking troops that had ridden on the sides and rear of the APCs now faced forward as the vehicles reversed direction toward the battle. These hitchhikers proved easy targets for prisoners who had once served their country as professional soldiers. The warders Grady and Mills were the first to fall headlong off their APC when a Russian POW saw them coming and squeezed off two perfect shots from a captured rifle. Any crewman caught peeking out the hatch of a tank or APC also put his life in danger. The two camp doctors, Nagy and Fell, who had examined me in the infirmary upon my release from the isolator, joined the casualty list when a Canadian sharpshooter pasted each of them in the forehead with a small-caliber round as they treated fallen troops in an area that minutes before had been under government control.

As the APCs came closer and the enemy commanders climbed out to direct their men in the final stage of this final skirmish, the defenders gave no sign that they intended to surrender. Instead, each of the surviving prisoners appeared to seek the highest and best use for his last bullet. For Gary Toth, the target worth dying for was General Jake Boscov. Toth spotted Boscov's broad chest protruding from an APC that barreled toward him and resolved on the spot that the General would draw his last breath before he did. He dodged the APC as it roared past and grabbed hold. Hoisting himself undetected onto the vehicle's side, he clambered forward in no time and caught the General in the throat with a fatal thrust of his Bowie knife. Toth raised his arm for a second thrust when a burst of submachine-gun fire felled him.

While this was happening, Glenn Reineke lay out of sight in a burrow dug under a barracks foundation. Bullets kicked up plumes of dust all around him but always wide of their target. His face wore an expression of quiet determination and, with a squad of attackers closing in, he appeared to be weighing the alternatives of capture or death. Then with a wild war cry he fixed his gaze on the shock trooper directly in front of him, scrambled out of his burrow, and fired. He no sooner rose to his feet than he toppled forward with a bullet in his chest.

Like Reineke, the handful of surviving defenders were down to their last rounds of ammunition and faced the same choice between surrender, capture, or death. Several veterans of the Manchurian War followed the example of Toth and Reineke and sprang forward to a certain death. Many younger men held out, clinging to life. Then a booming voice called out from beneath the same barracks that had sheltered Reineke.

"Hold your fire! *Hold—your—fire*! We surrender!" It was Colonel Marshall Majors. He emerged with his hands up and was taken prisoner immediately. Within moments, news of his surrender was radioed to the command post. Soon the tanks and APCs halted in place and the clatter of gunfire settled down.

"Drop your weapons and come out with your hands up," another voice ordered to those still in hiding. It was the no-nonsense little lieutenant who had escorted me to Colonel Tracy's tent before the attack began.

Slowly and cautiously, the defenders did as they were told. D.J. Schultz wept. Jimmy Vega's dry eyes smoldered with hatred. Others shuffled forward as if in shock.

The young lieutenant took charge of assembling the prisoners in the nearest open space and recording their names. A few minutes later Colonel Jim Tracy arrived in a tank to assume formal command. He echoed the lieutenant's order to have the prisoners lie on the ground with their arms outstretched, then strutted from prisoner to prisoner, cursing and insulting them and kicking those who dared insult him back.

One of those he kicked was the Texan, Jerry Lee, weakened from loss of blood but still feisty. Jerry Lee's friend and mentor, Ralph Knopfler, was at that moment being led forward with hands behind his head to join the other captured prisoners. Knopfler watched the strutting Colonel stand arms akimbo over the vanquished Jerry Lee and muttered a curse. In the blink of an eye, his hand drew a captured pistol hidden inside his coveralls and fired three shots that killed the colonel before he hit the ground. Knopfler lowered the pistol and didn't move until he, too, toppled from a burst of submachine-gun fire.

Having learned the hard way, the lieutenant ordered his prisoners to be searched for weapons. While the search was underway, the young officer mounted the nearest APC and conferred with his command post by radio. Moments later he ordered the APCs to resume their advance toward Division 4 and the camp jail, where the majority of remaining prisoners had gathered to surrender.

When the APCs arrived outside the jail, a self-appointed prisoners' committee assured the victors that all prisoners who had fled to Division 4 were unarmed and would cause no trouble. The APCs then surrounded the Division 4 parade ground while ground troops formed the prisoners into columns, ordered them to sit with arms linked, and recorded their names and serial numbers.

A short while later an APC delivered several of the deserters who had volunteered to help identify the revolt's ringleaders. An angry growl spread through the prisoners' ranks when they recognized George Perkins, Steve Bernstein, Kevin Gaffney, and other Unionist sympathizers. A second APC pulled up with Jack Whiting and a team of security officers whose job was to sort the prisoners according to their degree of involvement in the revolt: combatants, passive supporters, neutrals, and non-combatant thieves.

The identification process continued throughout the morning while the sun rose higher in the sky and temperatures reached the high eighties. No drinking water was offered. Tempers flared and from time to time a prisoner lunged at a deserter who had denounced him as a rebel. A young thief who had fought to defend the revolt spit in the face of his former capo, Frank Brancato, when Brancato accepted classification as a non-combatant thief. While Brancato would be returned to a conventional prison, the vandals who had been the revolt's vanguard faced execution or transfer north to Yellowknife with the politicals.

The vandals' hostility reached a fever pitch when Jack Whiting singled out Jimmy Vega and a half dozen other thieves as combatants. Jimmy seethed with rage but said nothing as long as the Wart remained at the front of the assembled group. But as Whiting paced up and down the columns in his search for rebels, Vega's right hand slipped inside his coveralls, as if hunting for lice. When Whiting came within three rows of him Vega pulled a pair of throwing darts from his waistband and hurled them one after another at Whiting's back. One hit Whiting over the left kidney and penetrated the full length of its four-inch, steel tip, while the other dangled from the back of Whiting's right thigh.

Whiting screamed in agony. His face turned dark as he reached behind him to remove the dart from his back and toss it to the ground in disgust. Then he pulled the dart out of his leg and examined it. But as he did, his nose twitched as if he smelled something strange and he held the dart by its fins to sniff at it.

"Oh, my God!" he wailed when he identified the smell. "Medic!"

To his horror, the Wart had discovered that the tip of the throwing dart had been smeared with feces like the blade Brian Gaffney had used to attack Glenn Reineke.

I watched the guards search for the prisoner who had tossed the darts but no one would betray him.

Jack Whiting left the sunbaked yard stretched across the back seat of a jeep rapidly slipping into shock.

I soared above the perimeter wall to watch Whiting's jeep cross the no-man's land, join the road toward Heber, then pass by a command tent where a crumpled figure in an orange jumpsuit lay under the tent's shaded entry. Coming in for a closer look, I recognized the tent as Colonel Tracy's command tent, where Jack Whiting had shot Skinner shortly before the attack, and the inert body as my own.

A few feet away, a helmetless foursome in desert camouflage uniforms played a raucous game of poker, their rifles propped within reach. The Kamas Valley was quiet now. The battle was over. The bosses had won.

CHAPTER 44

"I want you to know that everything I did, I did for my country."
—Pol Pot, Cambodian dictator

Thursday, June 27
Day 38

I turned my attention away from where my body lay and looked back across the no-man's land into the Division 4 parade ground, where 5,000 or more prisoners squatted on the ground in tightly massed squares. Security teams and their turncoat helpers strolled slowly up and down the rows, now and then culling a prisoner to send to the fringes of the yard where a queue of troop trucks waited.

Across the wall in Division 3, I saw warders stack the dead and wounded onto flatbed trucks, stopping only to finish off the occasional survivor with a knife slash across the throat.

I turned my gaze back toward the camp jail just in time to see George Perkins block the path of Colonel Majors as the colonel tried to slip past him. Without making eye contact or showing any sign of their former friendship, Perkins pointed his outstretched hand at the colonel.

"Here's the one you want," he said to a lean young captain holding a clipboard.

The Chief Commissioner had managed to remove all insignia of rank from his desert camouflage fatigues and looked up in astonishment when his former protégé betrayed him.

"You're certain this one is Majors?" the young captain inquired.

"Completely," Perkins replied, taking one last self-satisfied look.

"Then get him aboard a truck. They'll want him interrogated right away," the captain ordered.

"Oh, no, you don't," Majors challenged. "Get Doug Chambers over here. He and I have a deal. Or call General Boscov or Colonel Tracy. They'll know what I'm talking about."

"The Deputy Warden is busy. Save it for your interrogator," the captain said with a dismissive sneer. "Your days as a wheeler-dealer are over, Mister."

Majors didn't see the rifle butt that slammed between his shoulder blades and knocked him to the ground. In an instant a warder seized his wrists and bound them with a plastic restraint loop.

I thought of Doug Chambers and Fred Rocco and wondered how they would be celebrating their victory. The very next instant I found myself soaring across the no-man's-land and the rocky hills surrounding the Kamas camp toward the administration building about a half-mile away. There, on the building's ground-level balcony a modest buffet had been spread on a wooden picnic table. The food was simple, consisting of fresh bread, local butter and cheese, tinned meats, greenhouse tomatoes and cucumbers, with chocolate bars for dessert. A few steps away stood a card table laden with an ice bucket, plastic cups, and half-filled bottles of bourbon, vodka, and gin.

The Warden and Deputy Warden stood at the edge of the balcony basking in the warm glow of praise from their superior officers. Visiting from State Security Headquarters were Kenneth Cronin and General Gil Hardesty, both of whom had sat down with the rebels and had experienced their bloody-minded intransigence at first hand. Howard Barger from the Justice Department had also flown in, along with several lesser lights from Washington and the Denver regional office.

The happiest man in the group appeared to be Fred Rocco, who boasted that only thirty-two more workdays separated him from his retirement with full pension. Doug Chambers broke into a broad smile at

Cronin's announcement that Chambers would replace Rocco as Warden before returning to Washington for a substantial promotion in the fall. Hardesty injected the only gloomy note in an otherwise triumphant gathering by announcing the deaths in action of General Jake Boscov and Colonel Jim Tracy and the wounding of Jack Whiting, along with several dozen government troops killed and injured.

The camp bosses and visiting dignitaries showed hearty appetites after staying up all night early to follow the progress of the assault. Now that the spectacle was over and the battle won, they returned to fill their plates and glasses again and again before departing on wobbly legs.

As the last visitor left the parking lot, Doug Chambers excused himself from the Warden to make a phone call from his office. He let the telephone ring many times before giving up and returning the receiver to its cradle. The exhilaration and pride were gone from his face, leaving loneliness and dejection in their place.

As there was nothing left to see there, I left the administration building and returned in the blink of an eye to the spot where my morning's ordeal had begun, outside the command tent at the edge of the camp's eastern no-man's-land. For several minutes, I watched a pair of young soldiers probe and prod my inert body outside their command tent, disputing with surprising energy whether or not to hoist it onto a waiting truck stacked with prisoners' corpses. At last the taller and more forceful of the pair picked up my ankles while his partner stuck his hands under my armpits; then together they swung my body high enough for the warders inside the truck to pull it in.

I moved closer, not out of any sense of close identification with this lifeless form, but out of pity for the man who had inhabited it. Once he had been someone's child, had grown up and taken his place in the world, had married and fathered children, had been a decent and capable member of society. Then the Events had swept away the world he had known and had brought on the social and moral decay that had produced the camp system and the people who ran it.

I moved closer still and reached out instinctively to embrace the pitiable remains. But I could feel nothing. I had no legs for kneeling beside him, no arms for reaching, no hands for touching. Then I felt a sensation that started as a warm tingling. It rose to a dull ache, then to a stabbing pain, and all at once I felt my injured spine slam into the floorboards of the flatbed truck as the rear wheels struck a rut and roared off down the dusty track.

CHAPTER 45

"Of all the treasures a State can possess, the human lives of its citizens are for us the most precious."
—Joseph Stalin

Monday, July 1
Day 42

I opened my eyes in the infirmary. The only reason I knew this was that I recognized my nurse and the ward where I had visited Jon Merrill. At my insistence, she told me I had suffered a concussion, cracked vertebrae, and ruptured discs and had been unconscious for the better part of four days. In the next breath she cautioned me quietly to stay off my feet, not only to speed my recovery, but because any patient judged capable of walking would be included in the next prisoner transport north, expected to depart the next day.

But that afternoon, my wheel chair was taken away from me while I slept and I was obliged to use crutches to move between my bed and the toilets. It happened that new chief physician noticed me on my feet and promptly declared me fit for transport. So the next morning, less than an hour after the orderlies delivered our breakfast of oatmeal and heavily sweetened tea, a dozen warders arrived at the infirmary in a school bus to take some twenty of us patients to the Heber rail yard.

A handful refused to go, arguing that their injuries were too severe for work or travel. But the list had already been signed and any resistance was pointless. Those who refused to walk were carried or dragged onto the bus and deposited in a heap in the center aisle. I took up my crutches and walked as best I could despite the searing pain.

Although the ride from the camp to the Heber railhead lasted less than a half-hour, I tried to make it last as long as I could by paying close attention to every detail of my surroundings. The tufted green blanket of scrub oak covering the western slopes of the valley, the rippling surface of the Jordanelle Reservoir, the clouds of red dust rising behind us on the unpaved roads—all these were scenes I thought I would want to remember when we arrived at our new home in the tundra of the Yukon or the Northwest Territories.

From the first days of my captivity I had tried not to harbor unrealistic hopes about ever regaining my freedom. But the revolt had awakened in me a new kind of hope, one that I could allow myself to nourish without fear of disappointment, since the true source of the revolt's success lay in our hearts rather than our hands. Still later, the news that Claire was living nearby, that my family's exit visas had been renewed, and that I might be released to join them had created an intolerable tension between the hope of recovering my old life and the need to give meaning to my new life at Kamas.

Now the tension was gone. I had not betrayed the revolt in my heart and would rejoin my fellow rebels soon to share their fate in the frozen north. News of the transport came to me almost as a relief.

The bus turned off the Upper Provo Canyon road onto the main highway that ran through the center of Heber. A few minutes later our bus pulled up at the same rail siding where I had arrived on my first night in Kamas. Across the yard, the tanks and APCs that had destroyed the camp four days earlier waited now in well-ordered columns to be loaded onto flatcars. On a nearby siding sat a string of prison transport cars, their windows barred and screened. Inside I could see the outlines of prisoners huddled in the sweltering compartments until the locomotive arrived that would bear us on our long journey north.

I heard the rear door of the bus creak open and joined the rush to the exit to avoid blows and kicks from the warders. The men who were able to jump down did and then remained to help those who lacked the strength. I waited my turn and accepted a hand to avoid reinjuring my back.

No sooner had I made it to the ground than my helpers ran ahead to join the queue of prisoners outside the train, with warders in hot pursuit all the way. I looked over my shoulder half expecting a truncheon blow before I realized that I was alone on the platform except for a tall middle-aged man in a blue business suit and two camp guards. It was the Warden, Fred Rocco.

"Come closer, Wagner. I won't bite you."

I approached slowly, holding on to the side of the bus to keep my balance.

"I figured something must be up when Reineke seemed so eager to get rid of you," Rocco said in a jocular tone. "This morning Headquarters ordered us to send you to Philadelphia. Congratulations."

I leaned against the side of the bus for support. I had heard what he said but could not fully absorb it.

"I asked Doug Chambers about you," the Warden continued. "He told me the whole story. Including the part about Claire being your daughter. Remarkable, truly remarkable."

I bristled at the thought of a monster like Rocco speaking my daughter's name but let it pass.

"And have you decided what to do with me?" I asked.

Rocco looked at me with feigned disbelief.

"What's to decide? What Headquarters wants, Headquarters gets. Besides, with Claire and you both leaving the area, there will be less chance of any, shall we say, embarrassment for Doug's career. I think that's healthy all around, don't you?"

"Then I won't be going to Yellowknife?"

Rocco ignored my question.

"I've told these two fellows here to take you to the military airfield in Provo, get you cleaned up, and escort you onto the next military flight to Denver. Our people in Denver will take care of getting you to Philadelphia. Just do me one favor. When you see Claire, tell her Uncle Fred sends his best, won't you?"

I wanted to slug him but I lacked the strength.

"Don't just stand there, Wagner. Go home! We do release some prisoners now and then," he said with a jovial chuckle. "We're not monsters, you know."

Chapter 46

"And the generation that has seen the watch-towers of the Soviet labor-camp, and witnessed the repudiation of God, and heard the cry "without mercy"; the generation that has seen Bolshevism and Fascism, Nazism and Stalinism; the generation that has witnessed two climaxes—the climax of cruelty in tyranny, and the climax of self-sacrifice and heroism of those who love freedom—must draw these conclusions:

The end justifies the means? If you are faced with tyranny, do not hesitate to say: Yes!

Every end justifies the means? —No!

The end justifies all the means? —No!

Every end justifies all the means? —No, never!"

—Menachem Begin, Prime Minister of Israel

Wednesday, July 3
Day 44

Claire felt her distaste for Philadelphia rise the moment she awoke. Since the train had pulled into 30th Street Station the evening before, memories of her trip west came flooding back to her. Suddenly she recalled the terror and the anger of discovering that she was the only one in her family who remained free. She also remembered the gray skies, the crumbling brick buildings, the rusting bridges, and the sulfurous stench of Philadelphia's oil refineries.

Helen and Martha had reserved a room in a motel just south of the city, within reasonable walking distance of State Security's Philadelphia District Office. The motel was cheaply built and even more badly managed, being part of a nationalized chain frequented by government employees and other low-budget travelers. Since the collapse of tourist travel shortly before Claire's birth and the collapse of business travel a few years later, what had once been a glut of hotel space across America had become a permanent shortage. Now, merely finding a vacant room posed a challenge.

Having left Marie with Martha's parents, who drove in from New Jersey to meet them at the train station, Martha, Helen, and Claire settled into a room and retired for the night. They rose shortly after dawn, ate breakfast in the motel coffee shop, then took their place in the queue that formed each morning outside the Federal Building Annex on Broad Street. Nearly an hour passed before they reached the metal detectors. Then they waited for another twenty minutes at the reception desk to ask where to inquire about administrative detainees located within the DSS Philadelphia District.

"Registry office, second floor. Next!" came the answer from a heavy-set clerk in a leatherette swivel chair.

Helen Sigler led the way up the steel staircase. Upon reaching the second floor she spotted the word "Registry" on a glass transom at the end of a twenty-yard corridor. The queue stretched all the way from the door to where they stood.

After another hour of waiting, they reached a bank of six cashier windows. There Helen addressed herself to a pasty-faced woman of about forty with a huge head of frizzy orange hair. The woman wore the mask of boredom and indifference adopted by state employees throughout history.

"We're looking for Juliet and Louisa Wagner. We believe they were taken into custody on the evening of March 24 this year at the Philadelphia Airport."

"How do you know they're being held by State Security?" the woman challenged with narrowed eyes and an incredulous tone. "We're not the missing persons bureau, you know. Have you tried the Philadelphia police or the Port Authority? The airport is under their jurisdiction, not ours."

"A witness saw men in DSS uniform pull them out of the emigration line and take them into the security office," Helen replied patiently. "Also, your own Pittsburgh Field Office confirmed to me that the Philadelphia District Office has them in custody. Now, would you mind checking your records for us?"

"Relation?"

"I beg your pardon?" Helen replied.

"What relation are you to the missing women?" the clerk asked.

"None. I'm here with the prisoner's daughter." Helen pushed Claire forward.

The clerk snatched a printed form from a many-tiered rack of government forms and slid it across the counter to Helen.

"All right then. Fill out this form and leave it in the wooden box by the door. Then come back next Monday to any of these windows and, if the girl's mother is in our custody, we ought to be able to tell you more."

Martha Chambers stepped forward and held out her DSS identification card showing her as the spouse of an active-duty DSS field officer.

The clerk's expression changed at once from indifference to a sincere eagerness to please.

"I'm so sorry, Mrs. Chambers, I didn't realize—"

Martha cut her off.

"The problem is that we don't have a week to spare. Couldn't you do us a favor and look up their names in your computer while we're here?"

"The database has been down all morning, but I'll give it a try."

She entered some keystrokes on her computer and waited. Suddenly she raised her eyebrows in surprise.

"Okay, it's back up again. Do you know the missing woman's Social Security Number?"

"I'm afraid we don't. But we have Claire's. Could you use hers to cross-reference her mother?"

"I doubt it, but I'll do what I can."

Martha opened Claire's passport so the woman could read her name, date and place of birth, and other identifying data. For several minutes the clerk entered intermittent keystrokes and waited for the computer's response. At last she flashed a smile.

"Here it is. The database shows them in the District Detention Facility in Camden awaiting deportation."

"Deportation?" Martha replied indignantly. "That can't be right. They just had their exit visas reinstated a few days ago. They're emigrating legally."

"Yes, but since they tried to leave without valid travel documents, it was handled as a criminal matter. That's why it's coded as a deportation."

The woman's eyes remained fixed upon her computer screen as she scrolled through the record.

"Ah, now I see it. You're right. This time it shows their exit visas as renewed, emigration tax paid, and air travel booked for tonight. They could have gone out earlier, but the office in charge was still searching for the other daughter."

"That would be Claire. Now that Claire is here," Martha continued, "I'd like to arrange for her to travel on the same plane as her mother and sister. Could you double check whether her exit visa is still valid?"

"It probably isn't, but I'll look." She paused to pull up the appropriate record from the database. "Hmm, it says here that all four exit visas were extended last week."

"Is there any reason why she couldn't leave tonight?" Martha asked. The clerk shook her head.

"She still doesn't have her final release. For that she'll need to schedule a pre-release interview to explain her absence since February. And I know the Clearance Section is booked up for weeks."

"Could you put in a call to the head of the Clearance Section, please?"

The clerk looked askance at Martha but did as she was told. She asked the person on the other end of the line to have the section chief call her back as soon as he returned.

"You must understand, Mrs. Chambers, that the Department has booked tickets only for Juliet and Louisa. If you want to get Claire out on the same flight, you're going to have to book her ticket yourself."

"Fine. Can you tell me what flight they're on?"

"It looks like British Airways 867, departing Philadelphia for Gatwick at seven p.m. tonight. Now, here's what you do. As soon as we hear back from the Clearance Section, go on up to the sixth floor and ask for Neil in Room 614. Tell him you need a final clearance number and that I told you not to take no for an answer. Once you have the clearance number, go back down to the Documents Section, on the second floor, across the hall from Registry. Give them your clearance number and they'll issue Claire her exit visa and emigration tax voucher. You'll need to show those to buy your ticket and to get past the emigration counter. Clear?"

Before Martha could reply the telephone rang.

"Neil's back, but he only has fifteen minutes before he has to leave. You'd better hurry...."

"I can't possibly thank you enough, Mrs.—"

"Just call me Betsy." The clerk shook Martha's outstretched hand.

"Betsy, might I impose on you one last time?" Helen Sigler interrupted. "Could you check whether Claire's father is cleared to emigrate, too? His name is Paul Wagner, and he's been at the corrective labor camp in Kamas, Utah, since March."

The clerk stiffened.

"How do you know that? That's not public information."

"I live in a town near Kamas. Local people know these things."

"I can promise you we won't tell anyone," Martha added with a smile.

Betsy looked at Martha sympathetically, and then lowered her voice. "There's a separate classified database. Wait here a minute and I'll see what I can do."

400 | PRESTON FLEMING

She went to a computer terminal at the back of the room and logged in. The two women and Claire could see screen after screen pop up on the monitor. Then Betsy took a minute to read the contents of the last screen, logged off, and returned to her desk.

"I found a Paul Wagner from Pittsburgh. He left the Susquehanna Security Facility in February of this year bound for the Utah District. His case was up for review two weeks ago. The Special Hearing Panel commuted his sentence to loss of citizenship and exile for life."

"Then he's free to leave?" Helen asked excitedly.

"Not so fast. The Panel ordered him to be returned to this District for deportation out of Philadelphia, but there's no record of a response from Utah. It seems there was some kind of security hold at the facility he was in. No transfers in or out until further notice."

Helen thanked her, exchanged serious looks with Martha and took Claire by the hand to leave. Then Claire, who had said nothing through the entire exchange, spoke up.

"Do I really have to leave tonight?"

Both women stopped in their tracks to face her.

"Why wouldn't you want to leave?" Helen asked her. "Your mother and little sister will be at the airport waiting for you. By tomorrow morning you can be with your grandparents in London. You wouldn't want to miss that, would you?"

"No," Claire replied. "But I have this feeling that if I leave now, I won't ever see my dad again. He needs me here to help him."

"If your dad has made it this far, Claire, I'm sure he'll find his way back to you somehow," Helen continued. "Right now your mom and sister need you, too."

Claire nodded sadly and let Helen take her hand once again.

A few minutes later they found Neil at his desk in the Clearance Section. He resembled the prototypical bureaucrat, a jowly man in his mid-thirties who could easily pass for fifty.

"Are you the people Betsy called me about?" he began.

"Yes," Martha replied.

Martha handed Neil her DSS identity card. He glanced at it quickly and started typing on his computer.

"Could I see Claire's passport, please?" he asked without raising his eyes from the monitor.

Helen handed it over.

"On the strength of your association with the Department, Mrs. Chambers, I'm going to give Claire a clearance number. Can I have your personal assurance that this is not going to come back and bite me in the rear?"

Martha laughed.

"You have my word of honor."

They took the slip of paper with the clearance number and headed for the stairs. The queue in the Documents Section was mercifully short. Within fifteen minutes they reached the front of the line where a clerk entered Claire's clearance number in a computer and printed out her exit visa and emigration tax voucher on special forgery-resistant stock. The moment she handed Claire her documents, she put a "Closed for Lunch" sign in the window and disappeared. It was now precisely one o'clock.

Helen, Martha, and Claire flagged down a taxi and rushed back to the motel to pack their bags, eat lunch, and find a bank on their way to the airport. They reached the international terminal of the Philadelphia airport just after four and took their place in a ticket queue that stretched all the way to the next terminal. They left the ticket counter shortly before six and made a headlong rush to the emigration counter. While she waited for the woman behind the counter to stamp her papers she heard a boarding announcement for the seven o'clock flight to Gatwick and felt her skin crawl.

Too anxious to bear watching the immigration officer's expression as the woman examined her documents, Claire gazed down at her backpack and at the clothes that she had chosen for the trip. Despite the summer heat, she wore the same navy corduroy trousers, white turtleneck, blue cotton sweater, and green backpack that she had worn to the airport in

February. It was her way of turning back the clock and repeating that fateful night in the hope that this time things would turn out differently.

Claire heard a metal door slam shut somewhere behind her and turned to see a young male immigration officer approaching. He spoke with the woman who held Claire's passport, then addressed Martha and Helen.

"Would the three of you mind stepping into my office for a moment?" the officer requested.

"Of course not," Martha replied, casting a worried look at Helen.

The women followed the immigration officer through a heavy glass door into a cramped office furnished with a gray metal desk and four straight-backed chairs. Claire could feel her heart pounding. She watched Helen grow paler by the minute. Martha, too, seemed nervous but resolute. Through the glass partition Claire watched other passengers advance through the emigration line and move on toward the security checkpoint outside the British Airways gate.

"Damn!" the officer muttered as he pounded what appeared to be a stuck key on his keyboard. "Excuse me, but for some reason I can't seem to verify your final clearance number. I'll have to reboot."

Claire watched the monitor screen go black, then saw a white flash as the rebooting process began.

"If it's not too much trouble, could you tell us whether any other Wagners have come through emigration so far tonight?" Martha asked with a forced smile. "Claire is supposed to be meeting her family at the British Airways gate."

"Wait a second." A pause followed while the other immigration officer entered some keystrokes into a separate computer terminal.

"Here it is," he replied a few seconds latter. "The system shows two Wagners departing for London tonight: Juliet and Louisa."

"Any others? We're expecting Claire' father, too."

"Nope. Not yet, anyway."

"Would you mind if I made a phone call while we're waiting?" Martha asked. "My husband works for the Department and I need to reach him at his office." She held out her State Security I.D. card.

He handed her a telephone.

Martha thanked him, dialed, and waited. She hung up, dialed again, and this time got someone on the line.

"Is this the duty officer? I'd like to speak with my husband, Doug Chambers."

"What do you mean, 'not available'?" she pressed. "Is he on another line, in a meeting, or down at the camp? I need to reach him right away."

Martha listened and grew exasperated.

"Fine, I'd be happy to speak to the Warden," she snapped. "Yes, I'll hold."

Martha waited for several minutes without raising her head to meet Claire's or Helen's anxious stares.

"Hello, Fred? Is that you? I'm trying to get through to Doug and your duty officer is giving me the runaround. Can you tell me what's going on?"

Another long pause.

"I'm here at the emigration counter at the Philadelphia airport with Claire Wagner. Believe it or not, I've managed to find Claire's mother's records through the Department's District Office. For months her family has been waiting for approval to emigrate. Now their exit visas are final and they're leaving tonight for London.

"The only problem is that we can't locate Claire's father. It seems he's been in a labor camp but this month his sentence was commuted to exile. They tell us here that he's cleared to leave the country as soon as he's transferred back to Philadelphia. The reason I was trying to reach Doug is that—

"You already know...? Do you know whether Claire's father is still there?"

"Are you positive? When is he supposed to get here?"

"That's wonderful! Claire will be overjoyed—"

"No, we don't have much time, either. Got to go."

At that instant the immigration officer came over to the women waving a computer printout in his hand.

"Here's the clearance number," he said, handing the printout to Claire. "Take it back to the counter and you'll be good to go."

Claire took the paper and bolted through the glass door to the emigration counter with Martha and Helen not far behind.

A moment later, Claire heard the distinctive clunk of the self-inking rubber stamp marking her papers, then the sharp slap of the passport being returned to the counter. The young woman behind the counter cocked an eyebrow toward the gate, as if to suggest that Claire not waste any more time before boarding her flight.

Claire snatched up the passport and stepped briskly past the counter toward the security checkpoint, then abruptly threw her arms around Helen Sigler's neck.

"This time everything is going to work out fine," Helen assured her. "Will you promise to send me a letter as soon as you arrive?"

"I will," Claire answered with glistening eyes. She turned to Martha and embraced her.

"I miss Marie already," she told Martha, stifling a sob. "Can you send me a picture of her now and then?"

"Of course," Martha replied. "And we won't forget you, either, Claire. But you really must go now or you'll miss your flight. Quick, get on board and find your mother and sister!"

With Helen and Martha urging her on toward the gate, Claire turned around one more time, as if to imprint their faces in her mind.

By the time she passed through security and reached the gate, only a handful of passengers remained in the waiting area. The gate agents had already closed the departure counter and were preparing to shut the door to the ramp.

Claire was out of breath when she reached the door and handed the agent her ticket.

"Not a moment too soon," said the agent, a woman of fifty who smiled at Claire in a motherly way. "You're the last to board, except for the gentleman in the corner."

Claire glanced into the ill-lit corner of the waiting area, where a rail-thin man with a gray crew cut stood between two broad-shouldered giants in baggy blue suits. To her mind, the thin man's long-sleeved khaki shirt and khaki trousers made him look like a forest ranger or a gardener. She was about to turn away and enter the walkway to the plane when she saw one of the giants pull a key from his breast pocket and unlock the handcuffs that bound his own wrist to that of the thin man.

At that moment the thin man noticed Claire looking at him and stared back. He took a step forward and continued to return her gaze.

All at once Claire dropped her backpack and rushed into the thin man's arms. She looked into her father's laughing eyes, felt his bony ribs under her hug, then seized his callused but still gentle hands.

"Claire, Claire, Claire," he repeated over and over.

Paul Wagner held his daughter at arm's length and gazed at her with fatherly pride. His eyes now brimmed with more tears than all the ones he had shed during his imprisonment.

"Dad, is it really you?" Claire sobbed. "I tried to find you!"

"I know," he replied. "Thanks for not giving up on me."

Claire drew back from her father and laughed.

"Dad, you look so skinny! Mom's not going to believe it!"

Paul Wagner peered down at his legs and grasped a fold of loose khaki around his scrawny thigh. He neither smiled nor frowned, but instead gave a look of benign acceptance, as if the suffering of the last two years were being washed away. When he took his daughter's hand again a bright new smile started in his eyes and radiated lines of happiness not seen on his gaunt face since long before his arrest. He let out a soft laugh.

"Come on, Claire, let's go surprise your mom."

AUTHOR'S NOTE

I wish to acknowledge two sources of inspiration for *Forty Days at Kamas*. The first is a chapter from Aleksandr Solzhenitsyn's *Gulag Archipelago Volume III* entitled *The Forty Days of Kengir*, which inspired the title and plot for my novel. The second is a scene from Part One of Viktor E. Frankl's memoir, *Man's Search for Meaning*, which inspired the final scene in Chapter 18 of my novel.

Author's Biographical Note

I wrote *Dynamite Fishermen* and *Bride of a Bygone War* to clear my head after eleven years of government service in places like Beirut, Cairo, Tunis, Jeddah, and Amman. I had already decided to write novels at age fourteen, during my first year as a boarding student at Exeter. My English instructor, a World War II combat veteran, advised those of us who wanted to follow the path of Melville, Conrad and Hemingway to first go out and live some adventures so that we would have stories that people might want to read. My adventures started in the Middle East and continued in Washington, Europe, the Russian Far East, Maui, Utah, New York and Boston. Particularly in the Middle East and Russia, I saw failed states and failed societies but was often surprised at how much their people had in common with Americans. This made me think about whether America might someday suffer its own breed of failure. During the 1930's, Americans watched Germany, Italy and

Russia and asked, "Could it happen here?" Today, one might look around and ask the same. In writing *Forty Days at Kamas, Star Chamber Brotherhood* and *Exile Hunter*, my greatest concern has been that the novels gain a readership before the events they describe come to pass.

A Final Word: When you turn the page, Kindle's "Before You Go" feature will give you the opportunity to rate this book and share your rating and comments on Facebook and Twitter. If you enjoyed the book, please take a moment to let your friends know about it. Better yet, post a Reader Review on Amazon.com, Goodreads.com or LibraryThing.com. If the book gives others a few evenings of enjoyment, they'll be grateful that you reached out to them. And so will I.

With best wishes, Preston Fleming

OTHER BOOKS BY PRESTON FLEMING

Dynamite Fishermen

Classic Espionage. "Civil disorder in 1980s Beirut. An extraordinary novel, each page as eruptive as the city providing the setting." KIRKUS REVIEWS
http://www.prestonfleming.com/novel-dynamite-fishermen.html

Bride of a Bygone War

Realist Spy Thriller. "CIA agent in Beirut fears his past has caught up to him. An intelligent thriller teeming with vigor." KIRKUS REVIEWS
http://www.prestonfleming.com/novel-bride-of-a-bygone-war.html

Forty Days at Kamas

Dystopian Political Thriller. "A brutal portrait of a dystopian America, full of dramatic irony and shocking revelation." *KIRKUS REVIEWS*
http://www.prestonfleming.com/novel-forty-days-at-kamas.html

Star Chamber Brotherhood

Dystopian Assassination Thriller. "Dystopian thriller about a prison-camp survivor enlisted to assassinate the camp's warden. A full-bodied

thriller relayed by a consummate storyteller." KIRKUS REVIEWS
http://www.prestonfleming.com/novel-star-chamber-brotherhood.html

Exile Hunter

Dystopian Suspense Thriller. "Pure energy in print form, whether the characters are being pursued or simply talking." KIRKUS REVIEWS

http://www.prestonfleming.com/novel-exile-hunter.html